ARRANGEMENT
IN
BLACK AND WHITE

Blue Triangle Press

2014

Also by Fred Misurella

Fiction:

Short Time, a novella

Lies to Live By, stories

Only Sons, a novel

Non-fiction:

Understanding Milan Kundera: Public Events, Private Affairs

ARRANGEMENT IN BLACK AND WHITE

By

Fred Misurella

Fred Misurella

Library of Congress control number: 2014901218

The characters and events in this novel are fictitious. Any similarity to real persons, living or dead, is coincidental and not intended by the author.

Acknowledgments:

Thanks to Ann Misurella for permission to use her photograph on the book's cover, and to Beth Seetch for editing the manuscript. In all cases, mistakes are the author's. The author photo is by Volney Fray.

ISBN: 1494852128
ISBN 13: 978-1494852122

For Kim and Alex, as always,

with love.

"The business of love is
cruelty *which*,
by our wills
we transform
to live together."

--William Carlos Williams

CONTENTS

PROLOGUE:

1.

"MONSTER"

"It has big eyes, a huge snout, bulging, toothy jaws, and at night it comes out of its cave to devour little children in the woods..."

As the moon sank behind the trees, Margy wondered if that were true. She wondered, too, if she could find her way in the dark. But at the memory of her mother, running after her, cat-o'-nine-tails in her hand, she decided to stay. Mother was old, cross, ugly--angry at her for breaking something this afternoon, and by this time her father might be angry too. She would not go home until they forgave her.

She squatted near the tree, feeling the roots swell from the ground, bracing her back against the abrasive trunk. As the sky faded behind the leaves, she heard a soft, metallic rustle, heard the rustle build into a hum, and heard the hum fill the night with music. When the leaves moved, she heard a higher pitch of sound, a crescendo that tapered off, picked up intensity again, and finally quieted. Yet the original sound remained. Then she knew the hum was not the wind, but the waterfalls just beyond the hill on her left.

She stood for a moment, rubbing her hair against the bark. She squatted back on her heels.

"Tall and dark," said her mother. "With smoke coming from his mouth, fire burning in his eyes, and huge claws he uses to rip off your arms before he eats you. He has the devil's likeness."

"Only a story," her father said. Margy had not believed her mother yesterday, but she shivered at the description of the monster now. She heard a branch crack to her right, and although she hugged herself, the thought of the fiery eyes came back to her with hope. She would see the monster easily in the dark, and she could run away

7

before it found her. But where to? It was too dark to know where she was going. She sandwiched her head between her knees, wrapped her arms around her shins, and shoved her heels and seat closer to the ground. Would there ever be light again? Her mother had also said that someday the sun would go out; God would send all the wicked to hell and take a few good people to stay with Him in heaven.

"No warning; remember that, Margy."

She nestled against the tree, wishing it would bend over and whisper. She heard a creak, then another, but without a blaze of fire she convinced herself that there could be no harm. The falls hummed to the left, locusts shushed and wheezed all around, but, above, the wind was still. Two eyes came near, darting off when she jumped back at the sight of their two greenish halos. Something small nuzzled her ankles from behind. She felt it against her shoes before it turned and ran off with a rustle through the underbrush.

Am I dead? Will I ever see the sun again?

She thought of her mother chasing her this afternoon, holding one jagged piece of the plate Margy had knocked off the sideboard. She threw it finally, after Margy had dashed through the door of the butler's pantry and into the kitchen.

Escaping into the yard, Margy had stopped, not knowing where to run, for the moment startled as the glass broke on the pavement beside her, spraying off into the grass and around her feet. Her mother had shaken her fist, gone back into the house, then emerged from the doorway waving the cat-o'-nine-tails as if it were a wand. Margy had stood, paralyzed, backed against the lone maple tree that stood near the garage, and watched her mother come closer. She squealed, feeling the thongs break against her shins, and ducked, evading a second swing. Then she ran through the alley into the street and from there toward the end of the block.

"You will never come back," her mother had shouted. "Never!"

As Margy stopped at the corner, she saw her mother on her knees, lowering her head, almost hitting it on the pavement. "Go away! Don't come back. You little devil--"

8

Margy stopped, closing off the next few words, thinking of the two neighboring women who had come off their porches. In embarrassment rather than fear, she had run farther away, looking for a place to hide.

There were bushes, then the brook. Flowing behind a fence, the brook poured out from the woods where it began as a huge basin near the waterfall. She followed the brook, and when she came to the falls, bounded up the hill to the rock and elm that overlooked them. It was late afternoon, spring, the weather warmer than usual for this time of year, and she felt she could stay out overnight. Daddy might come after her, but she could hide from him. He would not think that she, afraid of the shadows at the top of the stairs, afraid of the very closet she kept her clothes in, would be brave enough to walk into the woods and spend the night alone.

She opened her eyes now, looking to see if things had changed. She saw patches, small white movements, but except for the ground and the tree, she did not know her place. She imagined the falls somewhere behind her through the trees, and, thinking of her father walking toward them now, she laughed: Wouldn't he be sorry? Then she held her breath, trying to listen above the hum of water.

She saw her mother lying in bed, pale, holding a Bible in her hands, calling out to God as if it were the time of Revelations. She would lash her head from side to side, implore Him to aid her in her suffering. She would scream, raise her hand to the ceiling, refuse medicine, throw it on the floor. Daddy would be there, patting her hand, whispering, hoping to make her listen to his gentle voice.

Margy crossed her fingers and arms. She covered her eyes, pretending she heard him whispering: clear, soft, loving, his voice wafted over the falls and wind, through the rustling of the leaves, until it was a pleasant sound in her ear instead of her mother's. She opened her eyes, spread her arms, ready to be taken against his chest. Only a great blanket of black surrounded her, only the faintest shadow of a movement when she looked up at the sky.

"Daddy... ?"

9

She said her first word aloud, expecting to make the woods start moving. She left the tree, took a few steps toward the sound of the stream, then stopped, floundered, lost her balance and almost fell to her knees. She backed three quick steps but could not find the tree.

"DADDY!" she shouted.

In answer there was a rustle to her right. A pair of large green eyes rushed toward her. She jumped back, felt something against her chest, tripped on a root. Falling, she hit her head against the trunk. She wrapped her arms around it, and as the eyes stopped, lingered, and swept past without even the recognition of a blink, she held her breath as if she were diving under water. She felt a warm, sticky substance when she touched her cheek. *Blood, it must be blood*, she thought. Whether from fear, or the blow from the fall, her grip weakened, her legs doubled, her hands slid down the trunk. As she sank to the ground, sound and touch became as dark to her as sight.

***

The wind misled her father too, but he followed the sound of water at his feet. Not a star out, and he cursed the luck that made it a moonless night. He strayed a couple of times, stepping into the water and then quickly hopping out in disgust, following the stream bed because he knew that was how she would go. Searchlight and a lantern: he swung one high, the other low and to the left and right. He moved slowly, conscious with each rush of something away from him, each plop of an animal into water, that in the woods he was at best a tolerated stranger. He hoped for something, anything, as long as it was dry and on land, and bet that the many visits they had paid to the falls would make it so.

"Ran away," muttered her mother, Beverly. "To damnation."

"Hiding," he had replied. "Looking for the security she doesn't get from you."

He cursed his wife, took it back, wiped away all thought of their argument this evening. Her screaming, her

10

wild, wide open eyes, her gray hair streaming behind her while she fumed about the house waving a piece of the paltry broken dish.

"My crystal platter, my favorite crystal platter."

She had repeated that over and over, like a litany, he thought. And he had not mentioned that they could buy a new one now, they could afford it without the slightest hardship. He had just stood in her room, looked at the table--full of unspeakable things: claws, dried intestines, medallions, candles--and shook his head as she ran past him in search of another fragment of broken crystal in the yard. "The damage has already been done, Beverly," he said, thinking of a more precious object.

"If she is harmed, if she is hurt in the slightest way--"

But he refused to complete that sentence now. Ten, fifteen, almost twenty years of married life, then, at forty, a child to bless his middle age: Margy; darling. He thought of her now, her silver-blond curls, her jeans, the lovely pink-lipped smile, the blue eyes that somehow sent a chill through him they looked so perfect; the arms and legs so graceful they seemed to float above the ground, the hands that always surprised him with their dexterity. He had seen her build things far beyond the abilities of an average girl her age, draw detailed pictures, bodies, arms, legs, fingers, full faces with full complements of features. Genius, he knew. Her hands were like birds, fluttering above a project, never seeming to touch, but nevertheless nourishing and leaving things exactly right: well-formed and in proper proportion. Just as she was.

If he, if only he-- But he crossed that from his mind and tried to concentrate on his search. Before him the incline jutted, humped like a frog in the evening light, and instead of following the stream around it, he decided to see if she were at the top. He turned to the left, around a bunch of thorny bush, climbing the rocky side instead of following the path. On the top he saw the lights of Waterloo Falls in the distance, but he found no trace of his daughter. The town was like a jewel that night, or a tiara, with a long row of streetlights filling up the plain, the jagged mass of roofs--especially the church--like a hand with a gathering of pointing fingers.

He searched the hilltop more carefully--behind a rock, deeper in some brush--and still saw nothing. Not the slightest trace of her bright hair, not the slightest artifact to show that she had been there. "The falls," he murmured. "She has to be there." He knew she loved them, their sound, the wonderful smash and rainbow of the water into the stream. He knew of her wish to fly from there, dive off the rocks above the falls and fly beyond the stream to the other side. "Even beyond the trees," she had told him once, but he had pulled her away, telling her not to think of that, not even in a daydream. Brooding, he moved quickly toward the hum of falling water. She wouldn't, no, she couldn't; oh, Lord, please make her not even pretend she is going to fly tonight. He pictured her tiny body poised above the falls, arms outstretched, her eyes down on the water, then across it and above the trees on the other side. She had drawn herself like that for him once, with a portrait of him and another girl-- another Margy, he reasoned--watching from a nearby tree.

"Deadless, like Deadless in the story you told me, Daddy. I want to fly to the sun."

Often he had to pull her back from the rock's edge, because beneath her impish, laughing smile was a certain seriousness that frightened him. She would really do it, she would really try to fly; she had told him that several times.

He stopped, just pulling his shoe back from the water. He swept the searchlight across the stream then over the field across the way. He saw movement, started, but then he saw it rush away. A rabbit, maybe a squirrel... He smiled. She did have a certain zaniness, a certain lack of inhibition that made her very special. But then he shivered because he knew that sort of character had attracted him to her mother once. With a sweep of his light and a toss of the lantern, he turned that from his mind. He called "Margy," several times, flushing animals as his voice cut through the silence, grinning to himself and remembering the sly, winsome mouth, the distracted look, the occasional insightful darting into his own eyes, as if she could read his thoughts.

12

"You're my girl," he told her often. "My one and only, my very special girl."

He cursed Beverly, the cheap religious books she read, the insane, scrupulous attention to Scriptural details that could turn her against her own flesh. "Dirt," she had called after her own daughter. "Trash. Off to a den of iniquity."

He entered the woods now, cutting through the lines of trees that shimmered in his light. He saw an owl look down at him, saw its broad, Raggedy-Ann face not even wink, then ducked when, with the slightest quiver of preparation, it spread its wings and took off above his head, its "who-who-who" a warning rather than a question, its stained splatter of lime falling through the light beam to his feet. He turned away and moved along the stream. If she were lost, if she were not at the falls, if on that rock she attempted... But he stopped again and tried to remember how far he had to go. For a moment he turned off the light and lowered the wick on the lantern. He could see nothing now, and as he tried an experimental step he found himself surprised, suddenly wet and cold, up to his ankles in water.

"God *damn* it!"

He pulled back, fingering his shirt pockets and slacks for a pack of matches. With the lamp on again, he felt he could pierce the maze around him, but he also felt terribly vulnerable.

"Margy!--Margy, honey!" The falls sounded nearer as he walked, and he listened for her reply above the constant sound. Nothing... A small, gray animal went by--a little muskrat or rabbit--and its eyes came into his beams like two perfect neon circles. It lurched to the left, changed to a mass of white, then stretched out and disappeared into the larger shadows of the underbrush. "My darling. My baby." But he checked himself as he moved ahead. The animal might have been running from her, and the image of her standing on the rock, arms outspread, ready to fly, became obsessive. It was a fall of seventy-five or eighty feet.

"Margy!--Don't move, honey. Just answer Daddy when he calls."

13

He hit a pebble, stumbled into water, found himself almost on his knees, just missed dropping both lantern and searchlight into the stream. He steadied himself, headed against the current toward the bank, and, soaked to his hips, marched through the knee-high grass, the wet squeak of his shoes sounding above the water. Margy came up to his hips, not even to his belt, and a single misstep like that... But he stopped and listened more carefully, taking exquisite pains to hold his breath. After at least a minute he was certain that nothing moved. The ground began to slope more quickly now, rising to the left along the stream bed, and the hum of the falls grew louder. He hurried, not caring about his own noise as he jogged uphill, depending on light and sight alone to find her. He swept the searchlight across the trees, over the stream bed, and carried the lantern awkwardly above his shoulder. The woods became a blur, a frieze, and he looked for a flash of white or yellow from the foreground of the bush. He reached a plateau, saw the falls shimmer as he passed the light beam over them, then shined it up the water to the rock. Nothing; no movement. He studied the banks around the basin, spotted the beam on the rocks, into any individual foliage he saw, even into the water itself and under the overhang of rock.

"God damn it, God damn it, *God damn it!*"

He screamed her name, but it was covered by the roar of the water. He climbed some rocks, reached the top of the falls and, as he expected, found nothing there. Not even a trace of something. Not a stick or stone she might have used to scratch a picture or message with. "My baby, my beautiful baby," he blubbered.

He sank to his knees and tried to think. From the pit of his stomach a cold feeling of certainty began to spread through his body. He had been so sure, so absolutely positive. Where else would she run in fear? Oh, God...

He shined the light down on the water, certain of something white bobbing in the middle. But it was nothing. He sat on his heels, turned out the light, tried to think with some direction. He should have got some men, he should have called the sheriff, he should have called the other

14

fathers of the neighborhood. But as usual his independence and pride—

Damn that sense of privacy you have, *damn* your fear of shameful public exposure, *damn* your wife who made it a necessary thing!--He pounded his knees, closed his eyes and moaned, trying to rescind the curse, trying to think himself into a rational peace. It was not Beverly's fault; it was not Margy's; it was not completely his either. People make their own beds, people sleep in them. But he stopped, trying to think more clearly about his daughter.

He stood, seeing three hundred and sixty degrees of woods. My life... *God damn it, forget your life and think about your little girl!*

The ground sloped downward to the right. Through the trees was a little cave he had shown her once. They had sat there through a rainstorm. Wouldn't she go there tonight? Could he, with his impossibly puny set of lights even hope to come near it in the dark? "Try," he told himself. "You have wasted time already." As he left the rock, climbed down a stairway made of stones, a horrible image of Margy evolved in his mind. She had floated past him as he came upstream. He had seen a brightly-colored object floating in the water, and he had thought it was nothing but debris. Fool!--Suppose it was her blouse, suppose it was her body, suppose... His daughter would be found tomorrow, he knew, just a block away from home, waterlogged, her poor skin aged, wrinkles over her whole water-soaked body.

They would lift her out of the stream, wrap her in a blanket, place her at his feet on the porch, and stare as he, flabbergasted then insane, would run into the largest house in Waterloo Falls, strike a match, and set fire to every piece of wood and paper he could find.

***

"*Margy*," he whispered.
"Daddy! Daddy!"

15

She woke, screaming, dreaming she was falling off a cliff and clutched at the bedpost, the mattress, even the clothes on her body.

She flapped her arms, listening for his footsteps coming down the hall. She cried out once more and listened a full minute before she realized she was not in her room. Her hand settled against a tree, her legs rustled inside a mulch of leaves. No light, no eyes; for the moment not even the rush and fall of the water off to the left: only the bump and scratch of the bark against her neck.

She stood, saw a curious glow in the distance, and then, more curious, a spot above it that seemed to wink in and out of the trees as it floated by. She stepped back, put her hands against the tree and held her breath. She circled the tree, keeping the trunk between her and the lights. Could they be the Devil's eyes? Could they be the monster's? She thought they must be, and in an unconscious twist of her earlier logic, she buried her face in her hands instead of running away. Even in the dark she could not get rid of that dreadful picture from the afternoon--or her mother's words, which were worse than her image of the monster.

Margy slid to the ground, huddled against the trunk, and tried not to cry. It was not her fault, it was not her fault at all...

"No, Mommy, no. Please don't--" But she had not finished that sentence.

There was the ball, the shattered dish, the crayons and paper. She saw the book with the pictures of Jesus and all the disciples in it, and then her mother, with an awful mixture of happiness and anger on her face, waving a piece of glass...

"Look what you did! Look what you did to my dish!"

Margy's memory went back a little further: The ball, bright and red, arcing beautifully from the molding in the corner, bounding into her outstretched hands after hitting the teddy bear's nose... She threw again, caught the ball, and started to throw it a third time, even though her mother was already calling from upstairs.

"Margy! You're playing ball! I hear you."

16

"No, Mommy. I'm not. I'm reading."

She ran to the chair and picked up the book of Jesus and the disciples.

"Don't lie to me. I heard something bouncing on the floor."

"I'm reading the book you gave me, Mommy."

"I don't want you to lie. I don't want you to scribble on those pages either. I told you, that's an expensive book."

Margy went into the living room to show it to her. Her mother came down the stairs. She looked at Margy carefully, and, as she often did lately, showing no emotion or anger, raised her hand and brought it sharply across her daughter's face.

"Remember that," was all she whispered. Back in the dining room with tears streaming down her face, Margy made one last throw.

"Damn you, Teddy!" The ball hit hard, bounced to the ceiling, ricocheted off the wall and, magically it seemed, so slowly and inevitably that her memory turned it into a slow-motion dream, fell onto the sideboard, bounded off the molding, just ticked the crystal platter--and the platter, leaning over in a more outrageous gesture, quietly floated to the floor.

"'*Margy*!'"

She had cringed, grabbed the ball, hid it behind her back, and retreated from her mother's footsteps. She ran to the end of the table and looked at her mother coming through the door. Beverly wore gray, a gray dress, gray apron, and even gray shoes. She wore glasses and, squinting through them, gasped when she looked at the platter. She took Margy's ear, dragged her to the corner and waved a fragment of the platter in her face. Even her hand was gray, Margy noticed.

"What did you do? What *did* you do? God will punish you. Don't you know that? Don't you know that God will send you to the Devil forever?"

"No, Mommy. Please. It wasn't me."

Once, twice, three times the gray hand with the fragment of crystal passed in front of her eyes. The jagged

17

edge of the glass grazed her nose. That made her giggle. She could not stop, even though she knew her mother would not like it.

"What? Are you laughing? Don't you dare laugh at your mother."

She slapped Margy, backed away, grimacing as if repulsed by something ugly, then went into the butler's pantry closet and returned with the black cat-o'-nine-tails swinging in her hand.

"I'll teach you to lie."

She swiped at Margy's legs. Margy ducked beneath the chair and crawled under the table.

"Stop! Stop, I said."

"No, Mommy, please!" She yelped, feeling the sting against her shins, and--crawling--slipped out from the table, through the butler's pantry door, then into the kitchen and out into the yard. The platter came through the kitchen door, caught a glint of the sun, and before she could see the pieces of it whole, shattered to bits of glass confetti at her feet.

"You'll regret this. I told you never to play ball in the house. Wait till your father gets home!"

The yard was flat, open, with only the spindly maple and garage in it, and behind them a seemingly endless field of wheat. She felt exhausted, paralyzed, ready to fall on her knees and beg, but when she saw her mother above her, felt the thongs burn against her legs a third time, she ran out of the cat-o'-nine-tails' reach.

At the end of the block she turned and saw a picture that she was sure would never go away: Mother, on her knees, gray hair falling, shaking her head and raising her fists in anger toward the sky.

"You little devil! God will punish you for this! ... I hope you die!"

***

If she is dead, if that poor child is really... He shook his head and threaded his way among the trees. He was careful not to trip on roots, yet he tried to keep alert for

18

signs. Bugs flickered in and out of the light beam, and he cursed as they veered off the searchlight and lantern, lost themselves in the dark, then made themselves known again with a dive bomber buzzing in his ear. "Like my wife and all her complaining," he grumbled to himself. He shook his head and waved his hands, thought the words *God damn that woman* and stopped.

How did this happen? How did two people, seemingly in love, twist their lives so that they could make a perfectly lovely child and then ruin her life? Money; career; temperament. He stopped when he reached the category of church. Every goddamn day, he thought, every goddamn day in that graveyard full of antiquated notions. We're all Christian, *all* believe in God--why make so much fuss? He thought of the people in town and how they went to the Methodist or Congregational church, why did she have to pick the only style of worship they would not abide? He waved the flashlight, saw the trees as pines, pines as stone buttresses of a building, then stopped to consider the wind and waterfalls as organ music. *My* kind of church, *my* kind of worship. He flashed the light into the underbrush, seeing little more than leaves. The cave was along here somewhere: he thought he recognized that boulder over there. Behind it was a sapling he remembered as an elm. Gnarled, delicate, turned over in filigree, its branches, birch-like, touched the ground before ascending for the light.

Survival, he thought, but at what dear cost?

He shook his head, still thinking of Beverly, but more especially of their child. How much have I kept away the light she needs? He shook his head, letting the lantern rest at his side, and looked to see if there were footprints in the earth. It was muddy here, a run-off, probably from the hill above the cave. He thought she must have come this way.

He followed it, stepping out of the path where the mud got too deep. He saw some animal footprints: a squirrel, maybe a rabbit, then another, probably a raccoon. But with all his probing and squinting, not a sign of a single human shoe. If she is not there; if she is ... ? He swung the lantern to the left and thought he saw a patch of yellow. He ran

19

through the bush, tripping as he fought through the underbrush and mud, but when he came to the other side, saw nothing. Just a frayed and yellow newspaper fluttering in the breeze.

Maddening. He looked at his watch and by the lantern saw that it was nearly midnight. Six hours, six and a half maybe. He cursed his wife, hoped she would choke on all her insane sputtering, hoped she would choke on her goddamn... He took that back and almost whispered, "I'm sorry," as he did.

My position in town, *my* disappointment, *my* obvious disgust at the way she handles her life. All because she was a nervous woman, "Sensitive," he used to say.

It's not going to be like you, Beverly. I couldn't stand it. It would make me sick. I'll see that this baby isn't like you. If I have to...

Yes, he had said that; not only in words, but, more important, in actions. And as he speculated on their child during pregnancy, he had seen his wife diminish before his eyes. She had become smaller, more than physically, more than in the deliverance of their child.

And you? And you?

He stopped, stepped onto the run-off again, flashed his light, and saw nothing but trees and a bend in the run-off's path. Funny how the trees look gray and black at night-- as if our light is unfit to reveal their natural colors. He thought of the elm that twisted like a birch, saw a huge rock beside the path, and knew he must be near it now. He felt certain when he saw an overhang of trees. The cave's opening should be just beyond them.

"Sensible. Damn sensible," he said.

He thought of her bright eyes, her robust child's voice that belied the surprisingly adult choice of words she sometimes made, and thought, of course, the cave is perfect. "I should have come here in the first place," he muttered, "since it was so dark."

He called her name, laughing in relief, then stopped to listen. She was probably asleep now, probably waiting for her stupid father to wake her up. He doubted, laughed at himself for thinking of the falls again, and began to trot up the path, around the bend, kicking mud and water as he ran.

"Margy! Margy, honey! Daddy's coming!"

He felt the water and mud tap against his ankles and slacks. He passed the trees, left the run-off for a grove of beech, and began to swing the searchlight and lantern to find the cave.

"Margy! Come here, come to Daddy ... now!"

Nothing; no path, no bush that he remembered. Then with a gasp he saw an incline coming out of the underbrush like a cantilevered roof. At once he knew it was the opening to the cave.

"Margy, *baby*!" He trotted to the incline, went around the underbrush to the other side. "*Please,*" he said, although he was trying to smile. "*Please.*"

He shined a light into the cave, held the lantern above his head, walked inside and pointed the searchlight toward the back—Nothing, not the slightest sign. *Why the hell did you come here anyway!*—He ran outside, screamed as loud as he could, and did not bother listening for a reply. If you had come here right away, if you didn't wait till after dark. If that monster that I'm living with didn't have to be taken to the hospital—But he stopped again, sighing... So she's not in the cave, she's someplace else. She's sensible. You trained her about these woods, she knows what to do, don't panic. Think. That's how you always destroy your life. Just five hours to sunup... I'll get a group of men. I'll...

He sat on a rock and buried his head in his hands. Oh, God, if she... If she... I could do it all myself. I didn't need anybody. I didn't want anybody. I can't have anybody find me out. He raised his fists and pounded them on his head. He pulled his hair, tried to slap his face but could not manage a sharp enough blow. You dunce, you *ass*, you *coward*! So they wouldn't know. So they wouldn't know you have a crazy wife. So you wouldn't have to admit that you're unhappy. As if the whole town didn't already know! He picked up the searchlight and lantern and tried to think about his next step. He turned the flashlight to the sky, then circled it around the

21

underbrush at his feet. Nothing. In a fit of rage, he lifted his arm as if to throw the searchlight into the bushes--

"*You will not panic. You will not give up. You will not do crazy, stupid things!*"

He took a deep breath, stood, and decided to walk back to the stream. He would check the rise, the trees, both banks, and the surface. Maybe she... He blotted that out and decided she had not gone near the stream. Oh, God, I hope there are no vicious animals out tonight. He thought of a boy who, in a horrible accident, had been attacked by dogs last summer. Immediately, he saw Margy torn to shreds. No. They would have growled; he would have heard them in these quiet woods. He took two steps, listened to the murmur of the wind and the slight whoosh-and-splash of the waterfalls, and screamed as he began to run down the incline through the trees. The falls, the water, *Margy*! He had not heard his own voice as he stood by the falls before. He had not even heard himself when he had screamed: *Margy*!

He went around a tree, barreled through some bushes, fell head over heels down an incline, landed on his back, screamed her name as he stood, actually ran into a tree and *Margy*! leaped up, groping for the searchlight beneath some bushes when, out of the corner of his eye, he saw something moving in the light...

Moving!

He stopped, fumbled with the lights, then held still. Something short and bright ducked behind a tree, then peered out from the shadows on the other side.

He whispered, questioning: "*Margy*?"

He caught a glimpse of yellow, a wisp of white beneath it, and finally what he was sure was a rosy, wily, frightened face. He did not move; in fact, he hardly breathed.

"Honey, it's me. It's Daddy."

She disappeared as he heard a rustle of leaves.

"Margy, don't! Don't go away--it's all right."

He stepped forward and stopped, seeing her full face in the lantern's glare. When she went behind the tree again, he trembled and almost began to cry.

"Oh, baby, we love you. We really do. I'm sorry you had to stay out so long. I'm sorry we're such a bad Mommy and Daddy to you."

She raised her hand to her face and seemed to shake. She looked exhausted. It occurred to him that she might be blinded by the lights.

"Honey, look! See? It's Daddy." He put the lantern behind him and turned the searchlight on his face.

"Why didn't you come out earlier? Why did you let me walk around so long?"

"I hurt myself," she blubbered.

Touching her cheek and forehead, she pointed to her face and looked at him with disapproving eyes. He saw dirt and perhaps a little blood. He lowered the light, crossed to the tree, and, with a sob, lifted her into his arms at last. Her eyes were wide and frightened. Yet she swung at him with all her might, striking him in the nose and ear as if he were some dangerous beast. He stumbled, almost dropping her, then shifted, clutching her to his chest.

"It's all right; it's all right; it's all right!" he shouted. He was laughing now.

As she swung toward him in a final, exhausted blow, she collapsed against his chest.

"I hate you! I hate you both!"

She pushed him away, screaming. Her palms were like little animals.

"I missed you," he whispered. "Margy Winters, I'm so glad that you're alive."

She wiped her nose and demanded that he set her down. Then, with a neutral, disinterested face, she began to walk away.

He followed until she passed the falls. Then, silent, he caught up with her, and they followed the brook until they saw the town ahead of them, a glow in the darkness of the plain.

I.

NEW BEGINNINGS: 1974

2.

TROMPE-L'OEIL

Almost thirty years go by: not exactly a flash, but not exactly an evolutionary transformation either. A few townspeople, such as the unhappy Emory Winters, might have experienced those years as centuries, but to a young, confined woman such as Margy they were a series of steps or squares that she, like a tumbling acrobat, hopped from one to another on. Meanwhile fellow performers followed suit, leaving one place, retrieving her present spot, then ducking as she prepared to leap onto theirs. Thus each year was a position, and as Margy looked back from an early spring evening in 1974 to a late spring afternoon in 1947, she retraced her movements and saw--as if in a wink of an eye-- that everything in her life had changed, even though with a second wink she could see that in fact everything had stayed the same.

A dark, unusually warm Sunday night. She heard a car pass the front of the house, the sound of its engine echoing off the walls of the buildings on either side and rattling the window above her easel. Her husband sat downstairs with his mother, brother, and sister. Her son was now playing basketball under the lights in the neighborhood school yard. Margy stood upstairs in her attic studio attempting to finish a painting.

She imagined the family around the marble coffee table, her husband at the projector, pushing the remote control button to change a slide while he retold the story of their trip to St. Croix in early March. It was his special version of the trip, she was sure: colonial rule, 18th century prisons, burned-out fields, black tee-pee shaped kilns his ancestors had died in and for, bringing, as he liked to phrase it, "the gold of sugar to white folks' pockets."

And nothing about themselves.

Everet, Everet Hamilton: "Black, though about a quarter of him is white—Italian-American," she would

25

immediately say whenever she discussed him with some new friend. Margy was white herself, of course, blonde, almost thirty-two years old, yet somehow (and this she would never discuss with her new friend) still a little girl, still trying to fly, still trying to paint pretty pictures, at the same time still trying to be the woman her adolescent experiences had made her want to be. In a few minutes she would go downstairs to greet her mother-in-law. She would kiss her cheek, call her "Mom," although the very word, raising visions of her own mother, was difficult to utter, and respond sweetly when Mrs. Hamilton patted her shoulder. She would greet Franklin and Cora, Everet's younger brother and sister; then she would sit on the sofa or floor and try to be a part of them, conscious that in this chiaroscuro family grouping, she was the odd figure out, the one whom they accepted, but as if she were a visitor.

"Everet--you'll enjoy this too, Margy--guess who I saw today in downtown Stoddard: an old fraternity brother of yours."

"Who's that, Mama?"

"Casper Giuliani."

"Jules the Cat! How is he doing?"

"Fine. He's working for the Mayor's office in New York City. I told him that you might need his services here in Stoddard one of these days."

Everet grinned. Mrs. Hamilton laughed, slapping her knees, her excitability a complement to Everet's. Franklin and Cora, a bit more self-conscious, stifled a smile as they looked at Margy who had just entered and sat down.

"Excuse me, Margy," Mrs. Hamilton said. "I didn't mean to bring up a sore topic."

"Nothing to excuse, Mom."

Mrs. Hamilton's first name was Ruth. A large, comfortable woman with gray, meticulously groomed hair, she had a preference for blue satin-finished dresses and sturdy, thick-heeled shoes. She was gracious, but, with Margy, always in a slightly guarded manner. After ten years they had resolved most of the color issues, but she frankly regretted Margy's habit of dressing sloppily (jeans and

26

sweatshirts in place of finer things), her occasional indifference toward cooking and homemaking in favor of class assignments, and, finally, the hours-long sessions in her studio making paintings that interested very few Stoddard people.

In rounded profile, glancing at Margy quickly out of the corners of her dark brown eyes, Ruth Hamilton made a memorable picture. Her lips moved expressively, as if she were readying herself to kiss, or just say something pleasant. She had wanted to be friends when Everet and Margy married, still tried to be friends, in fact, but Margy's sense of privacy was such that although they had a few years of moderate closeness, they finally decided, without ever discussing it, to go their separate ways. It was a shame, Margy thought; a good motherly influence was something she had never known.

"Are you going to the Democratic fund-raising dinner Wednesday?" Ruth asked.

Everet nodded. Franklin and Cora stirred in their chairs, while Margy maintained silence. Again, dangerous ground. With a wave of his hand, Everet added, "Margy hasn't decided yet. She thinks she may have to work that night."

Interesting, Margy thought, how men whose women start to do things other than be good mates adopt a tolerant but moderately disturbed attitude, as if life was out of synch. They only waited for the proper rhythm to assert itself again.

"It really isn't that at all," Margy said, "if truth be told."

Everet folded his hands and looked at her. "Do you want to talk about it now?" he asked, indicating his family's presence.

"Why not?" she said.

He inclined his head and opened out one of his palms.

"Well, I'd say that my attendance at the dinner depends on what Everet decides about the following weekend."

"The *following* weekend?" Ruth looked nervously from Everet to Franklin and Cora.

27

"Yes. We've planned for months to attend a retreat for married couples. We'd just about decided to go, but now Everet refuses."

"I'm not refusing! I'm questioning the value of it. You know that."

Ruth Hamilton moaned a little and asked Franklin and Cora to pick up Kennedy, Everet and Margy's son, in the nearby school yard. His name, his parents had agreed when he was born, would be perfect. Franklin shrugged and looked at his watch, saying it was still early, and even Cora, usually a docile do-gooder, seemed reluctant to leave her seat. With a look of disappointment, Ruth turned to Everet and Margy and asked them to talk about the problem calmly.

"Calmly or not, we've been through this before," Margy said, "and to tell the truth, I resent it. We don't need a peacemaker."

"No, you need to have some success with your painting."

"Painting?"

"Yes. That's what's bothering you. Admit it."

"My painting has nothing to do with this, and you know it."

Nevertheless, Margy raised her feet onto the hassock near the sofa and nervously folded her arms. The subject was definitely not a part of their usual arguments, and she did not like the sudden mention of it.

"At least the issue is clear," she mumbled, "from your point of view."

"From anyone's point of view. It's obvious," Everet said.

"Oh, children, please..." Ruth moaned again, shifting in the sofa and placing a hand on Everet's knee. "Somewhere along the line," she said, "I think you have forgotten some important feelings."

"No, *she* has. Her life--or her work--has become more important than what we mean together. The contract has changed."

He made the statement with a flourish, shooting his hands toward the ceiling, as though speaking before a jury.

Appropriate, Margy thought, especially since he had become an accomplished courtroom lawyer. Even in the house he dressed the part--tailored Brooks Brothers slacks with a vest, a blue button-down shirt, and a paisley tie. Any judge, jury, or client would be impressed.

Ruth glanced at Franklin and Cora again but said nothing. Margy simply stared at the ceiling and sighed. "My work has always been important to me," she said. "But for nearly ten years I've given it up for you and our marriage."

"It did us both good, and it didn't harm the world of art, I should add."

Margy looked at him, not willing to acknowledge the insult. "Well, damn it, I want to be selfish for a change," she said.

"Congratulations. You're succeeding."

"Not enough."

"You see--?"

Ruth, her hands in perpetual movement, stretched across the coffee table to pat Margy's knees. Finally, she asked for quiet and stared meaningfully at Franklin and Cora. After a few seconds they rose together and left the room. The three adults remained silent until they heard the outside door click shut.

"Mama, she's not getting..."

"I think as a woman you could..."

"Please! Children; children!--Let's talk about what we're doing here. I don't think the two of you are remembering what you've meant to one another."

"I remember clearly," Everet said. "Too clearly."

"I remember too, but it hasn't been that way for months--"

"Years, maybe. You see, Mama? And sometimes I feel guilty because she's unhappy."

He stood, walked around the sofa and sat down again. He loosened his tie and pounded his fist into his palm.

"Everet, I admit that I've been at fault, but I want help--to work things out this weekend."

"In one weekend?"

29

"Okay, several weekends--you know we need some sustained therapy. Even after a vacation to St. Croix we hardly talk to each other."

He sighed, shaking his head. Margy shot a glance at Ruth. She could see her struggling to maintain her customary even-handedness, although, Margy guessed, she probably favored Everet.

"Everet, why don't you show me some joy or anger now and then? All you do is play at being cool. You mention my painting, but all you think about is your career."

"I am not emotionally expressive," he said. "You know that. And as to my career, you married me knowing it was important. You accepted it."

Margy laughed. "Not so important that it ruled our personal lives."

He clapped his hands, mockingly. "Ah, yes! The theory of the richly emotional inner life. Along with the way to attain it by the famous therapy of the angry orgiastic scream. Forget about civilized restraint."

"Everet... "

"That's what we're supposed to do this weekend, Mama." He nodded his head and pounded his knee. "We're supposed to shriek, we're supposed to howl! Like good little religious niggers."

"It's not like that at all."

"The hell it isn't! Mama, do you remember that little store-front church we lived near in Norwalk? The Holy Roller Church? Those people stamped the devil from their souls just the way these people stamp it from their shrinking heads. It's old-time religion all over again. And it makes me sick!"

Ruth glanced at Margy, saying nothing. Clearly worried, yet sympathetic, Margy thought. Ruth's family had been moderately serious about religion, but kept a safe distance from fundamentalist beliefs. Everet had turned agnostic, his father, Douglas, had been a non-church going Christian, and Ruth had followed suit willingly, although since the death of Douglas five years earlier she had begun to attend services again.

30

"Everet, the brochures that I showed you, and the comments I've received from friends who have gone there already, show it isn't like that. You learn to listen to other people; you learn to listen to your own emotions too. That has nothing to do with yelling and screaming--or religion."

"It has nothing to do with us, either."

"It does."

"It doesn't. It's your painting. It's always been a problem, but I haven't seen it until lately. You've never made it, and now you're angry because my career is taking off."

"Oh, Everet..." Ruth looked at him, pleading, as if she were going to cry for Margy. There was even a sense of surprise at his behavior. "Don't be unpleasant," she said.

"It's true, Mama. She broke the contract."

Ruth looked puzzled.

"The marriage contract. She's not the woman I married. She doesn't want to be my wife anymore."

"I don't want to be the wife I was!"

"It's the same thing."

"I've changed; I'm sorry. But I'm also no longer in my twenties."

"Who is, Margy? That's what life is all about. But we make promises..."

Ruth put her finger to her lips, and just as Everet was about to shout something louder, they heard the front door open. Franklin, Cora, and Kennedy burst into the hallway. Short, chunky, Kennedy was about nine years old, while Franklin and Cora were in their early teens. The three stood smiling and breathless, having run home from the school yard, but the expressions of Franklin and Cora showed a trifle less exuberance. Kennedy dribbled a basketball and shot it across the couch as he stepped into the living room. Everet caught the ball, but with a forced smile he lobbed it back, reminding Kennedy that he should not play ball indoors. Kennedy went to Margy, kissing her cheek. She patted his curly brown hair, and then he kissed Ruth and Everet. With a short bounce of the basketball off Everet's knees, he left the room and ran upstairs. They were silent, hearing a *thump-thump* once or twice, then a door slam as Kennedy put the ball into his closet.

When the door slammed, Everet turned quickly to Franklin. "Just don't say anything about this, will you? Take him out for a walk. Take him to Carvel for ice cream."

He reached for his wallet and handed Franklin a couple of bills. Franklin nodded and went up to the second floor with Cora. As they waited in silence, laughter came from upstairs, then a stampede of footsteps on the stairway.

"Does anyone want ice cream from Carvel's?"

"No. It's your treat. Get what you want," Everet said.

"Anything? Oh, boy, you said that, Daddy. I didn't." Kennedy patted his stomach and, laughing, led the other two out while Margy, Everet, and Ruth waited for someone to start.

"How shall we begin?" Ruth said, forcing a smile.

"There's no beginning, Mama. We're in the middle of this already," Everet said.

After a moment, Margy muttered, "As I said, my life and my opinions have changed."

"Yeah, yeah. That's the subject, all right. But what about your word? What about our dreams? We shared them, but now the change has come at the wrong time."

"Wrong for you! Not for me!"

"For you, too! If only you could see yourself acting like a bitch!"

Margy stood, furious, and unable to contain herself, walked across the room to a pile of the day's newspapers. "Going to express yourself now?" Everet taunted. Groaning, she kicked them across the carpet. *The Wall Street Journal* fluttered momentarily; *The Amsterdam News* followed, along with *The New York Times* and several local papers.

"I'm tired of being seen by my husband as a newspaper item," Margy shouted. "It's time I started to live!"

Everet frowned and spread his palms before his mother. "I won't say that your behavior disgusts me," he said.

"But it does!"

He was silent, nodding his head as Margy wheeled on him. Ruth reacted also, turning away to look at the wall when Margy kicked the papers a second time. She turned to Everet and said, "Won't you try to understand her?"

"Understand her, Mama? What about me? And Kennedy? Doesn't our point of view count too?"

"Of course it does."

"Then why do we have to deal with this constant problem of hers?"

"But it's your problem too, it seems to me." Ruth folded her arms and looked stubborn.

"Thank you. Thank you, Mom, for coming down on the right side."

Margy smiled and threw herself on the couch. She folded her feet under her.

Everet glowered. "Okay," he said. "And what am I supposed to call your portion of this family problem, a female itch?"

"That's absolutely unnecessary!" Margy shouted.

He stomped his foot and shouted that it was. Margy rose from the couch again, stumbled, and in the process knocked a pair of ashtrays from the coffee table. She picked them up and, laughing for an instant, raised her hand to hurl one of them at the wall. Everet's eyes were serious though, and she could see his body--mother beside him or not--ready itself to strike. She replaced the ashtrays on the table.

"It won't disturb your career to go away for a couple of weekends with me. And it won't disturb Kennedy either. These things are considered normal nowadays."

"Margy's right, Everet."

"That's not the point, Mama."

"Everet, don't shake your head like that! We need help--you know that."

"Margy, we love each other. We've just got to let that feeling come through."

"Don't you see? We're not doing it?"

He sighed. Silent and agitated, Ruth stood to pace in front of the fireplace. Almost weeping, Margy sat down next to Everet again and took his hand.

"Honey, do it for me, please? And for your mother."

He shook his head. "I don't like creative listening and emotional outlet kind of stuff."

She slid to the floor beside his knees. She rose on her own and, in a last ditch effort, leaned across his lap to caress his cheek.

"Come on. One weekend isn't going to ruin your career. It'll get you in touch with your feelings. You need that--everyone does."

He shook his head defiantly. Margy dropped his hand and started to rise. He held her down by the shoulders. "Wait a minute. Let's think about this."

Feeling grim, Margy still tried to make a joke. "I think a deal is about to be struck," she said. "I can smell it."

Everet squeezed her shoulder with impatience. "Wait, I said. Will you go to the dinner Wednesday night? As an exchange?"

Margy shook her head. "We've discussed that already."

"Why?"

"Because, as I told you, after it you may change your mind about next weekend."

He nodded. "I might, if you don't act well. I don't want you to go into one of your artsy-fartsy numbers with my friends."

Margy rose; she walked around the coffee table and, after looking at the mantel clock, stopped at the hallway door. "I'm sorry that you've become so ambitious--for politics. It's ruined you."

His icy smile changed as he turned from his mother and replied, "I want a quiet, respectable family life, not an intellectual playpen."

Margy slammed the door and went up to her studio. She spent an hour there in silence, trying to work but actually accomplishing very little. When she heard Kennedy come in along with Franklin and Cora, she went down to say good-bye to the Hamiltons. Ruth was friendly as Margy kissed her cheek, but with an edge to her voice, even after Margy thanked her for her support. Franklin and Cora remained studiously neutral, while Kennedy, smiling and laughing as he pretended that he was leaving with the guests, seemed oblivious to the tension. Once the Hamiltons left, Everet sent Kennedy to bed and Margy retreated to her studio without a word. It was not until after midnight, in their bedroom, that they talked again.

"We can't go on like this," Everet said. "Even my mother is depressed."

"She should be. That's why I want to go to Wiltshire."

Margy lay under the covers, in her nightgown; the application she had filled out weeks before and given to him remained on the bureau, waiting for Everet's signature. Margy pointed to it again, and he went over to take a quick glance.

"That dinner is not for me either, Margy. But potentially it's important for my people. After all these years, don't you think you and I owe something to them?"

"Maybe. Don't you think you owe something to us?"

He nodded. "I do."

He went into the bathroom and came out again, wearing his blue terry-cloth robe. In spite of her anger, Margy gave a sharp intake of breath. One of the reasons she remained with him, she thought, was his capacity to move her physically. He appeared burnished, as if the blue of the robe brought out a warmer tone to his skin.

"All right. I admit it. This is important too," he said.

He went to the bureau, picked up the application and began to read through it. "Hey, what is this 'professional politician' stuff?"

"An occupation. Don't you like it listed that way?"

"I'm a civil rights lawyer, and a damn good one too."

"I'll change it."

He turned, grinning.

She raised her arms out to him. "Won't you come with me this weekend--please?"

"You know what I think. These weekends are for smart ofay--"

She dropped her arms. He put up his hand in order to stop Margy's cry.

"But I'll go! I'll go, goddamn it. I promise."

"Bullshit."

She turned over, burying her head beneath the pillow. He picked it up. "Bullshit, heh?—Where's my fountain pen?"

Dropping the pillow, he left the room, went downstairs to his office, and came up flourishing the application in his hand.

"No bullshit, baby," he said, pointing to his sprawling signature and placing the application on the dresser. "But you better be charming this Wednesday night."

"I'll do my best."

"Do better than your best. Be perfect."

He stepped out of his robe and modestly, in that bashful, simpering way he always had when naked, went to Margy as she pulled the covers aside. She trembled when she felt his body against her. It was warm and alive in a way that always struck her as marvelous, and a little sad.

"That's the only reason you'll go this weekend, to get me to that dinner?"

"The only one. Hey, Margy, it's reciprocal. You're as much a politician as I am."

She shook her head and pinched his buttock. He grinned, nuzzling her neck and reaching for her breasts. She pushed him away and, as he tried to pull up the hem of her nightgown, turned her back. That did not bother him. Immediately, he turned her over and kissed her, letting his hand slide down her flank and between her thighs. They made love. Afterward, with his softened penis pressed against her, his head settled into the pillow and, before Margy could close her eyes, he started to snore. That too was tinged with sadness, but she reached behind her back to squeeze a thank you to his leg. After ten years she had come to accept such little pleasures, although, as usual, she could not sleep, despite, or, perhaps, because of, his physical closeness. In a few minutes, she left the bed, went upstairs, and tried to work on one of her paintings.

36

3.

GOLDIE

"Hey, terrific! I like the way you got in all that action!"

Next morning. Goldie looked up from her journal, stopped, and in the middle of a blush, his smile began to fade. He turned back to the series of sketches in the notebook that Margy had shown him: Everet and his family, one or two of Kennedy, a half dozen neighborhood scenes--a couple of women at a backyard fence, a man dressed as a woman in the town shopping center, three or four girls and a boy playing jump rope.

"Sorry. It must have been painful for you to think about it all again. Was it after this that your mother became a bitch?"

"She always was--after that my father became awful too."

Margy took coffee from the stove, put it on a hotplate, brought two clean cups from the drainer. Goldie's blush deepened.

"Don't worry, Goldie. If I couldn't take your comments, I wouldn't have let you look through the notebook."

She poured coffee, took bread from the toaster, then went back to the table a little uneasy herself. She still felt strange talking about her past while in the kitchen. The more normal parts of her suburban life were absent: Everet, shaved and exercised, had driven off to work; Kennedy, dressed and overfed, was on the bus to school. Now, with Goldie up from the couch in the living room, where he had spent the night, her present life as a housewife and her former life as a young aspiring artist came together in a clash.

Goldie was seventeen years old. He lived next door with a guardian, his Uncle Dan, a widower whose wife had died some years before. Since that death, cancer-ridden and slow, Goldie's uncle had changed, and the Hamilton house

37

had gradually become Goldie's second home. To Margy, he looked like a teen-age Harpo Marx in certain ways: unkempt, yet charming--with bulging, bloodshot eyes, shirt-tail flopping above dirty, over-sized jeans, the smooth, hairless skin of his chest showing through an open, wrinkled collar, and, most of all, his blond hair a messy pile of yellow wool that fell into knots around his large, prominent ears and down his shoulders. As a flower child, he looked like a dandelion rather than a tulip; as a friend, he was a serious competitor in painting, as well as Margy's most reliable critic.

"I'm no expert, but I like these drawings, especially the guy at the center. It's like an Ivan Albright painting."

He rifled through the other sketches, glancing through the journal part of the notebook again and re-reading a passage or two. It was more than two hundred pages long, filled from top to bottom with small pen-and-ink drawings and Margy's cramped, almost illegible writing. She had been writing in it, along with many previous volumes, through most of her adult life.

"You've been working pretty hard. You intend to publish any of this stuff?"

She laughed. "I'm a painter, remember? And hardly a successful one at that. "

"That's what I keep telling you."

She waved, but could not come up with a better insult of her own. "Which ones should I try in the show? Do you have any preferences?"

He looked thoughtful for a moment, blocked his cigarette, then lit another and offered one to Margy. The show was a sensitive topic, and she was almost sorry that she had brought it up.

"Definitely the cross dresser," Goldie murmured, "and this one of the women talking. They both have a nice sense of movement. And feeling."

The sun came through the curtains behind Goldie, making it difficult to see into his eyes. They were bloodshot, Margy knew, and she could see by what light she had that his normally ruddy skin was a little pasty and gray. He had been out late the night before, had forgotten his key (which he did frequently), and when he came home his uncle, trying to impose strict curfew rules, had not let him into the house. After a long argument, Goldie rang the Hamilton doorbell, but neither Margy nor Everet had heard it. When Goldie returned home, he tried to jimmy his way through the back door, but before he finished, his uncle discovered him and they argued again. Finally, Goldie had telephoned Margy and asked to be let in.

"Did you sleep well?" she asked.

"Passing." He touched a bruise on his neck, and when she touched it too, he winced.

"I'm really sorry about your Uncle Dan. I must have been dreaming. I should have answered when you rang the bell."

Goldie shook his head. "I'm surprised you didn't hear the noise from the alley. He's been looking for an excuse to argue all week long."

He stood, dropped his cigarette into the ashtray, and with his legs bowed and arms out like a gorilla's, waddled around the table making grunting sounds. "'Wanna paint, huh? What, houses? Hitler did that too, and look what happened to him."

Goldie scratched his ribs and, with his mouth open, tongue extended, sounded an additional grunt.

"Then this number: 'What's a matter, truckin's too low-class? In your profession you get as much shit on your hands and none of the money.' He took my paints and brushes and tossed them into the garbage, second floor window to the pail in the yard. It was a good shot, but there are paint stains all over the driveway now."

Howling in frustration, Goldie looked out the window to the front of the house and shook his fist. Margy saw patches of red, purple, and blue, like bits of brightly colored paper, stippling the side wall, and, out front, one of Dan Goldstein's trucks. The logo was interesting--"If it's on the table, from Maine to Florida, Goldstein's Trucking brings it to you." Beneath it was an interesting painting too: a young child with blond ringlets smiling as he nibbled on a carrot. Goldie had posed for that picture when four years old.

"That's why I can't eat," he said, blowing smoke and pointing out the window. "If nothing else, I want to make it as a painter so I can make my uncle choke on that picture, truck by polluting truck."

Margy smiled. She took a few eggs from the refrigerator, scrambled enough for two, put bread in the toaster, and brought out jelly, juice and butter. When the eggs were done, she set a plate of them on each side of the table.

"Hey! Are you kidding?"

"You need it, Goldie. You didn't eat at all last night."

"Hell, no—food pusher!"

But he picked up his fork with a mumble and weakly poked at the eggs. After a few moments, he looked at Margy thoughtfully and said, "Did it really happen that way? I mean with your mother--exactly like you have it in the diary?"

She nodded. "As near as I can remember, anyhow. My father took her to the hospital that time, and when she came back she was more difficult than before. She had become a Catholic, she said, and not just for the fun of it. She wanted me to become a nun."

Goldie cringed. "What did your father say to that?"

Margy shook her head. "Not much. But he let her do anything to keep her quiet. He even beat my behind with a belt whenever she demanded it."

Goldie moaned. Margy spooned some jam onto her bread, forked some eggs on top of that and, nervous, put the whole thing into her mouth at once. Goldie, eyes wide in mock surprise, looked at her and patted her on the back as she choked, laughing and swallowing at the same time.

"Are you okay?" he said, as she tried to swallow and coughed again.

"Fine. Thanks. Everet says I'm a sloppy eater. I guess he's right."

He patted her back once more. "I'm really sorry, you know?"

"Don't be. It's over and done with and isn't worth the effort."

He shook his head. "I mean for the problems you have now, too."

She nodded. "Oh, well. We're going to try this weekend--at a sensitivity training conference up in Massachusetts. I hope it will do some good."

Goldie glanced at the notebook and shook his head, taking a small bit of his toast. He was very thin, and not just because of his uncle's business. Instead of eating, he smoked, he said. Although Margy never ate enough to gain weight herself, Goldie could make her feel hoggish whenever they had a meal together.

"That sensitivity stuff is okay, but it's not something I'd want to bet my future on."

"You aren't married," Margy said. "What would you bet it on--your talent?"

He nodded. "Maybe."

"Well, I hope you have better luck with it than I've had with mine."

Margy turned away and rose to go to the refrigerator. Goldie looked at her and closed his eyes. This, too, was a sensitive topic, and he started to apologize when she came back to the table. But then he simply inhaled his cigarette and let the moment pass.

"You going to class today?" he asked, as she poured a second cup of coffee for each of them.

"Sure. Aren't you?"

He shook his head. "I want to visit some galleries in New York. I also want to take a look at some of Foss's stuff. There are some new things at a gallery down in SoHo."

She put the pot on the hotplate and sat across from him. "Well, I have to work on my own stuff today, or else I'd join you. As a matter of fact, we'd better clean up so I can still get to Foss's drawing class on time."

They finished the coffee and washed and dried the dishes. Margy gave Goldie a towel so that he could clean up, and then she went to her room to dress. In a few minutes they met in her third floor studio. It was bright at this time of the morning, well lit from a window on the north end. It had bare plasterboard covering the beams, and its garret-like

41

quality was accentuated by a ceiling that slanted down sharply from the center to the floor. A large easel stood near one window. Above it hung a fluorescent lamp which Goldie had helped her install the winter before. He sat on the floor beneath it and looked through some canvases while Margy gathered together her equipment. Her desk stood beside a couch, at the opposite end of the room.

"Good landscapes and abstracts," Goldie said, squinting critically. "But that's usual. I still think you work better in watercolors." He looked through the smoke from his cigarette, and when she frowned, he grabbed a palette knife and slid it across the floor to her feet.

"So do oils, if you want. I don't care. How does Foss like this stuff?"

She looked at him and wiggled her hands. Goldie grinned.

Margy shook her head. "You know Foss. Today he likes them; tomorrow he won't say a word."

"I think you're good, Margy."

She waved. "Thanks, Goldie. But it's not necessary."

"It also happens to be true."

She nodded. He immediately dropped the canvas he had been looking at, blocked his cigarette, and looked at one of the slanted walls.

"You deserve credit," he said. "I owe you a lot."

She nodded again, then started to say something funny about the show, but stopped. While she continued to pack her things, she said, "I wish you were doing this show with me. I wish it was something we could share."

He waved and turned back to the canvases in silence. The show always seemed to create these moments between them; it had even produced the only disagreement they had ever had. In his middle teens, Goldie was considered something of an artistic prodigy, especially at Copperwood College of Art, a two-year school which he and Margy attended. He had dropped out of public high school in his junior year and, soon after, got into trouble with the police. Dan Goldstein had telephoned Everet and asked for his assistance. Everet had handled the police problems, and

42

Margy, knowing that art was important to Goldie, had shown his work to Foss and some of her other professors. They had liked his paintings and, after meeting him, they helped to get him admitted into Copperwood as a special student.

It was a complicated story, but that was how the problems with Margy began. In the middle of each year a jury of professors and off-campus artists chose a Copperwood College student to give a one-person exhibition over the summer. It was a prestigious event, bringing onto campus critics and patrons from New Haven, New York, and as far away as Boston. For two years in a row the choice had been between Margy and another student. The year before they had passed over her, even though her work seemed clearly the best in the school to many people. This year the choice had been between her and Goldie, and after some initial reluctance, she had decided to campaign for it actively, as the winner had done the year before. After some coaching from Everet, she went to Foss and other professors and pleaded her case. She had been at Copperwood longer, she argued; she was a good artist, also a conscientious student, and deserved some recognition for her work. Finally, the jury, which admired Goldie's work almost as much as hers, did choose Margy, but in a way that caused her trouble.

In their announcement, they said that Goldie was extraordinarily gifted, but young. He needed more time to mature, they said; and in a long, unusual comment, they virtually promised him the exhibition for the following year. Then, mainly because of jealousy, Margy thought, and partly because of Goldie's popularity, other students said that he had really deserved to have the exhibition. More important, they said that Margy had won because she was an attractive woman who got along well with Foss and the other male professors. After the announcement, Goldie argued with Foss and the rest of the jury; then he disappeared for days--from the college as well as Camels Back Drive. When he came back, he and Margy hardly said hello to one another, but after weeks of silence, he wrote her a note, telling her that she deserved the exhibition more than he did.

43

She looked at him that morning, remembering how relieved she felt after receiving that note; yet how guilty, and justified too, at having worked for the exhibition.

"You'll have your own show, eventually," she told him. "But for you it will be less traumatic."

"Why?"

"You're young." She raised her eyebrows. "And you already know that you're as good as anyone at the college."

"Thanks," he said, standing beside her and patting her back. "You're the only one who would say that."

She laughed. "Don't kid yourself. Everyone says it already—just not to you."

He shook his head, gravely. "I haven't been fair to you at all. You're the only person at the school who cares about the others, especially me."

She nodded, clearly pleased. "Well, at my age, and with my degree of success, I ought to have something to make me stand out."

She gathered her things, and as they left, Goldie helped carry her equipment. He leafed through the journal once again--she had left it on her desk--and before turning to go, he said, "To hell with our argument, with Uncle Dan, and your problems with Everet. We have the day ahead of us. Let's fill it up with movement and color, as if it were a canvas."

"Lovely," she said. "Let's try it."

She embraced him briefly, then led the way down the steps to the first floor. They went into the garage and drove to the railroad station in Stoddard where Goldie would take the train to New York. Before he left the car, he patted her arm and told her not to worry about herself or the exhibition.

"Whatever problems you've had," he said, "with me, or Everet, I'm always behind you. Remember that."

"Thanks," she said.

"I want you to know that I think you're tops."

She laughed. "Enjoy New York, my friend."

He squeezed her shoulder and ran through the traffic, across the street.

4.

FOSS

Stoddard and the section of town known as East Stoddard were in a lovely part of Connecticut. They had a shoreline on Long Island Sound; woods, which, westward, led toward the Berkshire Hills; and, south along the coast toward Westport, a sophisticated colony of artists and writers made up of ex-New Yorkers and old time Yankees. Stoddard was an amalgam of industry, several college campuses, and resident groups of blacks, Puerto Ricans, Italians and Irish, giving it a metropolitan, big city air, while East Stoddard had residential neighborhoods which combined the best and worst of suburbia.

In a sense, a map of the area formed a picture of Margy's life, and as she drove along Main Street and then down the turnpike toward Copperwood, she thought how lucky she had been to come here with Everet ten years before. She had not been ready for a career then, and in fact the small-town character of East Stoddard was just right to temporarily quiet--and nourish--her talent. She had the leisure time to think and be bored, a social position of sorts as the wife of a man who, although black, was obviously on the rise in the new, liberal world, and then finally, the fulfillment of motherhood, which also provided the perspective to see the limits of her fulfillment. While she loved Kennedy--would love him all her life, she was certain-- she found that being a wife and mother was not enough. Having the small, yet prestigious art college in Copperwood within a half hour's drive, she had made inquiries about it three years before, showed a panel of professors some of the work she had done while in her early twenties, and had been admitted to the college as what they called a "mid-career" student.

Copperwood had a good faculty, but the teacher of drawing and painting quickly became the most important person in Margy's artistic life. He was Sherman Foster,

45

known as Foss. Having studied with Pollock and de Kooning back in the fifties, Foss had taken up their abstract styles, made a quick and, as he called it, lucky success with them in the early sixties, and then in the last ten years had gradually worked himself back into a realistic style. It was there that his influence on Margy began. Because of that realism, he taught basic drawing at the college, urging all Copperwood students to attend his classes regularly so that they would not lose touch with the basics of line and form. Margy became his most faithful follower.

She pulled into the college parking lot and, checking her watch, found herself early by about ten minutes. She went into the life drawing studio to set up her easel, found no one there, and decided to drink a cup of coffee in the canteen. She talked to a few other life drawing students who stood at the coffee machine, and when they returned they found the class already in progress. The model--a large, big-breasted girl with lovely red hair--sat posed on a chair while Foss stood next to her, addressing the students.

"Keep your eye on the body," he said, as Margy strode behind the semi-circle of easels to take her place. "Draw the form you see. Look carefully, and let your mind's eye direct your charcoal without looking at the pad. If you look back and forth, you change the angle of your vision. And relax: remember, wrist and fingers extra loose."

Margy nodded, knowing that this was vintage Foss. In his late thirties, narrow-shouldered and intense, he had bright blue eyes dulled by alcohol and years of hard work. He had exhibited in New York for years and made a sensation at Copperwood several years before when he sold two huge canvases to the Museum of Modern Art. At that point the Guggenheim Museum became interested in him and bought two more. Then the Whitney followed, and after that several foundations inquired about his work. All through that spring there was talk that one of them would send him to Europe on a grant the following year. Yet, Margy knew, he was in a period where he was not producing very much.

"Be limp and humble," Foss said. "Allow yourself a little room for error. As one of my teachers used to say,

'Even the Sistine Chapel is going to crumble. All that fine technique will eventually pass away.' Try to get it right, but don't inhibit yourself."

He stepped back, acknowledging Margy and the other late students with a nod of his head. Then he studied the model's pose for a moment, readjusted her arms and, patting her rump and kissing her forehead, left the platform in order to walk among the class. Patient, he corrected the drawing technique of some of the newer students, gave the older ones encouragement--or a neutral stare, which they had come to know as disapproval. Margy drew quickly, loosely, first sketching the chair the girl was straddling. It was warm up time really, but when she came to the face she slowed down and worked more carefully. The model's expression interested her. She was heavy, but with a handsome, winsome smile, as if somebody had made fun of her weight and she wanted to show she really didn't mind. Margy tried to draw that quality in her, but although she had the technical skill, she felt too tight within herself. She had learned to expect that in the early stages of a day's work, especially when she tried to reach through to something soft and passive.

Foss came near, nodding when Margy said hello. But instead of talking, he returned to the model. He readjusted her position, and, when he turned back to the class, Margy began to relax more into her drawing. The model took directions well and, from the way she looked at Foss, Margy guessed that she was probably a recent lover. She followed him easily, smiling politely when he reprimanded her and again possessively patted her slightly bulging derriere. Margy ripped off the page, drew her outline once more, filling in the curves, the horizontal shadows of her flesh almost automatically. But when she got to the face she paused and had to concentrate on the smile. The girl had an intriguing frankness, and Margy ripped off the sheet again in order to concentrate on her face entirely. Foss stood beside her, stepped back with his chin in his hand, then came closer to offer his opinion.

47

"Margy, you have to get the lines better. Stronger here. More shadow around the lips. I think you're pressing too lightly on the charcoal. Keep your finger-muscles loose."

He held Margy's wrist, jiggled it in his hand, and grinned as his other arm circled her waist. "It's been a long time. Mind if I try something?"

"I certainly do."

He laughed, picking up the charcoal, and when Margy nodded he began to move it swiftly over the pad. A touch of charcoal to her eyelids, a trace of shadow under her chin, a heavy smudge of his finger beneath her earlobes. Technical, his changes had little to do with the inner feelings Margy had been working toward, but with just a few strokes, masterful ones, Margy thought, he had brought the face to life. Now there was an air of mystery to her portrait that Margy had intended to cut through.

"Nice, heh?" Characteristically, Foss smiled to himself as he stepped back to look at his work.

"Perhaps. But as usual I think you're a little bit too slick. *Playboy* would love that for a centerfold."

"Oh, come on, Margy." He thumbed his nose and drew a thicker line along the figure's neck. "You're better at landscapes usually, but I admit that occasionally you have a nice little line on your flesh."

He smirked, dropped the charcoal onto the easel rail and began to walk away.

"To hell with you, Foss," Margy said under her breath. Although she was sure that he had not heard her, he turned suddenly and waved his hand.

"It has been a long time, you know? Hey, don't be angry. I'm sorry about my crack."

Margy lowered her head. Although she was not sure which comment he meant, she said, "I'm sorry about mine, too, I guess."

He glanced around as he came closer.

"How's your show coming? You working on it yet?"

"Some. Not as much as I'd like."

He shook his head. "You're still uptight about those things. Well, I suppose it's natural. Maybe we should get together and talk about your work some time."

Margy nodded, half-heartedly. Foss stopped and stared, his mouth pursed with a trace of self-mockery. "Really, if you need some help, just give me a call. Like this afternoon? At my place?"

He was silent, grinning stupidly as he came closer, and all Margy could do by way of response was lower her head again. Other students concentrated on their work; Foss's little colloquies with female students were so habitual that they almost went unnoticed.

"Why your place, Foss?"

"Oh, come on. Why *not* my place? It's bigger. It'll be private and easier to work. I'm a busy man, Margy. I've got things to do. Look, you want to come around?--Say, about two-thirty?"

"I'll have to leave early, Foss."

"Yeah. Yeah. So do I. If you don't want to come, don't bother. I told you, I'm a busy man."

"I'll try," she said.

He smiled and put his arm around her waist. "For old time's sake, try, really. I'll let you go in half an hour. There's something I want to ask you."

Winking, he went back to the model, who had become slightly paler--a sure sign to Margy that she, at least, had been watching. Nevertheless, Foss put her into a new position so that she was almost standing over the chair. He became more cheerful and, spurred on by his livelier mood, the whole class began to draw more spontaneously. At noon when the session ended, they put their easels away, cleaned up, and ate lunch together under a willow in the yard. Afterward Margy went to work in an empty studio in the cottage, planning to leave at two o'clock so that she could stop at Foss's on the way home.

She thought of herself as a mediocre talent sometimes--especially in comparison to Foss and occasionally to Goldie--but Margy felt proud that afternoon when she opened her canvases and lined them around her easel along

49

the studio walls. Two and a half years of work: space, abutments, trees; she had a flare for those things, especially when she worked in watercolors, as Goldie had said that morning. The pictures that she lined up were images from the landscapes of her childhood, and they had made her troubled and nostalgic while she drew them. Generally, she was suspicious of emotion in painting, but she had tried to use it constructively in these works. There were haystacks in green, gold, and red, fields of corn that seemed to grade in color from pale green to mauve to rust, forest scenes with a genuine sense of gloom and dread, and small town skylines whose buildings showed the energy of progress in their lines, but whose blank sides betrayed Margy's sense of the emptiness behind them.

She set canvases on several easels and worked steadily on two or three of them at once. She completed one painting, touched up a second, and felt fairly confident about a third, which she left alone. She still felt proud, but in her general ambivalence with the show and Goldie, she was grateful for the opportunity to talk with someone who might be more objective--especially Foss.

She packed everything and started to drive to his place in Westport. He had a nice home there--in a converted barn on a little farm overlooking the Sound--with enough clear land around it to remind her of Waterloo Falls. The property was surrounded by firs and maples, which lined the drive on the way to his door, while clumps of rhododendron and spruce surrounded the barn itself. Margy saw Foss sitting on his front step as she arrived, and while she parked, he picked up a glass and gave her a little salutatory wave.

"Lovely," Margy said as she left the car. "When I go back to East Stoddard, I feel sick."

"Suburbia."

Foss toasted--not smiling--and drained the glass in one gulp. He had always been different at home, she recalled. Without a class in front of him he became more self-involved and, in Margy's opinion, much less in control. Inside the apartment, he immediately filled his glass with scotch and then poured a little for Margy. As she took the glass, she looked around the room. It hadn't changed: large and disorderly, with a bed in one corner, a red refrigerator and stove in another, and the rest of the space given over to a maze of tables, easels, and multi-colored workbenches on which he did his work. He took some books off an old brown couch, tossed them in the corner, and offered Margy a seat. When he took the chair across from her, he sighed, picked up an unopened pack of Camels and put it down.

"Well, as I said in class, it's been a while. You really want to talk about your stuff?"

Margy nodded. "Two years, isn't it? Since December, 1972."

"Christmas," he said. He reached for the cigarettes again, then pulled away and sighed. "Let's hold off on reminiscence, heh? It's been a goddamn long day, and I don't feel up to mourning."

He leaned over the back of his chair, reached behind a workbench, and flipped the switch for the tape deck and amplifier. Speakers from all four walls came on, filling the room with jazz. It was still Brubeck, Margy heard with surprise, and still his older sound. Foss had a preference for music that was low-keyed and controlled.

"How're you doing? You and Mayor Hamilton are still together, I see."

"Mostly, Foss. But struggling. You?"

He coughed on the scotch, grinned, rose to pour some more, then offered Margy the bottle. "You see the place. I don't think I could live full time with a woman again; not after that bitch, Carmina."

He sat, laughing, indeed almost cackling on Carmina's name. She had been his mistress for a year or so, a Puerto Rican girl whom he had used as a model, but she had left him in order to pursue her own career as a photographer. He had not yet recovered. Margy noticed a sarcasm in him that was turned upon himself. Increasingly, he expressed it as self-pity.

"You still love her, Foss, despite it all."

"Yeah, I love her."

51

He waved his drink, wiping his thin hair back from his forehead, then sat next to Margy on the couch. His arm went around her waist and she pulled away.

"Can't we talk about my work?" Margy patted him on the shoulder. "I have to get home early."

She picked up her portfolio, letting his arm slide from her waist, and began to unpack some things. She unrolled several canvases, then brought out some watercolors lying flat beneath them. With another sigh, Foss filled his glass and returned to the chair opposite her.

"Later. I spent the whole fucking day looking at student stuff, and I feel like I'm bleeding to fucking death."

Shoving the portfolio aside, he took Margy's arm and tried to pull her onto his lap.

"Come on, I said. Sit down. Talk."

"I have to leave soon, Foss. Kennedy will be home by four."

"Good for Kennedy. Good for little President Kennedy. Look, I want to sit down and have a conversation with you. That's all. As a man and woman. No squeezing or fighting, and no sucking me dry for my opinions."

He took another sip of scotch and leaned back, filling and lighting a pipe. Margy left his boney knees and returned to the couch. "Just talk to me--as a friend," he said. "In case you haven't noticed, you're all I've got."

She smiled. "How about the model in class?"

"Margy, I said *friend*. That's a chubby, pink-faced kid. What can I say to her?"

He drained his glass and smoked, filling the room with fumes from the pipe. There was a moist sheen on Foss's forehead, and, gradually, his cheeks turned pale, a pair of ghastly gray patches, if she were painting them. To Margy, the change was Foss's self-pity coming out in flesh tones, and she recalled the sense of loss and isolation she had felt on afternoons with him when they lay in bed together and listened to this same Brubeck music. Neither of them had been happier; but at least she had thought that they were being free. If she didn't know better now, she would have thought of her marriage with Everet and wondered what about her made men sad.

"Well, what is it, Foss?" she asked. "What can I do for you?"

"As a woman?" He flashed his big yellow teeth, and his hands dropped toward the zipper of his pants.

"Come on, Foss. Don't be stupid."

The grin dried up; the hand, midway to his lap, went back to his glass. He frowned.

"All right, don't do anything for me. What else can I ask for but talk? You always had something fine about you, Margy. Since two winters ago, the ass I'm getting isn't worth a cent."

He laughed, lamenting, screwing up his lips and blowing an obscene kiss at her. With a lump in her throat, Margy turned to the window.

"Foss, what do you want? We said we could still be friends. I want to help you as much as I can. But I did come here to discuss my work for the show."

"Sure." He changed the tape and came back to the chair with another glass of scotch. He began to talk, stopped. Then he took a deep breath and began again.

"I want you to help me with *my* work, goddamn it. I'm hitting this stuff pretty hard, as usual. But as you can also see, I'm doing nothing else." He looked around the room pitifully and waved his glass. "Empty. My guts are empty. I haven't touched a brush in over three fucking months. "

"That's nothing new for you," Margy said.

"It is when there's nothing stirring. I'm sick--"

Margy waved her hand. "You came to the wrong person to get you out of a slump, Foss."

"I know. I know. Goldie gave me the tragic news. 'Margy's choking up about the exhibition,' he says. ... Are you fucking that kid, Margy? He's a nice boy. I wouldn't mind him getting his share."

He stood, laughing at Margy's angry reaction. Then he tottered around the workbench, kneeled down behind it, and came back with a canvas in his hand. He unrolled it on the carpet at her feet.

"I never threw this away. Of course, I never finished it either."

On his haunches, pipe in his hand, Foss glanced up and smiled at Margy. It was an acrylic of her, nude, standing with a wreath of plain white flowers around her neck. It had been his attempt, two years ago, to construct a painting in the classical manner.

"It's still too mystical, too romantic," he said. "I want to knock out most of the mist and vegetation, give something of an urban background for balance. And I want to redefine the face, or change the pose of the head a little. I still think it could be good though, a modern Flora from *La Primavera*--without the Botticelli somberness."

"I thought we agreed that you work better with other models, Foss? Can't you let me go?"

He rolled up the canvas and angrily threw it into the corner with his books "Fuck it. God damn it, just say you don't want to pose. I don't need your fucking comments."

"I don't want to sleep with you, Foss."

He fell back into his chair, drained his glass, and threw an empty cigarette pack on the floor.

"Look, Margy, I need to work, you know? I'm an artist. I need to have some human contact--but for my *work*. We won't play around; I won't even touch you. Just come here a couple of afternoons to pose and give me a reason to begin painting again."

She looked at him and left the couch. He seemed sincere, but Margy did not want the obligation. She had enough of that kind of thing with him two years before.

"Foss, probably any girl at school would pose for you."

"I want to work, I said. Not fool around. Besides, that picture is you, not just any woman."

Margy shook her head. "Thanks. But I'm trying to straighten out things with my family. Everet and I are going away this weekend. I don't want to make things more confused. It's a sensitivity workshop. I want to feel I can tell him everything."

"Forget it. I'm sorry I bothered."

54

He got up, stumbled on the rug as he went to the red refrigerator for ice, and then filled his glass with whiskey. Hands shaking, he rummaged about the room for another pipe, and Margy saw that his whole body had begun to quiver. He tore open a pack of cigarettes, taking off the cellophane with a violent snap. "I'll never stop," he grumbled. "I'll never let you--or Carmina--go either." Suddenly his eyes glazed over, and he looked at her as if she were already miles away.

"Please, Foss. Can't you be civil? We said we'd always be friends."

"Bleed me. That's all you've ever done, is bleed me. You and every other cunt who holds a brush."

"I'm sorry, Foss. I'm just trying to keep things straight."

He took the bottle from the table, drained his glass, and poured it full again. He popped a pill and swallowed that down too. The look on his face became resolute but sickly, as the patches on his cheeks took on a faintly purplish hue.

"Fuck it," he said. "Go suck off that kid next door to you. Jack off your old man this weekend and keep things straight. I don't need you. I'll survive."

He took a long drink, a long puff of his cigarette, and closed his eyes as he let smoke out. Margy rolled up her canvases and replaced them in the folio, along with her watercolors. Bag on her shoulder, she was ready to leave when Foss opened his eyes and asked her to sit again.

"I've got to get going, Foss."

"Sit *down*, god damn it. Your kid will be all right if you're a few minutes late."

"I have to get away. I'm not going to be your pillow."

He started to shout at her, but then he stopped himself with a quick, deep breath.

"I'm sorry. I shouldn't come down on you like this. You're a fine woman, Margy. I 'm really sorry we broke up."

"I am too, Foss. Sometimes."

She turned away and felt ashamed. He had looked at her, come forward in his chair as if about to jump, but, after she said "sometimes," he sank back again.

"Look, can you come by tomorrow'? I need you. I need you for my *work*."

"I'll think about it. I'll let you know after class."

"Sure. Listen, before we come here we'll take a studio in the cottage, set up everything you've got and discuss it in detail. I know how uptight these exhibitions can make you. I'll guide you through it so it's nothing."

He stood, resting his arms heavily on Margy's shoulders.

"Thanks, Foss. I better go."

He kissed her. "Yeah. Go ahead. Get home to the kid. Maybe I'll see you tomorrow afternoon."

He sank into his chair, refilled his glass, and Margy, feeling troubled enough to run to him with open arms, went through the door. In the yard the light seemed darker, the shadows from the trees longer, and the sun behind the house looked almost out of sight. Something bad is going to happen to Foss--and to me, she thought. Beaten, with no sense of wholeness in either of us, no sense that we know what lies ahead.

She drove down a road with a pasture on either side and, crossing Westport's main street, headed toward the thruway. She thought of it as a ribbon wrapping up the Connecticut coast, making a gift of it to dump into the ocean. Cars hurtled through the heat and muck of the city, but the Sound remained pleasant through it all, a constant reminder--and fitting, for her present mood--of other, better things. The water was copper at that moment, and a warm breeze carried the smell of salt from the shore. In fifteen minutes, she had reached downtown Stoddard, heading east on the main thoroughfare toward home. Traffic was heavy at that hour, and as she waited through her third light in as many blocks, she saw Goldie crossing the street and walking toward the bus stop.

"Hey, come here." She beeped the horn and waved him toward the car. Immediately, she felt better. His youthful good looks always did that for her. He had his jacket off, his shirt was open to his stomach. His cheeks were flushed and shiny as he turned to face her.

"Wow, nice weather, isn't it? How was your day?"

"Good. I got *some* work done. How was New York?"

"Great. But I got tired of looking at paintings after a while. Even in New York they have so much crap around."

He winked at Margy, came up to the car and entered it. She turned off the main road, cut across the highway jutting through the center of town, and took a curvier, less travelled route than the main one. They talked about the paintings he had seen. There were two or three mediocre pieces by Foss, Goldie said. He sighed in disappointment as he described them, pulled his shirt completely out of his trousers, and opened it fully to the breeze coming in the window. When they arrived in East Stoddard, he buttoned it again.

"It's been a beautiful day," Margy said. "You want to spend the night with us? Kennedy won't be there."

He shook his head. "I've got to see Uncle Dan sometime. It might as well be tonight."

Margy shuddered.

"It won't be so bad."

"I know. But in case you have any trouble, I'll leave the key under the mat in back."

"Thanks. You--and Everet, too--are really being great. I want you to know I love you both." He leaned out the window and lit a cigarette. Margy would have talked some more, but they had arrived at the corner of Camels Back Drive, and Goldie, as usual after an argument with his uncle, got out so that Dan Goldstein would not see them together.

"Do you want me to come with you? I might be some help."

"You'd only make it worse. Uncle Dan thinks that you're a bad influence."

Margy grinned. "Only me, heh? No one else." Goldie grinned too, as he left the car. "Well, don't forget," she said. "The key is under the mat, in case you need it."

"I won't forget. See you tomorrow."

"I'll drive you to school, if you want."

"Sure."

57

"But I might go to Foss's after class. We're supposed to talk about my work."

She blushed, as Goldie's eyes widened, and he coughed. "The paralyzed leading the lame." He put his hand up. "Fine. If I can't do it, maybe Foss can. Thanks for the ride."

He waved and headed home. Margy drove down the street and turned directly into their garage.

5.

EVERET

The Goldstein home and the Hamilton home were the only traditional houses on Camels Back Drive. One-hundred-year-old twins, they once were owned by descendants of Carl R. Stoddard, the 18th century founder of Stoddard who, in his later years, built a family estate here. Each twin house had a grand entranceway with imitation Doric pillars in front and drives--typical of 19th century landscaping in Connecticut--lined with chestnuts, dogwoods, and maple trees. Their lawns had once taken up the whole block and even part of the woods in back, but, after World War II, the Stoddards had sold the surplus acreage to developers, and the newer, flatter, more sprawling buildings had been erected shortly afterward. The Goldsteins bought their house from the family in 1954; Margy and Everet bought theirs almost fifteen years later from the last surviving Stoddard, a frail white-haired, old man who had rented the house to strangers for years and then had to sell it against his will in order to support himself in a home for the aged. He died less than a year after Margy and Everet moved in.

As she looked at the two houses, Margy often remembered calls they had received during the first month or two. Anonymous voices referred to Everet and Kennedy as her "tar-baby" relatives and said that the Hamiltons would turn the neighborhood into a slum. Two owners on the block sold their homes immediately at outrageously low prices, but others stayed on, some even making efforts to be friendly, until finally the neighborhood stabilized. It was frightening, yet good too, because for one of the few times in Margy's life she had a public cause. And along with Everet and Kennedy she succeeded in winning friends all along the block. Even Sam Goldstein was on their side at first, and held neighborhood meetings at his home because, as some said, these meetings helped keep up the value of his property. But another reason, as others rarely admitted, was the

Goldsteins themselves had experienced an unpleasant reception when they first moved in. Jews, like blacks, were not a part of the Stoddard good-neighbor tradition.

The Hamiltons moved in during the spring of 1969, and it is that period which gave Everet his positive sense of their future in Stoddard. It was also the optimistic community spirit of that year, a sort of last breath of civil rights liberalism, as Margy thought of it, which he hoped to call upon in his political work. In the driveway that afternoon, on her way from the garage to the house, Margy wondered where her own optimism had gone. She felt she had become as self-pitying as Foss in certain ways, as if the six months or so that she had spent with him--all in the name of sensual and artistic freedom--still affected her, causing her to think of limitations in her work, rather than possibilities. Certainly she had learned at least a part of her pessimism in childhood, but with Everet she had forgotten that. For those few short months after they moved onto Camels Back Drive, all her past had seemed unimportant. She had worked especially hard to make the larger social issues implicit in their marriage at least seem invisible. She had stopped painting and ceased thinking about art because she had tried to channel her creative energies into social causes. But soon those causes were not enough, and within a year she became dissatisfied with her own development.

While Kennedy was still an infant, she began to dabble with brush and canvas again. When he entered kindergarten, she decided to work at painting more seriously. For a time her talent developed quickly. She entered several local contests for fun, won two or three first prizes, then applied to Copperwood where, immediately, everyone admired her work. Foss took her under his wing in the drawing class. He sponsored a picture of hers so that it could be shown and sold at a major gallery in New Haven; he sent some watercolors to Hartford in a state-wide competition: she won third place. He asked her to give special classes on drawing and watercolor technique when he had other things to do, or was too drunk to teach himself. And he began to take her to New York, to visit galleries and museums, and to meet people in the art world--first in groups, then alone. But certain negative feelings about art began to surface in Margy's mind. She felt guilty about Everet and Kennedy; then her drawing became mechanical rather than inspired. In despair over divisions between home and work, she sank into a weekend habit of getting high with Foss and some of his friends from New York. When, one early Sunday morning, she woke up laughing in her car after somehow driving from Foss's and found that underneath her coat she had no shirt or trousers on, she sneaked into the house, lay quietly on the living room couch, and after a restless hour and a half of desperation, confessed and apologized for her actions to an already knowing Everet.

Her despair crystalized one afternoon in one of those bizarre chance experiences that occur as if in a dream yet still affect us in real life. While standing in front of the house, Margy saw a slightly familiar woman walking along Camels Back Drive muttering to herself. She wore a cloth coat draped on her shoulders (her arms were not in the sleeves), and she hurried down the block through the cul de sac at the end, into the fields beyond until she came to the neighborhood septic pool, not far from Kennedy's school. She looked fragile, and something about her eyes and the carriage of her shoulders expressed Margy's sense of desperation and need. So she followed the woman, even though she could not say where she had seen her before.

The woman looked back occasionally as she walked, cocking her hand to her ear as if she heard Margy following her. Behind a tree, a bush, or a curve in the road, Margy remained carefully out of sight. She watched as the woman reached the end of the path through the wooded area, went past the rock, up a hill, and then to the other side of the hill where she paused at the wire fence surrounding the pool. Small, round, sand-lined as if it were a miniature ocean, the septic pool was camouflaged by trees and bushes as part of a neighborhood beautification project. At the fence the woman cocked a hand behind her ear again and turned, but Margy ducked behind a tree just in time to avoid being seen. She watched as the woman took off her coat and hat, kicked off

61

her shoes, and began to unbutton her dress. But she stopped, as though she felt chilled, and stood with her arms crossed in front of her as she looked around. Margy knew what she was about to do, but she felt such fascination that she could not bring herself to stop her.

The woman swung around, picked at a branch of a tree, and pulled a cluster of leaves off. She smelled the leaf, ripped it, chewed a piece and ran the rest of the cluster along her arm. Her smile was agonizing! Margy wanted to step out from hiding and run to her, but when the woman turned in her direction, she retreated, almost in a reflex. She waved again, her hand fluttering delicately by her face, then blew a kiss and started to climb the fence. Margy watched, trembling. She was sure now, but could not do anything. She stepped from behind the tree only to dash behind another when the woman--halfway up--twisted her head to look.

"Don't!" Margy finally shouted, stepping into the open and waving her arms. Whether the woman heard or not, Margy could not say. She smiled, not at Margy, but at the trees it seemed, then took another step to the top of the fence. Erect on two feet for an instant, she dived, fell, or simply dropped off with arms outstretched and, giving a little shriek, landed on her face and stomach in the sand.

"This is real, you dummy. This is not a dream!"

Margy raced to the fence and climbed it, landing on her feet beside the woman. She looked at her face and held it carefully in her hands. Blood streamed from her mouth. Her arm floundered spasmodically at her side. Her foot twitched behind Margy's hip, and her knees seemed to be burrowing in the sand.

"Are you all right? Can you hear me?"

The woman's eyes opened, but they did not blink, and the expression on her face had a highly unnatural stiffness. Margy spoke again, put her ear to the mouth, but heard no intake of breath. The woman remained on her stomach. With her ear to her back, Margy could hear no heartbeat. She climbed back over the fence and, turning for a final look, saw a sight she would never forget. The woman's hand stretched out along the sand above her head. Her fingers twitched weakly, as if digging in the sand. She reached for a pebble, grasped it, held it balled in her small fist. Then her eyes closed suddenly, her expression seemed to fade, and her body went completely still.

Fifteen minutes after Margy called, the police arrived and took the woman to the hospital. Her neck had been broken, yet, miraculously, she lived. In the newspapers next day, Margy read that she was a little-known television actress (her name was Brenda Salerno; classically trained, she could get work only in the soaps) who, for weeks, had spoken to friends of killing herself because she was aging.

"Sister," she whispered when Margy visited her at the hospital. "You give me hope. You give me a reason to live." Photographers snapped the two of them at bedside, and the papers next day spoke of the "miracle" produced by a good neighbor.

When Margy left the hospital that day, she wondered just how long that miracle would last. Brenda improved rapidly and seemed to be doing well when Margy visited her occasionally at home on a nearby East Stoddard street. Brenda moved stiffly at first, but gradually, with the help of therapeutic exercise, she regained most of her mobility. Soon she could walk with the aid of a cane. There was talk of writing her back into the soap. They spoke of their careers once while Brenda posed for Margy on the shore of Long Island Sound, and two or three times they made trips to New York City where, in a special car and wheel chair provided for the day-long trip, they divided their visit between the theatre and a couple of art museums.

Eventually Brenda walked without a cane and, as her spirits improved, she hinted at giving classical acting another try. But that spring, almost two years to the day after she left the hospital, she climbed out onto a jetty of the Sound in Bridgeport, sat for almost an hour according to witnesses, then slipped, fell, or jumped and was never seen again. People on the beach said she had simply stood up and disappeared. No note was found. Her family said she had given no evidence of renewed depression. In her notebook Margy made several sketches of Brenda lying on the sand near the septic pool; they show her hand outstretched and upraised, pointing--or, perhaps, moving--toward the water. One sketch shows her smelling those leaves from the trees. And as for the pebble she finally grasped in her palm, Margy drew her throwing it, desperately, somehow trying to make a splash within the pool of water.

Margy carried those images of Brenda within, and they were especially strong as she entered the house that afternoon--memories of life with Foss could bring her that close. She took a shower, put on a clean skirt and blouse, straightened the house, and then went into the kitchen. She was making Kennedy's supper--french fries, onions, frankfurters, all set off with a dot and dash of baked beans lying, as she liked to think of them, in a *gouache* of deep red sauce. Margy put on her yellow apron; her hair trussed up in a clean, *Good Housekeeping* bun; and into this cliché of Betty Crocker advertisements, a lovely mocha-colored son--an elf from a different myth--entered with baseball cap, glove, and book bag over his shoulder.

"Hi, Mama," Kennedy said. "What's for dinner tonight?" He came to the sink and planted a wet kiss on her cheek.

"Hot dogs, Honey."

"Again?" He dropped the bookbag heavily on the floor.

"Oh, Kennedy, they're your favorite dish. And I've made a batter for the onions, the way you like them."

"I'm only teasing, Mama."

She smiled, kissing him. "You're eating alone tonight. Then we're taking you to Grandma's. Daddy and I are going out."

"I know." He smiled, reaching out to put his hand in her apron pocket. Margy embraced him, for a moment holding his cheek against her neck.

"How was the game, love? Did your team win?"

"We crushed them, Mama, eight to one. I hit a homer."

He pulled away, carefully withdrawing from her arms. Then, posing with his hands interlocked, he swung, swatting

64

an imaginary ball and driving it through the window into the Goldstein backyard.

"Good for you, honey. How did you do in school?"

"The usual." He looked disappointed as he turned to her, let the bat disappear from his hands, and began to finger Margy's apron pocket again. "Tomorrow I have to do a report in American History. The economic system under Alexander Hamilton. I don't even know what an economic system is."

"Hmmm. That's something I know very little about, too. You'd better talk to Daddy."

"Oh, I'll get it. There are plenty of books on it. Sometimes school is so boring..."

He waved as if it were not important, then took an apple from the refrigerator and, biting it, began to go upstairs. Feeling a rush of something doubtful, Margy called to him.

"Kennedy?"

"Yes, Mama?"

"I love you."

"I love you too, Mama."

"I want you to be happy." She felt as if she were babying him, but she did not know what else to say.

"I am happy, Mama," he said. "Why wouldn't I be?"

He stared at Margy with a grin. His large brown eyes beamed clearly and with confidence as he bit the apple again, looking at her from the living room. She went through the hallway, fell to her knees in front of him, and hugged him tightly.

"No reason. But you know there are people who are miserable in this world. I hope you're never one of them."

He put his hand to her hair and pulled a wisp of it from behind her ear. She remembered other afternoons when she had returned from Foss's cottage with a great deal of guilt in her heart and would not be able to talk to him. She could feel his body shuffle against her arms, and then, after she kissed him, a burst of juice hit her cheek as he bit into the apple again.

"I'll do my best, Mama," he said. "I always do my best. As Daddy says, with half a break I should be okay."

She embraced him one more time and let him go to his room. Back in the kitchen, she opened more packages and cans, placed things on the stove and in the oven. An hour or so later, by the time Everet had arrived, Kennedy and his dinner were at the table.

"How's my family tonight?" said Everet, coming through the door. He smiled, embracing Margy while giving her a heavy, solemn kiss, and went into the den to drop off his attaché case. He left his jacket draped over a living room chair and, stepping around a hassock, returned with some mail that she had left for him on a lamp table.

"How's dinner, old man?" he said.

"I wish I had more of these hotdogs, Daddy."

"I'm keeping them warm in the oven. Finish those first, and you can have two more."

"Hey, sport, you're getting a little round down there. I told you, you're going to be sorry later on."

Everet patted Kennedy's belly, then, laughing, raised his fists and snapped a fake left jab which Kennedy pawed away.

"C'mon, boy. Down with the fork, up with them dukes. You're talking to Muhammad Ali."

He leaned in, jabbing Kennedy lightly on either shoulder, then took him in a wrestler's hold and lifted him out of the chair. Kennedy grasped Everet's hand, giggling. But when he was placed on the floor, he pushed Everet away.

"Oh, Daddy, stop. I got plenty of exercise today. We played a nine inning game."

"Hey! Great! How'd you do at bat?"

"Two walks and a homer. We even got a double play. The coach said I looked like Bobby Richardson at second base. Did you ever see him play, Daddy?"

"I sure did, sport. But you tell that coach of yours you'd rather look like Jackie Robinson. He was a whole lot better." Everet winked at Margy and ran his hand through Kennedy's hair again. "Anyway, you want to be hard and strong when you grow up. So you better be careful with your eating now."

"But I'm hungry. Can I have one more, Mama?"

Margy, who liked to feed Kennedy, looked at Everet, and he, frowning, told the boy to serve himself while he and Margy went upstairs. Poking Kennedy's stomach again, Everet embraced him and followed Margy out of the kitchen.

They took turns in the bathroom upstairs. Everet was first since he needed to shower, and while Margy manicured her nails, they carried on a conversation through the open bathroom door. Margy felt tense, as usual before formal affairs, and, as was also usual, she found Everet's cheerfulness before them more unnerving.

"I had a great day today," he said, "with some very productive meetings and some interesting new clients. How about you?"

"My day was all right."

"What did you do?"

She shrugged, not wanting to say anything about Foss. "Had breakfast with Goldie. Went to Copperwood. Tried to get some work done for my show."

"Sounds good. Why the hell are you so subdued? How is Goldie? He seemed pretty depressed last night."

"Okay. I just brought him home, and I suspect Dan will have a lot to say."

Everet grunted. For a moment Margy saw his face in the mirror above the sink as he started to lather his face for shaving. "He'll get through it. He always does. Listen, about Kennedy, I think you ought to feed him less. He's got a pudgy enough body as it is, and I want to make sure it's only baby fat. I know you love him, but try to give him more whole grains and vegetables--a lot less starch and meat."

"I do that already, Everet. I just thought that if he had to eat alone tonight, it would be nice to give him something that he likes."

"He's got to learn to appreciate healthier food. That's all in the upbringing."

Margy nodded. "Just give him time."

"It won't hurt to push him a little. Eating habits are formed very early."

She nodded again. Finished lathering, Everet had taken out a razor and begun shaving. When he finished, and then stepped into the shower, their conversation stopped. Margy finished her nails. As she laid out her evening wardrobe, Everet turned off the water, slammed the curtain aside, and came out of the bathroom with a towel wrapped around his waist. He looked at her meaningfully, glancing quickly toward the bed. She smiled, but he waved the situation away, going into the closet for his own clothes. He brought out two heavy paper bags, tearing them open and taking out the coordinates of his new tuxedo.

"It's lovely," Margy said, sitting on the bed. "Let me see you with it on."

"Just watch. Don't get too sexy."

He stood in front of the full-length mirror on the closet door and began to put it on. It was the first tux he had ever owned, and the first time he had ever worn it. Despite their argument of the weekend before, Margy felt the specialness of the occasion. He wore a shirt with a lacy collar, studded white rhinestones closing the front, pearls in his double barrel cuffs, and fitted satin-striped slacks. Kennedy called to ask for a piece of cake, and before Margy could answer, Everet impatiently yelled back that he should try a piece of fruit instead. Then he put on patent leather shoes, a cummerbund, and, after that, a silk bow tie.

"Does it look all right?" he said. "Is it straight?"

"Fine. You look better than I will."

He turned, almost oblivious to her, shot his cuffs, and went into the closet for the jacket. He came back, looked at himself with the whole outfit on, and sidled toward Margy from the mirror. He looked as though he were dancing, and when he buttoned the jacket, smoothed the lapels, shooting his cuffs once more, he smiled with an indescribable pride and joy.

"When I was a kid, Margy, if I had ever thought of owning a tuxedo--"

68

He stopped, pirouetting--reminding her of Kennedy for a moment.

"You do look fine," she said. "I wish I could feel as well in my dress. It's just not natural to me anymore."

"You'll look great. Come on. We have to be there in an hour."

"Oh, damn it, Everet ... "

"Come on. You know you're going to go."

He came to the bed, grinning, and tickled her ribs. She wore just a robe at that moment and, falling back while opening the robe, she tried to pull him on top of her. But after a short kiss, a quick pawing under clothes, he stood up and pushed her away.

"Come on, baby. You're sexy, but you're not going to get me now."

"Oh, no?" She threw off the robe and, laughing, snaked her hips at him while drawing close. He stood, impassive, as she moved toward him. When he turned toward the mirror again, Margy stomped into the bathroom and, although she did not want a cigarette, she lit one anyway to annoy him.

"Margy, will you please come out of there? You're already made up. All you have to do is put on your clothes."

She sat on the tub, squinting at her toenails to see if they needed trimming. Everet entered, caught a glimpse of the cigarette, then waved theatrically before stalking out of the room.

"You know, it gets a little tiring having this happen whenever we go out. Why do you have to punish me this way?"

"I'm not punishing anybody, you idiot. I'm trying to relieve the tension."

"Bullshit."

"I have to be charming, don't I? I *am* the candidate's wife."

He came to the door and showed unmistakable pleasure at the word "candidate." He stepped aside as Margy walked into the bedroom, and he stood watching as she pulled on her underpants and stepped into her dress. He

69

stood in front of the full-length mirror with her, hooking the dress behind the neck. She wore a short cocktail outfit--black satin brocade, with a flounced hem breaking just below her knees, a high neck and an almost non-existent back. He considered it very sexy.

"This is the last one, okay?" she said, as he kissed her shoulder blade. "I warn you. If you want to be a politician, you'd better find somebody else to escort. As of this night, I've had enough."

He was still pleased--so much in fact that he turned Margy around and kissed her while embracing her tightly.

"Just let me get the nomination, baby. That's all I want. After that you can stay home, sketch, and read every damn book in the house."

He handed Margy her wrap and they went downstairs. In the car with Kennedy between them, they followed the Merritt Parkway into Bridgeport, then drove the Black Rock Turnpike to Ruth Hamilton's house. She lived in a white, neat Cape Cod with potted geraniums set in the picture window, a large American flag flying from the overhang, and a gilded eagle roosting over the door. For Margy, it was always hard to imagine crowds demonstrating on the sidewalk, yet she knew that when the Hamiltons moved here in the 1940s, crosses were burned on their lawn, movers refused to take furniture from the van, and for months threatening phone calls disrupted their daily lives. Yet by the 1960s they had become one of the neighborhood's most respected families.

Ruth opened the door, embraced Kennedy, and clapped her hands when she saw Everet's tux.

"Don't he look fine? If your father could only see you now.--Ain't you proud of your daddy, boy?"

Kennedy smiled, sheepishly. Ruth took Everet's arm and turned him around, clapped again, and then led them into the living room where she tried to make them sit.

"Coffee, Everet? Don't you want any coffee, Margy?"

Margy shook her head apologetically; Everet held his mother off by walking immediately to the door.

"I can't be late, Mama. Especially tonight." He opened the door, took Margy's arm and pushed her onto the porch.

"We'll call around twelve-thirty tonight. But we'll let my man here stay with you till tomorrow morning. Okay by you, sport?"

"Okay, Daddy."

"Go out and get them, son. I want to address you as Mr. Mayor one of these days. It will make me so proud."

Everet choked up, then stepped back into the house to embrace her again. Margy saw him close his eyes tightly as he held his mother, and when he passed her a look both defiant and ashamed, she smiled. "We *got* to go now, Mama," he said, gently pushing her away. "We'll see you tomorrow." He went down the steps, waving, and, after helping Margy into the car, drove off to the dinner.

"I'm glad we're together," Margy said, feeling better now that they were on their way. "It's been a long time since we've been out alone."

"Yeah. It feels good to me, too."

He smiled, and, with genuine feeling, put his hand on her knee. Margy unhooked her seatbelt in order to move closer.

"Did things go well with Gray today?" she asked. "Did you get a chance to talk with him?"

He nodded, winking. "Keep your fingers crossed."

"What does that mean?"

He stared at the road. "I don't like to talk about it yet, but he's bending over backward to make me a part of his little clique of Democrats. They're close to supporting me, and with Gray's contacts and union power, do you know what he can do? Ten thousand votes, at least. Man, I can almost taste them coming to the polls."

"You'd be almost sure of winning in the fall, wouldn't you?"

"Who knows? Lots of things can happen. But the Democrats do have a strong majority in this town."

"You'd have it," Margy said.

He shook his head. "Maybe. But we'll have to be cautious."

They drove along the Merritt Parkway into Stoddard and followed Main Street into the downtown area. As they drove through the business district, they saw how the new highway--connecting downtown with the eastern suburbs-- gradually became a cover for the slums. Upon moving here ten years before, Margy had been surprised to find that the buildings were already worn, streets terribly littered, and cinemas and stores had joined the exodus to the suburbs. Things were no different that night, she noticed. In fact, they had become worse--despite a long period of urban renewal and a concern for cleaner air.

"Mayor Chambers' monument," Everet said, repeating his favorite theme as he pointed out the window toward the highway. "Energy shortage and all. I'm going to nail him on that come the election."

They passed one of the Stoddard University buildings, then drove east along the Sound until they came to the water. They stopped at a huge, red-brick structure, square and unreal on the skyline. It was a neon-decorated motel with an interior of large bare cubicles for dining rooms, molded fixtures for lights, and along the walls the inevitable bushels upon bushels of imitation ferns. Plastic was another Chambers legacy, because he had coaxed a new plastic plant into the city. The factory stank out the downtown area during the day, and on many nights, when the wind came in the right direction off the Sound, it could stink out East Stoddard too.

"When I smell this air and see this motel, Everet, I think you should be our mayor. If for nothing else, so you can clean it all up."

"Hmmm. I'll serve some purpose for you then." He looked at her seriously.

"Yes. You'll serve the purpose of making me want to bite you."

He laughed as she nuzzled him and poked his ribs. He took Margy's wrists and pushed her back to the opposite side of the car where he set her head against the back of the seat and kissed her on the ear. Margy caught his cheek and bit into it, making him jerk back with a howl as he let her wrists free.

"Hey, I don't want to go in there with any marks showing. Watch yourself."

"I'll mark you. I'll give you a lipstick hickey on the collar."

She lunged toward him, while he fended her off, and, chuckling, opened the car door. As they walked into the motel entrance, Margy felt awe and admiration. She clung to him, noticing that he seemed not to feel her weight against his arm. His mind was on himself, his image, extending to his cuffs, his rhinestones, and his tie. While she shrank behind, his shoulders fell back, his arms moved easily by his side. Quite gracefully, in a way she might have sketched him before they were married, he looked noble, naturally so. As with a dancer, his body appeared to float; his feet seemed just inches off the ground.

She kissed him. "Did you ever think of being a martyr, Everet?--Actually ascending into heaven for some cause?"

"Every day, Margy. With this skin, I have no choice. But you know me. I'll also do it to enjoy the results."

"Meaning?"

"Meaning in this day and age, there's no advantage in dying."

He smiled, opened the door, and followed Margy inside.

6.

PAST IN THE PRESENT

They were greeted by a flash of bulbs, a television camera, and two women with microphones who instantly stood next to Everet and directed questions at him or Fred and Emmy Gray. Everet talked about political plans, said something about the challenge of his experience as a lawyer in Stoddard, deferred comment on the Democratic primary to Fred Gray, then let Margy talk about how happy she would be to help on the hustings. He beamed when she gave the right answer, even though it was a lie: "It's the exciting part of a political marriage," she said, casting a pleased look at him as she talked. The Grays listened attentively, and after Margy checked her wrap they led the way into the bar where they took a center table. "Excuse me, Margy," said Fred Gray. "I want to introduce Everet to some important people over there. Emmy, you'll look after Margy for us, won't you?"

"Go right ahead," Emmy said.

Emmy took Margy's hand and looked at her with a deep, friendly smile. She was tall, elegant, Margy noticed with a touch of envy, her natural blond to whitish hair spilling over her ears in a, stiff cascade. "This must be exciting to you," Emmy said, as the men walked away.

"To tell the truth I find it a little overwhelming."

"Oh, we all do at first. I thought you handled yourself well with those reporters. You made a very positive impression."

Margy shrugged, thanking her. "I had no idea what I was saying," she said. "For all I knew, we could have been speaking French."

"You did very well."

Emmy patted Margy's forearm and waved to someone at another table. They ordered drinks, then passed an uncomfortable (for Margy) few minutes chatting about recent social events in Stoddard, some friends they might have had--but did not--in common, and current affairs in general. Emmy asked about Margy's painting, discussed Copperwood as if she knew something about its inner workings, then admitted that she had been an art student when she went to college many years before. "It was the most creative time of my youth," Emmy said. "I don't think I passed a day when I wasn't at least mildly stimulated." She shook her head. "Sometimes we just let those moments slip away."

Margy nodded, wondering if there were some light in that. But before she could reply, Emmy smiled and added, "Of course, there are other things to take their place. Politics are equally important, and I'm tremendously involved in Fred's life."

Margy nodded again and, not responding to her silence, Emmy glanced around the room. Everet and Fred stood off in a corner among some well-dressed men near the bar. Reporters, some with notebooks, others with cameras and tape recorders slung over their shoulders, waited near them, combing the air for quotes. One or two passed by the table to speak to Emmy Gray, and she immediately turned them over to Margy. The attention was flattering, but, as its meaning sank in, Margy became increasingly upset. Some important decisions must have been made already, she assumed, and she wondered about Everet's part in them. One reporter, a small, extremely thin woman with a heron-like head, sought her opinion about Everet's chances; another, older and squatter, wondered whether she liked being a political wife; a third, a man who was a photographer, Margy thought, hung back although she was conscious that his eyes were always on her. Emmy helped out, smiling affirmatively through it all, laughing appreciatively when Margy said that being a political wife could be confusing, and at the same time maintaining a careful reserve when she answered questions addressed to her. Wives, as Margy soon discovered, were Emmy's primary responsibility on the political trail, and so they came to her table in an almost endless stream, commenting on Emmy's hair and dress, asking advice, shaking Margy's hand with a reticent, professional air, and assessing her as the conversation progressed. In a way, Margy tried to place herself among them, and she was disturbed to find herself so unassuming. She really wanted to blurt out nasty comments, but she did not have the courage. Her hands trembled at times when she talked; she discovered as she tried to be sociable that her back, arms, and legs were drenched in nervous sweat. The drink relaxed her a little, but it also increased her confusion. At moments she found herself almost unable to respond to the ordinary chatter around her. By the time Fred and Everet returned to escort them into the dining hall, Margy felt sure that she already had cast doubt on Everet's ability to win the primary. Her reserve had insulted several women, she thought, and it had put the lie to Emmy's sense that she could make a good first impression.

"How you doing, babe?" Everet whispered as they walked through the bar.

"Awful. I hate myself already. More important, I hate you for putting me through this."

He looked at her, then over to Emmy and Fred. "You're terrific, you know. Everyone thinks you're quite a beautiful woman."

"I didn't come here to be gawked at."

"It can't be helped. It's the nature of the game. But you're doing all right; just bear with it for a while, okay?" He put his hand to her cheek and brushed his lips against her ear. A camera flash went off on their left and Margy clutched Everet's arm. "Don't worry about that," he said. "Just let them do their thing, and keep yourself calm. I need them if I'm going to make an impression on this town."

He smiled, waved at the photographer, but there was no second flash. Fred Gray came over and took Everet's arm, leading them to a little cordoned-off area beside the entrance to the dining hall. A cluster of microphones hung above a lectern like a stylized chrome and black bouquet, and about a dozen men and women stood in front of the lectern waiting. Two were reporters from the local paper, three or four were from a television station in New Haven, the rest came from Hartford and other surrounding communities. Emmy, Fred,

76

Everet, and Margy stood behind the lectern while a man named Grant Matthews, Democratic Party state chair, addressed the crowd. Surrounding them on the podium were other party dignitaries whom Margy did not know. Everet pointed out several state assemblymen, a United States Congresswoman, and mayors from Bridgeport, Westport, and Fairfield. Matthews introduced all of them, then stepped aside as each one stood at the lectern and answered questions from the press. It was Margy's first news conference, and she was surprised at the informality, the humor, and the easy camaraderie that existed between the reporters and the politicians. After an introduction, Fred Gray read a statement and answered questions, referring to each reporter by his or her first name. He joked easily, waved his cigar as if it were a scepter, and obligingly turned his head from profile to full frontal view each time a photographer or cameraman lined up a shot.

It was he, not Matthews, who introduced Everet, and when he did, Margy passed a few anxious moments in the spotlight. Apparently, Emmy and Fred wanted to show the Hamiltons together, so when Everet stepped up to the microphones, he squeezed Margy's hand and pulled her to the lectern beside him. "Smile, baby," he whispered. "Show what kind of trooper you are." She blinked when the overhead lights hit her face and, attempting to yank her hand free, she tried to step back into the shadows.

"Thank you. Thank you very much, Fred," Everet said into the microphones as he nearly broke Margy's hand while holding her close. "My wife, Margy, and I are happy to be here tonight in order to meet all the fine leaders of the Connecticut Democratic Party." He let her hand go, then gripped both sides of the lectern as she retreated with the stars of the camera flashes still winking in her, eyes. "Two years ago we fought a valiant but losing campaign which demonstrated that even in defeat Connecticut Democrats are willing to take risks in order to tell the truth, to promote liberal social policies on the local, state, and national levels, and to oppose corruption wherever it may occur--across the street from the White House in Washington, in the state

77

house in Hartford, or on our city pavements. We are living with the results of that loss today--as the red, sweaty faces of administration officials try to reassure us in Washington, and as our mayor in Stoddard tries to parlay political profit from social ideas that were bankrupt and outdated fifty years ago.

"I am proud to be associated with Fred Gray because he has always represented in Connecticut a rare combination of hard-nosed practical organization and the ideals of social reform—especially here in Stoddard. He may have lost to Larry Chambers in 1972 because of a wave of pro-Republican feeling that emerged from a misguided preference for charlatanism in the Presidential election of that year, but weren't we all here impressed by the fine, high-minded campaign that Fred Gray conducted?" Everet paused, nodding and smiling while loud applause resounded through the room. "That's right. He went among the people of Stoddard and spoke to them on their own ground, and he always brought a clear, plain-spoken vision to address the complex problems confronting all of our people--in the neighborhoods, the schools, even in our churches. Personally, I found his vision inspiring and his manner of conveying it instructive. As we begin the Stoddard mayoral campaign of 1974, I believe all Democrats will look to him again for leadership, whether in office or in campaign organization. So tonight, I'd like to personally thank Fred Gray for everything he has done and say that in the months ahead I look to him to lead the way to put Democratic power—both small 'd' and big 'D'--into the mayor's office again. I also hope, along with my wife Margy, that the state and federal representatives here tonight will recognize how important Fred Gray is to us at all levels of government. Thank you."

Everet stepped back from the microphones and, in an applause of lens shutter-motors, embraced Margy. He then turned to shake Fred Gray's hand. Margy heard a few hands clapping behind the podium and out front a few reporters and guests clapping as well. Confused, she started to leave

78

the lectern, but she felt Everet's hand grasp hers once more. He pulled her to his side as he waited for questions.

"Mr. Hamilton?"

"Yes, Mr. Rogers."

"While you look to Fred Gray for leadership, I am sure you are also aware of the rumors concerning your own candidacy. A black mayor would be historic in Connecticut. Do you have any statement to make about that?"

Everet stared at him. During a long pause, he took a deep breath and shook his head. "Not at the present time. There are a number of Democrats--Fred Gray among them-- who are worthy of the office. I am not sure I am the best choice among them. Mr. Di Francisco?"

"Thank you, Mr. Hamilton. If you are not running for the office of mayor, why are you the only local Democrat on the lectern tonight, with the exception of Fred Gray?"

Everet laughed. "Why *is* that, Fred? Are you forgetting someone you shouldn't?"

Smiling broadly, he glanced at Fred and Emmy, then turned back to the reporter. "Actually, as a delegate to the last national convention, I have some representation on the state level. We are all thinking, all the time, of the best way to build a strong Democratic slate for this year's election. I'm here because I would like to participate in the decisions on that slate. I like to think that I have an important contribution to make, but whether I shall be on the slate myself is a question to be decided later on."

"If it were offered to you tonight, what would you say?"

"Nothing, Mr. Di Francisco."

"What would your reaction be?"

"Astonishment. After all, there are primaries ahead. Besides, I'd have to talk it over seriously with my wife. Running might be very disruptive to our family."

That line of questioning continued, with some of the women reporters trying to draw Margy into the discussion with inquiries about her feelings. She deferred to Everet, and he handled every question professionally, as if he had been schooled. Gradually, Margy shrank back to be with Fred and

79

Emmy Gray because she feared that her presence might provoke a question she would not want to answer. In that moment--seeing him in the spotlight before her--Margy realized just how committed Everet was and how radically different they had become. She perceived him rapidly becoming a public, slightly artificial man, and, like the wife who sees her husband with another woman, she felt betrayed at first, and then envious that he should have a separate life.

"He's doing beautifully, isn't he?" Emmy whispered into Margy's ear. "It's as if he was born to be up there."

She nodded; Fred Gray reached across Emmy and squeezed Margy's arm with a wink. "You're both doing really well," he said. She nodded and reached into her purse to find a cigarette. As she tugged the pack from an inner pocket, Emmy put her hand over the purse and pushed the cigarettes back into it.

"No smoking up here," she whispered. "Not on the platform."

Margy looked across Emmy's bosom toward Fred, but just as he was about to raise his cigar to his mouth, Emmy reached over and held it down at his waist. "No smoking up here, Fred. Remember?" She motioned vaguely to their surroundings.

He nodded, his lips forming an "o" as he looked at the ceiling, and folded his hands behind his back. For a moment he looked like a London bobby with a smoking billy club in his hands.

"Wait till you see Everet when the going gets rough," Emmy whispered. "He has natural eloquence. Under pressure he seems to respond with greater force and authority."

The interview continued for another ten minutes and, luckily, the reporters raised no other questions concerning Margy. Grant Matthews stepped to the microphones beside Everet and reminded everyone that dinner would soon be served. With an eager bustle the crowd started to drift into the dining room, and Everet, beaming--like a trained, barking seal, Margy thought--stepped away from the microphones.

"You did fine," said Fred, shaking his hand and patting him on the back. "A pro could not have handled it better. Matthews and the others were very impressed, I'm sure."

"You were absolutely wonderful," Emmy said.

She touched Everet's shoulder, and, like a poor child unaccustomed to such praise, he bashfully lowered his head. Matthews, tall, white-haired, his small, half-glasses dangling at the edge of his craggy nose, stopped by on his way back into the bar. Brushing a lock of hair from his forehead, he shook Everet's hand and invited him and Fred Gray to stop by the head table during the evening. They talked for a few minutes until Emmy spotted Matthews's wife at the dining hall entrance and fairly floated over to greet her. After what seemed to Margy like hours, Fred and Matthews joined them, leaving Everet and her alone in an uncomfortable silence. She turned to him, brushing her cheek against his chest. Looking into his eyes, she saw an expression of resolution: Everet would make the run for mayor, she was sure. He couldn't care less if she did not like it.

"How's it going? You getting used to all this?" He shuffled his feet a little and looked toward the crowd gathered around Fred and Emmy.

"You did very well with the reporters," she said. "I was surprised to see that you have so much poise."

He grinned. "That's my Daddy in me. He handled situations a lot more difficult than this at work and in our house. It's just a matter of having an answer ready and not getting particularly excited. Reporters just want news copy-- they only attack when they see a person in the spotlight lose his cool."

"You kept yours very well. But--"

"You liked it, huh?"

Margy nodded. "You've decided to run already, haven't you?" she said.

"No--"

"Come on, Everet. You and Fred are like two cats with a mouse between you in a corner."

"Margy, we haven't decided a thing."

81

She walked away, turned in a little circle and came back. He took her shoulders and drew her close.

"I swear, Margy, nothing is completely decided. My inclination is strong, especially because of the atmosphere this evening. But there are lots of things to talk about."

"You seem changed to me."

"It's you who has changed. On the way here tonight you sounded downright sympathetic."

"I can't take these people, or the front I have to put up." She pulled free and, since the crowd at the dining hall entrance still milled about, decided to take a chair.

"You did fine, you know. For someone who's never done this sort of thing, you came off pretty well." Everet sat on a small bench beside her and, leaning forward, put his hand on her knee.

"I know," she said, brushing his hand away. "I'm an Emmy Gray in the making. Want to see me smile?"

"Now don't go criticizing her too soon, Margy. She has a lot of very fine qualities. She's been a source of confidence for Fred and me."

"Maybe you should marry her, and Fred can keep me as a tootsie. Blondes go very well with bald heads and big cigars."

Everet shook his head and looked away toward the bar. A couple of women passed, one in purple, the other in yellow chiffon, their gowns sliding behind them in a two-toned trail of gossamer. Margy turned back to Everet and this time reached out to touch his arm. "There are people who love this sort of thing, but you were never one of them before."

He shook his head. "I wasn't made to be a hermit, Margy. These people aren't so bad. Besides, they're a means to an end--something I want very much."

"So you *have* decided to run!"

"I've decided that I want to; I haven't decided that I will."

"What's the difference? The nomination seems to be yours for the asking. With Fred Gray on your side, how much more do you need?"

82

"Plenty. I want to make sure these people don't swallow me up. I want to keep my independence. I see what you see, Margy. But I also see that I don't have to become one of them. There's a whole range of other possibilities, but your bias makes you blind to them. I think you ought to lean back tonight and try to enjoy yourself. It might give you a completely different perspective."

She drew her hand away and, as if to satisfy him, sat looking at the crowd. Television and radio people had left, but several photographers and reporters from the papers remained. They formed a little island of casual expectation among the party members and their spouses, and they passed in and out of the groups with an observant, critical air--even though their own presence made the occasion special. Occasionally, Margy saw Fred and Emmy call two or three reporters over to make an introduction to Matthews, and with one in particular, they kept glancing back toward the Hamiltons and shaking their heads. This reporter had soft brown hair cut evenly at his shoulders and a trim mustache and goatee that contributed a sense of dumpy elegance. He looked familiar to Margy, but she was unable to place him clearly beyond a vague sense that somehow his clothing--a smooth, double-knit suit with a string tie and black cowboy boots--was out of character despite the goatee and mustache. Once or twice he glanced specifically at her rather than at Everet, and after a few minutes of conversation with the Grays, he walked across the room to introduce himself. As he stood before them, Margy gradually realized who he was.

"John Buford, Mr. Hamilton. I'm reporting for the *Stoddard Sun*. Fred Gray says you might be willing to spend some time with me."

"Fine. Fine. John, this is my wife, Margy."

She extended her hand, and Buford, as he took it, simply nodded his head. "Call me John. I think we know each other from a few years ago."

"At Copperwood--in Foss's class."

"Good memory. I was dabbling in the arts back then. Fred tells me that you're still at it."

83

"Still trying. Some of us never give it up."

"Some of us also have the talent. I never did, I'm afraid."

Everet pulled over a folding chair and offered it to Buford. He took it, crossing his legs and offering the Hamiltons a cigarette. When he lit Margy's, she recognized the lighter--a gaudy, gold-like brede affair--with a pair of silver crowns and ruby-red rhinestones on it. "Family heirloom," he said, when he saw her staring at it. "My father bought it when I was just a kid."

"It's very..."

"Gaudy is the word. I use it out of a special affection for my father. But also the damn thing has never failed to work in over twenty-five years. Let one of the phony brands on TV equal that."

He smiled at Everet, and when he turned back to Margy, she remembered the soft look on his face. It was bitchy but sweet, and used to make her wonder about his relationship with men--especially Foss--during the first couple of months that she and Foss were lovers. Buford had hung around a lot, going with Foss to the local tavern between classes, and once or twice even saying that he was jealous of Margy--although he was quick to add that his jealousy had to do with being her fellow student. He was the type of person who liked to be seen with teachers. Other students disliked him, either because they thought he was a snob or because they thought he was too ambitious. He had been clean-shaven but shaggier-looking then although there was always something sleazy about him. As an artist he had been mediocre, but Margy remembered that he never seemed to think that talent was important. He was the type of student who always talked about "contacts," and his favorite contemporary artists were invariably those written about favorably in the New York papers.

"So, you're still working down there, heh? Is Foss as crazy as ever?"

Margy nodded, slightly embarrassed as she glanced at Everet. "I think he's had some setbacks recently," she murmured.

"Oh? Not artistically, I hope. I see he's done quite well with the museum people in New York."

Margy looked away. "He's having trouble getting to work. I guess you'd say he was blocked."

Buford shook his head. "Is he hitting the sauce too much again? In my opinion that always was his downfall, even when he said it helped him."

"I don't know." She shrugged and again looked at Everet. This was an aspect of Foss that she did not want to discuss right now. Although Everet had met him once, she preferred him to think their affair was founded on a mutual interest in art. Everet's health obsessions far outweighed his moral ones.

"So, what are you doing at Copperwood now?" asked Buford.

"Still painting. At the end of the term I'm giving the annual student show."

"Very good." Buford nodded, pursing his lips as if he were impressed. Music came from the dining hall, and as Margy looked over to the doorway, she saw Fred Gray motioning to them. Everet called back that they would arrive shortly, and then he looked expectantly at Buford. "You wanted to talk to me? It's about time for us to go inside."

"Yes, sorry. But it just occurred to me that I might do an article on Margy's exhibition--on her art, in fact. It would make a very nice piece: The pursuits of a candidate's wife in her spare time."

"But I'm not a candidate yet."

"And I'm not worth the bother," Margy added.

"I think you are." Buford laughed. "And I think you're both being a little cagey. If you're not a candidate, Mr. Hamilton, why is there all this interest? The Democrats haven't got anyone else but Fred Gray, and he's obviously in your camp."

"Fred's in his own camp. Don't count him out."

"Oh, would you support him if he ran?"

Everet nodded emphatically. "Without reservation. He's helped my people, and he's been the one man the whole city can count on in a pinch. We've disagreed about certain

85

things, but there is no one who loves Stoddard and East Stoddard as much as he does."

"What kind of things have you disagreed on?"

Margy interrupted. "Is this an interview, Everet? Mr. Buford? I'm beginning to think the candidate's wife should leave."

"*Possible* candidate's wife, apparently." Buford smiled at Margy, then turned to Everet. Everet wore a determined look, as if in the face of all this clever seediness, he had to be particularly careful if he was going to come out all right. Since Margy would not make even a decent window-dressing companion for Everet, she decided he would handle the situation better himself.

"Is it all right if I go? I'd like to get some air."

"No, no. Hang on, Margy. I might have a question or two for you."

She smiled. "That's exactly why I'm leaving. Is it okay with you, Everet? I can meet you inside at our table--in fifteen minutes?"

"Meet me at the doorway--in twenty." He cast a cold, evaluative look at Buford. "That should be enough time, don't you think?"

Buford nodded.

"All right then. I'll see you in about twenty minutes," Margy said.

She shook hands with Buford, then left the two of them and went out to the hallway in order to go upstairs. The decorative motif, as in most public places along the coast of Connecticut, was sea and seascape, with nets, shells, and stuffed marine animals lining the walls. She took the stairs to the second floor, where a promenade overlooked the Sound. Several women turned as she walked through the door, one of them being Emmy Gray, who had been pointing to some stars in the sky. As she talked, the dot-dot-dash of a lighthouse beam flickered across the water, outlining Emmy's face in a silhouette, then disappearing over the water and beyond the horizon again. "Won't you join us, Margy? And I think you'd like to meet Estelle Matthews."

86

Margy nodded, smiling at the woman and taking her hand. Estelle Matthews was short, with dark hair and bright, lively blue eyes that imparted a sense of friendly energy to her face. "I've heard so much about you," she said.

Margy blushed, partly from a sense of embarrassment as Estelle Matthews smiled up at her with obvious warm feelings. "Good things, I hope," Margy said.

"Splendid. They tell me that you're quite the artist. Actually, I saw one of your things in a Hartford show a few months ago. It's nice to have an artist's point of view in a political campaign."

Emmy looked at Margy, her frown and slight narrowing of the eyes warning to take the next few steps with care. Margy simply nodded, not wishing to broaden the one topic that seemed to be hers for the evening.

"I paint too," said Mrs. Matthews with a titter. "Although not nearly with the skill that you have."

"We're just looking at Mars and Jupiter," Emmy Gray said. "They're quite high in the sky this evening. Luckily, there aren't any clouds. Estelle is quite the astronomer."

They took in the view for the next couple of minutes. Beautiful, Margy agreed. Although she knew little about astronomy, she could recognize the North Star way off to their left, the Big Dipper slightly to the right above them, and, in the distance over Long Island as Estelle pointed to it, Orion, bright and clear, chasing the Pleiades toward Rhode Island and the rest of New England.

"You have quite an easy escape to the sea here," Estelle said, enviously. "Unfortunately, in Hartford we have nothing more than industry and suburbs, with four-lane highways threading the borderline between them."

"We're getting there," said Emmy. "If Larry Chambers had his way this would become just like New York harbor."

They walked to the end of the promenade, where there was a small, enclosed pavilion. From it Emmy and Margy pointed out the ugliness of downtown Stoddard: the railroad tracks, the plastic factory, whose smell was slight, but unmistakable in the night air, and finally the row upon row of cranes and derricks along the shoreline to the north and south. Then they pointed to the highways--elevated over the streets like so many buttressed medieval walls--which soared through town from the Sound to the inner city and beyond to the suburbs in the west and east.

It was a pattern in Stoddard life that seemed unstoppable, yet when Margy saw it from the pavilion that night it reinforced her reluctant feeling that Everet should run. The history of this pattern went far back in his friendship with Fred Gray and showed, according to Everet, how much Fred had changed. In the late sixties, with the Democrats in power, Everet had participated in a Stoddard Model Cities Project report during the "Great Society" days and had presented the case for increased public transportation funds--for buses and trains--and an outlawing of automobiles within city limits during the weekdays. Town leaders, with Fred Gray prominent among them, had taken the report as criticism of the Democratic administration and had scrapped that section when they sent it to Washington. The result was that Stoddard and East Stoddard received increased Federal funds for highways and virtually nothing for public transport. Everet had been angry about their ignoring his work and had argued strongly in public and private against the federal decision. In this rather back-handed way, he initiated his relationship with the Grays because, as trouble-shooter for the Democratic machine, Fred had been asked to sell the city's plans to the people. He and Everet debated frequently at public hearings. Oddly enough, they impressed one another and formed a friendship that grew very close after Larry Chambers, a Republican, won two mayoralty campaigns. Then, at a public meeting, Fred Gray admitted that he had been wrong about the Federal funds, and his ties with Everet grew closer as they began to support each other on other issues.

Of course, Emmy and Margy did not discuss these things. They simply pointed to the development of industry and tsk-tsked along with Estelle when she commented upon its horrible aesthetics. They talked for several minutes, but when they heard the music from downstairs, Emmy and Estelle left the pavilion to find their husbands. Margy excused herself and crossed the second floor lounge to the ladies room. She stopped to buy some cigarettes from a machine just beside the door, and as she turned, she saw John Buford coming toward her from the stairway. He was alone, but he wore the same look of self-interest and purpose that he had had downstairs. She wanted to avoid him, but she could not walk past him once their eyes had met.

"He's free now," Buford said, "but I'd like to talk to you a few minutes, if I may."

Margy frowned. "I'm not fond of interviews," she warned.

"This is not an interview--I just want to ask how you are."

Smiling, he came close, taking the package of cigarettes from her hand, opening it and offering her one. He lit her cigarette with his gaudy lighter, and as she inhaled, he looked toward the promenade. "It's a lovely night out there--like that night we spent at Foss's. Remember?"

Margy flinched, inwardly, but on the outside managed--just barely--to hide her reaction. "I remember," she said.

He grinned. "One of my peak experiences. You know, it's a funny thing meeting you here. I've been covering Stoddard politics for more than six months and never once associated you with Everet Hamilton."

"Small world, as they say."

"It certainly is."

She saw a glint in Buford's eyes, and it was more than just an acknowledgement of Margy's little cliché. It was as if he glided into the situation, feeling more at ease, more commanding in fact, than he had been with Everet downstairs. She resented it.

"You're sitting with Fred and Emmy, Everet says. That's pretty powerful company."

"If you're interested in power. Personally, I hope we can have a little fun."

He grinned, turning toward the Sound and, although they were indoors, sniffed slightly, as if he were inhaling. "You remember that night? The air smelled just the way it

89

does now." He extended his hand and tried to touch Margy's arm. She pulled it away, instinctively. With his fingers splayed in mid-air, Buford looked at her and laughed without a trace of embarrassment. "You know, I had no idea you were married back then. I thought you were just one of Foss's usual student strays. Prettier, maybe; a little older. But he does--or did, certainly--have a way with women."

"Let's cut the slime, John. That's all over, and I don't want to bring it back. In case you're wondering, Everet knows all about my life with Foss."

He nodded. "I'm glad to know that. For your information, I wouldn't be the one to tell him anyhow. I'm a political reporter, not a gossip columnist. Besides, Fred Gray and I are very close."

"That's nice to hear--about you; not about him."

He shook his head, laughing. "I'll probably be around to interview you sometime. People like to read that first ladies have extra talents."

He laughed at that too, and this time his fingers caught Margy's arm before she could yank it away. "You do remember that night, don't you? I don't see how you could forget it."

"John, don't do anything stupid. I don't want to have to scream."

A foghorn moaned, and a wind swept through the room as it pushed open a door to the promenade; it also swirled the skirt about Margy's knees. Buford was speaking of two years ago, one of the last evenings Margy spent with Foss as a lover. There had been a Copperwood party at his place—with beer, wine, also plenty of pot and drugs--and at the end, the three of them, John, Foss, and Margy, were left alone. John had made one of his whining complaints about Margy's privileged position again, and Foss had--as usual--laughed it off, saying that his private life--with or without students--was his business, especially off the campus grounds. It was a boring topic. Foss liked to tease John about his own privileges occasionally, but that night after the party it seemed to make all of them nervous: Foss, when John and Margy talked of leaving together; John, when Margy decided

90

to go with him only if Foss allowed it; and Margy, finally, because she knew that she would have to stagger home and face Everet.

"Best head I've ever had, John. Bar none--and I've had my share."

"Yeah, well, so have I, Maestro. And I can get my own without your recommendation."

"Is that right, Margy? Can he?"

Foss was teasing Margy with his oily grin. "Fox," she often called him then.

"Will you two stop it? I can't do anything for anyone tonight. It's late and I'm high. I have to get home."

"Yeah. Margy has a curfew. Must get home to the family. Sort of limits what you can do, John."

Foss had fallen onto the couch, his shirt unbuttoned, his shoes unlaced. He carried a drink and a joint in his hand as he leaned back and surveyed the mess of his apartment. "I'm going to sleep, Margy. You and John take care of yourselves. Okay?"

"I'm going home, Foss. Remember?"

"Yeah... I'll call a cab."

"I've got my car. I can--oh, never mind."

His eyes had already closed. He had dropped his glass, and the homemaker side of Margy set it upright and gingerly removed the joint from his fingers. It was June, warm for that time of the year, and she had felt a breeze blow through the window in the same way that she now felt the one coming through the promenade door. As she lifted Foss's feet onto the couch and looked at John, she shook her head. The wind blew again; the sound of the leaves outside became so loud that she felt as if they were nesting in the branches of a tree.

"He's asleep. I guess I better go."

"Can you give me a lift? I really don't have any transportation."

"You can't stay here?"

Buford shrugged. Margy picked up her bag and without thinking about it, said he might as well come along with her. As they stepped into the yard, she felt his arm

91

around her shoulders. The smell of the air was sweet, mock orange mingling with the saltiness of the Sound. "I do want to make love to you, you know. Foss is always kidding me, but I do want to do it--tonight."

She remembered his hands taking her breasts and how her blouse seemed to open automatically to her waist. In the drunken fog of her vision, she looked behind and up and saw John staring at her hair. The moon reflected like a pair of cameos in his eyes. They seemed to fragment, switch, then gather together again as a matched set of silver coins. In a speed-of-light-like span of years, she looked up at him in the Stoddard Motel and saw the same thing happen again.

"I don't have my diaphragm, John," she had said. "And I've stopped taking the pill for more than a month. I can't."

He had pulled out her shirt, pushed down her pants, and, without preparation, she felt his soft penis bumping against her. Gradually, it hardened and became a ram. "Bend over, bend over and relax. This can be so easy. Oh, I want to fuck you now!"

She felt his tongue down there--the sensation strange, distant, like a very warm, very specific rush of air and rain. And then his finger had pushed up inside her. She found that exciting; she had never done this sort of thing before. Despite all her experimentation with Foss, this had never happened, and she felt surprised to find just how curious and willing she was. She also recognized how angry she was, and how appropriate it was for her affair with Foss that it should take place on his doorstep while he, drugged and in an alcoholic stupor, slept inside. "Fucking," she had said afterward. "Fucking, in all senses of the word, was going on."

"Relax, relax, mmm... " His arms wrapped around her hips; his fingers worked to manipulate her clitoris. She felt the cold teeth of his zipper against her buttocks, and, all the while he pushed, his wheezy, heavy breathing against her neck. He groaned, stuck his finger inside her vagina and caused her whole body to vibrate with it. She clawed at

92

Foss's front door, hooked onto its doorknob, and braced herself as she felt John pushing inside.

"Hey!--Take it easy. That hurts," she had said.

"Hold on--ohhh, hold on a little more ... Relax ..."

A fog horn moaned: outside the Stoddard Motel as well as in Westport on that distant night. Leaning against the wall for better leverage, John thrust inside more deeply, and Margy screamed when she felt something break inside of her. It was painful, but strangely distant.

Despite her cry and the surprising fear that she would shit all over him, she was somehow in control and enjoying it. On the water she saw a boat passing--Long Island glittering behind it through the firs and rhododendrons--and all around them insects were buzzing: into her ear, her nose, her mouth (each time she gasped, she swallowed a couple), her vagina too, she thought, as Buford's finger moved in and out.

"You ever sleep with Foss anymore?" he asked. That glint in his eyes again—here in the Stoddard Motel--with more than curiosity behind them. Margy remembered his soft thighs against her, his lips wet and sensual on her neck. As she looked at his pale skin, she found it hard to imagine a man like that wounding her. Yet he had broken something in her that night, and only part of it had been physical. His fingernails had scratched against her belly, his teeth had bitten into her shoulder, his lips had sucked so hard as he came and moaned, that she had a purple welt above her collarbone for two weeks. But the real pain was in her head, and it was not until this night in Stoddard that she understood why. It wasn't what men did that counted; it was her allowing things to happen, especially with someone she did not like.

"Daily," she said. "I still take his classes, so I screw him in the paint room between sessions."

He laughed. "Still have that sarcasm, I see. Well, very good. You're going to need a sense of humor for the campaign. Stoddard politicians are dirty."

"Thanks--I assumed that already. It seems quite fitting to your style."

He turned away, shuffling his feet and thrusting his hands deep into his pockets. In an offended voice he told her, "Hey, I'm on your side, Margy. I'm trying to give you and your husband good press." When she said nothing, he added, "I'll come around to take a picture at the table with the Grays. Later on, I'll come down to Copperwood and review your show."

Margy shook her head. "Don't bother. You won't have anything to write."

"But ..."

"I don't want any publicity, John. Don't you understand?"

"I won't--"

"It has nothing to do with anything from the past. I simply do not want a public life. Even when it comes to art."

She started toward the ladies room. Pushing open the door and pausing a moment, she looked back at him. Boyish, surprisingly less self-assured, he asked her to call him if she should ever change her mind.

"I'm at the *Stoddard Sun* office almost all the time," he said. "If I'm not there, leave a message. It doesn't have to be about a story."

"Sure. And I can see the headline written across your forehead, no matter what I say."

He sighed, his pink lips pursing as he turned away. For a moment the lights above his head reflected in his eyes and brought back the image of the moon as a pair of cameos before they broke up and left Margy with his normal steely coins.

"Just keep an open mind, Margy. You never know how these things work out."

"Find another way to make a career," she said.

He nodded. His hand brushed back his hair, his teeth bit on the corner of his mustache. With a careful flip, he rearranged the immaculate bangs above his forehead as Margy went into the ladies room. She urinated before a wall painted with figures of lobsters, fish, and crabs, and later, on her way to the first floor, she passed him as he talked to a group of other reporters. Compared to the lobster, they seemed like sea vermin. She said nothing. At the dining hall she saw Everet and waved to him as he rushed toward her with his hand outstretched.

"Hey, you told me twenty minutes. It's more than a half an hour. Let's hurry. Dinner's already on the table."

Smiling, she took his arm, brushed his lips with her own, and entered the dining room. In a distant corner, Fred and Emmy stood and waved them to their seats.

7.

THE GRAYS

Emmy Gray smiled, giving a reassuring pat to Everet's hand.

"Fred's right, Everet," she said. "There's no question that you could bring honor to Stoddard politics and still succeed."

Margy sat back and looked at her watch. The dining hall was large, a sort of square fishbowl, with sea urchins and sunfish swimming along blue walls behind green and yellow plastic ferns. Round tables, three couples to each, stood arranged in a U-shape about the dance floor while up front on the dais one long table had been set aside for party dignitaries. Dinner had been served, and to accompany roast chicken, dumplings, and a truly mealy mash of peas, the Gray party opened several bottles of champagne with the coffee and talked politics for most of the night.

Quickly, it became the kind of conversation Margy dreaded: the third couple excused themselves after dinner; Fred and Emmy Gray leaned over the silverware and china; smiling, effusive, they pressed her about the campaign, trying to trade off compliments for concessions, and debated with her, finally, on the value of politics in general. While she opposed them, politely at first, then with an increasing edge to her voice as she looked for a way out of the situation, Everet sat between them, eyes almost misty, so naive, in fact, that he seemed the perfect, seduced, middleclass black man. He had always dreaded that possibility.

Over their third cup of coffee, Emmy squeezed Everet's arm and sighed. "You'll be perfect," she said without a smile. "A knight in shining armor riding to make things clean again."

"Right you are, Emmy. And with a little practical organization, Everet would have little trouble winning. That's our part of the deal. The Hamiltons enjoy while the Gray family perfects the callus-making footwork."

96

Gray extended his finger and lightly tapped the table as he poured champagne.

"I'll need a lot of support, Fred. I wouldn't want the reputation of being a loser after my first campaign."

"Don't worry. I know you're no loser, and you won't be if you decide to make this run. Anyhow, mull it over. As for Margy," he added, "I'm sure she'll love it too. Emmy was reluctant at first; she wanted to raise kids and be a full-time housewife--even dabble in a little creative art, like Margy. Well, look at her now--the second best politician in the city. How's that for women's liberation, Margy?"

He laughed. Margy sat back, sipped her champagne, and stared, straight-faced. Gray was not unlikeable; in fact, she thought, he could be rather attractive. He had a pair of interesting, lively eyes, but, whenever he puffed his cigar, his bald head and wattled face made him look like the heavy in a grade B movie. If the movie were about boxing, she was sure, he would play the wise, yet money-grubbing manager, pushing a bruised and scarred fighter into the center of the ring and telling him to watch for his opponent's quick left hand.

In any case, the conversation had gone so far that her silence brought about an immediate apology from Gray--a graceful one, she had to admit—and, after glancing at Everet and Emmy, a suggestion to change the subject. Margy gladly agreed, and they turned to other things: children, Stoddard schools, books, Fred Gray's golf scores, Everet's jogging time, a recipe for tacos from Emmy, a foreign movie that all of them had seen in Westport. Earlier, Margy had told herself that Everet looked like a family pet while sitting in his tux and nodding to the Grays as they argued with her. At the time it may have been an extravagant image, but during the latter part of the evening, he seemed to justify it. When Grant Matthews introduced him to the audience again, he rose, waved, strolled to the podium, and, at Matthews's invitation, ad-libbed a speech that Fred and Emmy squirmed all through. He returned to the table with his chin down to his chest, and Fred, patting him on the back, took him to another room, ostensibly to talk with party officials. Margy felt sure he was giving him a pep talk instead.

Meanwhile, she spent another hour with Emmy and several table-hopping wives. Pleasant and intelligent, they showed more involvement in their husbands' affairs than she had imagined. Still, at 11:15, when everybody started to leave and Everet came to take her home, she felt profoundly relieved. The Grays invited them to join a small group for a nightcap at their house, but with a wistful look at Margy, Everet kept an earlier promise to take her directly home. "Margy is tired," he said. "Perhaps I'll take her home and come by myself." Somewhat flattened, he led Margy out the door with Emmy Gray's solicitude ringing in their ears. They retrieved her wrap from the hatcheck girl and walked out to the car. Everet said, "Margy, I have to go. And I might as well tell you that I'm going to make this run, so long as Fred Gray agrees to support me."

She was silent as they entered the car. He started it and drove out of the parking lot onto the waterfront road. The night was warm, their headlights cut through the dark, occasionally catching a moth before it crashed into the windshield.

"It's your decision," she said at last, "as I've always told you. Just don't forget that you have a private life as well."

"I'm very aware of that. More than you, maybe." He turned to her, coolly, then looked back to the road.

"Hmmm, that does sound intriguing. What does it mean, I wonder?"

"It means exactly what it says."

"Everet, we've discussed this already. Let's not continue now." But she looked at him and could not resist continuing: "I'm not messing you up for my career. I'm trying to hold us together through some difficult times."

He looked out ahead and spoke, as if to the road itself. "My career is very important to me, but it doesn't mean that you aren't. Look, I've already admitted that up to now our marriage has served my interests more than yours.

98

But you may be missing something with all of this anger of yours."

She lit a cigarette, opening the vent as he sighed and waved his hand in front of his nose. They drove onto the highway now and, after weaving in and out of traffic for a few miles, went the rest of the way toward East Stoddard in silence. They turned off at the exit for Main Street and followed that until they reached Camels Back Drive, where Everet drove to the end of the street and pulled into their driveway. Margy slid out and, with a house key in her hand, turned to face him. "Maybe you're right," she said. "Maybe we can have it both ways. But it's going to be hard."

He sighed. "Margy, it's got to be hard. We're trying to survive..."

"Oh, Everet, if that's marriage, what are we--?"

"Look, don't get shrill. I don't want to argue now. I want to drive to this little party and enjoy myself with some interesting and potentially helpful people. I'm sorry you can't come. I want you to come, but I understand why you can't. We'll talk about this some other time, okay?"

"Okay, okay, Everet. I'm the only real problem in your campaign, I see. Right now, I feel like you'd rather not come back to me."

He shook his head, asking her to make sure she called his mother. Without closing the door or answering, Margy turned away and began to trudge down the path between the garage and the house.

"Margy, didn't you hear?"

"Yes," she said. "I'll make the call to your mother. Don't worry."

"And if he's still up, say hello to Kennedy."

"What about it, Everet?" She turned to face him and spoke louder. "Would you rather not come back?"

He scratched his chin and, expressionless, leaned across the seat to take the door handle. "Please. Those are your thoughts. They're just going to cause more trouble."

"Am I your problem?" she shouted.

He shook his head. "I'll be back in a little more than an hour. I promise."

99

He closed the door, put the car in gear and drove away with a screech after he passed the yellow hydrant at the corner. Margy went up to her room and undressed, trying to relax by reading some recent magazines. She called Ruth Hamilton at midnight exactly and found that all was well. Kennedy had gone to bed at ten o'clock, and Ruth herself was bubbling because she had just watched Everet and Margy on the local television news. "He looked fine, Margy. Really commanding. And you looked like you just stepped out of a fashion magazine."

After they hung up, Margy looked into the mirror for a while (I am, therefore I must think, she always told herself) and then attempted to retreat from the night by going up to her studio. She worked for at least an hour--partly on her show, partly in her journal. She drew and redrew the face of the model in Foss's class. She saw that it had been the girl's good humor, together with her shyness and her evident need to please that had been so touching that morning. To Foss the girl had been an opportunity to work out problems of shadow and tone, but to Margy the face had been a reminder of her own vulnerable moments. And if Foss's lines of muscle and flesh were ultimately stronger and more stylized (formally more beautiful, Margy admitted) she had gotten closer to the girl's inner expression--the self that a man would have to deal with if he were to live with her successfully. Proudly, Margy told herself that her version was far better.

She drew the face again four or five times, abandoning any attempt to copy Foss's style. As the minutes went by, she began to feel more confident. With her fifth attempt, she at last grew tired of it, and in a triumphant bit of pastiche, she sketched in around the model's head a cartoon of the banquet hall that night--black-tied Charles Addams ghouls swooping down on various human prey, Fred Gray an Al Capp porcupine hurling poisoned darts, Everet as a Walt Disney wolf howling among the various sequined sheep, Emmy Gray as a white-haired Mother Goose, and Margy herself as a Saul Steinberg-inspired Little Red Riding Hood.

It was close to 1:30 by the time she stopped, and still Everet had not returned. She thought of telephoning Goldie but, looking out the window, saw that his room was dark. She hoped that he was home and asleep at this hour. She went down to the second floor and decided to get ready for bed without waiting for Everet. Just as she slipped under the covers, the phone rang twice and abruptly stopped. She stared at it, half out of bed again, wondering if it had been Everet or, possibly, Goldie. But she received no follow-up ring. She slipped back under the covers, and just as she reached to turn off the light, the phone rang again. Waiting for three rings, she got out of bed completely this time and picked it up.

"Goldie--?" She heard only silence at first, then the sound of heavy breathing. "Who is this, please?" she asked, about to hang up.

"Foss. You must be fucking that kid, Margy."

"Foss? It's nearly two o'clock in the morning!"

"I want you, Margy. I'm high, but I just want to tell you I'm serious about your work. Our work. Hell, everybody's work. I'll give you all the time you need tomorrow. Try to give me your time in return."

"Please, Foss, I told you. I don't want any interference now. I'm trying to straighten things out with Everet."

"Is he awake right now? Do me a favor. Tell his honor to fuck off."

He laughed, the rasping of his voice interspersed with a heavy, asthmatic puffing. Then she heard a series of quiet, gulping sounds and realized that Foss was swallowing a drink.

"Foss, don't do that to yourself."

"You're a fine, fine woman, Margy. I want you to know that. I may be drinking right now, but I know enough to say I need you and be sure of what I'm saying. Pose for me tomorrow--or the day after--and everything else is strictly hands off."

"I can't do it, Foss. I can't."

"You mean it turns you on? Hell, Margy, I have plenty of discipline. Everything's hands off, I'm telling you. I just

101

have to get back on that picture so I can work. Help me, please?"

"Foss, I'm trying to make things better here. We're going away next weekend for counseling. Why can't you leave me alone?"

"Margy, I've known you a long time. Things between you and hubby are never going to get better. You only think they are. He's probably sticking it to some black meat on the side."

"Sometimes I wish he would."

She sighed.

"Oh, boy, you *are* far gone!"

"Foss, please; you've helped me a lot, but I really don't deserve this."

She heard another gulp, and before she could admonish him, he started talking again. This time he sounded more insistent. "I can't paint without you, Margy. Without painting I'm afraid I'm going to die. Please--this once--so I can finish something again. Even for old time's sake?"

"No."

She heard something crash on the other end. "Margy, you got a lot of special attention from me a couple of years ago. And I don't mean just loving. Remember?"

"Oh, hell, Foss. Can't we talk about this tomorrow? I don't want Everet coming in on us."

"Hubby again, huh? It's either him or junior."

"Well, what do you want? I'm married; it's a fact of life."

He laughed. "I've never accepted it though, Margy. You paint. You're not a politician's hidden cutie."

She was standing beside the bureau now; at that moment she looked up and caught a glimpse of herself in the mirror above it. Surprised, she had not thought that she would look so worried—or sad. She collapsed onto the mattress.

"Foss, I'm exhausted. I can't discuss anything clearly now."

"Yeah, tomorrow. After class--in studio three. I'll give you the best goddamn art critique you ever had. Then we'll get to the painting."

"Good night, Foss. Thanks for calling."

"Good night. Keep your pants dry. Or should I say 'paints'?"

She lit a cigarette, breaking a resolution she had made earlier to cut down by not smoking except in her studio. Soon afterward, she heard Everet in the driveway and got out of bed to put out the cigarette and turn on the stairway light for him. There were a few moments of silence, then whistling as he opened the door, mounted the steps and walked past the bedroom, to the end of the hallway, before coming back. "I forgot that Kennedy wasn't here," he muttered, entering and walking to the bed. "I was going to look in on him."

He kissed Margy several times, squeezed her shoulder, and laughed woozily as he straightened up. Without further comment, he took off his tuxedo and shirt, neatly folding them over a chair. Then, tipsy though he was, Margy noted, he polished a pair of shoes and showed enough forethought to layout his track gear for the morning run. He brushed his teeth and, dressed in his blue robe, came to the bed and kissed Margy again. Instead of joining her, he said he had some thinking to do and started for the door. He seemed to move very carefully.

"Afraid the mattress will spin around?"

He grinned, hung his head and returned to the bed where, like a bumbling suitor, he took her hand.

"How'd it go?"

"Good. You know, the Grays are really being nice." He shook his head and, bleary-eyed, glanced down the blanket at the outline of her legs. Margy smiled.

"They make you feel like you're going to win, don't they? Nomination and everything in one sweep. That was obvious at the dinner."

"Margy, Fred's committed himself now--it's certain. Do you know what that means?"

103

She swallowed. Although she wished that she could change the subject, she thought of her conversation with Foss and decided to be understanding. "Then why so gloomy?" she asked. "You seem to have something on your mind."

He nodded. Slowly, he rose and went to the door, returned to the bed and held her hand again. From the look in his eyes and the confusion they showed, Margy suspected that he was about to dress her down.

"What is it? Come on. Tell me."

Perhaps it wasn't her behavior tonight, she thought; perhaps it was a problem with the Grays, or another woman. She was not surprised that that alternative almost made her glad.

"Fred and Emmy are having some people at their house—this Saturday and Sunday. They're important political people, and ..."

He stopped and looked at her. Margy shook her head: "Yes?"

"And Fred's invited us to come over and meet them."

She nodded. "Oh, it's too bad that we can't--"

"Oh, yes, we can."

She was genuinely puzzled at first, looking at the determination on his face. The confusion was gone, and she saw a certainty that was not from too much liquor. When it hit her, she could barely whisper, "Everet, no ..."

He slammed his open hand on the mattress. "Well, hell, didn't you tell me they give those sessions in Wiltshire every week?"

"Every *other* week, I told you. And if you cancel out, they sometimes refuse another appointment for months. They want to be sure the couple is ready."

"Now, don't get defensive... I'd really like to go to this thing, Margy."

"No! Go to the Grays the weekend after! Or the weekend after that!" He looked away. "Everet, you promised, and we have the deposit in already. It'll be June by the time they have the next session, and if I know you, you'll even be busier with your campaign."

"No, I won't. That's not till the summer."

"Well, you'll be starting. Don't lie about it. Besides, by June I'll be pressed for time myself."

"Fred Gray is going to support me, Margy. He's sending a TV reporter here to do an interview this week."

She sat up, lighting a cigarette and warning Everet not to comment on it. She took a deep drag, then another, blowing the smoke just above and beyond his head. Perhaps she was being selfish, she thought, but he was, too. He merely sat back and looked impatient in his own hard-headed calm. "This morning we said we wouldn't argue," she said, "so I 'm going to state my case as objectively as I can.--Our marriage is dying. No!--that's not objective. I'll change it. Our marriage is in trouble. We both admit it, but at this point only one of us is trying to make it better. I may have screwed up in the past--as I freely admitted. But if you don't come with me this weekend, you will have broken your promise and that will show something too."

"But we can make it another weekend, Margy." He bent forward, his hands extended toward her. She tried to concentrate on the cigarette. He slapped his knee. "I have to show Gray that I'm sincerely interested. My personal life can't get in the way."

"Well, Everet, if that's one of your problems, we might as well forget it--pack it in right now."

He rose, strode to the door and, once more, hesitated.

"God damn it, Margy. You know what this means. You have to accept the fact that I'm doing this. I want to work with you, but you have to accept that my campaign takes special consideration. I may not have another chance to meet these people."

"I don't care!—We're more important!"

He opened the door, closed it without leaving, then returned to the bed and lay down beside her. He pulled her close.

"Watch the cigarette, you idiot! You're going to make me burn the sheet!" He rolled away in a sulk, as she put it out in the ashtray.

"Come on, baby. Just one more delay. One--that's all. I promise, on the weekend after, absolutely nothing will stop me. Nothing." He raised his right hand and, as she turned from the ashtray, placed his left one on her breast.

"Get out of here!" She shoved him away and rolled onto her stomach. He patted her back and, cooing in her ear, tried to embrace her. Margy pushed him away again.

"You looked good tonight, you know? You looked great in that cocktail dress. A number of people told me that."

"Jesus, you are sick--Get your hands off me! You're giving me nothing but a homeboy's jive."

"Margy..."

"We had an agreement, Everet! Your shining knight's word!"

"And I intend to keep it. Just delay two more weeks. If I don't go then, you never have to come anywhere with me again."

"I may never want to go with you again--anywhere. You don't seem to realize how serious I am."

She slapped his hands as he reached for her shoulders and moved to the opposite side of the mattress. Her stomach was turning; her hands trembled and her arms and legs felt heavy. She tried to block out her nervousness, but she knew that it was not in her nature to deny such things; the struggle affected every muscle in her body.

"You're a prick, you know that? You're not even subtle about it."

He reached over, laughing, sliding his hand beneath her nightgown and along her bare thighs.

"Come on, Margy. I'm feeling good; you shouldn't have to be angry. I want you to share my happiness." His other hand slid onto her breast again, squeezing it. Then, probably because he thought she was crying, he turned her over and very tenderly kissed her eyes. She began to soften.

"Hey! That guy John Buford's all right. He's going to help us out. Fred's got him doing a story on us--both of us."

"Oh, God, you know you are really disgusting."

106

He fell beside her, laughing. Then he threw his arms across her shoulders and kissed her neck. "Kennedy's not home," he whispered. "We have the whole house to ourselves. You want to make love downstairs--like we used to?

"Oh, Everet--"

"To hell with it, baby! Let's have some jelly-roll--in front of the fire."

"No!--" But he blatted his lips against her cheek, tickled her ribs, then, as she screamed, picked her up and carried her down to the living room in the dark. She did not kick or beat his chest; she did not even laugh, stupid as she thought herself at that moment. She simply lay in his arms and let him take her where he would.

"I love you," he whispered, in front of the fireplace. "You know, you're more important to me than anyone else in the world."

"Go to hell, will you?"

Margy struggled to free herself, and he, laughing still, placed her gingerly on the couch. "It's been a nice night. Don't spoil it. This is a good way to top it off."

"I hated it, Everet. We were miles apart. And remember, you're the one who cares about how we feel."

He waved and went to the bin to get some wood for a fire. There were a few pieces of kindling and a couple of medium-sized logs left over from the winter. He lit the kindling and added the logs one after another; then he returned to the couch and slowly pulled off his robe. Undressed, he came to Margy, slipped his hand beneath her thighs, and lifted the nightgown over her head. She did not resist; in fact, by this time she was caressing his hand. The air brought goose-bumps to her skin, and he lay next to her, lightly massaging her arms and legs till they became warm again. Then he kissed her, and she felt that trigger something tender inside. Where before she might have cursed and cuddled him at once, now only the cuddling was left. With his arms around her, she held his penis, kissing it and watching it flower in the fire's orange glow.

107

"Cream. You're like rich, thick cream sometimes," he murmured. She kissed his lips; he leaned over, pressing her down and then, together, they slid onto the carpet in front of the fire. As usual, his body was slightly awkward, slightly stiff as he lay on top of her--as if this were completely new between them--but his hands were smooth and skillful against her limbs. They had made love thousands of times during their life together; yet she was aware that each time it was a little surprising and challenging, and always a little tense because it might spill over into routine. She also knew that there were marvelous times when their bodies broke free of their wills and seemed to move of their own accord, sweeping away everything in thoughtless motion. That was what she hoped for now.

Everet's legs squeezed between Margy's, while his lips and fingers caressed her upper body. She resisted at first, but, spurred on by her own need, she touched his back and ran her fingers down to his buttocks. How full and muscular they were! Despite everything, she began to loosen up a little more. He whimpered when he held her breasts, nipping them, lying on the left one with the nipple in his ear. Her heart opened. Like an infant, he kept time with its beat by tapping his fingers against her shoulder. Finally, he entered her and the look on his face was both childlike and passionate, wiping away completely the powerful resistance she had felt.

He pressed against her, biting her ear, sliding his tongue in and out of it, then groaning--straining suddenly, as if in terror--and just succeeded in holding back, with a motion that was both distant and intimate, bringing her up with him, pushing her back, then shoving her over the edge of something while he started quickly behind.

"Oh, God, I can't help this. It's so good!"

He moaned, as always; they pressed together, thrusting their upper bodies apart at first, then bringing them back together again. Margy's mind went blank. She heard him say her name over and over, and her only reply was a constant, climactic hum which, he had told her in their lighter

108

moments, emerged from her throat like a mournful diesel-engine's wail.

"I won't be able to leave you, Everet. I won't be able to get off this floor." She cried. Her body seemed to be moaning, almost convulsing with the rhythm of her sobs, ready to shatter at one point if she could not let herself come.

"Hold it, Everet. Please!" He stopped, pumped again, and continued. She hit his shoulders, cursing, calling his name. Gradually, he began to slow down, and that change freed something else inside her. She pressed against him, blurting his name, crying. With each cry she came, and when he called her name too, she came again and again.

And then one final time.

"Ohhh, God... " she cried. "I can't believe it! I can't! I could just keep going!"

They lay together a long time, keeping just below the level of yet another climax until, exhausted, Everet finally pulled away. He staggered to the hallway, giggling. Tripping over the coffee table, he sent a spray of perspiration all the way to the door. He went to the closet and came back, carrying a light gray blanket.

"What was that," he said, smiling, "number 2,876?"

"Seventy-eight," she replied. "I see you're counting too." She grinned, wiping his forehead with the ribboned edge of the blanket as he lay next to her.

"How many times do you think it is, really?" he asked, helping her spread the blanket over their legs and hips.

She rose, reaching across him to the couch for a pair of cushions. "Good and bad, or just the good ones?"

"Everything--about this, we can't dismiss a thing."

She considered. "Twenty-five hundred, maybe three thousand."

He sighed, settling his head into the cushion. Margy tried to fold hers to get more height beneath her neck. "You add up the time. Do you know how many hours that makes?--Almost two thousand in the sack. That's quite a lot of bumping and groaning."

She laughed, and he, after rising again to use the bathroom, put his favorite recording, Bach's "A Musical Offering," on the stereo. He took Margy into his arms. "Passion with control," he whispered. While they listened to the harpsichord and strings murmur to the flute and bassoon, he fell asleep almost immediately. She tossed and turned for nearly an hour.

***

Later, hours later, after a quiet, uncomplicated time of sketching and smoking in the kitchen, in the middle of what must have been a disturbing dream for him, Margy heard Everet call her name. She heard him moan, and, when she returned to the living room to lie next to him, he pulled himself on top of her as if he were her child.

This had happened many times before.

"Margy, Margy," he whispered, half-awake, half in the box of his dream. He tried to force himself inside her. She held him away at first, but then she looked up at his face and saw tears spilling from his eyes.

He clutched her arms. When she embraced him, his fingers gripped her elbows until she nearly screamed. Then he groaned--painful, horrible sounds--and she let him enter her, feeling him immediately spill over inside. Still asleep, he mumbled something which Margy could not understand, but which she took to be an apology. He left her, rolled to his side. In the silence that followed, he resumed his normal nighttime breathing....

Four o'clock. She stared at the clock on the mantelpiece and could not close her eyes. At last she took some pills and, lying beside him as still as possible, she breathed deeply and watched the fire die until just a coal was left to throw a grayish-pink glow across the blanket. The sounds of the house continued to stir her. What would it be like not to have thoughts or sensible impressions? Not to have to draw an imaginary line from the far left corner of the ceiling through the yellow stain in the lower quadrant, to the brighter middle where the light fixture hung?

110

What would it be like not to feel compelled to conceive of that line as the beginning of a form? Not to sketch another line from its middle?

What would it be like not to wonder about those shadows.

***

Morning light poured through the windows. Everet rose glumly, a dark patch of brownish-purple tripping over the blanket and Margy's legs before he stumbled up the stairs. She closed her eyes, trying to sleep, then opened them and saw him again--a gray and blue blur in his sweat-suit and jogging shoes.

In the hallway he performed calisthenics for a quarter hour. Then he greeted her in the living room with a kiss (but not a bead of perspiration), set the coffee-maker going in the kitchen, and, bending and stretching, throwing a few quick punches at his shadow on the wall, trotted outdoors to begin his morning five-mile run beside the Sound. By the time he returned (no more than thirty minutes later, he would tell her) Margy was on her feet smiling, groggy but good-humored. She had his breakfast ready when he came down from the shower.

"You slept well, I guess. Do you remember waking?"

He smiled. "Not a bit. I was really into my dreams."

"Good."

"It was fine making love with you last night."

She nodded. "I liked it too."

He stood, leaned across the table and kissed her on the lips. She started to speak, but it seemed unfair to spoil the mood by alluding to his nightmare.

"How could we talk about splitting up when it can be so good between us?" he asked.

"How can we? That's why I want to go to Wiltshire."

He paled, sipping herb tea and pouring milk onto his granola. "Ah, Margy." He took a spoonful of cereal while she sipped her coffee. "I'm sorry; you're probably right. But about this weekend—"

111

She waved her hand. "Forget it. I'll call the people at the institute to see if I can change the date."

"Great!"

And that was all.

After Everet left for work, smiling and penitent, Margy washed the breakfast dishes, poured herself another cup of coffee, then called the number at Wiltshire. She reached a woman named Sally Forrest, who said there might be problems with the change of dates. But after Margy expressed deep regret and pleaded an unexpected change of schedule, Sally requested permission from her superiors. They allowed an alternate weekend, the second in June. "Just this once," Sally reported.

Margy disliked Sally's tone of voice and almost cancelled the visit entirely. But when Sally said that they were looking forward to seeing her, and when she asked if Everet and Margy were certain about the second date, she sighed and humbly muttered yes.

Not really feeling sure, she went up to the bedroom for a twenty minute nap and slept well past noon. She missed Foss's class (plus his criticism of her work), lunch with Goldie (with more news about his visit to New York), and, most important, a planned afternoon hike by herself to a hilltop from which she had hoped to water-color a hidden valley near the Sound. It would have been perfect for the show: the Connecticut coast, just inland, in the middle of its annual change from black and grimy winter brown to springtime yellow, green, and blue...

Dark ship and colorless ocean,
We make waves, only to slip over them,
Slip over them, only to fall into their troughs...

II.

RUNNING

8.

AT THE GRAYS

Three days passed, during which it rained steadily, so that she could not get to that valley. There were two more arguments and an evening of love-making with Everet, an afternoon of conversation with Goldie, a short, unproductive session with Foss, and then preparation for their weekend with the Grays. On Friday night Everet and Kennedy slipped off to sleep early while Margy, almost as if to spite her efforts at composure, spent a long, arduous night. She tossed and turned until one, went up to the attic and sketched until three, saw Goldie's bedroom light on next door and made a short phone call to him on his private line. Then she slept, only moderately well, until dawn.

She was awake and surprisingly alert before the alarm went off, and, after Everet and she threw their bags into the car, they were on the road, with Kennedy between them, by nine o'clock. They drove through Stratford, reaching the local beach community, an aging remnant of 19th century Stoddard fishing life which wrapped around the town of Stratford like a lover's arm. Along the beach were dug-out channels, decayed and derelict wharfs, small Cape Cod homes with ceramic gulls over doors, windows, and garages, and, facing the sea, a series of widow's walks on the roofs.

This was the resort section of Stoddard, with a casual ambiance to its streets that made them more cosmopolitan than provincial. Soon, in place of the traditional Cape Cods, the party found themselves among a group of newer, sandstone buildings: sleek, square molds of concrete and glass, large and modern, constructed to blend unobtrusively with the environment. Few of the houses succeeded, but the Grays owned one that did, the last on a dead end street curving around an inlet and ending at the beach. The house nestled between dunes just at Stoddard's city limits, and, as they pulled into the Gray driveway, leaving the car and opening the trunk, they immediately felt a sense of space and privacy surrounding them--a rare thing in present-day Stoddard.

The sun was warm and the air dry, a relief after the last three days. The water looked calm and clear beyond the house, with a tint of green over the deeper layers of aqua-blue. As they set their gear on the sand, a tow-headed boy of about ten or eleven, a whirl of arms and legs, came running off the beach. Ignoring Everet, Margy, a bicycle, a sandpail, and a small, motor-driven tractor plumped to a standstill in a patch of tulips, he stopped with a skid of gravel at the car and shouted, without introduction:

"Hey! Can anyone here play right field?"

He glanced at Kennedy with large blue eyes. Kennedy looked at Everet with his brown ones. Everet rested a pink and tan hand on Kennedy's shoulders.

"He can play anything; anything you want."

"That true?"

"Sure."

"Well, let's go. You're just the guy we need."

Without a shake of hands or an exchange of names, they charged onto the beach and around the corner of the house, shouting. Kennedy carried a knapsack full of his own beach equipment.

"Fred Gray's nephew," Everet said.

"Good. That takes care of one of your problems. Now, how about me?"

"Come on, Margy... "

"Don't worry. I'll do my best. I know Emmy Gray will be my playmate for the day."

Margy turned, carrying an overnight bag in her hand, and saw Emmy waving from a chaise longue on a terrace near the beach. She looked awkward and out of place, wearing a blue one-piece suit, her legs fleshy and masculine as she waddled toward them. Obviously, her gown the other night had smoothed out some bulges. She led the Hamiltons into the house and turned over their belongings to a black man and woman who showed them to a room at the rear of the second floor. Though he refused to let the man carry his

115

bag or open the door for him, Everet showed little embarrassment.

"See?" Margy said, after they were alone. "I remember times when a black servant enraged you."

Everet frowned. "Fred and I have already discussed them, Margy. They are exactly why I'm interested in running for the mayor's job. If I win, Fred Gray--and others like him--will be my servants. Don't forget."

They changed into beach clothes and met Emmy outside fifteen minutes later. She took them onto the beach and pointed toward Fred--captain's hat waving in his hand--who was at the water's edge, coming toward them.

"Hey, Fred!" Everet called.

"Hello, Everet!--I'm glad you got here early enough to swim. Were those two streaks of lightning I saw across the beach my nephew and your son?"

He shook hands with Everet and gave Margy a surprisingly affectionate embrace. They discussed the air, the sun, and the clear sky, then decided to sit under an umbrella. The beach was clear for at least fifty yards to the south; there were no houses nearby, just a point and a jetty with a dune behind them that blocked their view of everything to the north and east. A small rowboat lay tilted on the sand, and a little way out in the water a motorboat with a tiny cabin rocked gently in the waves. Gray looked at it, motioned generally to claim it and the beach as his, then plopped down on a blanket and opened a thermos of lemonade.

"Goddamn hot today. You want some?" Both Margy and Everet nodded. He searched for plastic cups in a bag, filled them with lemonade and began to pass them around. "I want you to relax. You particularly, Margy: swim, sunbathe, feel free to use that motorboat anytime--but most important, I would consider it an honor if you would just make yourself at home." She nodded. "Everet told me that you cancelled an important appointment this weekend, and I'm grateful that you gave it up to come out here."

Fred leaned on his elbow and smiled genially. Everet reclined next to him in the sun, and Emmy and Margy, the

116

two fair-skinned ones, retreated to the shade of the umbrella. Noises came from the right side of the beach; Margy saw Kennedy and about a dozen other boys playing with a broomstick and a tennis ball near the water. Right field was the Sound, and Kennedy, wearing his swimsuit now, dove into the water repeatedly for fly balls hit his way. He seemed to enjoy it, laughing whenever he went in--a hearty, throaty laugh she always loved to hear--and during his first time at bat, he called for Everet to check on his form.

"Go ahead, I'm looking," said Everet. He watched Kennedy swing, hard but wildly, twice; then he cheered-- along with Margy and the Grays--as on the third swing Kennedy's bat connected, and he drove the ball into the sand so that it took a bad bounce and skimmed through the infield. One of the players near the water gathered it up just as Kennedy crossed first and turned toward second, where he stopped, sliding, then stood up and waved at Everet and Margy. She waved back and closed her eyes, proudly. But at the sound of the next shout, Margy looked up to see him being tagged out while trying to score on someone else's hit. Even Fred smiled as Kennedy slinked back to the sidelines, fell onto the sand, and looked miserably embarrassed.

"You tried. You wouldn't have got to second if you didn't try," Everet called. Kennedy buried his head in his arms, but his spirits picked up considerably during the next half inning. One of the players drove the ball far over his head into the water. It seemed impossible to reach, but Kennedy charged into the surf, doing a head-long belly-whopper when he left his feet. About thirty feet out, the ball, water and his frantic, upturned hand came together in one of those miracles of space and motion that seem to happen only in dreams. Kennedy stood up, ball barely sticking to his fingertips, water pouring down on his head from his outstretched arms, and shouted. Everyone on both teams stared at him in disbelief.

"You see that, Daddy? Did you see that catch?" he called.

"See it? How could I miss? You keep at it, son!"

117

Everet raised his fist when Kennedy's team came in to bat. Fred and Emmy applauded, and Margy sat, amazed and smiling proudly. She had never liked Kennedy to play sports; but she admitted that he came through them well, his good humor allowing for perspective.

As the game continued, Emmy left to make a snack, and Fred, preparing Margy for a long and difficult weekend, she was sure, invited her and Everet onto his motorboat so that he could teach her how to maneuver it. He rowed them out to the boat and, after they had climbed into it, he travelled along the coast until they were opposite downtown Stoddard. Across the water they saw the horizon of Long Island, but farther north (which, from the beach, had been blocked by the sand dunes and jetty) they saw water and sky, and a couple of gun-gray freighters looking as small as canoes passing in the distance. Back along the coast, Gray pointed to his house, then to a high bluff behind it, with bare sand leading from the water to a couple of dunes.

"Public property," he said, referring to the half mile of open space behind them. "I've been trying for years to get the city council to set up recreation facilities here, but the goddamn mayor and his cronies want to save it for industrial use instead. As if this water isn't murky enough right now."

They coasted closer to the shore. With the engine at idle, he showed Margy how to operate the throttle at forward and reverse; he taught her to read the buoys in order to stay in the proper channels. After demonstrating the use of the radio, he let her take the wheel, directed her to drive out to a distant point, then along the coast to the jetty and back to the rowboat, where he and Everet started to disembark.

"You think you can handle this contraption now, Margy? Everet and I have to go inside, but you're welcome to stay out here and practice as long as you like."

"I think I'll come in, Fred," she said.

He looked disappointed. "Oh, it's not that difficult. Just stay close to the shore."

"I'm not a sailor. Besides, I have a book with me, and I can lie under the umbrella and read. I'm getting burned."

He nodded, and Everet told him about the problems Margy had had in St. Croix: during their two weeks in the tropics, she had spent only dawns and sunsets on the beach; at the beginning of the vacation, one mid-morning in the sun had turned her a very painful red. Gray clucked sympathetically, dropped anchor, and after they transferred into the small boat, he rowed back to the beach where Emmy waited with sandwiches and cookies.

"We'll leave the ladies to themselves and talk inside," Gray said. He carried a plateful of sandwiches, and, after he led Everet into the house, Emmy and Margy talked for a while. But soon, probably taking the hint of Margy's reticence, Emmy excused herself and went into the house to prepare for that evening's party. Feeling uneasy, Margy read, but kept looking at the Sound. A white lighthouse stood beyond the jetty; in the open water a flurry of gulls hounded a passing freighter. Finally, instead of reading, she opened her journal, turned to an empty page, and spent the better part of the next hour putting together several versions of the view in front of her. Sketching could become obsessive, she knew, and she felt guilty for not having offered to help with the evening preparations. But a half hour later Emmy came onto the sand with her own sketchpad, and quickly the two began drawing the scene together.

Emmy had a strong line, Margy was surprised to see, and a real knack for capturing perspective. But she was weak on technical details: shadow and light, for instance, the cropping of mass with other mass outlines, and the echoing of small, formal relationships within the total composition. But she took Margy's suggestions well and improved on a sketch of the lighthouse considerably, allowing the curve of the beach to sweep up into the lines of the rock surrounding it and from there up to the beacon itself, so that the whole drawing had a continuous flow of movement from the lower right hand corner of the page to the upper left. The freighter became a small ship with a flock of gulls surrounding it; they gave counter-balancing shape in the upper-right hand corner to the boomerang of shapes in the lower left and added weight to the picture as a whole.

119

The women began to talk of other things, and gradually Margy perceived that Emmy was not simply feeling her out. She asked about the painters Margy admired, the kind of classes she attended, the types of subjects she preferred to paint. They had a long, interesting discussion about materials, and Emmy showed surprising awareness of the advantages and disadvantages of acrylics to oils, oils to watercolors, and so on. Not once did she mention the election, and when she had finally held up the completed sketch of the Sound, standing and dropping her pad to the sand, she winked at Margy and said, "Well, this certainly beats small talk, doesn't it? Especially the political kind."

Margy laughed, rising and embracing her for an instant before Emmy went into the house. She returned in a few minutes with Fred behind her. "I'm glad you two have kept busy. It's been a very pleasant morning."

He looked at Margy's page of sketches without comment and returned to the house. When he came back, he trailed Everet behind him, and then behind Everet, two other men, one of them being John Buford. Buford nodded to Margy while he shook Emmy's hand. He wore khaki slacks, a white short-sleeved shirt, and sandals. The other man wore jeans and a blue working shirt. They both faded off to the patio again while Fred went down to the game to call the boys.

"Hey, come on over to our place for lunch," she heard him say. "Winners and losers: we'll make a regular training table."

Most of the boys accepted, and back at the house Gray donned a chef's cap and stood in front of the barbecue where he gleefully grilled burgers for the players and chicken for the adults. Buford and the fellow in jeans left, saying they had a meeting in town, but they promised to come back for the party that evening. The adults shared a bottle of white wine with the meal and, after dessert, Everet ran off with the boys to join in the game. Several of the other fathers from nearby homes joined in too, and while Emmy, Fred, the maid, and Margy cleared the table, fathers and sons began a second game. Fred, balancing a pile of plates, silverware, napkins, and chicken bones in his hands, invited Margy out to the boat again. She refused as she carried glasses and a plate of leftovers into the house. But when she returned to the patio, he insisted, patting her on the arm. "I want Margy to get the hang of this boat," he said. Emmy gave a quick glance at Margy and smiled ruefully.

In the motorboat, Fred steered toward the jetty and the lighthouse beyond, until they lost sight of the southern part of Long Island. They glided past the lighthouse, following the buoys into a channel, which had been cut through the dunes and pebbly beach for almost a mile. The channel reached the Housatonic River, which they floated down toward Stratford, occasionally pausing in front of old houses and historic elms before they scudded through a group of sailboats and yachts along the eastern shore.

"That's the Shakespeare theatre down there--around the bend. It gets complicated beyond those boats; some low spots I'm not sure of. Let's head upstream, and I'll show you some of the older stuff along the shore. Everet tells me you're interested in local history."

They passed more sandstone houses, a bog of marsh grass, a small grove of gnarled trees, and then a huge, seemingly dying oak which was trussed up with iron braces at each of its three main limbs. Gray pointed to a rusty cannonball embedded in its trunk: "British iron," he said, "1778--When supplies and messages got through too easily from Boston to New York, they tried to seal off the Sound here in Stoddard. We were not as unimportant as some historians up and down river like to think."

He drifted into the cove and along the channel until they came to the lighthouse again. From there they moved into deeper water and, opening the throttle, Gray sped out to a distant sandbar and anchored. "Let's get out and rest, Margy. This will be dry for a while."

He jumped into the water and, with Margy beside him, swam--floated, rather--about forty feet to the bar, with a warm-up jacket, cap, and fuming cigar held well above his head. From the sandbar they saw small groups of people beginning to fill the beach and, near Gray's house, the

121

ballgame which, from the distance, looked like the busy organized movement of a dance.

"Have a seat, Margy. In case you haven't guessed, this is where you and I have our little heart-to-heart."

He patted the sand and lay back, pulling his cap, which he had not managed to keep completely dry, over his eyes. He had a pot belly, pudgy, muscular legs, and a confident, easy manner to his movements which Margy did not find unpleasant.

"You know," he said, "I admire him. I admire Everet very much."

She sat next to him and nodded, having decided to remain friendly but guarded. At the dinner in Stoddard she had already told him everything that mattered to her about the election.

"He's really a remarkable human being. His father was too; I knew him well."

She nodded. The sun was hot on her back; as she lay back, trying to make herself comfortable, Gray offered her his jacket, and she slipped it onto her shoulders. "If you want, I'll go back to the boat for a blanket to cover your legs."

"No, this is fine. I'll just keep moving it around. My skin is tender, but I can take the sun if I don't get too much all in one place."

He waved, rolling the cigar between his lips, then chomping it between his teeth as he lay back again and puffed. A mild gust of wind blew ashes and smoke directly out toward Long Island.

"You really don't want to help us very much, do you?" Gray said.

She looked at him, surprised at how direct he was. "I'm not sure I should," she answered.

"Of course you should. It means a lot to the town—and the country."

"Look, I thought we went over most of this the other night. Is there anything new?"

"No, but would you mind telling me what your real thinking is?"

"You already have it. You'll find that I'm rather open about my opinions, Fred."

"I mean about your marriage, of course. Everet and I have talked, in case you haven't guessed. He says it's basically sound, but that the reasons for your reluctance about the election run very deep. I don't know what 'basically sound' means, I must say. But he's got stars in his eyes as far as I'm concerned. I wonder if you would disagree."

She shook her head. "Sometimes they're very bright," she said.

Gray adjusted his cap as a drop of water rolled from its brim. "Well, what about you? It seems to me that you're much more planted in the earth. So just how 'basically sound' is your marriage?"

She looked at him, started to say it was, then thought better of it. She ended by shrugging and looking toward the shore.

"The same damn vagueness comes from him. That doesn't mean it's good, as far as I can tell."

"The issue is between Everet and me, Fred."

"No, it's Everet, you, and *me*. He's going to run for mayor."

Silently, Gray tossed cigar ash into the wind and turned back to face the shore with Margy. He wore red bathing trunks, decorated with white, spouting Moby Dicks. He sat on a few of them and stared into her eyes. "Let me tell you, Margy; whatever you think, I'm not a stone. I'm fond of Everet, genuinely fond. He makes me feel like a father sometimes, which is something I've never known before in my life. That's a very important feeling."

He adjusted the jacket on Margy's shoulders and looked toward a freighter in the north. Gulls fluttered and dove around it, their cries occasionally carrying to the sandbar with the wind. They stared at the birds for a while, then Gray turned to Margy and said, "In fact, that feeling of fatherliness is so important to me that it makes your reluctance to talk very painful. For his sake, would you mind telling me what your feelings are?"

123

"About what? You? Our marriage? This election? What the hell are you asking about, Fred?"

"Everything. Everything concerning Everet."

"I love him. I'm his wife, you know."

"Oh, very good, but you don't want him to succeed to his ambitions?"

"I'm his *wife*! Trust me, everything I say comes out of that."

"A *white* wife, let's not forget."

Gray leaned back and puffed on his cigar. A few gulls flew out from the shore, circling overhead. One landed, but seeing that they had no food, gave a little shriek and left.

"I want to talk and, by God, I'm going to lay all the cards on the table. If it'll do any good for our relationship, I'm going to let you know."

"Good. Lay your cards on the table. What are they?"

Another drop of water rolled down Gray's forehead. He took off the cap and tossed it onto the sand. He stared at Margy for a long time and said, "What do you know about John Buford?"

"Nothing." Again she was surprised at how direct he was.

"That's not what he says--John, I mean. But to tell you the truth, I'm not sure I can trust him."

"We were classmates; that's all. What has he said?"

Gray shrugged. "Nothing specific. It's all in intimations. Buford is a very ambitious man, and I get the feeling he's holding something back. But I wonder how important that information is? Would you happen to know?"

Margy shook her head, stubbornly. On the one hand she thought that Buford's knowledge was insignificant--it would be impossible to reveal in any respectable journalistic way, after all. But, on the other, she saw it through Everet's and Fred's eyes: Any sexual publicity would be unfavorable-- the vaguest story having the most powerful effect. Gray smiled, looking past her to Long Island, then turned back toward the beach. "I think Everet can win, you know, barring anything unforeseen. More important, I think he can be a goddamn good mayor, and I know the town needs him--"

124

"Oh, Fred, if this is your way of making me feel sorry, you're failing. I need him too, and right now he's not being a very good husband. He hasn't been for some time."

"How do you mean that? He seems conscientious as far as I can tell."

"He's very self-involved."

Gray puffed his cigar. "How so?"

"He is so interested in his career that he hardly has time for me--or Kennedy."

"Oh, so that's it. Margy, I've had this conversation with a lot of people, including Everet. But, as I told him, Emmy and I have had our problems too. I've fooled around; maybe Emmy's fooled around. In a way, I hope she has. But we never let that stuff stop our careers. It's just not that important when you consider the stakes we're playing for. People like us are the center of this city."

"Jesus, you are sick. I don't even know why we're talking here."

"If I have a good candidate who is in danger of getting cuckolded--at least as far as the public is concerned-- then I have to talk about it. Without his wife's loyalty, my man's a loser, and so am I."

"That's politics. I don't think it's as important as my personal life--certainly not our marriage. I'm talking about the foundation of the community; you're talking about what's hidden in the attic."

Gray looked at her sharply. "Yeah, and Everet just said that, too, about word for word. Strange, how you two have the same opinions but are so far apart." Margy shook her head. "He said he was never happy in his life until he met you. Margy--Phi Beta Kappa, Harvard Law School, a scholarship to study international law in France, citations from CORE, NAACP, an acquaintance with Martin Luther King, a fine mother and father who were very respected in this city and tried to give him everything. Yet he wasn't happy until he met you. To be frank, when he said that, I almost vomited."

"Nice of you to say, you shit!"

125

He shrugged and lay back in the sand with a self-satisfied smile.

"A shit? Why shouldn't I be? You haven't been so great to me--or to him."

"I don't want to talk to you anymore!"

"Good. Swim back to the goddamn beach. I'm just going to lie on this sandbar and get some sleep. Things are too complex for this dirty politician's simple head."

He turned over on his stomach like a great belly-whopping beast, set the cap back on his head, and, cigar still in his mouth, looked out toward the freighter. Margy felt stunned. She also felt selfish, and--true or false--it was a feeling that she never liked to admit to.

"And lately?" she asked, after a long silence.

"What?"

"What did he say about our happiness lately?"

"Oh, so you do want to talk about it, heh?" She glared at him, then turned away. "All right. I'm going to let you have it straight. He's as non-committal about things recently as he is about the 'basically sound' part of your marriage. He's confused, and, coming from Everet, that isn't a good sign. I've been checking around, and I have an inkling of what's happening between you two. You know, I know about Copperwood and this teacher, Foster. I know about the purpose of this trip that you and Everet were supposed to take this weekend. I also know about the flirtation with this kid next door."

"Flirtation?"

"Don't look at me like that. Dan Goldstein is an old friend of mine. Besides, regardless of your opinion, it's part of politics, and so it is my business to know about these things."

Margy shifted Fred's jacket from her shoulders to her legs. There was a sudden shout from the shore, and she made out Kennedy's mocha-colored body lumbering into third. He rounded it, then dove back to keep the base. Everet was up next, left-handed, and with the first pitch he lofted the ball very high toward the Sound. A land wind must have caught it because the right-fielder, stumbling into the water,

126

could not reach it on time. He waded in to his waist, stretched, seemed about to grasp it, but in a sudden spurt the ball streaked past his outstretched hands, bobbing up beyond him in a little wave. Kennedy was already at homeplate, shouting and jumping up and down. Everet had rounded second by the time the fielder reached the ball and threw it in. Then she saw Everet bend low, kick up sand at third, and dive into home head-first as the ball caromed off his shoulders.

"Bravo!--That's it. Keep it up!"

Gray clapped his hands and whistled. He was on his knees now, puffing his cigar with fatherly satisfaction as he looked at Margy over his shoulder.

"I'm not cuckolding him," she said. "With Goldie or anyone else. We've always had a rather loosely defined agreement about fidelity."

Gray winced. After a pause, he asked, "Do you love him, Margy?"

"I told you. He's my husband."

Gray nodded. "What about Dan Goldstein's nephew. Are you just satisfying an urge to be young again?"

She stared at him. Struggling with her thoughts, she looked toward the beach and said, "I don't want to talk about this, Fred."

"Margy, if I don't find out what's going on, the newspapers may, and then where will I be? John Buford is a friend--at least right now he's a political friend. But Dan Goldstein is different. He is not a very diplomatic man. I wouldn't want him to come out talking about his nephew--or that teacher--and you. I wouldn't be able to stop him. Now tell me, are you playing around, or are you serious?"

"What difference does it make—politically!"

She threw the jacket into his face, rose to her feet, and swam back to the boat. Gray looked at her, serenely smiling as he finished his cigar, and held up the key to the engine in his hand. Margy lay in the bottom of the boat and folded her arms. After a few minutes, she heard a splash and when she looked over the side, she saw him floating toward the boat with the cap and jacket above his head. He held onto the gunwale, told her to stand opposite, and carefully lifted himself over it.

"I really want to make this marriage work," he said, after settling himself in the bow. "I've been trying to think of a way to help you and Everet."

"Go ahead." She laughed. "Try something."

He shook his head. "I will. But it seems to me that you haven't really decided yourself. I think he really wants it to work."

"In theory, or in reality? For six months I've been trying, Fred. But between you and the election, I haven't been able to get through to him. That's why I want to go to an institute--for counseling and therapy. He just wants us to get along."

"Why do you see these other people then? Especially the painter?"

"I don't. Foss and I stopped seeing each other long ago. Right now, he's just a professional acquaintance. And Goldie and I are good friends."

Gray winked and then squinted doubtfully as he took up the oars. "You've seen Foster a couple of afternoons recently, I think."

"He's helping me with an exhibition. My God, what are you, the CIA?"

"I'm not spying. Believe it or not, this is just word of mouth. Besides, in politics, private life is an indefinable term. Ask the Kennedy family." He looked away, innocently, then turned back to Margy. "If you love Everet, why did you start playing around with this painter? Why are you posing for him now?"

"I'm not posing for him!"

Gray winced. "All right. But what about the past?"

"I told you, we had an agreement that allowed for such things."

"Come on, Margy. Let's be realistic."

Margy shrugged and turned away.

"Level with me. Has affection ever been a motivation--with Foster, or the others?"

She shook her head, in spite of herself.

"Ambition--was it ambition, then?"

"What do you mean?"

"Come on, you want to be a successful artist. Word has it that you wanted Foster to help you with your career. When it became apparent that he wouldn't--or couldn't--you up and left."

"Buford's the word!" she shouted, standing and almost turning over the boat. Calling out, Gray caught the gunwales, then choked himself into a coughing fit as he tried to pull Margy down into the seat. He looked back at the shore once or twice, and when she threatened to swim back to the sandbar, he patted her knees and grudgingly apologized.

"Sit down. *Sit down*," he said. "I'm sorry. I really don't want to be your enemy. I want the best for everyone."

"I loved him for a time, I think. But then it fell apart. He's a sick man. Buford is too." She stood up, then fell into her seat, almost tipping the boat again. Grimly, Fred started the engine.

"What about Everet?" he asked.

"I'm trying. I'm really trying, Fred."

He took them to the rowboat, glowering at Margy all the way. He dropped anchor, and as they transferred to the smaller boat he said, "I know something about your past-- the tough life you led with your parents when you were young--"

"Jesus. You are a rag picker," she said. "Be careful. I'm self-conscious about all that."

He nodded, lifting the right oar into the air and pulling with the left in order to swing the bow around toward the shore. As they started in, Margy saw Everet and Kennedy waving and waiting on the beach. "I know. I know that, too. I'm not that insensitive, you know. I can understand your bitterness, but all I can say is that in my opinion it would do you good to get closer to normalcy, rather than farther from it. This guy, Foster, is no good. Buford, I'm not sure about, but you don't seem to like him anyway. And Dan's nephew seems like a decent enough, though troubled kid. Maybe you ought to let him stay that way."

129

"What are you trying to tell me, Fred?"

"Why don't you try to patch up the normal things in your life?"

She looked away. "I'm trying to. I already said that I'm trying to."

"Contact your parents again--think of your husband. Take care of your fine son."

"What do you think I'm doing?"

"Do more of it. Work for Everet rather than yourself. Get involved in his campaign."

"You mean give up my unimportant career for his?"

"It's not unimportant. Just make it less important for a while."

"It already is. Since the beginning, our marriage has always favored his interests! What will he be giving up?"

That seemed to quiet Gray. He rowed closer to the beach, turned to steer around a buoy, but did not make an answer. Once they had got around the buoy, Margy repeated, "What will he be giving up?"

"Nothing, for now," Gray said.

"That's terrible."

"Let him make up for it later. Or count his acceptance of your affair with Foster as a debt you have to repay."

"For the rest of my life?"

Gray shook his head. "Just this part of it. Remember, in a political campaign you can't control everything. There are people who can make or break a candidate; he has to deal with them. Often that takes personal sacrifice, and right now Everet may have to give up more for others than he does for you."

"You make me sound like an inconvenience."

He looked at Margy, nodding. "I wish we didn't have to think of you at all. A doubtful wife is the next worse thing to a public scandal. Luckily, people are much more accepting nowadays of marriages that aren't exactly four-square. But--" At this point Gray took his hand off an oar and pointed directly at her face—"I don't want to test the people's morality too much. So for everybody's good, I'd be happier if you could force yourself to toe the line."

"That sickens me."

"Let it. But also, let it have some meaning."

"Bullshit!"

Gray shrugged. "Everet may be the best thing we have to offer Stoddard, Margy."

"You really believe that?"

"Of course. If I didn't, do you think I'd be working so hard?"

He looked up at the sky. It was clear, not a cloud or a bolt of lightning in sight all across the horizon. He winked, coasting in on a wave as he raised both oars. Although Margy liked to get in the last word during conversations like this one, they had come near the beach, and since she saw Everet and Kennedy wading toward them, she held her tongue. Just before they got within hearing, Fred said, in a low voice: "Go up to that camp in Massachusetts. If you think it will do you and him good, I think you should go. But don't think it's going to change things very much. He's a political animal. You're not. Those things don't mix in election years."

"Mama!"

Kennedy dashed toward the boat, and the two of them smiled as he lunged into it, almost turning it over.

9.

NIGHT GAMES

Grant Matthews was picture-perfect, Margy thought: hard, stinging blue eyes, lines that seemed to be chiseled into his brow and engraved along his cheeks, a long, lean body just made for blue serge suits, and a shock of white hair that framed his face as if it had been worked on for months. He had a reputation for precision, for cracking the whip, for ruthless, unsentimental decisions when it came to party workers, and his appearance belied none of that reputation.

"So, you paint," he said to her that evening, a hint of a smile coming to his lips as he twirled a scotch and water in his right hand. "My wife, Estelle, has some interest in that. She's over there somewhere, near the punchbowl, talking to one of the reporters."

Margy turned and looked toward the refreshments table on the patio. A large group of people stood there: Buford, Gray, Everet--in plaid dinner jacket and snappy white cotton slacks, almost acting the host to the others--Tommy Gray, Estelle Matthews (who, Margy saw, was talking to John Buford's partner), largely the same group of people she had seen at the dinner in Stoddard, plus others--local Democrats, mainly--who had not been there. A small steel-drum band had set up near the house, and the music they made came through the air frenetically. The weather was lovely, a perfect mid-spring evening with a touch of August heat in the salty breeze. Emmy Gray passed. Lifting a tray from a servant's hands, she offered *hors d'oeuvres* to people and paused a few moments to speak to Matthews. She reminded Margy of an amethyst that night: in flowing purple gown, white shoes, and white hair piled high with a silver tiara gleaming on top, she seemed to be the proper queenly partner for the party's state chairman.

"Well, how are you, Grant?" she said, a touch flirtatiously. "Are you recruiting for the next fund-raising dinner?"

"Do I have other functions?"

He laughed, brushing back a large dollop of hair that had fallen over his eyes, and chose a modest celery-stalk filled with cottage cheese. Matthews was the most conservatively dressed of the men--formal solid blue tie over a white-on-white shirt with a moderately spread collar, all that wrapped in the three-piece suit, as if he alone had worked that day and had by chance strayed into this party from his office.

He and his wife had in fact arrived early, as Everet, the Grays, and Margy sat on the patio dawdling over cocktails in the diminishing twilight. An outside door chime had sounded, Gray had leaped from his chair to go around to the front of the house, and before he returned, William, the husband in the Grays' servant couple, had escorted Matthews onto the patio through the back door. Emmy and Everet rose immediately, and by the time Gray returned five people were seated to watch Tommy and Kennedy play Frisbee on the beach. Red-faced and pleased, Fred had quickly ordered drinks, but before the first round was finished, Buford arrived with his partner, a fellow reporter named Bradley. Matthews and John Buford were already acquainted; Bradley had to be introduced. After a preliminary quarter hour of drinks and conversation, Gray led the men into the house for a conference, while the women stayed behind for the usual hour of small talk until the rest of the guests arrived.

"Well, are you enjoying Emmy's house?" Estelle Matthews asked Margy. She flashed a sly, appreciative smile toward Emmy Gray. "Her hospitality is rather legendary in the state."

"Oh, we've done fine. There was a lovely meal this afternoon, two baseball games and a volley-ball game with the neighbors, and hours just lying in the sun. Emmy's done very well."

Emmy nodded, pleased--and surprised, probably--by the compliment. "Margy has been a good guest, too," she said.

"Oh, no, Emmy..."

"But you have. This afternoon she gave me some fine tips about drawing." Emmy laid her hand on Estelle Matthews's arm. "I don't know how many times I've looked out at that water, tried to sketch it, and just ended up putting down my pad in frustration. Margy has a real gift for teaching."

"We certainly have a need for good teachers in this state--have you had any formal training, Margy?"

She glanced at Estelle, blushing, unready for such a pragmatic question. It sounded innocent enough, but Margy had the feeling of a deal--that if she made the proper response, she might have a job offer somewhere. Even Estelle must have felt the awkwardness, because she looked at Margy for a moment then seemed to withdraw the unintended lead. "But I suppose you would find that boring on a permanent basis," she said. "Real artists seldom have the interest or aptitude to teach--they're two different character types."

Emmy held the tray of *hors d'oeuvres* in front of Margy, keeping her other hand on Estelle Matthews's arm. "In what way?" she asked.

"One is unselfish and giving, the other is egotistical and self-serving. Artists seldom make good public servants."

"Why should they?" Margy asked, suddenly challenged.

"Indeed, why should anybody? Because public service is very important."

Margy shook her head. "An artist's work justifies itself. Sometimes the public benefits; if it does, that's just icing on the cake."

"Exactly," Estelle said.

She smiled, without a hint of rancor in her look. But something dark flickered behind her eyes, and Margy had the distinct impression that an item had been registered, filed away for future use. Emmy asked Estelle about some mutual

134

friends, and the conversation shifted to other topics. Margy remained with them for a while, but when another state-level official, this a small, wiry man with balding head and trim salt-and-pepper beard, stopped to discuss some developments in Hartford, she excused herself and left to talk with Kennedy by the punchbowl.

He looked fine tonight, she thought--bright, handsome, sociable, an important asset to his father. Standing with Tommy Gray, one hand in his jacket pocket as he sipped a Coca-Cola, he looked to be a perfect junior partner--if only in miniature. "How are you doing, honey?" she asked as she went up to him. "You having a good time?"

"All right." He grimaced clownishly, looking sideways at Tommy when he answered. Tommy held up a camera and without warning, snapped Kennedy and Margy as they turned toward him.

"Are you the official photographer this evening?"

"No." Tommy shrugged, "I just like to take pictures."

He raised the camera again. Getting ready for the flash, Margy squinted, but she realized he had someone else in mind. By the time the light went off, Kennedy and she had turned to the punchbowl and waited behind others for Margy's refill. The table was long, running the length of the house, with several large punchbowls and a dozen or so bottles of various liquors and mixers on it. As they waited, they heard Everet talking to a few men at the opposite end of the table. He seemed confident, Margy noticed, better than he had been at the dinner. His voice was loud and sure, and at the moment she could see no reason why he should not be that way. She herself had confidence in him for a change, the talk with Gray having settled her somewhat, since even he had admitted that a trip to Wiltshire would not do any harm. When Everet called her over to make an introduction, she brought Kennedy too, and for the first time in weeks--perhaps in months--she did not feel an automatic, defensive smirk come to her face upon meeting his new companions.

"Here they are," he said, "my wonderful, lovely family." He draped his arm about Margy's shoulders and

135

squeezed her. He ruffled Kennedy's hair and smiled as he introduced them to two state assemblymen. Margy forgot their names immediately and spent several awkward moments because of it. "So this is the woman who keeps you on your toes," one said. "I can see why." She bristled. Shaking hands, Margy felt their eyes look her up and down, and it did not help that they had harmless, good-humored faces. As with Buford and his partner, they seemed to be a matched pair, and the feeling they gave off to her was one of danger, despite a pleasant front.

They exchanged a few more remarks, but soon Everet and the two assemblymen withdrew while Kennedy and Margy went off to sit by themselves. Kennedy wanted to replenish his Coke, so she sat in a wicker chair at the rear of the patio and waited while he went to the refreshments table. He returned, smiling. When she asked why, he said it was because one of the two assemblymen they had just met had asked him about his politics.

"Politics?"

"Yes. He wanted to know if I was a Democrat."

"God... What did you say?"

Kennedy laughed, shrugging his shoulders. "I told him I was too young to think about that."

"Good for you," Margy said.

He smiled at her and offered a sip of his Coke. "I like people," he said, "so I guess I would like politics. But I don't know anything about the laws. I leave that stuff to Daddy."

She pulled a chair beside her and let him sit in it. The party moved around in front of them. Like a swirl of wind-driven leaves, it gathered in bunches and piles at various parts of the patio and beach. Everet was always the center of some group, and wherever he moved, good feelings seemed to follow. Gray beamed, making sure, Margy saw, to touch the hand or arm--as Emmy did--of every person he spoke to. Then he would introduce that person to Everet, and they both passed long periods of time listening to what she imagined were descriptions of problems in various Connecticut counties. Much as she disliked formalities, she also admired professionalism, and she had to admit that the

Grays and Everet were all very professional that night. Whenever Everet called Kennedy and her over for an introduction, she was impressed by the smoothness with which he handled it. There was a smile of warmth and possession for her, a doting, loving father's look for Kennedy, and at the same time a genuine sense of interest for the person they were meeting.

As they had dressed earlier (along with the usual pre-party nerves, she remembered), Everet had said to her, "This is an aggressive world. You have to be as assertive as you can. Don't let anyone bowl you over." A perfect formula for his behavior that night. Margy tried to imitate him at first, but she could not really pull it off. She worked through greetings and handshakes boldly enough, but after a few minutes of conversation, her conscience bothered her. She wondered what she was doing, why she, an ambitious artist, stood there talking when she had a show to complete, and she found herself walking away, embarrassed. It made her edgy and threatened her sense of self-control, especially since she had often become combative in similar situations when she was younger. Luckily, Kennedy performed much better. He talked easily, shook hands readily, showed that quiet, amiable grin that so obviously reflected Everet's, and answered all questions--except those about politics, apparently--with frankness and ease. In fact, by the end of the evening, he had clearly outdistanced Margy in social terms.

"He's such a doll," Estelle Matthews said as Margy held his hand and began to walk him to the house so he could prepare for bed with Tommy Gray. "And such poise! He handles all this attention beautifully!"

Margy nodded, grateful but ashamed because it brought to mind her own failures with publicity. To make matters worse, after Everet kissed him and made a great show of having him wave good-night to all the guests, Kennedy pulled his hand from Margy's and went off alone with Tommy Gray. She stood by herself on the patio for a few minutes, then entered the house and went up to the second floor. She heard laughter as she opened the door,

137

then a hushed silence as she stepped inside. Her own sense of estrangement seemed to be breaking in on them, and at that moment, she felt how out of place she was. When Kennedy looked at her, she saw something in his eye that made her go weak. She quelled a sob, then took his hand and held it on the powder-blue coverlet. With his finger tracing the coverlet's braided border of tridents, ropes, and harpoon hooks, he looked at her with a sadness she found surprising. Gasping, she embraced him, kissed him several times, and tried to say, without too much ostentation, that she loved him very much. He looked at Tommy and gently pulled away.

"Sleep well," she said, drawing the coverlet above his shoulders. "Tomorrow we'll swim and play some volleyball."

"We've been lucky with the weather, haven't we, Mama?"

"Very lucky," she whispered. She said good-night to Tommy, pulling up his coverlet too, then quietly slipped out of the room. She felt foolish after that, and on the patio where the party was still going strong, she tried to forget her overprotectiveness with a show of talkative, high spirits.

Some of the guests had begun to leave, but a few of those who stayed were now in a gayer, more festive mood, which cheered her. Some of the men had taken off their dinner jackets along with their shoes, rolled up their trousers, and waded into the surf. Women danced on the sand as the band played Jamaican tunes. She joined them, but through the music and dance she also watched Fred and Emmy gather together Everet, Matthews, Buford, Buford's partner Bradley, and some others on the patio. After a few words with Emmy, Gray led them into the house where they spent half an hour or so while Margy danced and, finally, talked to Emmy and two other women. She tried to do better than she had earlier, but by one o'clock, exhausted, she was relieved to see Fred and Everet emerge from the house and begin to sing, "The party's over," in unison as they waltzed around the band and drank from flute-style champagne glasses.

Grant Matthews followed them in a few minutes although he did not dance or sing. He simply called Estelle, joined Fred and Everet in a champagne nightcap, and then went off with his wife. Along with the servants, John Buford stayed on to help the Grays clean up. After they had piled everything into three neatly tied and wrapped plastic garbage bags, William and his wife entered the house, and the Hamiltons, the Grays, and Buford stood near the doorway. With Fred and Emmy looking haggard but pleased, Everet embraced Margy and proposed a walk by the water before bed. "This," he said, waving at everything from the sea and sand to the patio and piles of plastic bags, "calls for some domestic tranquility. We need to be alone for a while."

They wished the Grays and Buford good-night, took off their shoes and walked down to the water. When Margy shivered, Everet slipped his jacket onto her shoulders and, with a giggly laugh, dashed into the surf. Then he ran back to the car for a searchlight, and when he returned, they climbed onto the jetty, following the flashlight beam out to the end for a closer look at the Sound. The rocks were slippery and difficult to walk on; the tide had been coming in for more than an hour, and the water smashed against the rocks, sending up a spray that turned into a series of mini-rainbows through their light. At the farthest end, they sat on Everet's plaid jacket and embraced as they looked up at the sky. Everet kissed her, sighing deeply as Margy nuzzled his chest. A foghorn bellowed in the distance; the lighthouse from the opposite point made a dot then a beam over and over as it shined across the water. Everet lay back, cradling his head in his hands, and chuckled in contentment.

"How did it go? Or shouldn't I bother asking?" Margy said.

"Outstanding."

She squeezed his hand. "They said nice things, huh?"

"Better than I had hoped: 'Good man, sound tactician, interested in the party and the people.' I almost turned around to see who they were talking about."

"That's terrific. You deserve it."

139

He nodded. "And it wasn't just Fred. Grant Matthews patted me on the back as if I were an established state figure. Buford and the others looked impressed. Ten years, Margy. I've worked ten years in this town, and I finally felt the recognition I've been after. Fred was walking a foot above the floor."

He caressed her hand, trumpeting a foghorn yell across the water.

"They're going to endorse you then."

"No doubt about it." He grinned.

"Did they give you a commitment?"

"Matthews said he is with me all the way." He shook his head and held her tightly. Margy did not know if that meant yes or no. She assumed it meant yes.

"What did they decide about me?" she asked. "That I won't hinder you?"

He paused, laughed, and held her more tightly.

"Well, what did they say?"

He leaned back and looked at her. "What are you talking about, Margy?"

"Come on. I'm not so naive. Fred and I talked earlier. Did you agree to muzzle me?"

He dropped back on his elbow and looked at the lighthouse. "Margy, your name wasn't even mentioned. Don't be so self-centered."

In the dim light of the moon she found it hard to read his face, but as she looked she could not doubt the sincerity in his voice. Finally, she asked, "Are you sure?"

"Margy, I'm sure. Look, you're not that important."

She nodded, relieved, but feeling further diminished. She was also somewhat doubtful. "I'm glad--and relieved," she said. "For you and for me. I want to be kept out of this as much as possible. I don't think I'm stable enough to help."

He frowned, but his eyes lit up with pleasure as he looked away from her and stared up at the sky. The stars were bright, a handful of white flakes against a dark, dark blue. After a moment, he said, "They're not only going to endorse me, Margy, but they're also putting money into my campaign. One of the state people said it would be a test election. And he mentioned Congress in a few years--that is, if I do a creditable job here. Washington, D.C.! Margy, I must have bubbled over into Fred's champagne."

She felt sick, despite herself, dizzy with a sudden empty feeling in her stomach. She tried to suppress it and held his hand, even smiling.

"I'm going to announce the week after next," he continued, twining his fingers in hers. "Gray will support me publicly a few days later, and then Matthews and the county's Democratic committee members are going to back us right after that. The goddamn primary will be a mere formality."

He looked at Margy and squeezed her hand. Her smile weakened. "You better be ready for one busy nigger around the house, baby. And a happy one, too. When we started, I just wanted to make a social point. Now I want to swallow the whole damn pie."

She nodded, trying for enthusiasm, but this time the effort froze the look on her face. His own expression came down a degree in candle-power when he saw her shake her head.

"Hey, what's the matter?"

"Nothing." She slumped back and, on her elbow, turned away from him.

"Margy, stop playing games. What's bothering you?"

She pounded her fist on his knee. "This is such a goddamn little woman's thing, Mr. President. I'm almost sure I know the answer, but what day are you going to announce your vaunted candidacy?"

Without a blink, he said, "The 8th, of course, two weeks from today. So we can get it into the Sunday papers."

"Mmm, I see. And what weekend were we going to Wiltshire, Massachusetts?"

"To the Institute?"

"Yes, the Institute, Mr. Sound Tactician."

He sat up, evidently just understanding. He took her other hand and turned her to face him, holding her tightly while she tried to pull away.

"Margy--"

141

"I knew it would happen, but I didn't want to believe it--couldn't believe you would do this to us, Everet. But you did, and without even realizing it."

"Realizing? You think it was a mistake? Listen, Margy, the Institute can wait. This announcement can make or break me."

"And make or break your family life too, you fool!"

"Oh, Margy, this is my goddamn dream. Hey! Come back here; come back here, I said!"

"You knew it! You let them set the date even though you knew it was important to me. You're sicker than I've ever been."

He said something, but it was lost in the wind as Margy left, hurling herself over the rocks toward the beach. Her feet slipped once or twice. She felt a dangerous surge of water knock her on all fours as she stumbled about half-way along, and--perhaps for the pure drama of it--felt an urge to let herself fall from the jetty.

She reached the sand and started running toward the other point. About twenty-five yards from it, Everet caught up with her and gathered her into his arms. The water from her dress soaked through his shirt. "I'm sorry, Margy. Really. I was wrong, but you've got to understand."

"This is your dream! *Your* dream! What about mine? What about us?"

In frustration, she slammed her fists into her thighs and then, trying to break free, into his chest. But she could not loosen his hold. His eyes were wide, frightened, and for some reason that made her more angry.

"I'm sorry, Margy. Please. There was nothing else I could do. I was powerless..."

"Powerless?" She punched his shoulder. "Everet, those Institute people are rigid too. They're not going to let us reschedule this time. They are going to say that we aren't ready. And they're going to be right!"

"I couldn't go against Grant Matthews and the others. Neither could Fred. This is bigger than we are."

"No, it isn't! You're letting it be that way, because--*because* ..." His eyes turned toward the house, and he put

142

his finger to his lips. Margy felt the same sense of rage she had felt as a child whenever her father shut her up because of her mother.

"Change it, Everet!" she shrieked. "*I don't care about the fucking Grays*! Let them hear me!"

She finally found strength to pull from his arms. She ran a few steps, stopped, then whirled in the sand and pointed at him: "You better change that date, you mother-fucker, or I'm going to do something drastic."

"Margy... "

"Don't touch me! I'm not going to be pushed around by a bunch of shit-eating crooks--and that includes you!"

He reached her, took her shoulders and shook her. When he put his hand over her mouth, she hit him in the neck with her fist. She hurled herself at him, screaming. He stepped away, and, as she picked up a handful of sand to throw in his face, he turned his back.

"I won't accept this. I'm telling you, Everet, I will not accept this callousness." She threw the sand, covering his back with it. He turned again, came forward to embrace her, but she stamped her foot and screamed so loudly that he immediately pulled his arms away. He tried again, but stopped again, and whether he sensed her anger spilling into hysteria; whether it was the lights on at the Grays' house; or whether it was genuine regret for what had happened (she would never be sure), he withdrew. When she turned to look a couple of times, she saw his white cotton trousers flickering in the dark as he walked back to the house. Like the lighthouse beam, black then white, black then white, black then white, he was an eerie negative image becoming smaller and smaller in the dark.

143

10.

SKINNY-DIPPING

"I don't expect you to understand, Goldie, but it was just like that. He knew I was upset. I asked him for one last time to change the date, but one look at Buford, a comment from Gray, and he came back to saying he couldn't do it. If I had something sharper, I would have killed him... "

"Don't talk like that. You're not that violent."

"I'm afraid I am."

"No, you aren't. Get on with the story."

The sun, a bright red apple that morning, rose from the water. Fishermen stood on the jetty, casting into the surf, and two moved through the waves with a net between them, pulling it across the water onto the beach, where they dumped it free of shiners. Goldie and Margy sat in her car on a street overlooking the beach. Goldie had driven from East Stoddard after spending another night at the Hamilton house--because of an argument with his Uncle Dan. He had returned late from a party, and they had come to blows, forcing Goldie to leave.

"'Politics,' he said. 'You don't tell these guys you have another appointment when they're wheeling and dealing dates.'

"I screamed. I threw an ashtray at him, and the Grays came charging into the room after they heard it shatter against the wall. And guess who followed? Buford; the nerve! 'Yes, you can change the date!' I shouted. 'This has to do with our lives. Our family.' With the Grays, Buford, and Everet coming toward me all at once, I picked up a letter opener, lunged at Everet, but held back just as he ducked and I was about to slash his neck. 'See? See what you've made me become?' I dropped to my knees, with images of my mother before me. 'I don't want to be this way, Everet. Don't force me.'—Oh, God, I still can't believe it."

"Steady. Come on, you can handle it."

"I can't. Oh, Goldie, I can't."

144

She held her breath and closed her eyes. The whole evening came back and she started to shake.

"Margy, tell me what happened after--"

"Then... Then... Oh, God, then I heard whimpering, and when I turned around, I saw Kennedy looking at me from the hall. He was on his knees too. His mouth was open. And, and..."

"Easy..."

"And he had his hands up to the sides of his head as though he were in some horrible pain. I threw down the opener, ran to him, and cradled him in my arms. Goldie, I can't go on. This is too much."

"It's better for you to talk it out."

"I cried. 'Oh, honey. I'm sorry. Mommy's sorry. I'm really not like this. I'm really not this mean.'

"He pushed me away, screaming, saying I always spoiled things. He ran into his room across the hall, where Tommy Gray sat up in bed staring blankly at us. I tried to follow, but Kennedy slammed the door in my face, and I stumbled back to our room, stopped and saw Buford looking at me."

"Buford?"

"Yes. He had such a smug, all-knowing smile on his face that it riveted me. 'What are you staring at?' I said. 'What kind of smutty story do you want?' He licked his lips and broke into a grin. It was awful; I was furious."

"Easy now... "

"As he started to speak, I picked up the opener and struck at his face. He dodged, but Everet and the Grays came at me, and with my second swing I hit Everet. I pulled back, surprised. But I saw blood spurt out of his neck onto my arms and hands. It was like a fountain. He gagged, turned pale, and seemed to crumble to the floor. I looked at the Grays and Buford. No one was moving. There was just this general feeling of surprise. Then I ran down the steps onto the beach and out to the lighthouse. I think Buford followed me for a while, but I got lost. I don't know what the Grays did--probably called in some political advisors. Anyhow, then I telephoned you."

145

"Didn't you go back to see what happened?"

"I couldn't. But I watched from down the street for a while. There was nothing. No police. No sirens. Not even a car that might have been a doctor's."

"Amazing."

"You know those bastards will worry about publicity. Buford and his partner have probably written a covering story already."

Goldie sighed. He puffed a cigarette and looked out toward the water.

"Oh, God, I can't stand this. It's my own family all over again. I've actually become like my mother. Kennedy will always see me running toward his father with a knife in my hand!--He'll always think of me as murderous!"

Margy bit her finger, and the tears poured down her cheeks. It was a nightmare. She wondered if her mother had seen herself despicable through her daughter's eyes. Goldie patted her shoulder and embraced her. "There are other important things to worry about, Margy. I'm pretty sure Everet's all right, though. No matter what the publicity, if he was badly hurt, they would have had to call a doctor right away."

"Those people are crazy, Goldie."

"Look, I'm sure he's all right. Or at least not badly hurt. You have to think about yourself."

"Think about myself!" She gasped, and for some reason, that hit her. With pain in her stomach, she doubled over. Tears rolled from her eyes and soaked a pair of dark gray patches on her dress. She felt her arms tremble. Then her whole body shook with sobs. "This is the end of it," she cried. "I don't see how I can stay with Everet now. I don't know if I can go home anymore."

"Come on. Be reasonable."

"Goldie, don't you understand? I could have killed him. I *would* have killed him--or Buford--if I had a better aim. How can anything be normal again?"

Goldie muttered and turned to the window. He had a flat, tired look in his eyes, and his face was slightly bruised where his uncle had punched him the night before. In

146

addition to lateness, they had argued about his use of drugs, a former pastime, Goldie assured him, and his uncle had forced him to leave, telling him not to come back. He was no better off than Margy.

"I don't know about your marriage," he said, "but nothing can stop you from going back if you really love him."

"Love him? You sound like Fred Gray, Goldie. I don't even know what the word means. Especially if I can strike at him like that."

They were silent for a few minutes. The men in the surf had passed a quarter of a mile down toward the Grays. Suddenly, she turned toward the back seat and reached for a pile of rolled up canvases and drawing pads which she had left there after class on Friday. Sobbing, she started to heave them out the window. Wind swept across the sand, taking some loose water-colors with it. Like multi-colored kites, they floated up to the height of a small building, then were picked up by a gust and driven out to sea. Calling out, Goldie leaped from the car and gathered what he could. Canvases were easiest since they were heavy, but some of the pads blew down toward the water and, without any lift to them, plunged into the surf like de-feathered gulls. Goldie picked up what he could, bringing it back, dripping, to the car while Margy sat inside and cried.

"You're crazy--absolutely crazy. There's months, maybe years, of work right here."

As he opened the trunk and dropped canvases and pads into it, she stepped out of the car and stood next to him--tears still pouring down her face, arms and hands trembling, knees nearly buckling. She took a canvas from the trunk, stepped on it, and pulled with her hands until it ripped in two. Goldie shoved her away and slammed the trunk lid closed.

"Get out of here!" he yelled.

"You think I'm interested in painting right now? My son has seen me as a murderer."

She cried harder, louder. Goldie held her shoulders and shook her violently. Then she collapsed into his arms and fought to control herself. She would always remember

147

the next few moments vividly. She had a hallucination, knew it as a hallucination, but it affected her so strongly that she felt as if the environment sought revenge: a cloud washed over the sun, turning the sky dark gray. But then the cloud split and a meteor-like streak of white and green burst across it; the water became ashes, a sudden, overwhelming tidal wave of heat and dust. Rocks seemed to fall from the jetty; and as the sun emerged again, the cranes and derricks across from them on Long Island took on the appearance of flaming wicks. For a few short seconds, the Sound looked like a boiling, poisoned sea.

"Let's get out of here," she said, taking Goldie's arm. "This whole situation is driving me batty."

They left the car, walking down the beach road about a quarter of a mile until they came to a small cove, surrounded by a couple of sand dunes. There they walked onto the beach again.

"Goldie, do you think I just want to be a good wife and mother? In the end, is that what this is all about?"

He waved. She took off her shoes and, tears still streaming down her face, began to jog along the edge of the water, away from Stoddard and the Grays. Later she realized that she was close to a foolish attempt at suicide, and that Goldie, sensitive as he was, must have realized it, too. She felt terrible because he was also very depressed and showed it. Reluctant at first, he followed as she ran along the sand. When she giggled, taking his hand and pulling him into the surf, he began to laugh himself, throwing away his cigarette and taking them deeper into the water. She held back then, but he went out even farther until a small wave hit and she felt the sudden shock of it above her waist. It floated her dress up around her breasts, and she shrieked, laughing.

"No! Come back, Goldie." She took his hand and pulled him toward the beach.

"I wish I had my bathing suit," he said, as they reached the sand. "We haven't been in the water together this year."

She wrung her hem and smoothed it around her knees. She smiled at him, laughing. His eyes flickered for a moment, only to turn away.

"We went skinny-dipping around this time last year, remember?" he said. "You want to try it again today?"

"Are you insane? If we got caught--" He nodded, grinning as she motioned to the fishermen down the beach and the houses around them.

"It's early. Come on, nudes are in, as Foss likes to say. Besides, it will make us both feel better." He took off his socks and shoes and began to unbutton his trousers.

"Goldie, you're an idiot! See those houses down there? They'd have the cops on the beach before we got to the water."

"Not with my idea. Come with me."

They walked back to the car and, rummaging among the dripping canvases and pads in the trunk, he pulled out two ponchos. Everet insisted that she keep them there in case of rain.

"If you want to come in, put that on," he said. "We can take off our clothes beneath them and then go into the water. I've done it on the beach lots of times. No one will see a thing."

She looked toward the jetty fishermen and the houses behind them. She turned away.

"Oh, come on, Margy. It'll be nice. If we see Everet or Gray, we can tell them you rescued me. Or we're out diving for votes."

"This is no joke," she said.

But Goldie laughed anyhow, slipping the poncho over her head as they went back to the cove, where he got into his. Although she complained that the ponchos would drag them down, when she saw Goldie drop his shirt and trousers at the edge of the water, she pulled off her dress and slipped out of her underpants. They entered the Sound together.

"Come on," he said. As a wave washed over their waists, she sucked in air. With the ponchos clearly floating in front and behind, she began to feel more confident. They left their feet together, ducked under and out of the openings,

149

then floated on their backs, kicking water toward the beach. It felt wonderful. The chill sent a charge of energy through Margy's body, and it seemed to quicken her nerves.

"EEEEaahhh! Bare-assed in the Sound!" she shouted. "Did your uncle ever think of doing this, Goldie?"

He laughed, spitting water and swimming beside her now. Looking toward the jetty as he stumbled past some shallows near a sandbar, he began a slow, graceful butterfly toward the open water. She held the end of her poncho--light plastic, it was easy to support--and backstroked out a little farther. The water calmed her. She went under, head-first. Goldie watched her legs up to her buttocks, then smiled as her head surfaced before she swam underwater back toward him. She treaded water and checked for people walking on the dunes.

"Keep it flat; flat out. The poncho will almost float itself," he said. "As long as no high waves come in."

"I know; I'm doing it. It's working."

She dove under again, swam away, then surfaced where he was treading water. Goldie grabbed her arm and kissed her hand. She turned over without saying anything and towed the two ponchos to a buoy, where she hung them as if on a coatrack. Returning, she splashed him, laughed when he swam around to tickle her feet, then moved out to deeper water. They swam about one hundred yards together, until they saw the lighthouse, the fishermen--all considerably smaller now--and way off to the south the golden hump of the Grays' sandstone house plus the wall that separated their patio from the public beach. It still looked very quiet.

"I want to swim east, Goldie. Past Long Island, out into the Atlantic Ocean. To Europe!"

He swam closer, then, pausing a moment, looked into her eyes and embraced her. "I love you. I love you when you're like this. I feel like we could make it if we swam together."

He kissed her--still on the cheek--but when she turned her mouth to his, their lips met and they clung in a long embrace, until they found themselves completely under water. Margy pulled away, panicking, splashing him with a

150

slap of her feet and hands, and when she re-surfaced, she saw him heading back toward the shore.

"Hey! Where are you going?"

"In," is all he answered.

"You weren't insulted, were you? Goldie, I got scared."

"I'm just cold," he mumbled.

"Wait a minute. Please, don't run away."

"I'm not running. I'm just going in."

At the buoy, he supported a poncho with his toe, lifted it off the hook, then swam in front of it toward the beach. A large patch of seaweed preceded him. Margy swam to the buoy, unhooked her poncho, and swam in, trailing it behind her. She was more tired than she realized, and the poncho felt heavier than before. But she worked hard to catch up to him and reached the shallows of the sandbar just a few seconds after he did. The water was near their waists at that point. Bashful about her breasts, Margy ducked under the poncho and slid it over her head before standing up. Now it felt heavy. Looking hard at her, Goldie dived under again, dug his hands into the water, and shot straight out--away from the beach. Swimming quickly, he looked to be aiming toward the sun--it was hovering just above the horizon by this time--and free of the poncho and his clothes, he looked as if he might at least reach Long Island. He waved at her, swam out a little farther until he seemed to be a yellow ball bobbing on the water, then began a slow, careful butterfly back to the shore. He rode a swell or two, floated on his back, his head becoming a whale's hump throwing up a foot-long spout of spray. After five minutes or so, he flipped over and dug in deeply again, not stopping until he had come into the shallow water near the sandbar. He was breathless.

"Come on, Goldie," Margy said, flattening out the poncho as he floated in. "People are starting to get up--they'll be on the beach soon."

"What's the hurry?" he asked.

She shrugged, pointing to some children near a house beyond the cove. He disregarded the poncho, slowly slipping past the opening before standing out of the water. His body was smooth, attractive, very much a piece of the morning light. His blond pubic hair glistened around his pink genitals. Margy caressed his arm, following him onto the beach-- wearing her poncho, feeling foolish carrying his--and at the car, dried herself as they both dressed quickly.

"Let's get out of here," she said.

"What for? No one's around." He seemed to be mocking her.

"Goldie, I know what you want. We've talked about this before. I don't want to be the older woman in your life."

He laughed. "'Then don't start anything, if you can't complete it," he said.

She nodded, reluctantly, not sure who had started what. He slid behind the wheel of the car. After she entered the passenger's side, they drove along the beach road, cutting across town toward the highway. It was Sunday morning, without much traffic at that hour, and just before slipping onto Route 95, she asked him to pullover. He turned into a parking lot of a diner. "Let's talk about this," she said, as they watched the traffic pass along the street. "It always bothers me."

"What's there to talk about? It's already settled."

She looked down at her feet, taking a cigarette that he offered her, then using a book of matches on the dashboard to light both his and hers. "I know we have something special," she said. "But I thought you agreed that it was too risky to try."

"Try? We've never even given it a thought."

"That's not true, Goldie. I'm twice your age. I have a son. I have a husband and a married life I'm trying to keep together. I had a bad experience with Foss. I've given it a lot of thought, and I can't handle any more. You have to understand that."

"Then don't tease me. Don't cock-tease me," he said. "I can't stand it when you get that way."

"I know. I know... Goldie, I think sometime in the future, when all this is settled—"

"Let's not talk about it, okay?" He started the car. "I'm unsettled. You're unsettled. Let's get back to the house

152

and think about what we're going to do today--not next year--or even next week."

He drove onto the highway, heading toward New York, and they arrived in East Stoddard in minutes. The streets were completely empty. But instead of turning directly into Camels Back Drive, they took the precaution of driving to the next block, turning around and coming slowly back. No police were on their street. To their relief, they saw absolutely no sign of life. Goldie turned the wheel over to Margy and started to walk home through the backyards. "I'll call in about half an hour," he said, "if the coast is clear."

She waited for fifteen minutes, to make sure that Dan, if he was home, would not see them together, then drove down the street and parked in their empty driveway, feeling like a fugitive sneaking into the house. The air inside was stale, probably from the cigarettes Goldie had smoked the night before. When she opened the windows, she saw his head bobbing above the hedges outside and called to him.

"What's up?"

"Door's locked. I still don't have a key. I tried every window, and they're locked too."

"Your uncle isn't home?"

He shook his head. She opened the kitchen window, let him in the back door, and gave him Everet's robe to wear while she dried their damp clothes in the downstairs dryer. She put on slacks and a blouse, and then began to make coffee in the kitchen. They both felt chilled now, as well as uneasy. They hardly talked, and to give them some warmth, she opened the oven door and turned on the gas. Goldie sat up close. After starting the coffee-maker, she joined him; but just as she sat, the phone rang and continued for at least a minute. They looked at each other; the sound brought them together almost instantly, but they did not answer. Stopping, it immediately began again, this time ringing at least two dozen times. At the end, Margy found herself shivering.

"Let's get out of here. That was Everet--or the Grays. I'm sure of it."

"It might have been my uncle," Goldie said.

Margy reached for the phone. It stopped ringing, and even in the silence she could not bring herself to touch it.

"Goldie, it was Everet--or about him. No one else would let the phone ring that long. Even your Uncle Dan isn't that stubborn."

She felt her knees buckle as she sat down. Goldie went to the window to look at his house and came back to the table.

"I had to sneak by that place once today," he said. "If he finds out what happened and sees me with you--" He clenched his fists and held them in front of his chin.

"Let's go. We have to go," she said.

She turned off the coffee-maker and went down to the basement for Goldie's jeans. They were completely dry now. After he put them on, Margy packed some things for each of them, made sure she had some cash and charge cards, and led him out the back door. As Goldie slid behind the wheel of the car, they looked at each other again and shook their heads. "Two of a kind," she said, almost laughing. "Fumblers and copers, nothing else."

"Where to?" Goldie asked, without a hint of a smile.

She shrugged, saying that she did not know or care. When he said nothing, she laughed again. "My God, what a pair of nuts! We can't just sit here."

Goldie raised his hand and told her to be quiet. A car passed the driveway, turning at the *cul de sac*, paused a moment in front of the house, and continued toward the end of the street. For a moment, Margy thought it was the police.

"Start the car. Let's get out of here."

He tapped the wheel impatiently, thinking. "Some friends of mine have a farm in Massachusetts," he said. "It's near Worcester. They have a cottage we can stay at, but it won't be permanent."

"Good. Let's go. Start the goddamn car."

"We may have to sleep in the same room, you know."

Margy pounded the dashboard. "Goldie, don't start that. Let's just get going."

154

He waved his hand. "Well, think about it. What are we going to do when we get there? Do you want to sleep together?"

She nodded, not in agreement, but to acknowledge the point and get him going. "We'll do what we have to do when we get there, that's all. But does your uncle know about this place? If Buford or Gray--"

"He knows about it," Goldie said.

"Well, then how can we go there?'"

"They won't mention anything to anybody now. And unless he hears about Everet, Uncle Dan won't think of us as running away together. He and I have been through this lots of times."

She stared at him as he finally started the engine. When he put the car in gear, she reached out and touched the door handle. It was the first time she had thought of this as running away, and it made her want to stop immediately. It was going away for a few days, maybe, but not running. Shaking her head, she opened the door and started to leave. "I can't do this," she said.

"Margy, come on! This is ridiculous."

"I can't run away from my family."

He reached across the seat and tried to pull her back in. "You see how this one phone call affected you? Besides, maybe your family ran away from you. At least Everet has."

She shook her head. "I simply can't do it, Goldie." She felt numb. She had the door open; one leg dangled toward the pavement while tears welled up in her eyes again. Goldie turned off the ignition switch and, gripping her elbow tightly, draped his arm across her shoulders. He drew her close.

"Margy, it's only for a few days--to cool things off. It works with my uncle when I have to leave. It will work for you and Everet."

She shook her head again, and Goldie turned away.

"Kennedy is not going to be ruined because--"

"How would you know?" she shot back. "You sound like Foss!"

155

He laughed, letting his arm fall to his side. "Pardon my cynicism, but I've been an orphan since I was Kennedy's age. I know something about this stuff."

She raised her fist to stop him from talking. As she rested her forehead against it on the car window, she thought of her father and what he might think of her and began to cry bitterly. Goldie apologized, putting his arm around her again. After a few minutes, she sat up to dry her tears. Looking into his eyes, she kissed his cheek. He sighed.

"What do you think?" he asked, even more ready to drive.

She shook her head. "I've messed up everything so much by now that one more blunder can't hurt."

He nodded. "Are you sure?"

"No," she said. "But I don't want to think about it anymore."

As he started the car and put it into gear again, Goldie kissed her--also on the cheek. "It's the right move," he said. "It will give everyone a chance to cool down."

She smiled, not really believing him, not being sure what they had to be cooled down from—whether Everet's injury or her own.

She felt tense during the early part of the trip. Goldie switched on the radio for local news, and when they heard nothing about Everet, Margy, or the Democrats, they began to relax. As they approached the Berkshires, traffic thinned out considerably, and Goldie drove faster, pulling out his shirt, while Margy took down her hair. Letting the wind blow through it, she put her feet up on the dash and began to feel at ease. She lit a cigarette, passed one to Goldie, and touched his knee as he grinned at her.

"You're going to make me drive off the road," he said.

She laughed, squinting through the glare from the sun, and leaned out the window to look up at the sky. The farm--owned by a couple named John and Carrie Appel (pronounced "Apple," Goldie told her, the husband's nickname being "Mac")--was situated on a lake in the center of the state, about five miles northwest of Worcester. The Appels were older, in their early forties. They had been

156

friends of Goldie's parents and had in fact been one-time next door neighbors since the Goldsteins' summer home had been adjacent to their property. "They have something," he said, speaking of their marriage. "It's really special. You'll like them."

Margy sighed, not needing a comparison with her own life right then and uncertain about meeting anybody new. But as the trees passed, in odd colors and shapes, almost like a beautiful abstract film clip, a part of her responded, and that seemed to ease her doubts.

After they crossed the state line and drove more deeply into Massachusetts, Goldie turned onto Route 15 going east. Here the hills were lower but with bushes and trees in thickets that seemed to bring them closer to the road. On the far side of a town called Beasely, they circled a farm of apple orchards and followed a narrow, rocky path for another mile and a half until they came to a clearing, where they stopped before a narrow, tree-lined lake. A couple of water-skiers crossed in and out of the wake of a motorboat, and, not far out, a large island, which Margy thought at first was part of the mainland, separated the lake into two main bodies of water, like two raindrops, forming mirror images of each other. Goldie drove down the hill, through a grove of oak and chestnut trees, and then pulled to a stop beneath a pine near a small wooden house. "This is it," he said, pointing to a house, a woodshed, and a ramp for setting boats into the water. "Mac and Carrie's place is just over the hill in back of the car."

Margy doubted again, breathing deeply and clutching her bag as she watched a robin fly across the windshield. "This is the cottage we're staying at?"

He nodded. But instead of getting out, Goldie turned the car around and went up the hill behind them. He followed a switchback past the cottage and, after several sharp turns, halted at an overlook. From there they saw the cottage, the two drops of the lake, and the island. Beside them the Appel house stood in the middle of a field of corn. It was a white, three-story building with strings of blue morning glories running from the ground to the porch overhang and a pair of

157

large pines that towered above it. Goldie turned off the road, pulled the car to a stop beneath one of the pines and laughed when a pair of dogs appeared from somewhere in back of the house. Barking and whimpering, they circled the trees and came at the car with their tails wagging.

"Hey! Hey! Hi ya, Brandy! Hello, Scotty! How're you guys doing?"

Goldie opened the door and went down on his knees to embrace them--a shepherd and a collie--sticking his chin into their muzzles so that they could lick him. Bounding off his knee, the collie leaped at Margy, and she, always leery of dogs on first acquaintance, did her best to push it down as she left the car. She petted it--tan, black, and white, it was very friendly. Then she had to push the shepherd off too, and she gave up at last, dropping her bag and petting both of them at once as she fell to her knees.

"Where's Carrie--and Mac?" Goldie said, half to himself and half to the dogs. He went to the porch, called out, and, with no answer, tried the handle to the door. It was locked. Slipping a note into the crack behind the doorjamb, he said they should go back to the cottage.

"It *is* beautiful, Goldie," she said, as they entered the car, with the dogs bounding and weaving around them. "I'm glad we came."

He grinned and pointed past the overlook to the island in the lake. "That's called 'The Nest'," he said. "We'll go out there later. But first I want to let you see the town."

He drove down the switchback and parked near the dock, opening the door to the cottage by means of a key in the mailbox. Goldie pulled the sheets off the furniture, opened the windows, and, after showing Margy the rooms, turned on the electricity and water pump. When he returned, they went to a shed behind the house and pulled a rowboat out along with two ten-speed English racers. Dragging the boat along the dock, they set it in the water to swell and then, deciding that it would take an hour or two to become tight, looked at the bikes. Goldie pumped air into the tires and adjusted the chains so that they could ride into town. It would be a three mile trip--beautiful for a bicycle, Goldie said--along more or less level roads partially around the lake and through the outskirts of a forest preserve. The town, called Evergreen, was small and quiet. When they arrived, Margy saw a street of shops, a large municipal parking lot, and two banks.

She bought some eggs, chopped meat and salad vegetables in a corner grocery store and, at a bar, some German beer for the Appels. Near the town's park, they visited the municipal building and the local schoolhouse, which had an interesting statue of the Howe brothers in front of it. Goldie showed it to her because Mac Appel had done the statue. It showed Elias bent over and squinting into the workings of a small sewing machine while his brother looked over his shoulder with a nicely rendered expression of awe. They toured a few other sights--the firehouse, the library with a painting of Hawthorne, Melville, Emerson, and Thoreau in a Mount Rushmore type frieze over its front door ("Mac?" Margy asked. "Carrie," Goldie answered, wincing. "It's not that bad," Margy said.). Then they rode back through town to the cabin where they ate lunch and spent the afternoon on the water.

Goldie rowed past the island into the open half of the lake, and from there he showed Margy a good view of the Nest's darker side. They saw lots of brush, a few spruce and fir, and two tall, mast-like oaks in the center, making the island look like a ghost ship caught in a harbor. They rowed along the shore for a while, then returned to the island and anchored in the sun just beside it. Goldie pointed inland to a beech, which, hump-backed and deformed, spread its limbs as if it could not decide whether to be a shrub, a vine, or a tree. There was a series of pegs driven into its lumpy, disease-scarred trunk about fifteen feet up to where it forked, the two main branches stretching in opposite directions for light. A small tree house rested in the fork, its boards unpainted but solidly fitted together.

"Come on. I haven't been here in a year."

They climbed to the house, skipping over a couple of pegs which looked loose or had been broken off, and entered a square room with one vacant window facing the outer lake.

159

Another opening, more like a door, faced the house on the mainland. There were two mattresses and several moldy blankets on the floor, with a couple of weather-beaten paperbacks in the corner. Goldie climbed over the mattresses and sat at the window overlooking the lake.

"My dad and I built this," he said. "It was supposed to be my library and summer studio. I used to sleep here during July and August, whenever the weather was dry. My parents' house was right over there."

He motioned through the opposite opening, toward the rise where the Appels lived. The house had been set into the hill near the top of the switchback. It had burned down a couple of winters after his parents died, when its woodstove had exploded. "Mac was taking care of it when it happened," Goldie said. "After the fire, he bought the land from my uncle, but he told me that I could have it back whenever I wanted it."

They had used the house often. Goldie and his father had come up to snowshoe during winter weekends; and they had hunted pheasant in Mac Appel's cornfields every autumn. He pointed to some drawings on the walls of the tree house-- birds, animals, several woodland scenes--and said that they were the first things he had drawn outside of a classroom. Except for one odd, clumsy sketch of a man on a raft, the drawings were large, rounded, and richly shaded, with strong lines that showed detailed muscular movement.

"My father did the raft," Goldie said. She nodded, startled at the contrast in the drawings. Goldie had done his between the ages of seven and ten, and, when his father drew his, he must have been in his early forties. Yet a viewer looking at the two easily might have reversed the ages of the artists. The animals were closely observed, rendered with such minute detail that no average eight-year-old could have done them.

The drawing of the man on the raft had none of that skill, and so it was difficult to believe that its artist could have fathered the other, more skillful one. Margy tried to recall the work she had done at a similar age, and she realized that although she had been very good for the normal

160

Waterloo Falls student, she would have been ordinary compared to Goldie.

That realization was a surprise to see--or to admit-- and, together with the other things that had happened in the past twenty-four hours, caused her to fall silent. She could express an abstract vision of planes and forms in her landscapes; she had developed a way of seeing things well, inside and outside. But she was never good--at least not as good as Goldie--at making her drawings subjects themselves, with their own breath and light. Even at seven or eight Goldie could do that.

Margy withdrew into the corner, told Goldie how moved she was by the drawings, then smiled when he pointed to something carved into the lower wall near the doorway. Within a crude flourish of trees, flowers, and awkwardly drawn abstract figures were three adolescent carvings: "John luvs Lucy forever," "Sarah + Bobby= Dream," and, finally, a strongly embellished one clearer and more deeply cut than the others: "G and M, 1968."

"My, my," she said, "you *were* precocious. I wonder who 'M' could have been?"

He blushed, good-naturedly, turning toward the water as she took his hand. He kissed her lightly, embracing her, and she began to feel guilt again. Although she regretted having attacked Everet, especially after having, she thought, failed him miserably at the party; although she felt awful for having abandoned Kennedy as her mother and father had abandoned her, she now also regretted that she had worked to be awarded the show at Copperwood instead of turning it over to Goldie. A breeze blew off the lake, rustling the leaves of the trees surrounding them. She lay near the doorway, and, taking Goldie into her arms, stared out at the sky above the Appel house. He stirred against her. She held him off, surprised by the strength of her regrets: warnings and charges that caught her unaware.

"Maybe we're lucky, Goldie," she said. "Despite everything, maybe we ought to be grateful for the way things are."

161

He turned his head and looked at her, one eye closed. "You mind telling me what you're talking about?" he asked.

She shook her head. "I'm in my thirties. I've gotten nowhere. You deserve much better than me."

He turned away, silent for a moment. Then they heard barking and saw the two dogs on the shore. They were sniffing around the tires of the car, their tails up, as if they were stalking an animal. Goldie sat up. Speaking softly, he ticked off each item on his fingers: "You have a lot of ability. Technically, you know as much as anyone I've ever met-- including Foss. But you also have responsibilities, even though you want success so badly. It's unfair, but with some people it takes more time."

She shook her head again. "I plug away, plug away, and... Nothing."

"You're very good, Margy. What do you mean?"

"You've got so much more potential. It's hard to bear."

He shrugged. "I'm younger, that's all."

"Yes, but you already know as much as I do. It's in those drawings. It's part of your blood."

He grinned, scoffing a little. Then, catching his breath as he was about to speak, he poked his head out the door. A man stood on the dock with the two dogs now. He waved when Goldie called out to him. "It's Mac," he said. "Do you want to go back to shore?"

She nodded, but, as they rose, he took Margy's hand and led her onto the porch. He added, "About blood—that's really silly. Talent is what you do. There's no other way for us to measure it."

He turned, but she pointed across the treehouse room to his drawing of a squirrel nibbling on an acorn. Next to it, a Black-capped Chickadee in the middle of its S-curve flight hovered, as if above a flower. And then a large raccoon, discovered at some theft, began to slink back into the water with its head thrown back. They seemed to leap from their poses, as if she were pointing with a gun.

"That speaks for itself," Margy said.

"For what?" He stepped out to the limb and started down the pegs.

"At seven you were as good as I was at seventeen."

"And at seventeen?"

He smiled. She shook her head.

"We'll discuss it later," Goldie said, laughing as he continued down the pegs.

"No. I'll say it now. At seventeen you're better—much better--and you should be giving the Copperwood show."

From the ground, he looked up at her and turned away, still laughing. "We'll talk about that later too," he said, starting for the boat.

On shore a tall, pot-bellied man with a beard and long white hair swinging down to his shoulders met them. He wore bibbed overalls with heavy oil-resistant boots and waved a curved calabash pipe as they floated up to the dock. With the dogs barking and nipping around and between his legs, he pulled the boat toward him, tied it to the dock's main post, and extended his hand politely when introduced to Margy.

"Well, you made it, I see. I've been wondering where you were."

"You have?"

"Sure. We've had several phone calls already."

"From Uncle Dan?"

"Yup. Who'd you think, the CIA?"

Goldie winced, looking at Margy. Then together they followed Mac into the cottage, where they gathered food and beer from the refrigerator and brought them up to the main house.

11.

A GARDEN OF EARTHLY DELIGHTS

Margy swung the bar over a cow's head and locked it into place. "Not bad," Carrie said, pulling the milking machine down the center aisle. "Why don't you give them some hay? Mac is always stingy, and I think the ones down at the end haven't had much to eat this morning."

Carrie connected the hose to the cow's teats and inserted the other end into the flow pipe which hung above the floor for the length of the barn. "It looks as if you've done this stuff before," she said.

Margy nodded, crossing the walk and hopping over the waste trench to lock the second cow into its stanchion.

"I had a friend in high school whose father owned a dairy farm. Sometimes I helped him do the milking."

Carrie shook her head, "Iowa farm girls—that's one of Mac's fantasies." She hopped over the waste trench behind Margy and attached a hose to the second cow. The cow shuffled a little, tail swishing a fly, and let out a quiet, mournful moo. Carrie patted its hip and murmured, attaching the other end of the hose to the flow pipe.

"Twelve more," she said, as they proceeded down the line, locking the rest of the cows in while the first two were being milked. When they had finished, Margy went back to the barn door where a bale of hay lay broken open. Its sweet, musky smell mingled pleasantly with the heavier odor of the animals. She picked up a pitchfork, jabbed the tines into the hay for a forkful, then carried it the length of the barn and deposited it in front of the last cow. It shuffled and mooed, its white snout and pink tongue immediately shifting from the grain to explore the new offering. As Margy returned for more, Carrie worked on the next two cows. She smiled and pushed a wisp of dark hair back from her forehead.

"It's the best part of the day for me," she said. "I love this kind of work."

She wore jeans, boots, and a long-sleeved cotton flannel shirt. Her hair was drawn back into a pony tail, and she moved among the cows with an attractive country girl's gait. When she rolled up her sleeves and spoke in flinty New England tones, Margy perceived a sense of toughness and independence that she admired. Carrie was younger than Mac; to correct Goldie's judgment she would have guessed that Mac was in his early fifties, while Carrie was still in her thirties--perhaps late thirties, but certainly not yet forty. They had four children, a boy who was visiting friends in New Hampshire, a girl who was away at school, and a pair of twins, a young boy and girl, who were out with Mac and Goldie feeding some of the fowl they kept for food.

Margy went to the bale three or four times, each time bringing a bit of hay to the cows at the opposite end from the door. By the time she finished, Carrie was milking the fifth and sixth cows and adding shovels full of grain to the hay. At just after six, with the sun barely edging above the horizon, the breeze blew a pleasant chill through the open door.

"Have you known Goldie for long?" Carrie asked, as Margy passed with an extra forkful for the last cow.

"About six years. We're really next door neighbors."

"That's right. He's mentioned you to us once or twice."

"Really?"

"Oh, yes, at times when he's getting away from his uncle. I believe he calls you his in-town mother. I'm the one from the country"

Margy laughed, hopping over a hose and leaning the pitchfork against the wall. The milking machine began to make bizarre slurp, slurping sounds, indicating that the cows were done, and Carrie removed the hoses in order to go on to the next set. This time Margy helped attach the hoses. Carrie smiled and showed her how to set a teat into a sucking cup. She was a rather laconic person, typical for New England, Margy thought, and so her actions now were on the side of expressiveness. The night before she had remained silent, letting Mac do most of the talking while she went about the house doing things: cooking a really fine meal,

165

supervising the twins setting the table, starting a fire in the living room, getting sheets and pillow-cases for Goldie and Margy. There had been something of a to-do over that-- whether Goldie and Margy should go down to the cottage or stay in the house--and, when they elected to stay in the house, whether they should share the same room or sleep separately. Since even Margy was non-committal about that, Carrie had set up two rooms off the kitchen on the first floor in order to give them, as she said, "a chance to make up your minds." Margy liked her a lot although something about Carrie made her feel that she was being measured.

They moved on to the next cows together, and, when the machine started to slurp again, they moved the hoses once more. In about an hour they had finished the cows on both sides of the stanchion, and so Carrie rolled the machine and hoses back to the entrance and began unhitching the bars. The cows started toward the door, two or three of them needing to be prodded, as Margy helped.

"Come on, Rosie; you, too, Mona Lisa. You'll get more to eat outside," said Carrie.

They shooed the cows into the yard and then through the gate into a pasture with several shade trees, a gentle slope, and a large dug-out pond for the drinking water. After cleaning out the waste trench, Margy and Carrie started for the house, skirting the cornfield as they walked down a narrow path beside a field of vegetable seedlings. Beyond the house the lake shimmered in the morning light, its still water reflecting the hills and oaks. To the left and slightly beyond the island, they could see a green pasture with a stone house on a hill that was almost a mirror of the Appels'. Carrie stopped to inspect the corn, her fingers expertly turning over the leaves of each plant to see if there were any damage from beetles.

"You ever run a tractor?" she asked.

Margy laughed, shaking her head.

"Well, we're going to cultivate this field very soon. I thought you might want to help us."

"I'd like to try."

166

Carrie pulled one or two weeds by hand and smiled. The corn was about calf-high, its leaves a washed, pale green color that was quite appealing, the soil a lovely deep reddish brown. Carrie breathed deeply through the nose and sighed as she looked out over the field.

"Mac's my usual helper," she said, "along with John Jr.. But maybe the women can do it this year."

"That would be nice."

"We'll see how it works out."

Margy nodded, not saying anything as Carrie placed her hands on her hips and looked up the hill behind the house. Over that hill toward the west, the Appels had a couple of pastures along with a fallow field, and it was there that Mac, Goldie, and the twins were feeding the chickens. She wondered about Carrie's relationship with Mac, who seemed equally shrewd, equally measuring, but, on the surface at least, a little less intense. He enjoyed the ownership of the farm, not the work, and seemed more at home at their roadside produce stand than in the fields themselves. He performed his share of the daily tasks, but he seemed to do so with the end in mind. The day that they had arrived, for example, while Goldie and Margy had helped him repair a fence around the dairy pasture, he had stuffed his pipe constantly, talking about Frost's "Mending Wall," and discussing the economic and ecological independence which he and Carrie had gained by becoming farmers. Meanwhile, Goldie did most of the post-digging, and Margy trimmed lumber and helped fit it into place. Mac supervised from a distance, offering a hand here and there, making occasional suggestions but rarely getting involved. But when Carrie did something, she performed it thoroughly, obviously because she enjoyed it. It was as if farming were her natural talent.

"Were you raised on a farm?" Margy asked.

Carrie nodded, pointing to the north and saying she had been raised about ten miles away. She had gone to college in Boston, taken up fine arts and then met Mac, who was a graduate instructor. Together they had planned a life of working and teaching in the arts. Carrie laughed. "But somewhere along the line Mac got distracted. He read a book

167

on farming, put it together with what he remembered of Thoreau and Emerson, and decided that the two of us ought to give it a try, for the sake of self-sufficiency."

Margy stood next to Carrie as they looked out on the lake. "That must have appealed to you," she said.

"I guess. But I think I was just a little homesick." Carrie shook her head, ruefully. "I had been away for five or six years by that time, and I sort of felt the call of nature. We pooled our money and bought that little piece of property up on the hill there. In those days real estate in this part of Massachusetts was still relatively cheap."

She waved, wiggling her fingers as if to say that those days were long gone, and turned to look at the house.

"We had nothing like that at first. Mac just built a little log cabin--we both did, I guess--and spent a year and a half farming before we showed any profit. Then an uncle of Mac's died and left him some money. We bought up more land around here; then this house, the barn, and those fields became available. After buying them, we started to farm with a little more commercial intent."

"It's a nice life. You must enjoy it."

"I wouldn't have it any other way, even if I were alone."

"Good for you. Keep it."

Carrie smiled, and together they continued down to the house where they had a cup of coffee and waited for Mac, Goldie, and the twins to come home for breakfast.

12.

MAC

"Be careful with that, Mac! He could fall off the axle-casing."

Carrie slammed the head of the hoe into the ground and stood with her hands on her hips. Together, she and Margy watched Mac drive the tractor from the barn to the cornfield. Goldie was standing behind him, hands on Mac's shoulders and grinning as Mac zig-zagged across the road.

"He's a nut. He just doesn't realize that these are machines. Mac! Be careful!"

The tractor swerved around a rock, just missed rolling into the roadside ditch, and finally righted itself as Mac, giggling and roaring, with his hair blowing in the wind, twisted and turned the wheel.

"You ninny! You're going to hurt somebody one of these days. Goldie, you'd better get down from there before that monster does something moronic."

She stood in front of the tractor and Mac, after a gritty show of teeth, as if he were going to run her over, brought the machine to a halt just a foot or two in front of her. Carrie had not budged an inch. He shook his head, saying, "Damn you, woman," as he stomped his foot on the fender and yanked his pipe out of his mouth. Goldie, his hands off Mac's shoulders, put fingers in his ears and closed his eyes as if he were afraid of what was going to happen next. Carrie simply looked up at the two of them and shook her head.

"Mac, I love you, but this machine is not a toy."

"Then what am I doing with it?"

She frowned. "It's a tool. Carelessly used, it becomes a weapon. You know that."

Goldie hopped off the axle-casing and stood behind the tractor. Mac, swiveling on the seat, rolled over the large rear wheels and landed on his feet in front of Carrie. With a

169

huge grin, he wrapped his arms around her and lifted her off the ground.

"Ah, Carrie, my love, bitch that you are, neurotic mother of the earth that you try to be, I adore you."

He let her down, kissing her mouth while she sought to turn her head away.

"Yech! No! I don't kiss dummies, and I'm not going to kiss you!"

She freed herself and turned, laughing, to run when he began to pursue her. Squealing and giggling, the two of them raced along the road, around the tractor, and across the ditch into the field. Goldie and Margy watched, grinning as Mac finally caught up with her and pulled her down to earth, the two of them rolling and flailing at one another among the corn plants. Carrie screeched, Mac roared as she bit his hand, and suddenly she was up and running back to the road until she came to the tractor. Mac lay on his back, pulling a pipe out of his pocket, lighting it, and sending up great clouds of smoke.

"I'm done with you, woman. Done! I won't take this anymore."

Carrie brushed back several wisps of hair and looked at Margy and Goldie with a blush. She shook her head, then seeing that Mac intended to remain supine, backed up the tractor to where an iron cultivator lay and began to attach it to the tractor. Margy watched as she set it into the hitch and tightened the bolt. All business again, Carrie climbed into the driver's seat, started the engine, and began to steer it toward the field. "You want a ride?" she asked Margy, who stood at the edge of the field with a hoe in her hands. Margy shook her head. Carrie smiled when Goldie hesitated too and assured him that she would drive carefully. With a doubtful look, he climbed behind her and placed his hands on her shoulders as he had done with Mac.

"Look at the two of them, twins," said Mac as he rolled to his knees, stood, and walked toward Margy. "Two shriveled peas in a pod."

He picked up a hoe and joined Margy in chopping weeds between the rows of corn. The tractor was to run the length of the field, with the cultivator getting most of the weeds lying along the vertical rows; the hoes were used to get the weeds the cultivator missed. A large black crow flew overhead as they began to work, and Mac stopped for a moment to look at it. It dipped to the earth, landing on the other side of the field, but when the tractor turned and headed in its direction, it took off with a caw-caw and flew over the hill toward the other pastures. For a moment Margy saw the collie and shepherd charge over the hill in pursuit.

Mac continued to hoe and moved nearer to her so that they could work together.

"Slap down hard," he said, puffing on his pipe. "You have to take out the roots, and it's the downward pressure of the blade that cuts to them."

She nodded, already knowing that from her childhood. Mac was large-boned and tall--her head only came up to his shoulders--but he worked the hoe with a deft hand. He watched her for a bit, puffing on his pipe and leaning on the handle. Meanwhile, Carrie and Goldie came chugging down the rows of corn from the opposite direction. Carrie looked at them both with mock horror, as if she were out of control. Goldie rested on her shoulders and peered at the rows in back of them to make sure the cultivator got weeds and not corn plants as they rode.

"Look at her," Mac said, shaking his head. "She rides that like a quarter-horse--just trusts it to know the way itself."

In fact Carrie did seem rather casual about the direction, Margy thought, only using the wheel when she came to the end of the row and had to turn back to go the opposite way.

"Why does she do that?" Margy asked. "Isn't it dangerous?"

"Simple. Though it's a weapon, she thinks she's a hotshot--which she is, of course. She also thinks that the Earth Spirit is showing her the way."

"Earth Spirit?"

He nodded, seriously. "That's the way she sees it. Put to proper use, the tractor doesn't need any steering if the

171

right person aims it correctly from the beginning of each row. If she watches for rocks, she hardly needs to steer."

Margy widened her eyes and slapped the soil to pull out a weed. Mac stood beside her, his pipe smoke wafting across her face in a sweet cloud. Carrie and Goldie passed in silence, going back down the far end of the field, and she and Mac hoed until they passed again. Goldie beamed this time. When the tractor reached the end of the row, Carrie stopped, dismounted, then let him sit behind the wheel and stood on the axle-casing herself while he headed down toward the other end. Her one hand rested on his shoulder, the other was on the wheel, helping him to steer as they proceeded gingerly among the corn plants.

"That doesn't look very much like a spirit is doing the steering," Margy said.

"He's a novice; she has to guide him. He'll become an expert quick, you watch. Then she'll let him alone."

Margy shook her head. "I doubt it. He's got too much city and suburb in him. Besides, he wants to paint."

"Ha. What do you think I want? Carrie's the only true hayseed around here. That's why this farm works. When we started it, I didn't know a pussycat from a pussy willow, much less how, when, why, and where you hoe. You learn because you have to."

He smiled and shook his head. Margy looked at the tractor and then past the pines to the house. It was nine o'clock, the sun already high in the sky, and the air was warming. They had finished breakfast about half an hour before. The twins were off with friends learning how to water-ski on the lake. During breakfast, Dan Goldstein had called and, according to Mac, seemed to know that Goldie was there. In fact, according to Mac, Dan was pleased because it meant Goldie was not in trouble. Also, Dan had indicated that he knew nothing of the incident between Everet and Margy, telling Mac only that it was quiet on the street and that Copperwood College had called to ask about Goldie's absences. And even the absences were good signs: Dan thought they showed that Goldie might not return to school--a trouble-spot, according to Dan, in relation to Goldie's behavior.

The one ominous note was that Dan seemed to think Margy was with them, too. He mentioned frequent phone calls, people asking for Margy and then calling again, even though he had told them she was not there. "Tell that nephew of mine that the phone and bed are still here, so long as he stays away from the Hamilton woman and all the other Copperwood types. Tell him that even the painting can be arranged, provided he doesn't cause me too much aggravation."

He had hung up soon afterward. Margy was impressed that Mac had been serious, even interested, yet had given hardly any information. And without lying. She had the feeling that, if Dan had asked to speak to Goldie, Mac would have turned the phone over to him. But he seemed to direct the conversation so that the request was never made.

"Here--you take the cross-path over there," he said now, pointing to the row next to his. "I'll take this one. The field is too narrow for us to run a tractor up and down in both directions."

She moved over and plunged the hoe into the soil around the corn plants. It was pleasant work, bringing back her childhood when she hoed in a backyard garden with her father. The earth felt rich and comfortable beneath her feet, and the sight of the sky, surrounding land, and the lake behind them reassured her landscaper's eye. Margy's mind wove between the whirl of events in the last forty-eight hours and the calm she felt upon arriving here. She had resolved herself into thinking that Everet was out of physical danger--although the sight of him falling to the carpet at the Grays' had kept her awake through most of the night; but she had come to think of separation from him as inevitable now. With a surprising sense of relief she wondered what path her life would take. They had been intimate once, at first because of the stares of disapproval from their families as well as the public when they had made their relationship known, and after that because they had come to love each other a great deal. They had married to prove to themselves

173

that they were committed to each other beyond physical attraction and bias, that somehow their own personal, intense feelings had triumphed over social limitations.

Of course, that intimacy had changed now, and the thought of independence loomed ahead like a storm cloud in an El Greco landscape. She understood that she had wanted to reinstate the original premises of their relationship at Wiltshire, but working beside Mac at that moment, she assumed that reinstatement was no longer possible. Their lives had drifted too far apart.

As Goldie and Carrie passed for the fifth or sixth time, she nudged closer to Mac.

"You like it here, don't you? Even though you paint and sculpt."

"*Used* to paint and sculpt." He shook his head. "Now I'm a farmer."

"All right, used to. But you like it here, don't you?"

"Love it is more like it. I wouldn't have it any other way."

Margy sighed, smiling in admiration. Mac put his hand on her hoe to stop it from moving. He squeezed her wrist. "You're going through a bad time now, aren't you?"

She nodded, looking down at her shoes and suddenly trying to hold back tears. She and Goldie had told him and Carrie very little about her reasons for being there.

He shook his head. "Just remember, there are always other things than painting."

She almost laughed, noting his instinctive agreement with Everet and Gray and wanting to tell him that painting was not the real issue in her life. Instead, she took a deep breath and said, "Like what? I'm no farmer. I'm not even a decent housewife. I've never been anything in my head except a painter. Now I'm not even sure of that."

He laughed, comfortably. "You know as well as I do what else there is. Living: kids, books to read, friends to spend weekends with." He grinned, and for a moment his good feelings lifted her. "And, for me, sometimes there's even this farm. It's a living, as Carrie likes to say, and I can sculpt or paint when I feel like it, not because I have to."

Margy smiled at him. "It doesn't upset you to have to think of other things?"

"Hell, no. It's a relief."

"Some relief," she said. She kicked a root and chopped at it with her toe. He stood beside her and patted her arm.

"Listen, I think a person has to make a decision if he is going to survive. Only a few can be an artist and nothing else—and they're the lucky ones."

"Like Goldie?"

Mac nodded, pulling out his pipe as he glanced at the tractor again. "He's special all right. I'd hate to see him taken off his tracks by any of this decision-making. He needs all the time and freedom he can get."

He looked away. Margy nodded, going after a weed near his foot and clanging metal against metal as their two hoes met. She felt confused.

"I think he saw you as a model once," Mac said, "mainly because you are older and just as committed to painting as he."

"Not as talented, I'm afraid. Nor as likely to develop."

Mac glanced at her, clearly surprised, and asked if she was sure. Margy nodded emphatically. Mac said, "Goldie thinks you're pretty damn good. I think your work is an influence on his. He showed me one or two things once, and I liked them."

She blushed. Mac smiled, and she felt flattered because she liked the paintings hung throughout their house. There were things by Carrie and Mac--Carrie's were undoubtedly inferior, Margy thought--some early stuff by Foss and Goldie, and other artists. There was a lithograph by Robert Rauschenberg and a small, realistic oil by Jackson Pollock that must have been found in a shop somewhere and was now worth a lot of money. For farmers, they had a sophisticated collection.

"What about you?" she asked. "Aren't you his model too?"

Mac glanced up from the earth and shook his head.

175

"I certainly hope not," he said. "Goldie knows that I gave up years ago. Much as I clown around, farming is really where my talents lie. Carrie and I do all right here. She's got the practical daily knowledge, but it's me who keeps us going on the longer view."

"With philosophy—Thoreau and Emerson?"

"Don't laugh; it's very important. Remember, in college we were educated to think this kind of life is very dull."

"It isn't?"

He grinned, snapping his hoe at Margy's shoes and bumping her with his hip as Goldie drove by with a wave. When he came to the end of the row, he made a quick hand-over-hand turn, swinging the tractor to the right and out toward the vegetable patch, then back to the left where he headed into the next series of rows. Carrie did not have her hands on the wheel this time. She leaned over his shoulder, talking into his ear in order, Margy presumed, to give him directions. The tractor swung into the field and without hesitation went through the corn perfectly, not damaging a single plant. Mac shook his head and held his pipe while he watched.

"He's an expert already. That kid has some pair of eyes and hands."

With a great puff of smoke, he waved at Goldie. His expression changed; he leaned over the hoe and his voice took on a more serious note. "There's something I've been meaning to ask you," he said, taking the pipe from his mouth.

"Yes?" she said, trying not to frown. Her flesh rose, but she could not say why.

"What's the real situation between you and him?"

"Goldie and me? Nothing. What has he said?"

Mac puffed his pipe and played a bit with his beard. "Nothing either--except that you're a friend who needs to be away for a few days."

"A *few* days..." She was a little surprised. She had thought that they were going to be here, not permanently,

176

but for a while. She had assumed that they would soon move into the cottage.

"That's right," Mac said. "Of course, it's none of my business, but I was just wondering."

"Well, does there have to be something more?"

"Not as far as I'm concerned," he said. "Carrie says that both beds were slept in last night. To tell the truth, I didn't expect it."

Margy paused before she spoke; she thought immediately of Fred Gray's spying. The tractor passed two or three rows in front of them. As they looked up, Margy saw Carrie wave and point to the other side of the cultivator. Mac advanced about six rows while Goldie proceeded to the end of the field. Margy followed and together they watched Goldie make his turn and drive back toward them, trailing the cultivator through the last few plants.

"Mac, you haven't done a damn thing," Carrie shouted. "You've been talking too much."

"Haven't stopped working yet, Carrie, my dear."

"Haven't stopped talking, you mean."

Margy smiled, ruefully, calling out that it was her fault. "Everything is my fault," she added, angrily. As the tractor sped by, Mac let out a puff of smoke and kicked at a weed that would not work out of the soil. He reached down, jerked it from the earth with his hand, and threw it to the side of the road.

"Let's drop it," he said. "It's none of my damn business."

"It's absolutely normal. Everything I do seems under suspicion these days."

Mac shook his head. He went to the road, picked up two extra hoes and walked them across the field. There was some laughter and joking, which Margy could not quite hear and which increased her bad feelings. Mac gave Carrie the hoes, and, as he left, she swiped at his rear end with the handle of one of them.

When he stood next to Margy again, she said, "I know Goldie's an adolescent, and I'm very conscious of my responsibilities--despite what Dan Goldstein says. I've never done anything with him that I'm ashamed of."

"Are you sure?"

She hesitated; then she said, "I'm absolutely certain."

"Well, Carrie has," he said. He took his pipe from his mouth as Margy looked at him.

"Meaning--?"

"You know very well what I mean," he said. "Why do you think she knew about the different beds?"

"You mean Carrie and Goldie--?"

Mac nodded. He looked ill, but a smile, partly sardonic, partly ashamed, covered his sudden paleness.

"No question about it," he said. "But now, take your hoe and let's see if we can beat those two to the other side of the patch."

13.

FINDING A WAY

That bit of information colored everything, making her feel ashamed and vengeful. And that evening, when Fred Gray called to ask specifically if Margy were there, it almost made her wish that the Appels would expose her. The phone was in the kitchen, and Carrie answered while the rest of them sat talking in the dining room.

"No," they heard Carrie say. "Mr. Gray, she isn't. I, uh ... Mr. Gray, look, I'll have my husband call you as soon as we have some appropriate news."

There was a sudden pause in the dining room conversation. Goldie blushed and looked at Margy. They sat at a large, linen-covered table, surrounded by dark furniture, surprisingly lightened by paintings of food, food-processing, and farming that covered all four walls. Mac scratched his beard and drew on his pipe; the twins looked at each other and then at Mac as if to ask what was going on. Margy and Goldie walked into the kitchen where they saw Carrie standing at the door, speaking as if into the top half of it, which was a window. Margy went to the counter, leaned over a note pad and wrote the words, "Fred Gray?" in large block letters. Still listening, Carrie nodded her head and turned away to the door again.

"Mr. Gray, I wish I could help, but I really don't have any news. What? Yes, I'm sure he's all right. You know, he's done this before. I'm sure he just wants to think things through. From what Dan Goldstein tells us, they must have had quite an argument."

She nodded once or twice, impatiently blew her breath as she started to speak and Gray interrupted her. Then she took the phone from her ear and turned to Margy with a look of distaste.

"Yes, Mr. Gray. Look, do you want to speak to my husband?--Well, he'll tell you the same thing I did, but maybe you'll believe him."

179

Just then Mac entered the kitchen, closing the door and shooing the twins back into the dining room. He tip-toed around the table, stoking his pipe and peering intently at Goldie and Margy. Carrie took the phone from her ear and looked at him, her hands out in supplication, as if she were begging him to talk. He shook his head and motioned her to continue.

"Yes, Mr. Gray. I understand. It must be difficult for a businessman to raise a child by himself--especially a boy like Goldie. But I would not say that he is a trouble-maker--he is simply restless.... He's very talented; he also had quite a shock when he was young. Not everyone can tolerate the sudden death of both parents."

She shook her head, glancing at Goldie, waving at Mac as if to tell him to keep still. He was tapping his pipe stem on the checkerboard tablecloth, then motioning like a television director to tell her to draw it out. She pouted a little, with a hand on her hip, but she nodded and talked into the phone.

"Margy?--Yes, yes... He's mentioned her to us before, but so has Dan... No, no, I didn't know it was that way."

Carrie glanced at Goldie and Margy and flushed, her tongue sticking out slightly in a little pout. "I really don't know anything about their relationship, Mr. Gray, and, to tell the truth, I don't want to. It's none of my business."

She looked at Margy, an angry expression on her face as Margy motioned to get her attention. She turned away. Margy tapped her shoulder. She leaned over the note pad again and printed Everet's name with the words, "Any news?" Carrie stared at the pad, listening to Gray, and then looked up at Margy with a whispered "who?" on her lips.

"My husband," Margy lip-synched. She flipped the page and scribbled, "Does he mention my husband's name--Everet?"

"No, no, Mr. Gray," said Carrie, shaking her head at Margy simultaneously. "But doesn't she have a family? Do you really think she has the time? Well, that's insulting. I didn't know women were that anxious for affairs anymore.

180

They're trying to develop themselves in other ways, aren't they?"

She nodded. Goldie stood nearby and took Margy's arm. Carrie shook her head, telling Fred Gray that he had a jaundiced view of women.

"Well, if she is absent, then I admit it looks like Goldie and Mrs. Hamilton may be together. But it could also be a coincidence. Maybe she and her husband had an argument at the same time Dan and Goldie did. That's not so unlikely, you know."

She took the phone from her ear once more and held it to her breast, whispering that he was impossible as she took a couple of breaths. Finally, she put the phone to her ear and without listening, said, "Mr. Gray, this is tiring. My husband will call you as soon as we get some news--if there is any news. But I assure you that Goldie is all right. One thing about him is that he knows how to take care of himself. That's an aspect of his character that Dan has never fully appreciated, I think." She nodded once more. Mac came to the phone, reached for it, but Carrie pulled away and finished the conversation herself.

"Yes, he is a teenager, and he is Dan's responsibility. But remember, Mr. Gray, he is also rather capable. Give him some credit, whatever their disagreements."

She smiled. "Fine. I'm glad that Dan will feel better. If we get any news, we'll call immediately.... Good-bye."

She shook her head and hung up. Goldie, Mac, and Margy stood as if stunned, waiting for an explanation. Carrie went to the oven where two chickens lay in the final stages of roasting, checked the meat thermometers, then turned off the oven and pulled out the birds.

"Well, come on, Carrie. Don't hold us in suspense; what news is there?"

Carrie glanced at Mac, then turned with annoyance to the counter, on which she had been cutting vegetables for a salad.

"Is there any news of my husband--or anyone else in my family?"

181

Carrie glanced at Margy, frowning, but did not move a muscle. She cut into a large hothouse squash as though it were a piece of sausage, then threw down the knife and lowered her head.

"What's the matter, Carrie, my love?"

Mac was by her side, his arms around her shoulders as he waved Margy and Goldie out of the room. Goldie started to leave, but Margy held her ground.

"Is there any news about Everet?" Margy asked. "If so, please tell me." Goldie stood by the table now, running his fingers along his arm as he looked from Mac and Carrie to Margy.

"You didn't tell us this would be ugly," Carrie said to him. "You didn't tell us that this could have something to do with the law."

Goldie gasped. Margy held her breath. Her knees trembled as she thought of Everet, and she felt the panic clutch her throat as she held back a cry. "Everet," she said. Finally, Mac turned Carrie around and made her look at Margy.

"What happened? Is my husband hurt?"

Carrie shook her head and looked at her hands.

"Well, what is the legal problem?"

"Carrie, tell us," Goldie said. "It doesn't do any good to keep things secret."

"I don't know. He didn't say anything clearly. But they know that Margy's disappeared, and they think she's with Goldie."

"Oh, so that's all." Margy breathed a sigh of relief, nodding at Goldie, yet not really knowing what it meant.

"Gray wasn't clear, but the police may be looking for you," Carrie said.

"For what?"

Carrie shook her head. "He said that Dan is gloating because of the Mann Act."

"The Mann Act?"

Goldie looked at Mac for an explanation, but Mac merely stroked Carrie's neck and kept his eyes on her face.

182

"That's transporting a minor across state lines," Carrie said, pouting a little, "for sexual purposes."

Goldie looked hurt, and then insulted. Margy put her hands to her face and looked down at the floor. "It's used to protect young women," Carrie continued, "but Gray thinks it might apply to Goldie."

"This is impossible. They're not going to pick me up for that."

Carrie flashed a look of anger. "This is Massachusetts, honey. There are some awfully ancient sexual laws still on the books."

"But it's a federal law," Mac said, innocently. "Federal officers would have to get involved."

"It's also a very big bluff," Margy replied. "Dan wouldn't want Goldie associated with that—it's not manly enough. And I'm sure Everet and Gray wouldn't want me associated with it either. They have as much to lose as we have."

"That's right, exactly." Goldie nodded, but he still wore a worried look.

"Just what is going on?" Carrie snapped. "Even if Gray is bluffing, don't you think you should tell us the cause? Is it something about Goldie?"

Mac laid his pipe on the counter. The twins came through the kitchen door, and the pair of them--a boy and a girl about Kennedy's age, fair, straight-haired and long-limbed like Mac, but with Carrie's unmistakable grit in their expressions--wondered what was keeping dinner. Carrie shoved Mac away and turned back to the squash. She told Mac to ready the chickens for carving, and ordered the twins to start putting silverware on the table. With an ominous glance at Goldie, she mentioned the salad, and he and Margy went to the refrigerator for the ingredients.

"There is a slight problem in my family," Margy said, trying not to sound ironic when she said "slight."

"Yes?"

"I'm not sure I handled it correctly, but Goldie and I thought we needed to get away."

183

"We assumed that already," Carrie said. She threw slices of squash into the salad bowl, shoved it to the back of the counter, and chopped into the second squash as if with a meat cleaver.

"Now, now, Carrie. Let Margy tell it the way she wants to."

Goldie winced, coming to the counter with a handful of tomatoes. He began to slice them as Margy rinsed the lettuce under the faucet.

"My husband and I had an argument," Margy said. "In the course of it, I... I..."

She looked at Carrie and Mac and could not continue. Mac picked up his pipe and began to light it. Goldie went to Margy's side and pulled a chair behind her. She sat down as Carrie turned. Hoping for sympathy, Margy looked up to find genuine hostility in her eyes.

"I'm sorry to pressure you this way," Carrie said. "But if Mac and I are going to be implicated in this, it's better for us to know what happened."

"There was no crime," Goldie murmured. "I'm no goddamn minor."

"If there was a crime, it was absolutely unintended-- and it wasn't a kidnap statute that I violated."

"That might be debatable. You have to be careful."

"And I ran away only because I thought it wasn't serious. There is nothing to worry about."

Mac looked at Margy hopefully and nodded.

"I--I--" She slapped her knee. "Goddamn it, I just can't say it to you."

"She stabbed her husband with a letter opener--"

"Stabbed him!"

"Accidentally," Goldie added.

Mac and Carrie spun about and stopped. Then Carrie's expression gradually changed, becoming normal, while Mac, placid, took the pipe from his mouth and contemplated something disappointing at his feet. *Girls will be girls*, Margy could almost hear him say.

"How badly was he hurt?" Mac asked.

184

Margy shook her head. Goldie squatted on his haunches and placed his hand on her knee. He told them that there had been some blood, but that as far as they could tell from the lack of activity around the Gray house, the wound had not been serious. Mac nodded, but upon hearing that Margy had stabbed Everet in the neck, he cringed and said such a wound had to be dangerous.

"Goldie, you really have to call your uncle," Carrie said.

"I can't. I have nothing to say to him."

"You must. The more we know, the harder it is to lie to him. Or to this Gray character." Carrie looked at Margy with distaste.

"Besides," Mac added, "if Dan and the others don't hear something soon, they're going to come up here to look for themselves. And that won't do anybody any good."

Goldie nodded and turned to Margy for a reaction. She put her hands to her head and looked down at her feet. The twins came through the door, and, when they saw Margy, they stopped, closing the door and standing against the wall as if they were hiding.

"I don't know what to say," she murmured. She began to slump to the side. Goldie held her arm, and again she felt the enormous weight of the weekend with Everet.

"I'm tired," she mumbled. She rolled off the chair, doubling up as if in pain and lying on the floor with her knees under her. She started to cry. As they surrounded her, a plate fell from the counter near the salad bowl.

"Get some salts, smelling salts," Mac shouted to the twins, who were busy looking after the dish. As if from a distance, Margy heard the gathering of pieces into a pan.

"Let her lie there," said Carrie. "Open some windows. Matthew, Lucy, go get some salts."

"Margy, Margy..." Goldie was leaning over her, his lips almost brushing hers, his hands pressing her shoulders as he placed her on her back and gazed into her eyes. His own eyes looked plastic, like buttons--wide open and seemingly motionless as she searched for understanding in them. She blanked out, came to, then blanked out once more.

185

"I'm sorry. I really fucked up ... everything."

She felt him embrace and caress her; then, unaccountably, he was no longer there. As if she were in the Sound again, she felt herself go under a huge, soft wave.

14.

LEAVING

She liked to think of herself as a realist--in painting, it was the legacy of Foss; in philosophy, it was her own character development. She admired consciousness, and she had lost it only three or four times that she could remember, feeling each time as if she had been transported, struggling and kicking, into another world. So she fought to return that night, and when she came to she was lying in what had been her bedroom the night before--a small, old-fashioned room with an antique chest-of-drawers, a lumpy bed, and the smell of mothballs which, she thought, came from the blankets that Carrie had kept in storage until they arrived. She was alone, but outside the door she heard voices, and in a few seconds Goldie and Carrie entered. Carrie held a small bottle of smelling salts.

"We don't need that!" She jerked her head away from the smell. "I'm awake now."

Carrie turned as Mac stuck his head through the door and asked how Margy was.

"I'm fine," she muttered. "Just keep that stuff away." Goldie smiled as he leaned over the bed. Mac pushed through the door and, waving a couple of books, sat on the edge of the bed. He puffed his pipe.

"Nothing to worry about, Margy. You're going to be all right."

She stared at him, then turned to Goldie.

"How are you feeling?" Goldie asked.

"I'm fine. It wasn't serious." The twins came into the room and again played their trick of shutting the door and standing close to the wall.

"I'm sorry," Margy blubbered.

"Don't mention it. You're right; it's not that serious," Goldie said.

Carrie and Mac glanced at one another, and Mac took Margy's hand, squeezing it as he leaned over the bed. She

187

began to feel even more miserable, and, looking up at him, was very grateful.

"You know, you people are really wonderful," she blubbered. "Especially you, Carrie." Before she could say more, she burst into tears. Carrie shooed the twins out of the room while Goldie and Mac sat beside the bed and tried to comfort her.

"Easy, easy," Goldie said.

Mac left the room, returning with a bowl of water and a rag, which he used to wipe her face. "I feel so awful. God, I'm sick of all this crying."

"It's probably good for you—as a cathartic," Mac said. "Don't try to stop."

He wiped her neck and forehead, dipping the cloth into the water and continuing the conversation all the while. His hands were gentle, surprisingly expert, the look in his eye extraordinarily caring. Carrie stood in the background, a neutral look on her face. When Mac placed the bowl of water on the floor, she picked it up and took it from the room.

"Feeling any better?" Goldie said.

Margy nodded and tried to settle her hands which, she suddenly noticed, had been trembling at her side.

"Don't worry about a thing," said Mac.

Margy glanced at Goldie who, with a morose face, blushed and squeezed her hand. Carrie came back into the room with a bowl of water and set it on the table next to the bed. It was an odd moment during which no one knew what to say. Carrie took the cloth from Mac and, dipping it in the water, wiped Margy's forehead again. Gripping her arm, Margy pulled her closer. Still neutral, Carrie glanced at Margy and Goldie, then quickly turned away as Margy held her breath. She said nothing. Carrie threw the cloth into the bowl of water and left the room. Goldie and Mac looked at each other, ashamed.

"Don't worry about her," said Mac. "Carrie's emotional about things she can't control."

"I'm going to call Uncle Dan," Goldie said. "I'm calling him tonight, and I'm going back home in the morning--if he'll have me."

Margy looked at him. "So be it," she said bitterly.

"Don't say that. You can stay here if you like."

Margy shook her head.

"Think about it," Mac told her. "I assure you we can handle this."

She looked at him. She did not know how much of Carrie's behavior was jealousy, and how much self-righteousness. On the other hand, she did not know about her own feelings either, and she decided that she could not bring them up. "I'll go back home, too," she said. "I might as well face up to what I did back there. My son—my whole family--deserves at least that much."

She rose, slowly, and sat on the bed, feeling more embarrassed than weak. She stood, uneasily, patting Mac and Goldie on their shoulders. They offered to help her walk, but she shook them off, and they went into the dining room where the twins and Carrie sat. Carrie rose and offered Margy her chair. When Margy took it, Carrie smiled—with some tension--and offered to bring something to eat. Margy nodded, and soon they all sat down to dinner with her.

After a while, Goldie telephoned Dan and, in a conversation that was more benign than difficult, said that he would arrive in the morning. Dan agreed, satisfying everyone, especially Carrie, and they went into the living room to have a night cap. Mac started a fire, the twins brought out a tray of glasses, brandy, and calvados. Drinking, they talked about local painters and galleries--and farming. Carrie played Gershwin on an old stand-up piano tucked under the stairwell. Margy listened to the talk and the music, glanced at the Appels and, thinking that her life might have been like theirs had she stayed in the Midwest, decided that the price would not have been worth it. Good as the rural life might be, Mac would never do anything important with his art, sculpting and painting clearly mere hobbies now. And Carrie's work--examples of which were all around the house--was direct and efficient enough, but certainly uninspired. How much of her limitation was environmental and how much a matter of talent, Margy could only guess.

189

But she knew that she herself would do little more in the same situation.

Exhausted, she drifted off in the middle of a conversation about a cider press that the Appels were about to buy, and nearly two hours later, around midnight, Goldie woke her so that they could go to bed. They were alone. Since they had not slept together here, there was an important decision to be made at the door to Margy's room.

"I'm sorry about going back," Goldie said, as he kissed her good-night, seeking her lips but only getting her cheek. "But remember, you don't have to go with me."

Margy laughed. "You don't understand jealousy, my friend—especially for a woman."

"What do you mean?"

"You know very well. Mac told me about you and Carrie. And last night--right next to my room! I thought I heard voices."

Goldie, his hands on her shoulders, dropped them to his side. His chin began to tremble. Slowly, tears filled his eyes, and she ran her fingers through his hair, kissing him— this time on the lips.

"Don't tease!" he said, turning away as she tried to hold him. "It didn't mean a thing. With Carrie it's not like it is with you."

"I'm not teasing, Goldie--I'm glad you were with her. It must have been nice. When the time is right for us, it will be nice too—I hope."

He gasped, pressing against her. His expression moved her, but she pushed him away and then down the hall. For a moment they heard footsteps in the hallway on the second floor and stopped. "It's nothing; it *was* nothing," Goldie whispered. "I promise you." Without a word of protest, he watched her turn out the lights and close the door.

For the next few hours, she listened to him in his separate room. Restless and wide awake, she tossed and turned through most of the night, thinking about what she would do when they got home. She slept very little, but was

190

happy to note there were no further sounds of footsteps coming from upstairs.

15.

A NEST AGAIN

Mac and Carrie glanced at one another by the door. Goldie, who had virtually stopped smoking since his arrival, searched his pockets for a cigarette, then decided to forget it. Margy stepped onto the porch, embracing Mac and telling him how much she appreciated his help. Carrie stood beside him, reluctant. Margy embraced her too, kissing her on the cheek and saying how much she had enjoyed helping milk the cows. Carrie laughed, but in her tight, reserved way still held something back.

"I'm sorry to have caused you and Mac trouble," she said. "At the moment we left Stoddard, I just wanted to get away."

Carrie nodded, her face still composed, and told Margy not to worry. "Things will be all right. I just don't like to lie."

Margy looked at her. "I don't either. Somehow, my life has worked out to make it necessary."

Carrie blinked. Margy saw a spark of protest flare in her deep blue eyes, but with a look at Goldie she put her arms around Carrie and wished her luck with the farm.

"Come again, whenever you want," Mac said, shaking Goldie's hand and stepping around a morning glory vine in order to go to the car. "There's room and, lord knows, Carrie can always use the help with the work around here--the little she gets from me."

"So long," said Goldie. "I'll be up again sometime this summer. I'd like to do some landscapes from the hills around here."

"Good idea. Around late July and early August, I start getting the itch to feel the brush again. We can help each other work."

Carrie nodded, and Goldie embraced the twins. With a last wave and a quiet honk at the dogs, they got into the car and drove away. Margy would remember Carrie's forlorn look as she laid her head on Mac's shoulder and then turned about as the car pulled away. "Nice people," she said. "But complicated. I hope we didn't twist their lives too much. Especially Mac."

"They can take it," Goldie said. "Mac's a rock. He can handle just about anything." He smiled at Margy and started down the switchback.

They stopped for gas just outside of Evergreen, following the Massachusetts Turnpike to Interstate 91 and going south until, by mid-morning, they had reached the smoke and brick skyline of East Stoddard. They had an eerie drive across town toward home. Margy felt ashamed and culpable, partly because of Carrie, but especially because of Everet and the Grays. Goldie seemed affected too. He drove nervously and kept his eyes rigidly ahead for fear of seeing someone he knew.

About eleven they arrived at Camels Back Drive and circled the neighborhood for signs of police. Nothing had changed. There were no signs of trouble, no evidence of Gray, Buford, or the police. The sprawling lawns and the stair-like split-level houses remained peaceful in appearance, yet, when they finally pulled into the driveway, Margy felt something gone wrong. Goldie left the car, started to his house and came back.

"What now?" she asked.

He shrugged, grinning. "No keys, remember?"

"Oh, hell."

"And Uncle Dan always locks the doors when he leaves."

"Come on in. You can stay with me until he gets home." She stepped out of the car and started toward the house, but Goldie shook his head.

"What's the matter?"

"I'd rather go down to the warehouse to get the keys."

Looking up at the vacant windows of her house, Margy frowned, curious to see the inside of it again. Everet had apparently gone to work after sending Kennedy to school, and through the windows the interior looked

193

absolutely lifeless. Normal, she supposed, but that very normalcy seemed to corroborate her sense of something gone wrong.

"Can you take me to the plant?" Goldie asked.

"All the way downtown?"

He shook his head. "Uncle Dan's building a new place. I bet he's at the construction site on the Stoddard marshes."

On the marshes, the land more or less washed away into the Sound. Arriving there, they saw no trees, just beach and sea water, with the elevated Thruway dominating the scene. Along the stretch of sand between the highway and the Sound, a series of low buildings looked newly erected. They crossed over the mouth of the Housatonic River, and, like a dune buggy for a while, followed a makeshift sand road for a quarter mile. They bumped along a rusty railroad track that had served East Stoddard and Stoddard during the 19th century, then, crossing it, threaded their way through piles of steel and brick beside the road. Margy would remember a roar, a sort of primeval belch of sound, beginning in the distance then swelling all round them. Trucks chugged back and forth along the sand, heaving loads of dirt and brick for masons, and great Caterpillar machines ate up marshland and grass, dumping the residue in one place or another as if it were animal droppings.

They circled the Caterpillars, arrived at a complex of buildings away from the tracks, and saw a newer, smaller building half-erected. Beside it stood one of Sam Goldstein's trucks, and behind the truck was a dumper unloading bricks.

Goldie left the car, running around the wall and talking to one of the workers. A steam shovel hissed, covering them with a drop of its shovel, but on its rise she saw Goldie nod, disappear behind the wall again, and emerge beyond a second pile of bricks. This time she saw him talking to his uncle.

Dan Goldstein seemed calm, almost friendly, although she could not be sure at that distance. Even so, when he suddenly waved one of his massive hands and pointed toward the car, Margy slid down and ducked beneath the dashboard. She sat up as another dumper crossed, dropping

194

a pile of sand and, for the moment of the dump, standing between Margy and her view of the Goldsteins. With a great screech it shifted the burden on its back, turned to the left, and again revealed them talking together. Dan raised his arm again, but only to gesture at one of the mason's brick-carrying helpers. He seemed to shout, piling more bricks onto the man's wheelbarrow. Then he pushed him along and complained to the mason before coming back to Goldie and, after a few seconds, handing him something from his pocket. He even embraced Goldie who, with a broad, embarrassed grin, disappeared within his uncle's arms, nodded several times, and trotted around the wall and back to the car.

"Oh, my Uncle Dan," he said, as he caught his breath. "He actually bawled out that guy because he could have carried two more bricks."

He jingled the keys in his hand.

"But I got these," he said, with a wry face. "And we're going to have a long talk later on. He actually seemed happy to see me."

Margy nodded, starting the engine, and, feeling guilty, asked if Dan had said anything about Everet or her.

"Nothing. He must be all right, Margy. Uncle Dan would have said something if he wasn't."

She sighed. "I hope you're right," she said and drove away from the site, following a slower, more scenic route back home. In the driveway, Goldie opened the car door and stepped onto the pavement. Swallowing, he started to leave. "I love you," he said, "no matter what happened up there. It'll be hard going back to what it was before."

She nodded. "It was a great two days. I hope something positive comes out of them for both of us."

Smiling, Goldie leaned into the car and, without looking for witnesses, kissed her lips. "There's something positive," he said.

She laughed, smacking her lips and nodding.

"I want you to know I think you're wonderful."

"Oh, Goldie... "

He held up his hand. "But you were right last night. I shouldn't have had Carrie in the room, especially with you

195

next door. And I shouldn't have put pressure on you. We have a special situation. I wouldn't want it spoiled for a moment or two of... "

He sighed, grinning broadly, and Margy turned away, sad for a moment. "What is it?" he said, touching her arm. She shook her head, but he took her shoulder and held it.

"Come on. No holding back," he said.

"Oh, I don't know, Goldie."

"Come on, say it."

"I want you too. I admit it. And, yes, I'm jealous—a little jealous, anyhow--of Carrie."

He blushed, laughing softly, and she suddenly felt like crying again. He merely looked at her, a sad smile creasing his rosy face.

"There is no one else I can talk to," she murmured, "or feel close to. At least about painting—and other things."

He touched her arm. "We're still free. There are still great possibilities for both of us."

"It's wonderful--" She could not go on.

"I hear a *but*," he said. "A big one. What does that mean?" He held Margy's shoulder now, and she looked away.

"*Special* is going to be difficult to keep, considering my house, my family, our town."

"We'll work it out. Okay?" Goldie stepped back, swallowing. Margy started to say something, but he stopped her by putting his finger to her lips.

"I can't think negatively right now, Margy. It would kill me. Things are too much up in the air."

"Go ahead--into the house," she said, finally. He waved, turning away quickly, and as he walked into the Goldstein yard, she circled her house on foot, entering through the back door.

16.

OLD LOVES

She felt a chill, a strangeness, upon entering that took her breath away. In the kitchen she felt choked, as if something poisonous were in the atmosphere. She closed the outside door, inhaling deeply once or twice, and went into the dining room where she found a letter that added to her sense of menace. The letter was from Everet: hand-written, neatly folded, and leaning against the sugar bowl in the center of the table. She glanced at it for a moment, but something made her turn away, and, with visions of dead bodies in every corner, she checked the downstairs rooms and then the bedrooms on the second floor. She went back to the dining room and sat at the table.

His handwriting--bold, clear, with an extreme slant to the right--raced in front of her, tripping over itself to reach an end. ("You are ambitious," a graphologist had told him once, "and impatient. You want to succeed in everything very quickly." He had practiced his handwriting ever since in order to maintain that same appearance.)

Her name was at the top of the letter, an initialed "E" at its bottom; hardly a satisfactory word of tenderness in between:
Margy:

I don't know what to say to you. I was shocked the other night; that you would abandon us this way, your son, me, your responsibility to an injured human being--and the Grays. I can excuse the violence. It was a burst of anger, and I did do something pretty nasty. But I can't excuse the running away, the forsaking of our child and home. I don't know what you're doing (I don't think you do either), but I do know that you'll probably come home soon--probably penitent, probably very humble--a chicken returning to its roost.

Buford has agreed to keep the whole thing quiet. Along with the Grays, he is committed to my election, and we will probably be able to use his services should I win the primary. Fred thinks some payoff will have to be made in the fall, but I find it hard to conceive of embarking on a public career while my private life is being held hostage. I respect myself and my constituency too much to allow that. I am thinking that I may not run.

I left Kennedy at my mother's, and I, of course, am about my work. I don't have time to worry about your safety or your life. From now on I intend to be selfish. Thus, I expect you'll take care of yourself and will not need me although I must admit I am deeply hurt that you left. I am deeply worried and also somewhat ashamed.

Dan Goldstein called--I told him that you were visiting friends and that I hadn't seen Goldie for a couple of days. (Yes, we know that you were with him.) And then that character, that wise-ass from Copperwood, Sherman Foster, telephoned. He wants to see you about your show, and he wants you to call him back.

You know you have always been free, and I sincerely hope that you do call him back. I hope you resolved something with Goldie, and I hope you start to work again. After this latest escapade, I also hope we can settle down to routine. I'll go to Wiltshire with you--when I think the time is right. For now, we've had too much upset in our lives, and I think it's time for us to fulfill ourselves and make a family unit for our son. We can do it, but only if we stop running, accept one another and begin to deal with who we are.

I don't know if that makes sense to you. I can see you standing at the table, laughing, ripping up the letter in that dramatic, angry manner you sometimes have; or I can see you sitting down and equally dramatically crying. Whichever it is, so be it. I hope you finish reading it, though, because what I want to say is that until we really listen to each other, until we really face each other *within the given limitations of our mutual life*, all the encounter groups in the world are so many mills for gossip, so many audiences for us to perform for, so many opportunities for us to escape ourselves. Sure we're unhappy. But you know, there's something beautiful in us too. Inside me there is someone who would like to chase that beauty, catch it, and hold onto it especially for ourselves. I love you. I wish you could say that, too.

At any rate, I want to deal with our problems, but I want to deal with them with you--alone. Then we can go to Wiltshire with a purpose.

Final note: we didn't send Kennedy to school today. He was too upset. I feel bad that he has to suffer through our troubles too.

E.

She dropped the letter on the table, stood up, then sat down and read it through again. So, he was all right--he had to be--but he had not been changed very much. That troublesome, two-sided love was typical of Everet--slapping her wrist with one hand, patting her on the shoulder with the other. "I love you," he could say; meanwhile, "I, of course, am about my work."

She felt a rush of pleasure at the beauty section, but without finishing the passage a second time, she crumpled up the letter and tossed it onto the table. "Oh, God," she cried. "I am so sick of this double life, this home, so sick of the neighborhood and our ordinary lives." She saw it all as based on unrealizable hopes, false, plastic-coated dreams, all falling apart as the rocks of the jetty had fallen apart in her vision the other day. Yet those hopes and dreams were precious too, and still that ambitious bastard would throw them away for a couple thousand votes. What kind of love and beauty was that?

She washed her face, changed her clothes, and then, lighting a cigarette, entered her attic studio. She gathered together some notebooks and paints, bringing them along with several changes of clothing down to the car. She felt angry. When she entered the dining room again, she began to think about her mother. She remembered her during an argument once breaking dishes, throwing vases, smashing a mirror above a sideboard, and then she realized that her mother might have done the same thing today--perhaps

199

because she would finally sense how little real value owned objects (including crystal platters) had.

Margy sat down and let that memory run through her head once more. The idea seemed plausible, but it changed a whole life's conception. It was as if the things Beverly Winters had owned (particularly crystal platters) did not harmonize with, in fact seemed to cancel out, the things she knew or had known; as if in an algebra equation both sides were true and unequal at the same time. And all because of family. Beverly had struggled with her own imbalance, seeking things, destroying them; wanting Emory, then hating him; loving Margy, then dismissing her. And in a house on Camels Back Drive nearly thirty years later, her daughter tried not to be like her mother at the same time she tried not to dislike her mother for what had been.

Margy wanted to talk, but she felt she could not call Goldie, and she certainly did not want to speak to Everet. Inwardly, she struggled. She might have wrecked his office and laughed, torn apart the house with all its accumulated bric-a-brac and felt no shame, but she simply could not permit herself that kind of excess. In a final, quiet gesture, she did absolutely nothing--broke nothing, scrawled nothing on the walls or windowpanes--and, like an animal running from the butcher's knife, slipped out the door, closing it against all those dangerous, pointed things.

She trembled upon entering the car, and after fifteen minutes of absolute blankness, thought of driving into the garage, closing the door, and leaving the engine running. She conceived of it as resting, "sleeping it off," as if her life had become a simple hangover. But even at that moment, with those thoughts, she could not do it. Finally, she drove away, stopped at a street phone somewhere in Stoddard, and called Foss in order to ask him if she could visit. He was surprised but happy to hear from her and, after asking about her frame of mind, told Margy to come over right away. Taking some back roads to Westport, she threaded her way through a cool mid-day light that turned the blacktop green as it curved beneath the leaves of boxwoods and maple trees. When she followed the drive up the hill to Foss's place, arriving finally at the parking space beside his cottage, she found him lying on a net hammock strung between two pines. He held a drink in his hand, a sketch pad in his lap, but no charcoal or pencil. He waved airily when she pulled up, but he soon reacted purposefully. Margy thought it was because she stumbled as she left the car, hanging on to the door for a moment before standing straight and walking unsteadily toward him on the pebbly ground. Immediately, he squirmed out of the hammock, dropping the sketch pad, cigarettes, and matches.

"Are you all right?" He ran up to her, uncharacteristically embracing her and kissing her warmly on the forehead.

"I'm fine. Leave me alone."

He embraced her again, and, as if struck in the face, Margy began to cry. "Come on. Come on inside," he said, tightening his hold when she tried to pull away. Together they stumbled through the open door to his cottage, nearly collapsing when Margy felt her legs turn to rubber.

"What's up, Margy? I thought you sounded strange on the phone."

They tottered to the couch with his arm around her waist; then he let her fall into it. "What am I doing, Foss? Why am I here?"

He sank into the sofa beside her. She buried her face in his shoulder and suddenly felt her whole body go weak. A wail of despair burst from her throat; she could not understand why. She tried to speak, pronounce individual words but could not.

"Whoa!--Relax. Take it easy." Foss trotted to a liquor table in the corner.

His hands were a blur above the table. All thumbs, elbows and feet, he moved in different directions as he found a glass, searched for ice, poured some scotch, went back to the bucket for ice, and added a splash of water. Juggling his drink (on the rocks) and Margy's (with a splash of water) together with, for some strange reason, an unopened can of peanuts, he returned to the sofa and collapsed into it.

"Hey, take it easy. Easy, I said."

She gasped, shaking, yet like a child observed her broken grown-up self. She began to feel silly, and, when Foss dropped the can of peanuts to the floor clutching her glass while almost losing his own, Margy burst out laughing. He patted her back, asking repeatedly if she had had an argument with "the Mayor."

"Stop! Stop that! It isn't funny anymore, Foss!"

Yet she giggled, choking as she did, and, when she pushed him away, she began to sob again. He leaned awkwardly over her, holding her head back, and started to pour whiskey, slowly, down her throat.

"I don't want any. I don't *want* any, goddamn it!"

She saw his swollen face, his tired, red eyes, the reddish-purple lines around his nose and mouth. He fell onto the couch again, and, when he gulped another drink, Margy felt ashamed that she had come to him.

"What a pair of incompetents!" she cried, remembering that she had said practically the same thing to Goldie. "We're both sick!"

He looked at her, placing his hand on hers, and with a dour face said, "Margy, I'm sorry you feel bad."

"I don't feel bad. I feel terrible."

"I'm sorry you feel terrible then."

Foss nodded. Margy turned away. Noting the edge in his voice, she was not at all surprised when she felt his hand slide over her hip and begin to fish between her knees.

"Hey! Get out of there, you... bastard!"

Hands to her face, she left the sofa and, in a coughing fit, tried to compose herself as Foss returned to the liquor table. Leaning against the wall, he stared, blank but seemingly comprehending. Margy took a handkerchief from her pocket and, thinking that she ought to leave, wiped her mouth.

"Two of a kind, Foss. Right?"

"Two of a kind, Margy. That's us."

"And fucking is the salve that takes away the mutual pain."

He nodded, raising his glass as if in a toast. "To the good, rousing mutual mess of our massage."

202

"But it's no fun for me, you bastard. What do you do for my pain?"

He stopped, nodding. "I've done plenty for you in my time, and you know it."

Margy laughed. "For free, Foss?"

He grinned--leered really--raising his glass and saying, "To that mutual massage."

He crossed the room, slid his hand onto her breast, and sighed.

"I have to leave," Margy said.

"Wait."

She clutched her bag, pulling away from him. Later, she supposed that this was where her passivity--her fear of life, she sometimes called it--betrayed her, because, despite the need to be overpowering, she could not muster strength or courage. She felt cowardly. She did not hate him enough, even as she walked to the door and he insolently stood in front of it.

"Come on, Margy, sit down. You can't drive." He patted her hand, led her to the couch, and pushed her down, saying that she could not be trusted by herself. She could not resist him. After a few weak attempts to stand on her feet, Margy settled back when he offered another glass of scotch.

"Did I drink the other one already?" she asked.

"Yes. Here, take this one."

She reached for the glass, but things had gone so hazy that she could not find it. He shoved it into her hand, and she drained it immediately. She chugged another, choked, and during her coughing, Foss seemed to slip away. Laughing, he came back, and instead of quieting herself, Margy continued to joke, as if it were a game.

"You look charming," she murmured, her head lolling back as she stared past the rim of her glass.

She took his hand. He kissed her, falling on his knees and grinning.

"Prince Charming," she murmured. "My lovely, drunken Prince Charming."

"May I claim the honor of my dear lady's hand?"

203

She saw the lines around his nose, like the decaying red lines of a dying leaf, looked at the skinny legs and the flabby, withered muscles of his arms. She could not resist a nasty remark.

"Take anything you like, my lord, but not mine honor. I doubt that you can make the mount."

He stood, stumbling as she spoke, then fell to his knees again with a shocked, pained expression. His face changed immediately, and when she put her hand to her cheek, she began to understand why. It was not her words, at least not totally; it had to be her face. Her palm and fingers came away glistening, completely soaked.

"Tears, Foss? Are these real tears?"

He nodded, burying his face in her lap.

"No! Get away from me!"

She pushed his head away, but he took her hand, squeezed it, and at the same time her whole body seemed to empty itself of liquid: pouring off her forehead and her chin. She could feel it running down her arms and legs, between the cheeks of her buttocks. It was as if she had fallen into a pool and was just emerging into the air.

Muttering disjointedly, Foss led her across the room, pushed her onto a bed behind a screen of easels, and feebly wiped her forehead with the end of a soiled pillow case.

"I think I've pissed my pants, Foss. I think I've actually pissed my pants. Jesus!"

He looked concerned, tender. He shushed her with his finger, and then, grinning, went to get another whiskey. Fumbling with bottles and glasses on the table, he lit a cigarette. The match exploded. Its huge flame seemed to streak, then blacken the whole room as he blew it out and dropped it to the floor. Rubbing his fingers to cool them, he lit his cigarette with another match and, when he came back to the bed, he reached for Margy's jeans and started to pull them down.

"No, don't!"

"Come on, Margy. You're going to catch a cold."

She pushed him away. Smiling, but sighing at the same time, he leaned against an easel.

"You better get out of those things soon. You're going to catch a bad chill—and stink."

She shook her head.

"Go into the bathroom at least. You've got to get dry."

He took a blanket from the footlocker in the corner and tossed it to her. She kicked it to the floor, lying back and opening the top of her jeans.

"Hey! What are you doing?"

"I can be gross too, Foss! The same as you; the same as John Buford! Come on, let's see what you can do."

She laughed, humping up her pelvis and pulling down the top of her jeans in order to flash her underwear. He leered, cocking his hand behind his ear, and for some reason Margy laughed so hard that she could hardly speak. The laughter tipped her balance. She began to lose control completely. Laughing harder, so much that she lost her breath, she would remember very little of the next few minutes. She remembered rising, waddling across the room with her jeans around her knees, gasping for air, and then, without a misstep, collapsing suddenly to the floor, laughing the whole time. She felt degraded. She did not lose consciousness, but, as she regained her breath, everything seemed to happen strangely, menacingly, as if in the shifting images of a nightmare.

She knew she was with Foss, but it was John Buford, not Foss, who leaned over and asked if she needed help. Buford took her hand, lifted her up and placed her, jeans and feet dragging across the room, gently on the bed again. And then it was Everet who went to the liquor table, opened a bottle and fixed her a drink; yes, Everet who took his own clothes off, slowly, and then, white and hairy instead of black and smooth, returned to the bed, looking a lot like her father, then Goldie, and at times, even Goldie's Uncle Dan. "Gentle," he whispered, as he sat beside her and brought the whiskey to her lips.

She drank, kissing him. They watched smoke rise gently from the stroke of white and gray that formed her cigarette.

"Grass?" she asked. He nodded.

205

"You never broke training like this before," she said.

"Jelly roll," Everet replied. But it was Foss, not Everet, nor Goldie or his Uncle Dan, who took the joint from her fingers and twirled it, smoldering, in the fading afternoon light. When he looked at her tenderly, she embraced him, and he kissed her graying hair back from her pale forehead.

She felt his fingers, pink and loving against her gentle skin. She heard his voice, deep and soft as he murmured in her ear. When the wet clothes rolled off her body, she put her arms around his neck, caressed his thin but muscle-rippled back, pulled his balding head to rest upon her breast.

"Gently, gently," she whispered. Gently was the way they kissed. Gently was the way he touched her breast.

Gently was the way she let him disappear...

***

She was a large head, a balloon, until something pricked her suddenly, emptying her down to size.

"Wake up, Margy! Hello; wake up!"

She did not have to fight back to consciousness this afternoon. She felt a slap and saw a man above her. Not her father. Not Everet. Not Goldie or Fred Gray. Foss, clothed in denim shorts and shirt hanging loosely on his gaunt frame, slapped her yet again, and she pushed him away as she turned over on the bed. Light glared through the window, forcing her to cover her eyes.

"Leave me alone."

She buried her head in a pillow, sank down into a gray, gloomy mist that seemed a part of her body's inner weather, then turned over and looked at the clock.

"Four o'clock. Time to get up."

He slapped her again, and she moaned. Her head felt terrible. If he had hit her harder, the gray matter of her brain would have exploded like the feathers of a pillow to the opposite side of her skull. Gloom rolled over her, like fog, though the afternoon light seemed to counter her sense of doom.

"Here. Take this. It should help."

206

Foss handed her a cup, lit a cigarette, and stuck it between her lips. She pushed the cigarette away. He sat beside her, and, as she sipped what turned out to be coffee, she was surprised to find that all her clothes smelled fresh and dry.

"When did you put these on me?"

He shook his head.

"What do you mean?"

"You never took them off."

He looked at her and winked.

"Come on, Foss."

"That was quite a little sleep you had," he said. "You must have had some very sexy dreams."

She stared at him, trying to read the expression on his face. "Didn't we... Didn't we...?"

He waved. "Of course we did."

Laughing, he winked again, draping his arm around her shoulders and shaking her.

"You're good, Margy. You really have what it takes."

She pulled away, sliding to the other side of the mattress. "Did you... Did you make love to me, Foss?"

Her head felt muddled. She looked at the room through what seemed like a smeared, gray lens. It blocked out everything in middle distance, yet as if someone from far off were staring at her, the light from the window assaulted her eyes. Foss raised his glass, and when she saw him guzzle the whiskey, the thought of having been to bed with him again filled her with disgust.

"Did I pee in my pants earlier?" she asked. The event still seemed vivid.

He nodded, pointing to her underwear on the floor beside the bed. "You have clean stuff on. I brought it in from the car."

"Thanks." Then she looked at him and asked, "Are you kidding me?"

"About what?"

"About... about making love."

He shook his head, but the blush and grin of pleasure on his face made her wonder.

207

"Are you sure?"

"Margy," he said testily, "if it's that hard to remember, why bother to ask?"

"You're a bastard, that's why."

He shrugged, turning to the window and gazing at the sunset. Two hills came together in the distance, and at this time of day the sun had the look of a shining red ball ready to roll down one hill and up the other. Rising, she stumbled past Foss and stood at the kitchen sink. Full of brushes and paint, it stank of oils--linseed, turpentine and others. Nearly throwing up, she crossed to the bathroom in the back and, after closing the door, washed her pasty, bewildered face. She tried to clear her head, tried to remember the reality of the afternoon. Her pelvic muscles hurt terribly, her body smelled sour, as it often did after sex, but she wondered if the soreness was just her period coming on.

She stripped completely, bathed at the sink, then dressed again, combing her hair and washing her face. After returning to the living room, she sat on the couch, and, when she saw Foss coming toward her, she understood what had happened. Knew it. Assured, complacent, he looked as though he had something on her. In a moment she remembered his face over her, his tears, or sweat, something disgusting washing off her forehead, and then his body, weak and spent, rolling away.

"You all right now?" he asked, reclining beside her.

She nodded; then she went to make a drink and tried to remember more. As she reached for the ice bucket, he came up behind her, embraced her, and pulled her away.

"Not now. You don't want any of that."

"Why not?"

"You can't handle it. You have to drive."

He patted her shoulder, telling her to sit down. "You have to drive back to Stoddard, don't forget."

"Since when have you started worrying about my safety, Foss?"

"Come on, put that liquor down."

She stared at him, puzzled. She saw an expression of genuine concern on his face now, and for a moment that put her off guard.

"I'll make a drink for you, nice and light. You had quite a bit this afternoon."

She stood at the table thinking, and he stepped in front of her, edging her toward the couch with his hip as he reached for the seltzer bottle. His actions puzzled Margy at first, but as Foss turned he knocked over a small, brown bottle next to the whiskey. It rolled off the table, and, when she picked it up, he slapped it from her hand.

"Hey!" In a scramble of arms and legs, she reached the bottle before he did and at that moment remembered him fumbling around the table earlier while she lay in bed. "Did you?--Oh, no, Foss! Did you put something in my drink?"

He grabbed for the bottle, grappling with her fingers, but she hid it behind her back. Turning to the window, she read the label in the light.

"You idiot! You're sick!"

"Now, Margy... "

He edged away from the table, nervously holding his hands before his chest as he came toward her.

"No wonder I was... Jesus, Foss, you could have poisoned me."

He shook his head.

"That stuff won't hurt--"

She ran into the bathroom, locking the door behind her this time. She felt nauseated, but the feeling went away immediately. Her eyes looked dull earlier, but as she stared into the mirror, she was surprised to see them brighter now. Her complexion was also clear, and she felt pretty much in control of her arms and legs. She flushed the pills down the toilet, and, when she returned to the living room, she threw the empty bottle at Foss's feet.

"What's your next trip, Foss? Gang rape?"

He waved his hand, saying she was exaggerating the strength of the drug. "I wanted to calm you down. You were pretty upset earlier. Remember?"

209

"How much did you give me?"

He flushed, turning away.

"A celebrated artist. Maybe getting a Guggenheim next year. I should be angry, Foss, but, you know, I pity you instead. It's the last resort of an impotent man."

He picked up the bottle and hurled it at her head. She ducked.

"Fuck you, bitch. If you don't like it, you can go fuck yourself. You had a good time too, you know."

"That's right--the earth moved; I think I heard bells ringing."

"Yeah--you liked it!"

"Foss, to tell you the truth, I didn't even feel it. I was in another world."

He drained his glass and smashed it on the floor, but, when she went to the bed for her bag, he dropped to his knees and from the middle of the room whispered her name.

"Margy... please, stay with me. I need you."

"I can't, Foss."

"I mean it."

But he was mocking now. She saw it, and, when she crossed the room, she found the energy that she had lacked earlier and slapped his face. He fell to the floor--giggling. He crawled after her toward the door and, as she stood and gasped, lay at her feet. Despite the laughter, he breathed heavily, and he had such an expression of hatred in his eyes that, when Margy turned to look at him, she had to back off.

"Foss, don't do this. Get up, please?"

"I love you; I want to can you, Margy. I want to stick it in your ear."

"Foss, you're making me sick."

He kissed her toes, her ankles, embraced her knees and thighs. He looked up at her, pathetically. She saw tears--real tears, no laughter behind them--rolling down his cheeks.

"Please, Margy. I need you. Just a little--just a little bit--"

She trembled, almost embracing him. Pawing at her knees, he giggled shrilly and slid to the floor. He kissed her shoes again, licked them, taking the buckle between his teeth and sobbing. Margy had to pry his hands from behind her ankles. When she tried to lift him, his mouth opened into a high-pitched wail that took her breath away. She choked. He laughed ghoulishly when she knelt beside him, shrieked when she embraced him, and then lowered his forehead to the floor when she pushed him away.

"Get up! Get up, I said. Get up!" She stood above him, tugging at his arms and shoulders. She pulled at his fingers, tried to get his arms from around her waist. He was like an octopus, and suddenly she was on her back, he on top of her, pulling the shirt from her jeans, holding her down with the other hand, somewhere, somehow, unzipping his fly with the other.

"No, please. No!"

She screamed, putting her hands onto his face and shoving him away. He rolled off weakly, and quickly she rose to her feet. He crawled to the liquor table where, reaching for a glass, he accidently tipped a bottle over. It was uncapped, and the whiskey poured onto the floor.

"Margy," he called. "I need you. I need you for my work."

"I'm going, Foss. I can't let you do this."

He considered her a moment, eyes apparently clear and sane, then lowered his head and licked the whiskey from the carpet. There was no laughter, no sarcasm. It was a studied, careful effort to shame himself—and perhaps, she thought, her too.

"Foss, don't... Please."

"You want to eat me. You want to bite off my cock. All of you want to take my guts and suck them out. Well, I'm not going to let that happen. Go home to your kid, to the mayor. Go get your fucking nourishment from them."

He buried his face in his hands. Hesitating at the door, Margy found herself wanting to ask his forgiveness. When he looked at her, she saw that his eyes had become blurred again, and she knew she could not talk to him.

"Good-bye, Foss. I can't stay with you anymore."

She heard him wailing as she stepped outside, heard him even as she stood for a moment in the yard. Although she felt like returning to offer help, she turned toward the car.

"His misery is NOT MY FAULT!" she shouted. "Remember that!"

She started the engine, drowning out the noise of all his crying, then pulled away with a burst of tire-thrown pebbles against the house.

17.

HOME AGAIN

It was darker now. The sun setting behind her turned the Sound and the buildings along it a rusty mauve. She drove toward the Thruway and, impatient, stopped at a booth to telephone Goldie. There was no answer, and, when she called home, she received no answer there either. She followed the Thruway toward Stoddard, took the ramp to Fairfield on a whim, and followed Route 1 through downtown. She had no plan, but she was restless and wanted someplace to go. She stopped in a fabric shop, bought some muslin, and, although she had not sewn for more than a year, selected a pattern for a dress. From the store she called Goldie again, received no answer, and the same happened when she called her house.

Six o'clock. Kennedy must have been at Ruth's; Everet must have been working late. She returned to the car, took the Thruway up to Bridgeport and drove out of the downtown area to the Hamiltons' home. It was in an old neighborhood--exclusively Italian until the Hamiltons moved in. A trellised field of grapevines grew beside the house, and on the street a group of boys and girls played hopscotch in the lamplight. She saw no ballplayers, no bats or balls, no football being lofted along the telephone wires. It was dark by this time, but even in that light she knew that Kennedy normally would be playing. It was quite probable, she figured, that he was not in Bridgeport. The Hamilton house was dark, with no doors or windows open, even though it was still warm out. Not wanting to risk embarrassment, she left without ringing the doorbell.

In downtown Bridgeport again, she parked near the university campus and walked down to the beach. It was quiet there as always although she saw several groups of people in the middle of early season cookouts, the burnt smell of the meat sickening her as she approached the water. Margy felt lonesome yet realized that if anyone but

213

Goldie were there, she would not be able to talk without screaming. She looked at the horizon, threw down her cigarette and stamped it out, returning to the car and driving along Route 1 through Stratford, Stoddard, and Shelton. Then she turned back and took the back roads to Westport again. Once or twice she pulled over to the side of the road and tried to clear the fog in her head. At one point she almost returned to Foss's house, but she stopped when she realized what she might have to do if she saw him again.

The sky grew darker now, adding a twilight grimness to the air that seemed to match her mood. On impulse, she stopped at a roadside phone, but when she called Goldie's number, his uncle answered and she hung up. Still no answer at home, and none at Ruth Hamilton's either. Desperate, she called Everet's office, where she had some luck--although luck is not what she would have called it.

A young woman answered. Then around a murmur of "One minute, Mrs. H," Margy heard her speak over a muffled phone. There was a giggle, a click, then humming silence during which she was certain she had been cut off. Finally, the woman's voice returned, purring with the information that, "Mr. H is on an important call."

"Would you like to wait?" she asked. "Or should I have him call you back?"

"I'm at a pay phone," Margy said. "But I'll wait."

She sat in the car, lighting a cigarette and fidgeting as she timed him. When the Bell operator came on she added another dime, and Everet came on just as that one ran out. She told him that he would have to call her back.

"Where are you?"

"A phone booth."

She gave him the number over the operator's annoying warning clicks and worried that he would not dial it. When the phone rang she immediately picked it up.

"Where is that phone booth, Margy? Stoddard?"

"On the Thruway, in Westport--Where's Kennedy? He's not home or at your mother's."

"I'll take care of him. Don't worry. I'm not going to let you take him away."

214

"Everet, don't!" But his voice broke over hers in an enraged howl:

"Don't give ME any *don'ts*! Don't give me ANY ultimatums!"

"I never--"

"Piss on it! You make me sick."

She hung up and in the silence found herself wanting to drive away. On the other hand she kept thinking her life was at stake, and when the phone rang she picked it up.

"Everet, please. I called to talk, not to argue."

"Call somebody else then. You'll run from me anyhow."

"Everet--"

"Piss on it, I said! Goddamn fuzzy confrontation weekends, art, artists, and your career. Piss on it all!"

"Listen, if you're going to continue ..."

"If you ever gave me a chance, gave *me* a chance, Margy, instead of worrying so much about yourself and your fartsy artsy friends, we could have made a go of it a long time ago. As it is, I feel nothing but contempt for you all."

"Stop! Stop it, I said!"

But she stopped herself, trembling, ready to hang up again, fighting to hold the telephone to her ear. She felt it happening again, the paralysis. Even with Foss the guilt had almost turned back on her.

"Are you there!" he asked. She said nothing. "Oh, for Christ's sake, Margy, are you there?"

"I--I'm here." In the reflection of the phone booth's glass, an alien face seemed to loom before her. It was her mother's, and the only response she felt inside was silence.

"Oh, come on. If you want to talk to me, talk. I'm a busy man. I'm down here late because I have things to do."

"Everet, why?" She could not raise her voice above a whisper. Because as light played on the image in front of her, it seemed to contort her features into a terrifying scowl.

"What? What did you say? Goddamn it, Margy—"

"I said I didn't know you hated me so much, Everet. I didn't know you were so ignorant of my feelings."

"Margy, I am not ignorant, and I do not hate you."

215

"You certainly sound like you do."

"Listen, I love you. I don't want you to play this guilty shit on me."

"Who's trying to make you guilty? If you could listen to yourself, if you could hear the tone of your voice..."

"To hell with my tone of voice! Listen to *what* I say. How about your own snotty way of talking most of the time?"

Tears came to her eyes. She turned away from the image in the glass and looked at the traffic passing in the opposite direction.

"Well, are you there?"

She was silent. Enraged.

"Well, say something, Margy."

"It's about time we faced it, Everet. You can't stand me. You regret the day we married."

She stopped, listening, absent-mindedly reading the exit sign across the highway as cars whizzed by. In a calculating manner, Everet broke in: "You're saying that, you know--the regret part. Not me."

"But it's in your voice. It's in your letter. It's in the way you treat me."

She would not look back at the face before her. It occurred to her that, in fact, she was loathing herself.

"It's not in my voice, or that letter! Now you're pulling something, Margy. You must feel this hatred yourself, and you're trying to shift it on to me. Do you know why?"

"No. Tell me, since you know all about emotions."

"Oh, Jesus, you're trying to make me the fucking scapegoat. You hate yourself—*yourself*—and you're trying to blame that hate on me. The fucking black boogie man!"

"Oh, wonderful! Put in a dime and dial a pop psychologist. What else have you got to say to me, Uncle Remus?"

He was silent. She could almost feel the anger coming at her through the phone. Then he said, very quietly, "Honey, you're a coward. You can't handle life, our life—or you have trouble with it--and you ought to begin to understand that right now."

"I do understand it. How could I not? But the fear doesn't come from my light skin, Siggy. It's from your office, with those pictures and awards, and that lovely pickaninny secretary. You can't stand my guts, and you wish I'd never become your wife."

She stopped, frozen, too paralyzed even to cry out because, to her surprise, Everet still talked on the other end. It was as if he had not been interrupted. As if he had not heard her words at all.

"... We have to understand each other, baby. We have to know each other too. But we have to do it in our daily lives, not on weekends in the country."

He stopped, hearing nothing, and then filled the silence. "Hey, Margy. Are you still there?"

She moved, at least enough to take out a match and strike it, lighting a cigarette that was dangling and--without her knowing it--trembling from her lips.

"Well, are you there? Are you going to keep me in suspense?" But he was being ironic, playful, and the only thing she could do was throw it back.

"I'm here. I've made enough noise already, haven't I? Maybe too much for you."

"Not enough right now," he said.

"What was that you said once about a quiet, respectable family life?"

He chuckled, relaxing a little. She puffed her cigarette and blew smoke into the phone, grinning. She imagined him, handsome, feet on the desk, white shirt against the brown leather executive's chair. Then she imagined him leaning forward to listen to her breath.

"Hey, what's going on there? What's that sound?"

"I'm smoking, Uncle Sigmund Freud. If we were together now, you'd throw open the windows or stomp out of the room!"

"Bullshit, Margy!"

"Oh, Everet, you're blind! You're trying to make me lead your kind of Mr. Clean life, and lately you make me very tired."

217

She almost hung up then, but a glance in the glass showed that face again, and she did not want to be alone with it. She switched the receiver to her other ear.

"I have to work, Margy. I have things to get done-- tonight."

"Good. That's what I thought. Just keep on working."

"Can we talk another time?"

"Why not? When there's nothing important going on."

"I hear that, Margy. I hear what you're saying. But it's true. There are things I just have to get done tonight."

"You always have things that have to get done."

"This is particularly important," he said, peevish.

"Fine." She could be peevish too, she thought. "Are you going to be home eventually--with the little wife and quiet family?"

"I'm going to have dinner at my mother's. If you want, I'll bring Kennedy home right after that."

"Why can't we get together now?"

"I don't know."

"Because I want to; isn't that it?"

"Oh, hell. If that's all--"

"Isn't that it?"

"Suit yourself, Margy. Suit yourself. All I have to say is that we don't really need you. So... "

"So you don't give a shit what I do." She was tired, a little desperate. After a deep sigh, she looked into the glass and, seeing more of herself than her mother now, murmured, "Oh, Everet, tell me, were you ever going to Wiltshire with me, really?"

"Margy, what I wrote in that letter is true. I think we have to do it all ourselves."

She took a deep breath and sighed again.

"You never did try to save that date, did you?"

Now he was silent.

"Well, did you?"

"What do you think?"

"No." He said nothing. "Well, then I'm justified in everything I've done. Good-bye, Everet."

218

She smiled to herself in the glass, but to her surprise, the phone clicked on the other end before she hung up.

She entered the Thruway again and, furious, drove toward home in order to pick up some equipment. She called Goldie from her attic room, but his uncle answered again, and, when she looked out, she saw that the second floor bedroom light was out. She gathered notebooks, a couple of sketchbooks and clothes, threw them into the car and, without leaving an explanation, took off again. Her first idea was to go to Massachusetts--either to the Institute or the Appels--but it was too dark for a long ride. Besides, she did not feel like talking. She took the Thruway, got off in the center of Stratford, and drove through it to the marshes and the Dan Goldstein construction site. The shovels were silent, the trucks still, the sound of the water and highway echoed over the empty, flattened dunes. Down the road she saw a small motel, The Caliban, overlooking the Stratford beach, and, since she felt like being near the water, she decided to take a room and stay the night. She would call Goldie in the morning. Perhaps she could convince him to return to Massachusetts with her--or just to live together somewhere for a while. After checking in, she carried her bags to the room. It was on the second floor, with a beautiful view from a hill overlooking the beach and some private houses. The sky was completely dark, and she watched the water reflect a purple sheen. She went downstairs, walked on the beach, and watched the whitecaps breaking against the shore. Then she went to a diner for some supper.

She had not eaten all day, and the food she consumed that night actually moved her emotionally, bringing a mixture of sorrow and relief that broke through in tears just as she was putting a forkful of salad and tuna in her mouth.

Fighting for control, she finished the meal in silence, paid her bill, and in an attempt to treat herself well, decided to go to a movie at the only movie theatre in Stratford. It showed a suburban farce, the kind that she scrupulously avoided on TV, and by the time Mom and Dad had solved their third cute problem with their two cute, lively kids, she

219

left the theatre. But she felt better, simply for having gone somewhere, and it occurred to her that maybe something positive *had* happened in Massachusetts. She was beginning to feel that she could care for something--more important, that she could really matter again, to herself.

In the motel room she took off her clothes, smoked a cigarette, and tried to understand these new, optimistic sensations. Curious that an emotional change could occur without her awareness of its process. She felt an old motion inside; it arrived as a current, a strong rush of life and time sweeping her onward, outward even--toward something positive. She could ride with it, but she also saw herself as strong enough to swim against it, should that rush turn out to be a false sensation.

Wrapped in a blanket, she sat on her room's balcony and looked at the Sound. She thought of her old friend, of Brenda, and understood at that moment why she, Margy, had needed to come here. Extending from this portion of the beach she saw the same jetty Brenda had fallen from. She wrapped the blanket tighter around her shoulders as she remembered. This is the present, she told herself. There is the water, but here is the notebook in which I will be drawing and writing. I ran away often as a little girl. In certain ways I have been running ever since.

Margy went inside, put on her clothes, sat at the lamplit desk, and began to write instead of sketch. Words poured out of her pen. When lightning flashed outside at one point, she looked up in alarm and saw water coating the window in front of her. It made a stippled mirror for the room and her. The sponges, seaweed, and fish painted on the walls floated behind her head. A shark seemed to plummet from the left, above her, near the ceiling. Almost thirty years before, she had run away, and her father had brought her home. Ten years before, she had run away again, and another man brought her home. Signs, she thought, not necessarily the clearest. When she ran away this time, with Goldie, she did it because she had begun to take her own acts seriously.

Yes, something *had* happened ...

220

"For the first time in my life," she wrote, "I believed that my actions mattered, and I ran away."

As she put those words down, she glanced up at the window. The shark balanced above her. The sponges clung to each other without a millimeter of shift. Fish and seaweed circled her head in a guilloche of movement that seemed to isolate her face at the same time it made her a part of its watery design. Both artist and object, she closed the curtain and returned to her desk, continuing to write—and sketch-- as she felt herself go whole.

III.

PARIS: 1964

18.

LEAVING

"You will be good. God bless you." When her father, reborn Christian and banker that he was, offered Margy a trip to Europe before her senior college year, he offered it in a tour, a Christian Youth Fellowship tour, with chaperones, clergy, and visits to church in a pre-established itinerary.

"But I want to go for art. How will I meet artists? How will I get to their studios?"

"Boys. Boys. That's all you're interested in. I'm glad you're going away."

Her father took his hand from Margy's forehead and placed it on Beverly Winters' shoulders. Thin, with the arched nose and boney eye-sockets of an anorexic adolescent, she glared at Margy as if to counteract the blessing her husband had just given.

"God needs to give His blessing to the likes of you," she said.

Years later, her mother's voice would still cackle in Margy's dreams, and when it did, it had the same quality as on that day. In front of the globe in the waiting room of the Cedar Rapids Airport, her face loomed close to Margy's, covering the model world as it spun around, and her mother's voice rose above the whine of the plane outside: vindictive, hateful. Except for a shadowy kind of insight now and then, Margy had never been able to see why her mother acted that way.

"Thank you, Mother," she said. "I love you, too."

She carried an overnight bag in her hand, a ticket in her pocket, and in her eye the image of the leader of their group as he motioned to line up at the gate. On the runway stood a giant TWA jet, its red and white colors glinting in the sun, its hoses and ladders sticking out like so many intestines. A monster catching her at last, it would swallow her up, drop her in Chicago, then pick her up again to leave the continent and spit her out an ocean away.

223

"Good-bye, Margy honey. We'll miss you."

Her father bent over, smiling whimsically as he kissed her cheek. When he straightened, she saw a tear roll from his eye.

"Bye. Thanks for everything," she said to him. "And thank *you* for nothing."

She glanced at her mother, but did not offer to kiss her. As she went through the gate to the plane, she thought she would never see either of them again. She would miss her father. In a strange, hopeless way, she would miss her mother too. But good riddance in spite of that; she did not wave, and when she walked onto the plane, she did not even bother to look back.

19.

LANDING

Margy ducked when the cab passed her tour leader waving his hand. The taxi rushed out of the airport and onto the highway, hurtling in and out of traffic lanes toward the city. She settled back in her seat, watched, and waited.

She saw apartment buildings, huge cranes above them, setting up the steel skeletons of many more. And no flowers, just great blossoms of concrete, a stone horizon moving closer and closer to the road, like a sculptured jungle engulfing everything around. They came to an entrance ramp and crept for twenty minutes past a wrecker picking up bits of glass and chrome that littered the site of an accident. A truck lay on its side; two cars, crushed nose to nose on a dividing island, stopped traffic in both directions; a blue wagon, "Ambulance" printed on its snout, was parked across two lanes, three bodies covered with blankets lying beside it. A woman sat weeping on a curb while a young boy, thumb in his mouth, leaned against a crumpled fender. Margy had to turn her eyes as the cab rolled past.

The cars looked like little sinister toys, and her driver, handling the cab with the carefree aplomb of a boy smashing his Christmas truck against a wall, must have thought the same. Past the accident, resuming normal, hurtling speed, he swerved into the third lane, switched back into the second, then cut into the third again--all with a rush and a juggle of arms that had her lurching from side to side--and broke into an open stretch like a colt loping through heather fields, until more high risers shrank them down to metal again. She waited for signs--gentility, grace, culture, aesthetic promise-- it was Paris after all; and slowly high risers gave over to shorter, squatter buildings black with soot and filigreed in typical Le Notre rococo style.

"C'est Paris, Mademoiselle. C'est Paris."

She saw an el, a *carrefour*, and beyond some buildings a large parking lot that looked like an American

225

shopping center. And beyond that she caught a glimpse of water. The Seine? Beret on head, cigarette dangling from his mouth as though in a Godard movie, the driver turned off the highway, burst onto a boulevard, passed through several miles of markets and small boutiques, circled a marble lion, then screeched to a halt at a red light and glanced into his rear-view mirror. He muttered something, and she, not understanding, vaguely nodded her head. He said something again, pointing to the street, and she looked out the window to see where they were.

"Paris, Mademoiselle. Paris."

A waiter swept the pavement in front of a small cafe, an old woman hobbled by with a basketful of bread. Quaint, she thought, like something from Utrillo. But the woman looked at her and, as if to spite the painterly reference, leaned over the curb and blew snot out of both her nostrils.

"Où allez-vous exactement, Mademoiselle? Où allez-vous?"

She turned to the driver, realizing that he had been speaking for quite some time. His giant Gallic lip thrust out as if it were a second tongue; his eyes bulged behind a pair of rimless glasses, and his irises, pointed in different directions, seemed to stare around, rather than into, her eyes. He spoke so fast that she could barely catch his words.

"Mademoiselle... "

"Je ne sais pas. Where, ah, *où*... Ah, *où sommes nous?"*

He doffed his cap, pointed to the sign next to the cab and smiled. A gold tooth glittered among the tobacco stains. *"Le quartier Latin, Mademoiselle. Comme vous m'avez demandé. C'est le Boulevard Saint-Michel."*

She looked at the street sign and fought against a sudden rush of panic. Right; it was Boulevard Saint-Michel. She had read about it often in French classes, but she had no idea where to go from there. It had been labeled as a student quarter, but nothing looked remotely collegiate to her eye.

"Mademoiselle... "

"You mean... You mean, this is it?"

226

The driver, with a giant droop of his lip, looked out the window and sighed magnificently. He waved to a gendarme, but he--blue cape on shoulders, cigarette in his hand (another Godard movie)--simply nodded and walked across the street. She breathed a sigh of relief and wondered if her parents had been informed already that she had left the group.

"Mademoiselle... "

"*Vous ne... Vous ne parlez-pas anglais? Ahh... Vraiment?*"

The driver laughed, shaking his head, and she stifled a desire to order him back to the airport. Raising her hands, she clutched them against her forehead and spoke in a pleading tone:

"*Oh, je ne comprends rien... Je suis perdue. J'ai besoin d'un hôtel. Salle de lit. Pension.* Everything."

The driver grimaced, smiled at the way she tossed her head when she said, "Everything," then reached over the back of the seat to pat her hand.

"*Hôtel... pension... concierge... petit déjeuner. Everyteeng...* " he said, the last with a strong upsweep of his hand.

To which she could only answer, "*Oui, et pas cher.*"

Condescending now, the driver turned off Saint-Michel, headed down a side street called Sommerard, then down another, smaller one called Champ Marseille. The sides of the buildings seemed to creep closer to the car, almost scraping the windows. Where was the post card she was supposed to ride into? Where were the lovely vistas of the Seine? Instead she saw soot and blowing papers; her stomach recoiled at the sight of a drunken man lying against a building as they inched by.

"*Engleesh. Ici on parle Engleesh.*"

Stopping in front of an old stone building, the driver pointed to the hotel door. A sign on it said: "Rooms for rent." Then, "English spoken here."

"Yes?--Okay?" He smiled, shrugging his shoulders and raising his hands, while his eyes went pleadingly, and separately, she noticed, skyward. Her first thought was to

227

run inside and scream for help, but feeling Waterloo Falls still tugging at her heels, she resisted, shaking her head and saying she wanted a real French hotel.

"*Uh hôtel français, vraiment français,*" she said.

"*Mademoiselle, il est français. Mais on parle un peu anglais aussi.*"

She shook her head, and the driver, annoyed now, put the car in gear and roared down the street. He whipped past old buildings, more old men stumbling into littered gutters, more old ladies with baskets of bread swinging from their arms. Tires shrieking, he barreled into what looked like a back alley, turned left when he reached the end of that, and jerked to a halt in front of an even older building than the former one. Pockmarked (bullets? she wondered) it had great hunks of cement torn from the outer walls. Windows were cracked, geraniums sat on the sills, and a lonesome, faded French flag flew above the doorway.

"*Ça, c'est français.*" Without waiting for a response, the driver took her baggage from the trunk and set it on the pavement. She paid him, held open a palm full of change to let him choose his tip, then stuck out her tongue as he spat on the curb and drove off in a cloud of smoke.

"*Touristes,*" an old man muttered as he waddled past her on the street. Another snort, and snot shot out of his nose too.

She looked up at the hotel building. Tall, gray, narrow, as derelict as the rest of the area; however, five floors of geraniums, each double-blossomed plant framed by a cracked, unpainted window, gave it a certain neighborly charm. No name appeared on the door, but the bell for the third floor had *pension* printed beneath it, and, although her knees shook, she decided to give it a try.

"*La vie bohème,*" she laughed, trying to make a joke of it. "*On visite... On visite Paris* once in a lifetime." She pressed the pension bell and waited.

"*Bon jour, Mademoiselle.*"

"*Bon jour, Madame. Y-a-t-il une chambre pour une personne?*"

228

She congratulated herself; a language textbook author could not have been more proper. The *hôtelière* nodded and led the way up three winding flights of stairs. Tiny--about five feet tall--with long, absolutely white hair, a grotesque cataracted right eye, and a bad limp which made her hobble laboriously, the woman spoke no English and could hardly understand Margy's broken French. But she jabbered constantly as she led the way up the steps.

"*Est-ce que la mademoiselle va rester longtemps?*"

"What's that? *Je ne comprends pas.*"

The *hôtelière* shook her head and waved her hands. That clarified nothing, but Margy, nodding as if she understood, smiled with comprehension. On the third floor, the woman motioned to set down the bags, and then they struggled up two more flights to a dark hallway. A picture of de Gaulle hung in a dusty corner, a bust of Napoleon sat on the table in the middle, and, oddly out of time and place (like herself, Margy thought), a photograph of the late President Kennedy smiled at them both.

"*Vous la trouverez bien, j'espère.*" The *hôtelière* opened the door, motioned Margy into the room, then shuffled around the bed and swung open the windows to a little balcony at the front. On the wall were a crucifix and a World War II photograph of the military cemetery at Omaha Beach; she noted a basin and pitcher on a table, and a bed and chair jammed around the corners of an old armoire. Out the windows, she noticed the stone building across the way. Looming pock-marked and brown behind a geranium plant on the balcony, it blocked her hoped-for rooftop view of Paris.

"I'm really tired," she said, not even trying to cover her disappointment.

"*Mademoiselle?*"

"*Je suis fatiguée. Très, très fatiguée.*"

The *hôtelière* clucked her tongue and sympathetically smoothed out the bedspread so Margy could sit on it. The mattress felt lumpy, hard, the bedspread rather grimy to the touch. She would take it, she thought, as she lay back. But when something tickled and she looked to see a two-inch daddy-long-legs dart across her arm, she leaped up, screaming, then picked up her purse and ran shrieking from the room.

"*Mademoiselle! Mademoiselle!*"

"Shut up! I hate you! I hate you all!"

"*Dix francs par jour, mademoiselle. Toute compris. C'est pas cher, n'est-ce pas?*" Her voice rasping like a boat horn, the *hôtelière* tottered down the steps, grabbed an overnight bag and waved it at Margy from the third floor landing.

"*Mademoiselle, mademoiselle! Vos bagages. Vous oubliez...* "

But the rest was lost in the pounding of Margy's heart and feet. Into the street, running past cars, old men, doorways, *pissoires*, a little man grabbing at her arm--"No!" Then she stopped suddenly, realizing what she had left behind--her traveler's checks, clothes, books, paints-- everything she treasured or needed was in those bags.

"Damn!" She made herself turn around, hesitated, then forced herself to go back. When the hôtelière saw her at the entrance, she closed her one good eye, shook her fist, *pff*-ed a profound French fricative of disgust, and stepped aside finally, slamming the door after Margy walked into the hall. She found her bags--stacked neatly on the third floor landing. She picked them up, and with one valise under either arm, hobbled back toward the English-speaking hotel.

"*Il y a une chambre pour une personne?*"

The textbook French was already better.

"Yes, miss. How many days?" The owner, a good looking, polite man, took her money, filled out the official fiche from her passport, then led her to a small but pleasant-looking room. Ironically, it faced the back of the building she had just run out of. But the bathroom signs were in English and in French; the *International Herald-Tribune* (in English) lay on the breakfast table, and the comfortable sound of American voices filled the halls. She found a well-lit dining room and smiled at a couple of Impressionist-looking reproductions on the walls. Finally, a creamy Renoir brightness permeated her room, and for three mornings she basked in it, thinking she had found a magic land laid out just for her. She practiced French, visited museums, explored the streets and alleys of Paris, and hardly thought of home. She even met an English boy, Michael, who moved into the room next door. He had just finished college, and he said he was going to travel for a year in order to find out what he wanted in his life. They slept together the second night they knew each other; in the morning, with the special light pouring through the windows, he asked if he could take her to see the bulls run in Pamplona. Margy accepted, happily buying a Spanish-English dictionary so that she could learn the language. But the night before they were to leave, her parents called, begging her to come home again. It was upsetting enough to make her break all appointments.

"No, I will not rejoin the youth group on its tour," she told them. "Yes, I plan to stay in Paris--indefinitely. No, I don't think I'll ever see you again. I really *want* to stay, that's why."

She started to hang up just as her mother came onto the extension wire and screamed. Her father asked her to think of their family happiness.

"Family happiness? Are you kidding, Daddy? I want my own. I hate her. I even hate you. I hate my whole goddamn life..."

Then, typically, she bit her lip and tried to apologize across five thousand miles of suddenly disconnected wire. Michael lay on the bed. As she dropped the phone, he opened his arms to receive her. She turned away and sat down on the corner chair instead.

20.

STREET LIFE

She withdrew from people and spoke to no one for ten days. At least her father, she kept thinking, would call again. He didn't, and, disappointed, she began to prowl the streets. She visited the museums again, the parks, the boutiques. She tried to become one of that band of knowledgeable Parisians who knew where to dine on four and five course meals and still pay less than three dollars. She ate in Vietnamese restaurants on rue Monsieur-le-Prince. She sampled couscous and Sidi Brahim wine at Algerian restaurants near rue de la Harpe. In late July, Michael came back from Pamplona and took her to some of the plainer French bistros around Les Halles, where they had onion soup, pate, sausage, cheese, and wine for under two dollars. He showed her the small Jewish quarter around rue des Rosiers and escorted her through the quaint back streets of "La Butte" in Montmartre. But Michael stayed only one more month, and it was clear to Margy that, although he wanted her with him in London and they had a good time touring Paris, he had an efficiency and purpose about his life that she could not yet match. London would have to come later, she decided, and so, seeing him off at Gare du Nord in late August, she cashed in her few traveler's checks and took to the Paris streets alone again.

She dressed in jeans and walked to Montparnasse to spend evenings in the cafes near Boulevard Raspail. She talked to artists who drew pastel copies of paintings on the sidewalks and left little bare circles of pavement to serve as collection plates. She followed buskers in and out of cafes and Metro stations, and, since her money supply had diminished, she sang along with one group and passed the hat for another in order to share the proceeds. With her long blond hair trailing behind, she looked typically American, typically adventurous, and for a time developed her own little following.

In early September Margy met a girl from Cedar Rapids and sold her the return portion of her airline ticket. Then she relaxed a little, sharing a car with a young American couple to see Versailles, Fontainebleau, Brittany, and Normandy, coming back to Paris while the couple drove east toward Switzerland and Rome. She took up her street life again, spending more time around Boulevard Saint-Michel because, with summer vacation over, she found more students there. It was in one of those cafes, at the river, across from the Notre Dame, that she first talked to Everet.

He looked familiar, perhaps, she thought, because she had seen him around the hotel. He nodded as she entered the cafe, but she looked back with a blank expression. He sat with two friends. One was short, stocky, with sideburns and a tightly knit body that seemed on the verge of breaking into a trot when he looked at her. The other was tall, lanky, with an attractive, but ingratiating, smile and large boney hands, whose jacket sleeves barely covered his wrists. Everet wore a red and yellow dashiki.

"*Bon jour*. What a lovely night for a walk beside the Seine."

The tall one spoke, taking her arm, and cast an approving glance toward the river. "Would you like to join us?" he asked. She shook her head, pulling her arm away, and passed to an empty table.

She sat in the corner, signaled the waiter, and then glanced back at them. They looked like three crouching leopard cubs, she thought, their dark complexions a rich recessive color that seemed to fascinate the entire cafe, which, in atypical Parisian fashion, turned toward them rather than the people on the sidewalk. The tall one walked over and, introducing himself, again invited her to sit with them.

"My friend is American also," he announced in French, vaguely motioning toward Everet. "You will have something in common."

A breeze swept off the river, pushing a newspaper before it, and near the fountain across the way a horn tooted at several pedestrians. She shook her head, took out a

233

paperback novel, and stared at it resolutely while he, shifting his feet, studied her.

In English he said, "What's the matter, miss? You don't want to be--how do you call it--sociable? Is that how one says it, Everet? Sociable?"

"Yeah. That's it—sociable."

Everet smiled across the tables, but out of the corner of her eye Margy could see him change expression slightly as if he were embarrassed. Now she remembered that she had seen him once, in a bakery near the hotel, and another time, along with some friends of his, while she worked with one of the buskers. They may even have exchanged a word or two in a cafe near Montparnasse as she passed the hat, but nothing more than a polite greeting.

"Do you have problems with dark skin?" the tall one asked.

"No!—And stop that—you don't need to touch me!"

She stood immediately, shaking his hand off her wrist, shocked that he had broken in on her so easily. He did not smile. The whole cafe seemed to smile, however, and, as if to upstage him, she shook her head, pushed him aside, and walked quickly to their table. She felt brave, but also very anxious.

"*Je vous présente Denise Songolo et Everet Hamilton. Il est Américain, lui. Moi, je m'appelle Josef Mamadou.*"

"Hi. I'm Margy Winters," she said.

She shook hands--one sharp French tug with Denise and Josef, and a quiet squeeze, with an American double-pump, from Everet. She took a chair, wondering what she was doing there. Something about them challenged her. Something about their carefree French-immigrant style fascinated her, especially in Josef, and she wondered what it would be like to be among their friends. Somehow they, not the various Parisians in the cafe, held the key to legendary Bohemian life.

They talked for an hour over coffee, strolled to the Ile Saint-Louis and back, and at Denise's suggestion agreed to meet in Montparnasse the following night. The men went off to the north--to Les Halles, they said--to meet some friends, and Margy walked south, back to her hotel alone. They had invited her along, but she had refused. She felt intrigued, nevertheless, and saw them each of the three following nights. Then Everet, attending the Ecole Normal Superior for the year, dropped out of the group to study, and soon afterward Denise decided to study too. Finally, she saw Josef Mamadou alone for the next few nights.

He was pleasant to her, yet she did not feel the romance with him that she felt when the four of them went out together. She also did not feel comfortable with him alone, and, although she constantly warned herself, she regarded that as intriguing. During the third evening out with him, after a few passionate kisses, she had to firmly refuse an invitation to his room. He turned loud and abusive, even shouting at her in the street, and abandoned her in an unfamiliar neighborhood around one a.m., after the Metro had closed and with no taxis in sight.

She decided to keep away from him, but in about two weeks he called to apologize and invited her to an exhibition of Cameroonian art, folk songs, and dances being held at a theatre in the suburbs. He and Denise were from Cameroon, and she accepted, primarily because she felt lonesome, but also because she hoped to learn from their exotic background. Josef brought some flowers for her hair, took her to dinner at a lovely restaurant, and at the exhibition introduced her to friends. It helped that he spoke English and could translate for her. A party of Cameroonians and Margy rode back to Paris together, and then they went from cafe to cafe to drink cognacs and coffee before returning home. It made a wonderful evening, gay in the way she had always read about Paris nights, and it made her feel more comfortable with Josef. But he changed suddenly when he took her back to her hotel. As they stood at the front door, Josef placed his hand behind her neck, grabbed a fistful of her hair and, drunkenly, covered her cheeks and forehead with kisses. Mutely, she pushed him off. Still he persisted.

"Hey, come on, Josef. Hands off."

The street was dark, as usual after midnight. She felt frightened, but she had twisted out of his arms so many

235

times and with so many techniques two weeks before that she thought of this moment as a well-rehearsed *pas de deux*. Yet the grip on her hair felt earnest, and so she had to take his fingers, carefully force them apart, then hold his hands firmly against his chest.

"Josef, I like you, but this is too much."

"Margery, in my country you could be queen."

She laughed, nervously.

"It is true. I promise you."

"Who said I wanted to be queen?" she said.

She leaned forward, wanting to let him know that she did feel some affection. He took her hand between his palms, kissed her fingertips, and gently rubbed them against his cheek. A cold shiver ran down her spine, and she tried, very firmly now, to pull away.

"Is there someone else? Someone in America?"

He laid the back of his hand on her shoulder, and she felt his dry, cool fingers edging toward her face

"Not now. Come on, hands off."

"Tell me about him," Josef said

She looked into his eyes.

"Go ahead. Tell me."

"How do you know it's a him?"

"Oh, I know," he said, smiling. His legs pressed against her as he giggled. She edged away and turned into the alley beside the hotel. The front door was closed. The owner usually locked it at twelve o'clock, giving his late night guests a key to the side entrance. With Josef whispering behind her, Margy walked down the alley and took out her key.

"What?" she asked, as she approached the door.

"Not 'what'--white," he taunted. "Was this boyfriend of yours white?"

"Josef, why bring that up now? I'm not a racist. Never have been."

"Everet has informed me that you were with a white boy for a few days. One of the singers."

"A busker? Oh, that was nothing."

He motioned toward the building behind hers--the first hotel she had looked at in Paris--and pointed four or five flights up to a dimly lit window. It was Everet's room, she knew. They had walked home together from Montparnasse the second evening she had gone out with them. Denise and Josef had walked off giggling on what they called a secret mission to Pigalle.

"Everet has told me that he saw you with a man for weeks. Was that your lover?"

She shook her head, knowing he spoke of Michael, but, as she edged toward the door, Josef darted in front of it.

"Is it not my black skin?" he asked, rubbing his forearm.

"Oh, stop it, Josef. I don't see this as funny."

"I assure you that all Africans are color-fast," he murmured.

Chuckling, he reached for her arm, but this time Margy stepped away and began to walk back toward the street.

"You try too damn hard, you know that? If you would just let up a little bit... "

He snickered as she stopped beneath the street lamp. They both tried to be polite although perhaps for different reasons. Margy made an effort to smile to hide her sudden fear. Josef lapsed into polite, formal English, perhaps to defend himself against her fear. "I have learned one thing during my brief stay in Europe," he said. "If a black man does not strive--for money, possessions, or a woman--in this white man's world he is cast aside. I am not a child, Margery. I will not have you, or anyone else, treat me as one."

He dropped his hands to his waist and pouted. Because of the tension, Margy reached out and chucked him under the chin.

"Hey, Josef. Cheer up. I didn't say 'never,' did I?"

He smiled. She took a deep breath and, not wanting to appear prejudiced, leaned forward to kiss him--lightly, this time--on the lips.

"Good night. Sleep well," she said.

Immediately, he gathered her into his arms.

237

"Easy! Not so fast!"

She pushed him away, but he took her hand and, beaming, pulled her down the alley, past the side entrance, to the building in the rear of the hotel. Picking up a pebble, he tossed it at the window four or five flights up. It looked dark now, but after a few throws, the light went on and soon Margy recognized Everet's head leaning out.

"Brother, I hope the studying was good," Josef said.

He laughed and Everet, trying to see who they were, peered into the darkness.

"Is that you, Josef? I can barely see you."

"Look under your window, brother! Two well-wishers want to say hello."

Josef stepped back into the rectangle of light from the window and pulled Margy next to him.

"See?"

"Margy! Is that you?"

"Yes," said Josef. "I have my own American affiliations."

She said nothing. Josef laughed, but she heard--or thought she heard--a touch of malice in it.

"Won't you come down for a drink, Everet, my friend?"

"At this hour? You must be kidding."

"The cafes on Boulevard Saint-Germain are still open," said Josef.

Everet sighed. "Look, I've got loads of work to do. I'm studying for exams. I'll return the compliment some other time. Meanwhile, good-night, Margy. And take it easy, heh?"

He closed the window and turned out the light immediately. As she went back to the side entrance, Margy felt embarrassed--and abused. She did not want Everet to think of her as frivolous. "You're not coming up with me," she said, loudly, to Josef. "No matter what you think, I don't like being shown off."

"Oh, Margery... "

He pressed her from behind. He spoke in French and even went so far as to use the formal *vous*.

"Don't do that. I've had it," she said, pushing him away.

She opened the door, stepped inside, and on second thought gave him another good-night kiss--this one on each cheek. When he tried to embrace her, she stepped inside and closed the door.

As she looked through the gauze curtain in the window beside the door, she saw his angry, disappointed face. It looked ready to kill, or at least break in, she thought. But then Josef did something that went to the root of her inability to understand him whenever she thought about him: Hardly changing his expression, he shrugged, placed his hands in his pockets, and, with a carefree whistle and step, walked down the alley and out of sight.

21.

CRUISING

She saw him just twice after that, and eventually they drifted apart. In later years she looked at Josef as a preparation for Everet, a preparation which she never quite completed. She had to make a living, she decided, because money was getting short, and by October she started to do odd jobs, wherever she could find them. She tutored students of English--several of whom she had met with Josef at the Cameroon exposition. Two days a week she babysat for a French family, taking the children to the Luxembourg Gardens to watch pétanque games and tennis while she talked to them and tried to give them at least a listening acquaintance with English. She also worked as a typist-receptionist at a small consulting firm on rue de Chevreaux. She did not eat out frequently, instead buying fruits, dairy products, and cheap cuts of meat at the neighborhood market and keeping perishables in a drawer of the hotelier's refrigerator. He also allowed her to cook supper in his kitchen. From time to time she met Everet in the market or at the local kiosk where they both bought *The Herald-Tribune* in the morning and *Le Monde* at night. They exchanged a few words, but that was all. She was interested, but he seemed wrapped up in his studies.

On her part, Margy was determined to learn French well, and she took evening courses at Alliance Française, hoping eventually to earn a certificate to teach. But her graphic work suffered. She did no painting, only occasional drawing in a notebook she carried--using it as a diary, sketchbook, and log for her expenses and income. It was a habit she would continue for the rest of her life.

Her artistic block was simply a matter of too many expectations. When she thought of all the Monets, Utrillos, Lautrecs, and Picassos she had seen that perfectly captured her sense of Paris, she froze. Yet when she walked through the city, looking at buildings and people, she almost wept at the visual possibilities the city offered. Keeping the masters out of her mind, she thought she could do anything; she had the sense that something important would occur, some event that might change her life. Perhaps it would make her paint.

Occasionally she wrote to her father--a postcard or two from Brittany and Normandy--a note when she had read a good book, accomplished something important in French, or simply seen some Parisian scene that moved her. One evening when she walked through the market at rue Daguerre, she heard a couple of buskers sing American folksongs, and, when they ended their performance with Woody Guthrie's "This Land is Your Land," she cried from homesickness. Returning to the hotel, she wrote a long, apologetic letter to her father in which she expressed regret for her last telephone conversation and her behavior at Cedar Rapids Airport.

Still she heard nothing from home, and, while she accepted that with relief in the mornings, the silence upset her at night when she felt alone--either in her room or at some quiet cafe. She tried to draw or study French through it, but she got nowhere. She took long walks up Saint-Michel to Boulevard Montparnasse, Montparnasse to Raspail, then the long, lonesome, eerily dark blocks up to Saint-Germain where she could turn toward Saint-Michel again. She felt threatened, especially on Boulevard Raspail, but she could not help herself. She even crossed the river into Les Halles, occasionally walking up rue Saint-Denis where the prostitutes stood in groups of three or four on almost every block. No respectable woman would go there alone after dark, she knew, and she was harassed constantly, yet never enough that it kept her away. In fact, something of the egalitarianism and economic forthrightness of rue Saint-Denis appealed to her. She felt a sense of freedom on the street. The prostitutes survived by doing what she could not do in similar circumstances, and she imagined them as morally independent while in fact they were merely women who had found an age-old way to make a living. She talked to some of them in a cafe near the arch at the boulevard and became disillusioned. She was not surprised to see how

241

carefree and uneducated they were--but their mental simplicity troubled her. They knew very little about anything but sex and romanticized popular music. They thought of the United States as full of cowboys and rock and roll and expressed admiration for American cars, television, and styles of dress. Margy could not connect her attitudes toward them with *Les Demoiselles d'Avignon*, and she was surprised to find that the pinnacle of their ambitions was to star in a film, preferably a Hollywood film, although a pornographic piece "would do," one of them told her. She, of course, had always wanted to be the maker of art, not the object to be made.

One of the more friendly--and intelligent--girls was named Marie-Thérèse. She was considered the intellectual of rue Saint-Denis because she read pot-boiler novels and had ambitions to write one herself. Marie-Thérèse did not sell her body, she said; she rented it out simply to get material for her book. Margy envied her spirit, her experience, and, most of all, her attitude toward men. Men were conveniences to Marie-Thérèse, nothing to get excited about unless you had the bad luck to fall in love with one. She had no pimp, or *maquereau*, as the French called it, and as she stood on the corner of rue du Cygne in her tight jeans, low-cut blouse, and high-heeled shoes, holding a pet schnauzer close to her breasts, she seemed to Margy to be the ideal of feminine independence. Whenever a man stopped to pet the dog and discuss the price of a visit, Marie-Thérèse would look directly at him with clear, friendly eyes, toss her long mane of straight black hair, and smile with an expression of complete professional confidence. Men would know she was worth the price, Margy imagined, and from the naiveté of her seat in the window of the cafe across the street, she became jealous of that obvious competence.

She watched as Marie-Thérèse walked down rue du Cygne, trailing the man behind her at first, then slowing down and, with a flash of happy eyes, moved beside him so that they could talk. She liked to make them comfortable, she had told Margy, because they were often nervous at having to pay for love, and she found that they were much more generous if she helped them to relax. She invited Margy up to her room once or twice, and Margy was surprised to see how clean and respectable it looked. Carpeted in red, with a double bed in the corner, a radio, a shelf full of *romans noires*, a poster of the Golden Gate Bridge in San Francisco on the wall next to the bathroom, and a little cushioned box for the schnauzer in the corner opposite the bed. She made coffee in the kitchenette, and they drank it sitting at the two windows overlooking the rue du Cygne. Marie-Thérèse came from the south of France and had lived in Paris two years. She said she hardly wrote to her parents, but that at Christmas and Easter she sent them large checks from her earnings. They thought she was a waitress at the Tour Argente, across from Ile Saint-Louis, and they wanted her to send them stories of the famous people who dined there.

Sometimes Margy fantasized taking up prostitution herself. But when she spent a Sunday afternoon and evening in the cafe watching the procession of short, fat, sometimes drunk and unkempt men that Marie-Thérèse led up to her room, she decided she could not. She did not like men enough, she thought, nor did she have that much need of sex. In addition, many of Marie-Thérèse's clients looked physically repugnant, and she could not imagine herself disrobing in front of them, having them disrobe in front of her, or allowing them to lie beside her in a bed. That night she dreamed of standing in a room full of naked, bearded men with canker sores all over their bodies.

While they talked one afternoon, Marie-Thérèse convinced Margy to pass an hour in her room while she worked, and, although reluctant at first, Margy agreed to do it. They set up a room divider outside the kitchenette and placed a chair behind it. Marie-Thérèse said that when she arrived with a customer, she would ring the downstairs doorbell twice. Then Margy could hide behind the screen and watch through one of the cracks where it folded. She thought she would stay in the kitchenette to listen and not look, but the first customer went in and out so quietly that she had to peek through the crack for the second one.

243

It was a pleasant surprise. She saw a small, handsome, talkative boy from Toulon whose golden thighs and buttocks set Margy fantasizing about nude sun-bathing on the Mediterranean. Marie-Thérèse mothered him, her long, delicate hands caressing his neck and arms as she helped him undress, leading him into the bathroom where, although Margy could not see it, she performed the obligatory washing of genitals and checking for signs of syphilis. It made her uneasy and excited, and the sparkle of conspiratorial laughter that came from the unseen couple in the bathroom increased the feeling. When they came back into the main room and Margy saw Marie-Thérèse naked for the first time, her hands started to shake and she had to pull back from the screen to avoid knocking it down. Marie-Thérèse did not have a pretty face--certainly, if they were to walk down the street together more men would look at Margy than at Marie-Thérèse--but she had an earthy quality that Margy completely lacked. Her hips were rounded and full, and the movement of soft lines up to her moderate breasts reminded Margy of some classical Greek sculptures. About her waist she wore a single gold chain. It had no clasp and, in fact, she told Margy later, it had been soldered together by a former client who was a jewelry maker. Her legs were muscular but shapely, and, as she turned, pushing the boy onto the bed and kneeling beside him, she showed a pair of smooth, full buttocks and then a curly, well-groomed triangle of dark hair between her legs.

Margy felt revolted seeing her friend like that, but nothing compared to what she felt when Marie-Thérèse went down on the boy. She had done it herself occasionally, but always under the cover of drunkenness or passion, which never quite hid the disgust she felt if the man came and she had to deal with the warm, oyster-like mucous she wanted to swallow, but that invaded her throat as if it were a slimy, hot-footed tape-worm entering her. Marie-Thérèse seemed clear-headed and clear-eyed, however, smiling and cooing happily as she kissed and nipped at prick and balls. Margy stared at her elbows and knees, marveling at how easily they had gone down on the floor and mattress. When Marie-

Thérèse moaned, an obviously feigned sound to excite the boy, Margy looked away and went into the kitchenette. In there she became aware of her clothes, and as Marie-Thérèse's moans grew louder and more rhythmic, Margy felt like screaming. Then there was a pause, a faint giggle from the boy, a murmur of approval from Marie-Thérèse, and the quiet shoosh of mattress and bedsprings. Margy sneaked back behind the screen, seeing through its cracked folds (as if it were something primal and forbidden) Marie-Thérèse's hands push the boy's buttocks as he mounted her. Her thighs opened, slammed against the mattress with a dull thud, and then enveloped him. Surprisingly, the boy almost disappeared, like a small child in Marie-Thérèse's arms. The schnauzer, obviously used to such human behavior, shuffled its paws on its own little pillow, yawned, and closed its beetle-browed eyes. Rooted at the screen opening, Margy tried not to knock against it, tried not to gasp in despair, and tried very hard not to take off her own clothes, stepping into the room and joining the happy confusion.

When he was done, the boy collapsed onto Marie-Thérèse with a loud sob and held onto her flanks, as if he were trying to survive. She chuckled, smoothed his hair with a sigh, and stroked his shoulders, at one point grinning and waving to Margy behind his back. After less than a minute, she left the bed, went into the bathroom and began to wash herself off, singing some bit of American popular music while the boy, bewildered, lay on the mattress and stared around the room. He seemed old suddenly, putting on his clothes slowly and with rickety movements. When he had finished tying his shoes, he stepped into the bathroom, only to back out immediately as Marie-Thérèse, business-like, came out pulling her shirt on over her head and, picking up the schnauzer, led him to the door. At the last moment she winked at the screen and walked into the hall.

Margy stepped into the room with a sigh. It was the first time she had watched a couple making love. As a matter of fact, it was the first time that she had seen a naked woman because in college and high school gyms the girls had their own individual cabanas to change and shower in and in the art classes the models always wore body stockings. She stopped at the bed, touching the wet spot in the middle of the sheets (she always avoided it in her own encounters), then rubbing her fingers before her nose, sniffed the acrid smell which was not so disgusting after all.

It was also the first time that she had ever seen a woman in a superior role to a man, and that intrigued her too. She returned to Marie-Thérèse's place one or two more days, always feeling guilty and perverted at first, yet finally reveling in the good fun her friend seemed to have. She viewed the visits as lessons, and she began to think of men differently. They could be beautiful, she knew, physically strong, occasionally intelligent, certainly sensuous and even charming. But from that Toulon boy on she saw them as children rather than as fathers. She understood them as servants to a physical urge for women that was larger than themselves and which made them malleable in the right, tender, motherly hands.

She looked upon her father's pathetic relationship with her mother in the same grudging light; and she frowned upon Josef's and even Michael's presumptuous command over her because it masked their real desire to be taken care of. Restraint, she decided, was the essence of civilization, and from what she knew and saw from behind Marie-Thérèse's screen, it took women to impose it on men. Despite their bodies, their muscles, their independence--or possibly because of them--they were the much more needy half of the race.

22.

JOSEF

Fall and winter were long, and Margy grew lonesome. Just before Christmas--her first ever away from home--she met Everet at a local cafe and invited him to her room for coffee and a piece of fruitcake that she had found at a store on the Champs Elysées. He was studying for exams, however, and, for the holidays themselves, he had been invited down to the Mediterranean by some French friends. Spending a solitary Christmas and New Year's Eve, Margy called Michael in London several times, but he was always out and never returned her call. She wrote a letter to her father about her jobs and her progress in French and did not mention her painting. He never replied.

It was the most difficult time of her year in France. The days were short and dark, the sun not rising until nearly nine o'clock and then setting around four. In addition, the weather blew bitterly cold, the skies showed gray with none of the cheerful Midwest whiteness of snow falling from them, and her poorly heated and insulated room nearly froze. She spent days and nights huddled in a blanket near the small radiator beside her desk, trying to read the newspapers, some French novel or poem, or listening to a small portable radio she had bought used from a student at Alliance Française. Non-existent as it was, mail became important to her, and she began to write to friends in Iowa. One girlfriend replied around New Year's day, writing with envy of Margy for having broken free; and then a boy, Chris, whom she had dated a few times at the university, sent her a card from New York where he had gone to live and find a job as an actor. He was not envious. Rather he wrote with a sense of complicity, saying that they were together doing something bold and unusual to define their futures.

Reading that, Margy felt a pang of remorse. Wrapped in her blanket, having no sense of what was to come except for her next day's job, her next meal's food, or her next

French lesson's rules, she had no sense of self-definition. Still she wrote back to Chris, telling him about the people she had met, the places visited, and the French film and theatre she was, on occasion, seeing.

She spent Christmas morning by herself, then went with Marie-Thérèse to a friend's house where they ate Christmas dinner. It was a small, light-hearted meal. The friend was a Bretonne woman, and she made a dinner of seafood crepes and rice, adding wine and salad, along with several plates full of steamed clams and broth. For dessert they had sweet crepes with cooked fruit and butter on them, and, after coffee, Margy, Marie-Thérèse, and the friend exchanged small gifts before taking a stroll in the Tuileries Gardens.

But on New Year's Eve, Marie-Thérèse, of course, had to work ("The best night of the year," she called it), and Margy spent it alone, wrapped in her blanket, sipping cognac directly from a bottle, and drifting off to sleep shortly before midnight with a copy of Zola's *Le Ventre de Paris* in her hands.

Next morning she awakened depressed, and, as she walked through the quiet gray of a Parisian New Year's dawn, she tried to vow herself into action. This year she would work to accept the present, to live in the moment, and not to worry about her future so much. But her past still grated, and aloneness left so many empty spaces in the present that she could do nothing but hope for the healing effects of future days. She tried to paint again, but decided she would get nowhere. That afternoon Margy took her notebook to the Luxembourg Gardens and drew some of the isolate souls standing around the basin. Then she concentrated on the fountain that poured into the basin, its frozen spray blossoming into snow-gray cantilevered plumes as if it were a sculptured candle. She also went to a cafe near Odeon and drew street scenes, but, she realized, she showed no spark or energy in the drawings. She felt empty and for the first time in her life understood that she had insufficient self-love—either to sustain her through her work or through such difficult emotional times. She decided to look up Josef again, and as she rode south on the Metro to Cité Université, near which he lived, she had to fight against her self-doubt. She was relieved to find he was not at home, but when he came to her hotel a few days later (responding to a message someone had given him: *"une blonde, américaine"* had knocked on his door), she could hardly find voice to speak.

She threw her depression off and began to see him, trying to make sure that others were present when they went out. They saw his classmates at the university, political acquaintances who were becoming active with him in radical causes, and many Africans who were in France, as she was, trying to make something of their lives. Among Josef's friends were a large number of hawkers from Senegal, Cameroon, and Chad. They sold African crafts mostly, carrying them into cafes or placing them on blankets along the avenues where tourists walked. She and Josef would chat with them in the cold near their blankets. They laid out carved ivory tusks, musical instruments made of boar skin and bone, and occasional pieces of jewelry combining ebony and exotic stones.

They looked out for police at Metro entrances, and, if they saw any mounting the steps, then she, Josef, and the hawker gathered up the merchandise and walked off in three different directions--each with a cache under his arm. Nights were bitterly cold. Although Margy and Josef shivered in long wool coats and scarfs, these young men wore nothing but second-hand European jackets and slacks made of the thinnest gabardine. Generally, they wore mufflers and wool knit masks, but they carried no gloves, no sweaters, no heavy boots to protect their feet and, according to Josef, only the flimsiest of underwear. They smoked incessantly, and Margy always noticed how violently their hands trembled when they lit a match.

She asked Josef why they stayed in France and could only wonder when he said that their life here was more comfortable than back home. When she asked about his own life at home, he would only shrug and say that it was not as bad as theirs.

249

She and Josef went to cafes with some of the hawkers, and, as during her first nights with Everet, Josef, and Denise, Margy felt very conspicuous. Perhaps, as many Parisians said, the French had no racial prejudice, but they did have ideas about blonde women, and Margy had no doubt that in a procession of five or six tall black men with bright, dark eyes and short jacket sleeves and trousers, she was something of a pink and gold curiosity. Heads turned inevitably, and eyes followed her in the resulting hush. She felt like a target—exotic, yet still a target—and, when Josef placed his arm around her shoulder or waist, she allowed him to draw her close though she tried to look indifferent. People considered her to be Josef's girlfriend, she knew, and she accepted it when she felt how comfortable it was and, remembering Marie-Thérèse's customers, how easily she could handle him.

He drank too much, making him unpleasantly loud on occasion. He also grew increasingly angry in politics, and, while she found that interesting at first, it ultimately bored her. In February, they slept together for the first time, the long abstinence since Michael making it exciting--and awkward as well. He was a competent, but somewhat impatient, lover, with a surprising tendency toward peevishness if things did not go as planned. They fumbled all over each other's clothes and bodies in the small unheated fifth floor walk-up where he lived near Porte Orleans and achieved approximate jointure beneath a hand-loomed African rug which he also used as a blanket. Afterward she slept, shivering next to him all through the night, hoping that the small electric space heater at the bottom of the mattress would not tip over and cause a fire.

She felt excited, but not enough to consider her affair with Josef lasting. She worried about that, wondering about possible prejudice in her feelings, and whether she was blocking emotion simply because she knew her parents would disapprove. She tried to force her feelings at first, but finally she told herself that the right chemistry was just not there. Michael had possessed class, style, and gentleness, and her parents, especially her father, probably would have heartily approved. Still she had felt no movement in her center when she spent time with him--in bed or out. She had felt that movement a couple of times in high school and once, hugely, as she put it, in a brief affair with an art professor at the university. She had felt it again, momentarily, in Paris upon meeting Everet, but his brown eyes, darting as though he were thinking of other things, as if the feelings he sensed between them were a disturbance, kept her at a distance. Like many men he rarely joked and never discussed his emotions. She wondered, sometimes, whether there was a heart at all beneath his bulging chest.

Realizing that in her mind Josef substituted for Everet, she recognized, clearly for perhaps the first time, her own dishonesty in making love. It frightened her because she had always counted on a certain moral superiority over men, especially in sex. Still, Josef had little to complain of. Even though she occasionally imagined another face above her in bed, they had fun together. She was a good companion, and, she realized, she was also interesting enough to make him proud among his French and African friends.

But his possessiveness inevitably caused trouble. During the alternating periods of soft rain and brilliant sunshine that March and April, Margy began to want to break away and get on with her own life. She started to visit museums again, hoping for inspiration from the works she saw in them. But her body, as in her love affair with Josef, did not respond to the paintings, and she did not feel eager when she held a pencil in her hand. Although she still sketched daily, creating a kind of graphic diary of her Parisian experiences, Margy recognized that there was too much busywork in it, too much effort at discipline in the things she drew. She thought of traveling again, and by luck a company for which she worked briefly sent her to Florence to type and take dictation at an eight-day conference. Although she was required to attend meetings daily, she did visit the museums and public sculptures on the weekend. At the Academia she admired Michelangelo's David, but the unfinished statues of Saint Matthew and the slaves that lined the hall on the way to it moved her more than anything she

251

had ever seen. They seemed to stir themselves when she studied them closely, the figures emerging from stone in her imagination and taking on organic life. Meanwhile the more famous statue, polished and complete, struck her as perfect but frozen. She returned to the hall three times during the weekend and received permission from the guards to sketch the unfinished stones. She filled a dozen pages. There was an eye on one of the slaves that was barely visible in the marble, yet each time she sketched it, she swore the pupil moved and she understood the human character beneath it.

Returning to Paris, she spent a week drawing and painting in her room and did not see Josef. When he finally persuaded her to go out again, he remarked at how distant and uncaring she seemed. Margy apologized and saw him again the following night, managing to be more relaxed and cheerful. She had to work as an *au pair* for the next few days, and by the end of the second week her artistic momentum had disappeared. It was a matter of will, she concluded, recalling the stories she had read of the solitary, tortured lives that Michelangelo and Leonardo had led. She decided that she was not ready, that she was a woman of body rather than of spirit, and, while she kept at her daily sketching, for the moment she gave up all thoughts of larger projects.

That decision lasted until May when she and Josef had a noisy fight because he wanted her to live with him. They started arguing in a cafe, continued while they walked along the quais of the river, and concluded on the Pont des Arts near the Louvre. Josef took her arms, threatening to throw himself into the river and take her along with him. Frightened as she watched heedless passersby, she shook her head angrily, and, when he dropped to his knees, gripping her legs and burying his face in her pelvis, she broke from him, dashing across the bridge and along the right bank quai until she joined a group of tourists entering the museum.

Josef did not follow. She left the tourists as soon as they entered the main hall, and all through the afternoon she looked at Italian paintings, trying to decide as she studied them if her affair with him should be over. She did not want

252

to become lonesome again, and she wondered if it was worth holding on to Josef for a while. Yet there was her art, and she knew that could sustain her if she worked harder at it. She made copies of two Botticellis and one detailed drawing of the Giotto *Saint Francis*, then left the museum, determined not to see Josef again.

Twenty minutes later, however, as she turned the corner into her street, she saw him standing near the hotel. He did not come toward her. Instead he retreated into the alley, and, when she passed, she saw him at the end of it near Everet's building. He laughed when she stopped, pulled the shirt out of his pants, and in a slow, absolutely lewd gesture, rubbed the flesh above his genitals. She reacted badly, recoiling at first, then making up for it by stepping into the alley.

"You don't even want to die with me, Margy. Americans have no feeling for romantic love."

"Josef... "

"Margy, please. I am at least your friend. Don't run away from me. It is not fair."

There was his oddly formal English; she heard it whenever they had an argument. He started toward her and, whether from the hand on the flesh or the look in his eye, she became frightened again. Breaking into a trot, she raced out of the alley and to her building's front door, but Josef was so quick that he arrived there at the same time. His hand covered hers as she took the door handle.

"Please, Margy. Please... "

"I don't dislike you, Josef. I just want to be on my own."

He touched her face, closed his eyes and, after a moment, kissed her lips. Despite herself, Margy embraced him quickly before turning again to the door.

"I may call you again?" he said. "Perhaps in a few days?"

She shook her head, but he was grinning instead of sorrowful. The shirt draped over the waist of his trousers now, and his hands touched the doorjamb on either side of Margy's head.

253

"Please, I am not all bad, am I?"

She shrugged, attempting to smile a little as he touched her shoulder.

"May I call you again, Margy?"

She shook her head, tentatively.

"May I please?"

"Not for at least a week," she said. "And I'm not being a coquette. I really mean what I say."

"Perhaps we can take coffee together some afternoon?" he asked.

She nodded. Then, thinking she might want to see Everet instead, she changed her mind. "We'll have to see," she said. "Damn it, I have to start organizing my life. I have things to do."

He let her go, smiling, and she went inside with a sigh of relief. She did not bother to say good-bye as she heard him whistle down the street.

23.

QUATORZE JUILLET

It was a hot, humid June, leading to an early *canicule* in July. Cobblestones seemed to bake, throwing off damp waves of heat as Margy walked down alleys and crossed tree-lined squares. Since her room was hot and had no breeze, Margy spent all her non-working hours outdoors. She sat in the shade near the tennis courts at Luxembourg Gardens and wrote letters, read, or filled pages of her sketchbook with drawings of the players and spectators. Around the fountain basin in front of the Senate building she watched with mild surprise as visiting students turned the gardens into a city beach: one girl opened her top and let the sun shine on her belly, her breasts covered by nothing more than the blouse hooking over each nipple; and a boy took off shirt and trousers to sit in a chair with a maroon bikini swimsuit that looked very much like cotton underwear. Gradually, she became less inhibited herself, rolling up her jeans or pulling up the hem of her skirt so that the sun could shine on her thighs. And, braless in the afternoons, she always left three or four buttons open at the top of her blouse and pulled it off her shoulders.

She had not seen Everet since March, and, when she went to visit him at his hotel, the lady with the cataracted eye, not remembering Margy from the year before, could only tell her that he had finished his exams and left the city. She did not know where he had gone, but she thought he would be back sometime in July.

For company she visited Marie-Thérèse about twice a week, but she no longer stood behind the room divider to watch her friend at work. Once Margy had watched an African hawker with Marie-Thérèse. He was a friend of Josef's, and it had upset her to be in the same room with him. At the moment of climax, as she started to retreat into the kitchenette, she tripped and stumbled into the screen, luckily catching it before it fell. But the hawker stopped,

255

looked across the room at the schnauzer, and asked Marie-Thérèse if anyone else were in the apartment.

Mortified, Margy decided to keep out of the room from that day on. Instead, she met Marie-Thérèse in the cafe across from rue du Cygne, or they stood chatting together on the corner while Marie-Thérèse waited for a customer. She no longer felt nervous about appearing in the district, especially during the day. She met one or two acquaintances, friends from Alliance Française, a Moroccan student whom she knew through Josef, and frankly greeted them. There were plenty of neighborhood women on the streets, and none of them seemed ashamed. With market baskets in hand, perhaps a child tagging along beside them, they walked down to the market at Les Halles and, showing no hesitation, stopped to talk with the girls who stood empty-handed and childless, obviously waiting for men.

According to Marie-Thérèse, the people in the quarter assumed that the prostitutes worked at a job, as everyone else did. "They know that most of us go to church on Sunday, just as they do. This is the way of the world."

She talked to Marie-Thérèse about many things: politics, Parisian life, her drawings, her occasionally troubling lack of a man, and Marie-Thérèse's planned but still unwritten book. They talked about the boy from Toulon who was Marie-Thérèse's regular customer now. In fact he was so regular that he was known on the street as her *petit ami*, or boyfriend, and no one else tried to solicit him. "He pays--he pays very well," Marie-Thérèse said with a knowing smile whenever anyone joked about falling in love. One day she introduced him to Margy. His name was Gerard. He was very polite and certainly attractive with his young, baby-smooth face, close-cropped hair and tight slacks perfectly accenting his short, muscular body. Margy remembered his thighs and buttocks and tried not to be envious. He was more sure of himself now, she saw, and, when he left them at the cafe, he frankly and firmly kissed Marie-Thérèse on the mouth.

Thanks to people like Marie-Thérèse and Gerard, her French had become more fluent. She put it to use when Marie-Thérèse announced that she and Gerard planned to share an apartment and then invited Margy to a party to celebrate it. The apartment, larger than the room where Marie-Thérèse worked, was a three-room walk-up on the fifth floor of a building overlooking Boulevard du Strasbourg in the northern part of the city. Gerard's brother and some male friends attended, along with several of the girls from rue Saint-Denis. Margy liked the easy camaraderie between the women and the men and was sure she never would see anything like it in the United States. Marie-Thérèse's Bretonne friend (the only woman there, along with Margy, not a prostitute) made crêpes, Gerard's brother played the guitar and sang, and Margy provided her own entertainment, making quick pencil sketches of all the guests and presenting the finished drawings to them.

An interesting evening, she thought, one that brought her pride in her French and French relationships. She was tempted to write home about them, especially to her father, but he still had not responded to her Christmas letter, and she had decided to stop waiting for it. Sometimes she worried about supporting herself without his help, but she had made sure that her room was as reasonably priced as possible, and she now earned enough money through teaching, babysitting, and secretarial work to get through each month comfortably.

Occasionally, along with other artists, she posted sketches and paintings on the fence surrounding the Cathedral of Saint-Germain des Près, and on weekend nights she could make three- or four-hundred francs from her sales. Marie-Thérèse laughed at that since she could earn that much in an hour. But, to decorate her new apartment, she bought several of Margy's sketches at full price, and once or twice exchanged sketchbook for schnauzer to show Margy's work to other girls, a wealthy client, or one of the local merchants. The owner of the cafe across from her station asked Margy to sketch his storefront, and upon seeing the finished drawing, offered her a thousand francs for an oil painting of the same scene. She could live for almost two months on a thousand francs but, more important, as Marie-Thérèse said, the sight of the painting behind the bar would

257

encourage others to buy her work. In just ten days she painted the picture, and, after she collected the check from the patron, she gave up her *au pair* job as a reward to herself.

After that the days flew past because without a job she could paint more regularly. Still she worked as a secretary occasionally, and, to relieve the boredom of those days, she took lunch-hour strolls through the Latin Quarter searching for people and things to draw. One day, upon entering the Luxembourg Gardens at rue de Fleurus, she circled the Senate to study a statue near rue des Ecoles. Then she walked toward the front of the building and, taking a chair at the fountain and basin, saw Everet and Denise. They sat on the opposite side from her, on the lip of the basin, their trousers rolled up and feet in the water. As she walked around to greet them, Denise called out and, with one foot hopping on dry ground, took her hand. Energetic as ever, he was distinctly friendly, and, to her surprise, his animation affected Everet too.

After they dried their feet in the sun, Margy walked with them on the path around the gardens. Everet tossed pebbles from one hand and gestured frequently with the other. He looked refreshed and relaxed, wearing a red, obviously new, African cap and a white dashiki, also new, with black, stylized designs on it. After his winter exams, he said, he had spent time in eastern France, then had traveled south to Greece, crossed the Aegean into Turkey, cut across Africa in May and June, and journeyed north into Spain. Still excited by the trip, he insisted that Margy visit central Africa in order to paint the landscape there. He had traveled to Cameroon and stayed with Josef's family. According to Everet, they lived well and were politically conservative, having a mountaintop retreat and several important political contacts in government--this despite or in contradiction of Josef's radical views. Then, in early June, Josef had flown down also and decided to stay with his family through July. Laughing, Everet added, "I had to travel back alone through the northern deserts, then up the continent to here. I could have used some company."

258

"But he will return by mid-July, won't he?" Denise asked. "At least I hope so."

Everet shrugged. "He said it would be the end of the month, I think."

Denise shook his head. "He will be here by the night of the 13th, I'm sure, so that we can celebrate Bastille Day properly. It is a tradition of the foreign students to have a party."

Both Everet and Margy nodded, and Denise invited them to attend. Margy hesitated, almost refusing to avoid Josef, but she accepted on hearing Everet say he would be happy to go. They finished circling the gardens, and, after fifteen minutes or so at the gate near rue de Fleurus, she left them to go to work.

Shaking her hand warmly, Everet said good-bye, bending to kiss her on each cheek. "Nice seeing you again," he said.

She nodded, squeezing his fingers firmly. And because his happiness made her bold she added, "We should get together for coffee sometime. I'd like to hear more about your trip."

He smiled, burying his hands in his dashiki pockets, and promised a drink next time they met at the kiosk. Margy nodded. Smiling herself, she pumped Denise's hand and started for the office.

In about a week Denise called to suggest dinner together before the party. A good idea, she thought, assuming Everet would be with them too. But when she asked about him, Denise replied that Everet had other plans. A professor at the Ecole Normale Superior had invited him to spend the night with his family, and Everet had accepted. "If there is time," Denise said, "he will come to our party afterward."

Margy could not hide her disappointment, and Denise sensed it. "He seemed so excited the other day," she said.

"He was. However, this is more important. Everet is very political, my friend. You should know that."

"I know it now. I wish his politics would turn in my direction."

259

Denise giggled. "I have some news that may interest you," he said. "I have received a message from Josef. He will be in Paris on the 13th--as I had hoped—and with an important announcement to make."

"An announcement? Now who's sounding political?"

Denise laughed. "From Josef it will probably be a joke. But in any case, we have invited some American girls to the party. I can assure you that you will not feel bored or lonesome."

"Fine," Margy said. "I'm looking forward to it."

In fact she did look forward to the evening because she hoped to see Everet during the latter part of it. On the 13th she met Denise at a small restaurant around nine o'clock, and after dinner they took the Metro to the eastern part of the city. Lightheaded from food and wine, they walked down the side streets near Place Nationale, and on rue Clisson--a meandering old street that had seen a lot of fighting during the liberation of Paris--Denise put his arm around her and kissed her. She towered above him, giggling as she turned her head away. But he took her hand and pointed to a balcony five or six flights above them.

"The party," Denise said with a grin. Several people on the balcony waved, and from behind them the sound of string music--a mandolin, Margy thought--drifted through the air. One or two people leaned over the railing and called out to Denise. "It is a tradition among us," he said, "To kiss our friends good-night before we go to a July 14th party because we may not be with them when we leave."

"An important tradition," Margy said, leaning over to kiss him again. "Maybe I should have had more wine for dinner."

Laughing, they mounted the stairs, stopped at a door on the fifth floor landing, giggled at the word "*Enfer*" painted on it, and, after one more kiss, entered without knocking. Denise shouted a general greeting and then introduced Margy to some friends, quickly excusing himself to go to another room.

The apartment was large, she saw, skylit, with a couple of windows overlooking a block of buildings and a little yard in back. Scattered about the three rooms Margy walked through a variety of Mediterranean people, mostly Africans, and a few Asians. In a small company of Greeks, one man played, not a mandolin, she saw, but a kind of lyre which he plucked and scraped with a bow while others around him sang. Most of the women in this group looked southern European: olive-skinned, dark-eyed, lively, while the men were small-boned and handsome. Also at the party were large African women with corn rows in their hair, a half-dozen men and women in soft Indian dress, and many men and women wearing African prints. It was what she liked most about Paris, the variety of the people, like the city's wonderful gothic buildings providing shapes, faces, and images--new perspectives to evaluate and a sense of unlimited human forms. But when she saw two American girls huddled together in the corner of the second room, that sense of variety faded, and she instinctively turned away. Drinking ouzo and smoking, they looked hard, too harshly lighted and unreal. Without greeting them, Margy turned away and entered the kitchen where she found a table filled with couscous, meat, fruit, cheese, and nuts, most of which had been left untouched. She was about to take a piece of fruit when she felt a tap on her shoulder and turned around.

"Hi, I'm Becky. This is Tanya."

"Hi," she said, sipping some wine from her glass.

"We're from New York," Becky said.

Margy nodded, taking in the slim brunette who extended her hand and gave a friendly smile. She admitted to herself that in the present light Becky did not look so harsh. Tanya, the darker-haired one, did, however. Short and round, she stood beside Becky with a slightly frightened, slightly bewildered look, as if the tradition of saying good-night before coming into the party had made her want to scream. After they shook hands, she pushed a bottle of ouzo toward Margy and said, "Why don't you come over and join us? There's nothing much to do in this room but eat."

Margy nodded and followed them back into the other room. She sprawled on a cushion and talked to them while they passed the bottle of ouzo among themselves. One or

261

two of the men stopped to share the bottle, but because of language (Tanya and Becky could barely speak French), or lack of interest, they inevitably wandered off.

Still, as she had experienced with Josef in cafes, people stared at them from a distance, as if they were unusual objects instead of the three ordinary pieces in a roomful of exquisite things. Denise joined them for a while, and a little afterward a tall, lanky boy from Senegal, Becky's date apparently, sat on the floor in front of them. He tried English, tired of it, then after some difficult moments in French (Margy could hardly understand his accent--which was native, but strange to her Paris-trained ears) he kissed Becky and went off to sit among the Greek singers.

Soon Denise left as well, and, although she was bored with the girls, Margy knew she would feel awkward following him. While she sat there, Tanya went off to find her boyfriend, and, when she led him back a few minutes later, she had three other African men, all stumbling drunkenly over bodies and feet, behind her. Doubtfully, Margy acknowledged to herself that the party was just beginning.

"Ouzo! Ouzo!" Tanya shouted, holding up the bottle and rolling her hips. "We're going to do something with it!"

The four men sprawled on the floor, one of them shouting, *"Les Américaines!"* as he leered at Becky and Margy.

Two carried bottles of Pernod, and one, Daniel, who was Tanya's boyfriend, had a small hipflask of gin. In addition, they passed around a long, narrow pipe, carved from a bamboo-like wood that contained a ball of smoking keefe. After puffing it, Tanya became more giddy, laughing and shrieking as she called to people at the other side of the room. In a few moments a group of nearly a dozen people joined them, and they made a lot of noise. They carried more liquor and a second pipe that they passed around. Wobbling, Tanya stood up and attempted to make introductions in French. She mumbled Margy's and Becky's names (*Marzhee* and *Beckee*, she pronounced them), then screamed out Daniel's, with the accent on the *Yell*. But with most of the

262

others she either clownishly mispronounced the name or drew a blank.

"That's all I remember," she said, covering her mouth and burping. "*J'oublie les autres*" came out, horribly, as "Joo-blee lohtrahs."

Most of the men responded with grunts and groans. Daniel tugged the hem of Tanya's dress and clumsily pulled her to the floor beside him. He stood, and in a loud, genial voice rattled off the names of the people Tanya had forgotten. Finally, faking, he fell flat on his face to loud applause, embracing Tanya and, with a howl, rolling on top of her.

"You like to drink, yes? American girls like to drink?"

Margy turned to see a bronze-colored man sit and, without asking, pour ouzo into her empty glass. He said he was from Athens. "Yes, we like to drink," she said. "But I've had enough already."

"*Californienne?*" he asked, observing her blonde hair and the sunburn she had nurtured so carefully in the Luxembourg Gardens.

"Iowa," she replied, shaking her head.

"*A-wah-ee?*" He gave her a puzzled look and made wavy hula motions with his hands.

"No, no, no." Margy laughed. "*Ee-oh-wah*," she murmured, pronouncing the state in French. Then she added, "*Le centre du pays.*"

"Ohhh," he said. "*Le pays du football, n'est-ce pas?*"

She nodded, laughing again and feeling exhilarated as she turned from him to the surrounding crowd. Two or three men, hearing her speak French, offered to pour wine on top of her ouzo. She prudently refused, and after some talk about her stay in Paris, they began to ask her about the United States. Margy had already discovered the European fascination with America at that time, especially among the young. The Greek, a law student, had already made plans to spend a year at Stanford, another was going to Berkeley, and several others wanted to attend an eastern university, preferably in or around New York. They were surprised when Margy said she had never seen New York or California, but they were even more surprised when she said that she did not want to return to her country. She would have explained herself, but at that moment something else caught her attention: the figure of Josef.

As she talked, a loud voice broke over the other sounds, and, when she turned toward the doorway, she saw Josef smiling directly at her. Her heart skipped for an instant. She thought it might be Everet, but if the tall, lanky, relaxed frame had not confirmed it, the ill-matched, ill-fitting blue suit with sleeves barely covering his forearms and cuffs hardly reaching his boot-tops certainly would have. After what Everet had said about Josef's family, Margy saw the suit as a proletarian pose.

"Ah, my friend Margy and the United States again," he said. His bright, bloodshot eyes made his face arrogant and observant. He crossed the room, loudly adding, "She has nothing positive to say, my friends. It is not a rainbow. There is not even a pot of gold, primarily because they have no rainbow. We should all stay in Africa, on our--what do you Americans call them?—reservations."

He raised his glass and proposed a toast to "Margy's fair country." He spoke French now, but he said the word "reservations" in English, and pronounced the word "fair" in English too. Whether they knew the word's double meaning or not, everyone shouted, drank, and Josef raised a second toast, to the "fair" women of New York City. As he squatted to the floor, Tanya, lolling beside Daniel, gave a titter when her dress hitched above her thighs, and Josef, quick to notice, proposed a third toast, to "*Les* fair *culottes!*"

"*Aye, les culottes d'une cocotte!*" Daniel shouted.

The whole group laughed, and the cry carried through the apartment immediately. Some of the men singing with the lyre player in the corner picked up the call and surrounded Tanya with a burst of cheers. They danced in a circle about her, pulling up their trousers cuffs as they moved, and she, first giggling next to Daniel, suddenly howled when he rolled on top of her and pushed him off, screaming. When the dancing continued, she pulled down her dress and, covering her face in shame, charged from the room. The lyre player continued, but, except for Josef, the dancing stopped. Becky, Margy, and several of the other women followed Tanya into the living room. When she left the apartment, slamming the door behind her, they stopped, shook their heads, and returned to the group in the second room.

"Margy," said Josef, quietly sliding his arm about her waist as she stood next to him. "*Ma belle amie.*"

He kissed her, and Margy quickly slipped from his arm. The party became noisy again, and no one paid attention. Becky lay on the floor between a young Frenchman and her boyfriend, and beyond the three of them students began to dance to the lyre--even Daniel, who clearly did not miss Tanya. The player accelerated the pace of the music; the dancers moved faster in a circle until, with a final burst of startling speed, they literally ran to keep up with him. Josef slid his hand up Margy's back after they sat down, kissed her again and, feigning sleepiness from his trip, lay back, mumbling something affectionate as his head rested in her lap. She slid away, leaning her back against the wall. In a few minutes Josef fell asleep (his head pillowed on his rolled-up jacket next to her thigh), and she yawned, feeling tired enough to join him. The party was slowing down, boring her. At nearly twelve o'clock, she assumed Everet had decided not to come. She sat until chimes struck, and then stood with the others on the balcony to watch the fireworks display light up the city. Even then she could not deny her disappointment, and around one she got up to leave since she had planned to see the Bastille Day parade in the morning.

With no word to Josef or Denise, she groped for the hallway switch outside the apartment. It did not work, and the entire staircase remained unlit. Feeling her way along the narrow steps, she extended her hand along the wall and descended slowly, hearing a quiet sniffle below. It grew louder after someone blew a nose, and, still in the dark at the landing three flights below, she stumbled across a pair of human legs. The owner yelped, and from the timbre Margy knew immediately who it was.

"Tanya? What the hell--"

"It's none of your business!"

Margy found an open door along the wall and, just inside it, an electric switch. It turned out to be for a hallway WC, and, when the lamp went on, she discovered Tanya in front of the toilet, her back against the wall, as if she were a poorly hidden corpse. Margy stifled a smile, but when she saw tears in Tanya's eyes, she offered her a tissue and squatted beside her.

"Hey, come on, cheer up," she said. "It was only drunken fun."

"The bastards!"

Tanya moaned. In spite of herself, Margy had to suppress a sympathetic sob. "It was really only fun," she said. "Coarse, but you seemed to enjoy it until you ran out."

"If you think that was fun, you're as sick as they are."

Tanya turned her face to the wall and wiped her eyes with the tissue Margy handed her. "Let Daniel come down here now," she said, viciously, "or Josef!—I'll make them eat their jokes!"

She blew her nose and, tossing the tissue into the toilet, looked at Margy, her eyes wide and tearful.

"You think he likes you, don't you?"

"Who?"

"Josef—don't you?"

"Honestly, I wish he didn't," she said.

"Well, don't believe him for a minute. They just want us because we're white meat."

"Oh, Tanya, come on. That's pretty strong."

"I mean it. We make them look good."

Margy shook her head. With a shrug she patted Tanya's shoulders and said, "Anyhow, no harm done. It's all the alcohol and drugs."

Tears rolled from Tanya's eyes. "You don't understand!" she cried. "This always happens. You haven't been to their parties before. They humiliate me all the time. Especially that prick, Josef."

She gritted her teeth and blew her nose. As Margy handed her another tissue, Tanya looked at her and said,

"You'll get yours. You should hear what he tells Daniel about you."

She started to rise, fell heavily onto her knees, then sat back again. Thinking some air might help, Margy took Tanya's arm and pulled her to her feet. They started down the stairs, using the light from the WC to guide them. As they stepped into the street, Margy asked Tanya if she felt any better. The girl nodded, looking up toward the balcony and the sound of the voices coming from there. With tears welling from her eyes, she smiled wistfully as they started toward the end of the block. It had been a strange night, and Margy could not resist asking more from it.

"Tell me," she said, "what does Josef tell Daniel?"

Tanya wiped away a tear and, looking over her shoulder, shook her head. "It's not important," she said.

"Come on. Don't be coy."

She shook her head again. "He tells Daniel everything, so what do you think?"

"I don't understand," Margy replied.

Tanya looked annoyed. "They're men. Compatriots. They don't hide much from each other—especially about women."

Margy stopped a moment. "What could he say? That we've slept together? I thought everybody knew that."

Tanya laughed. "You *are* out of touch.--Not only that you've slept together, but that you went to bed with him the very first night you went out."

"So what?" Margy said. "It isn't true, but so what?"

"Well, if that doesn't shock you, how about that he told a whole group of them at a cafe that you work the streets near rue Saint-Denis?"

"The streets?"

"You know, sell yourself?" Tanya smiled, shaking her head almost vengefully. She rubbed her thumb on her fingers as a sign for money. "Ask Becky, if you don't believe me. There are others who saw you there, too. You should have heard the toasts they made that night!" Tanya laughed as Margy fidgeted. Then she added, "Don't worry, Josef likes prostitutes now. It's a sign of political correctness,

267

apparently. He said he loves you. Loving prostitutes is a very liberated thing!"

Margy groaned, not knowing what to say. She had always wondered what her friends might think if they saw her on rue Saint-Denis. She thought it would be obvious she was just visiting or, maybe, sight-seeing. For a moment she felt frightened; then remorse slowly replaced her fear, and, in a strange way, she imagined punishment for watching Marie-Thérèse from behind the screen. "That's awful," she finally muttered. "I thought these people were my friends."

"It sure is awful, and, in fact, most of them still are your friends. Daniel thought Josef would announce an engagement to you tonight. He said that in his last letter to Denise although Denise didn't believe him."

"An engagement?" Margy shook her head. Tanya held onto her arm as slowly they crossed the street and turned down the block toward Place Nationale.

"That's grotesque. Are you sure Josef told Daniel these things?" she asked.

Tanya nodded. "I heard him talk about you in the cafe. He even mentioned another girl he saw you with. He said that once he had fucked her too, for comparison. But he had to pay her, and she wasn't worth it."

Margy shook her head. "Marie-Thérèse... "

"I don't remember names, but if I can believe Daniel, you are a chastened woman. You are to marry Josef this fall and go to live with him in Cameroon. Together, you're going to revolutionize the country."

"Revolutionize!" Margy cringed and began to feel sick to her stomach. "Does Everet know about this?" she asked.

"Everet?"

Tanya looked puzzled. Margy clutched her purse and stopped to study her. "Everet Hamilton, an American—black--who is a friend of Josef."

Tanya shook her head. "I don't know any Everet," she said. She seemed absolutely straightforward, and that relieved Margy a little.

"Well, then, is Daniel the type to make up stories? As a joke on you?"

Tanya shook her head again. "He wasn't making this one up. As I say, I heard Josef myself."

They continued to circle the block, Margy wondering when Josef had seen her on rue Saint-Denis and how much that should concern her. She asked again about Everet, but Tanya knew nothing. The girl's honest if somewhat lack-luster face reassured her again. Tanya did not think that Everet had been with them at the cafe when Josef had spoken.

They discussed these things quietly, circling the block until they arrived at rue Clisson again. Tanya refused to go back to the party, but Margy, not wanting to return herself, felt that she had to see Josef. They walked down to the apartment building together, but Margy went upstairs alone, leaving Tanya in the alley to wait. Her legs shook as she mounted the steps. She tripped in the dark once or twice (the lamp in the WC still furnished the only light in the entire hallway) until, finally, she came to the door with "Enfer" painted on it. Margy entered and found Josef where she had left him. He was awake now, groggy but sprightly, sitting up and pouring out the last of a bottle of wine.

"Margy!" he called. *"Mon amour!* I thought you had left without the traditional good-night kiss." Eyes wide in mock surprise, he puckered his lips and motioned to the cushion beside him as he raised the glass. She stood above him and shook her head.

"I want to talk with you, Josef. Can we go into the hallway for a minute?"

"A little private minute?" he said.

She nodded, and Josef giggled, fighting to rise to his feet. "Oh, my, this sounds very interesting!" he said. "But I can't seem to walk very well."

Leaning against the wall, he pulled on the hand Margy offered, but with no success. She tried to lift him herself, her hands beneath his armpits, but the dead weight of his body seemed to resist instead of rise and brought them both to their knees. Embarrassed, Margy looked around to see several people watching them.

"Come on, Josef. Don't start that nonsense." Playfully, she punched his shoulder and stood back. Grabbing for imaginary ladder rungs, he fell completely to the floor. "Get yourself up," she said. "You're not that far gone!"

Struggling, he knocked over his empty wine bottle, lunging toward the wall as he reached his feet.

"Do not do that again, Margy," he said, regaining his balance. "Don't raise your voice. I am not your field-hand negro."

Steadying himself, he stepped from the wall, then, gingerly, hands on chairs, couch backs, and table tops, he followed Margy through the living room into the hallway. Half a dozen people were out there now, most seated in the dark on the staircase leading to the roof. With more dignity than Margy thought he could muster, Josef straightened his back on seeing them and, without support, moved in front of her to lead the way down the steps. Three flights lower, at the landing with the WC, he stopped and almost collapsed as he leaned against the doorjamb.

"Now, what is it you want to say in this very private minute?" he asked.

"Plenty—much more than a minute's worth," she said.

Josef giggled and chucked her under the chin. "'Plenty.' An American idiom, I believe. It means 'much'--the amount I love you."

He chucked her under the chin again and smiled.

"Stop that! What are you doing?"

He swayed drunkenly, letting his hand drop to his side. "I am listening to some of your charming criticisms." He caressed her shoulder and winked an eye, as Margy, disgusted, stepped away and looked down the stairway.

"I have two things to say," she said, "and neither of them is charming. You know I'm no prostitute--and since when have we become engaged?"

Slowly, he put his finger to the corner of his eye and squinted. She was about to shout, but quickly now Josef put his hand over her mouth and caught her wrist when she tried to push his hand away.

"I have warned you, Margy. You must not raise your voice to me. Especially someone with friends on rue du Cygne."

"Oh, stop it," she said. "You're sick."

"I have seen you with her. I have seen you go into her apartment. I have not been idle."

He took her wrist, twisting it when she tried to yank her arm away. She continued to pull, but he held on and increased the pressure of his grip. When she thought the bones in her hand would break, he let her go and sprang aside. For someone supposedly drunk, she saw, he moved with considerable speed.

"An African can tell a whore when he sees one, Margy. Even an uncivilized savage. Are you in love—with her?"

He held his head high and, turning, started up the stairs again. Margy ran ahead of him and reached the fifth floor landing first. "Enfer" was just above her shoulders as she stood before the door.

"Josef, I swear, I'll embarrass you if you go in there now. I want an apology."

"You are mine, Margy. Whether you like it or not, you are mine."

He stumbled suddenly and, with a wobble, leaned against the doorjamb. She didn't know if he was fooling, but he took her hair, wound a thick skein of it around his fist, and slowly pulled her toward him. She tried to jerk away, but he held on. "You must learn to love men again," he said.

"You're crazy!" she shouted. "I don't know what you're saying."

"You will. I'm certain of that."

He pulled her closer. As if he were lifting her scalp, Josef made her stand on tip-toe, kissed her, lightly, then leaned against her and the wall, breathing heavily, obscenely, in her face.

"Josef--"

He held onto her hair and put his other hand over her mouth. Incredulous, she saw several men and women, Denise and the Greek law student included, stare from the stairway to the roof just beside them. No one spoke although

271

she noticed even in the dim hallway light that all of them looked embarrassed. She tried to say something but could not. Even in her later experiences with Buford and Foss, she would never feel quite so abandoned.

"The more you struggle, the more you will be mine, Margy. Isn't it wonderful?" He had noticed the people at the stairway, and with a proud glance toward them he said, "It's all right. Soon we will be married."

Margy tried to shake her head and work herself back toward the apartment door. Josef leaned on her again. When someone inside, whether responding to the sound of their bodies or searching for the WC, suddenly opened it, she lunged backward, falling into the apartment and pulling Josef with her. They tripped over Becky and her boyfriend, sprawled together just inside the doorway, and as Margy and Josef rose, flailing wildly at each other, the whole party, including the blaring lyre, came to a sudden halt.

"I'm not yours! I never have been and never will be!" Margy shouted, landing squarely against a table. She swung at Josef with her purse, clipping him on the chin. "And I would never even consider going to bed with you!"

She heard catcalls as she rushed from the apartment, and some people on the stairwell laughed at her now. Downstairs she saw Tanya waiting in the hall, and catching her arm on the run she pulled her onto the street.

"What happened up there, Margy? I heard all that awful noise."

"Come on. I want to get the hell out of here," Margy said.

They ran down the block together and at the corner turned toward Place Nationale, this time to find transportation. They heard no footsteps behind them, and, since the Metro was closed at this hour, they slowed down, deciding to walk toward home until they came across a cab. It was gloomy, of course. Even with a clear sky and a bright half-moon, Paris had a way of looking sinister, and the events of the party did nothing to help them shake off that feeling.

"Margy, tell me what happened. You're taking this kind of hard. "

"How the hell do you want me to take it?" Margy said.

She wrenched away from Tanya's arms and moved into the gutter. Tears of anger and frustration rolled from her eyes. "How could he say that? How could he say that I wanted to be a whore—or fall in love with a woman?"

Her knees trembled. For some reason she kept thinking of her father and what he would say about her now.

"God, this is what we came to Europe for, isn't it?" Tanya said. "Adventure. Why does it have to be so horrible?"

Margy put her finger to her lips and turned the corner at Place Nationale. They crossed the square. At the opposite side they flagged a cab cruising past and rode in silence, via Place d'Italy and Denfert-Rochereau, back to the Latin Quarter. Tanya got out at her hotel, and then the driver took Margy up Boulevard Saint-Michel and around the corner to Champ Marseille. She paid him, conversing easily for a minute. And reflecting on the sophistication she had developed since her first cab ride into the city, she began to feel better.

"Merci, mademoiselle. Bon nuit."

"Bon nuit, monsieur. Au revoir."

As the cab drove off, she dropped some coins onto the pavement. Bending to retrieve them, Margy thought she heard a noise in the alley next to the hotel. She peered into it. Except for the cab and a motorcycle's roar in the distance, everything was silent. She remembered that the front door would be locked, and, as she began to search for her key to the side entrance, she tried to stave off an uneasy feeling.

She saw no lights in the windows, and even on the night before the fourteenth the neighborhood remained eerily still. The lamp above the side door was out, and staring into the shadows she was sure she saw something gray move through the dim light from the street lamp. She paused, a chill seeping down her neck as she thought of Josef. After a deep breath, she walked to the door, inserted the key and turned it sharply. A piece of metal clanged just as she heard a whisper of movement beside her, and she jumped.

Something rubbed against her ankle, and she saw a pair of eyes, two pale circles of bluish-green light looking up at her, move toward the street after a whimpered, kittenish meow. Laughing, she turned to watch the animal and saw, immediately beside her, Josef.

"I want to talk," he whispered.

"Creep! Leave me alone!" she cried.

She reached for the door, but he rushed forward, struck her forearm with his fist, and she fell away. While she held her wrist and retreated to the opposite wall, he pulled the key from the lock and dropped it into his pocket. Margy opened her mouth but, even more quickly, he stepped forward and put his hand up to quiet her. He did not seem drunk at all.

"You have no idea how much you hurt me at the party," he whispered. "You have no idea how much I feel betrayed."

"Come on, Josef. It's late. Leave me alone."

He took her arm, and with his other hand he covered her mouth. Breathing heavily, he moved against her, but, when he squeezed her injured hand, she struck out with her purse, angrily stepping back and kicking at his groin. He buckled over with a little moan and then, viciously, slapped the purse to the ground while he took her arm and twisted it behind her back.

"No," he said, quietly, as he pressed her against the wall. "We have had enough of that. This is not America, *ma petite.*"

He covered her mouth again, pinning her against the wall with his entire body, and she felt his hand release her arm, slide around to the front of her neck, and squeeze it. Then, as if on second thought, the hand went down beneath her blouse and touched her breast. He turned her around to face him. She could say nothing. He towered above her, and she could hardly breathe with his hand on her mouth. On the street a car appeared, slowed down, and for a moment she struggled because she heard voices. But no doors slammed, and, when the engine accelerated again, its roar fading away as it turned the corner, Margy began to cry despite herself.

"Please, Josef. Don't hurt me. Please."

"Such lovely memories, Margery. Such lovely times. Why did you spoil them?"

He bent over and kissed her eyes. She opened her mouth, but his fingers clenched her jaw and locked it shut. Forcing her to straighten, he leaned against her, unbuttoned her blouse and gently pulled up her bra. She struggled, but he held her firmly against the building.

"No, no, no. We are not in your country now, I said."

With hands still on her mouth and breast, he pulled her from the wall and tripped her. Shoving her to ground, he dropped on top of her, while Margy clawed at his shoulders to keep him off.

"There are no men in white sheets here," he whispered, grinning. "You'll have to let me have my way."

"Josef..."

He pressed harder, hurting her, although she tried not to react. Later, she would come to see this as some sort of parody, and she wondered if the idea had struck him too. At present, she hoped that some sweet memory would touch him, and so, as she let him unbutton her skirt and pull it down to her feet with one free hand, she offered no resistance. She even let him roll her underpants down to her ankles and did not fight. When he pulled them off, she half-expected him to excuse himself, as he used to on the mattress. But he showed no awkwardness or timidity, and as he unbuttoned his trousers, crudely manipulating his penis to make it hard, she tensed up and vowed to resist. She clenched her fists to her side. His hand briefly slipped off her mouth, and she tried to scream but could only gasp for breath before he covered it again. She struggled, but he pressed harder still, and, when a light went on at the end of the alley, he did not notice it at all.

"*Que t'es belle, Margy! Que t'es belle quand tu pleures!*" he whispered, pressing her head against the pavement. A window slammed, and suddenly he bit her ear. When a second light went on, he noticed it and froze.

"Who's out there? ... *Qu'est-ce qui se passe?*"

275

He leaned on her mouth, pushing her head against the pavement so hard that she thought her scalp would burst. But it had been English; that first phrase had been English, and she remembered it as a sign, especially as, in the flash of a third, brighter light, someone stepped into the alley from the building at the end. Before the light went out again and before Josef could recover, she found herself thrashing about to throw him off.

"Help! Please help me! Help!"

She could scream at last, and screaming seemed to give her force just as it seemed to weaken Josef. He shoved her head back, but she caught his hand in her mouth and bit a finger. He shrieked. She bit harder, almost howling; and, tearing himself away (literally, because she would not let go with her teeth), Josef darted toward the street. Margy rose, groaning. But the person chasing Josef knocked her down, cracking her elbow against the pavement as he rushed past. She grew faint with the pain of her mouth and arm. Collapsing to her side, she saw them both stop, pass under the street lamp, stop again, and turn left toward Boulevard Saint-Michel.

"Help!" she called. "*Au secours! Appelez la police!*"

Her teeth felt like they were falling out.

"*Quel bordel! Qu'est-ce qui se passe? Qu'est-ce qui se passe?*"

Window lights went on. Patrons from the two hotels streamed into the alley.

"*Cette une femme! Une femme! Viol! Appelez, la police!*"

Someone shined a flashlight, and a gasp went through the alley as perhaps a dozen or fifteen people in robes, pajamas, and nightgowns gaped at Margy. She felt ridiculous, cowering against the wall, her torn blouse and unhooked bra the only garments she still wore.

"*Oh, le pauvre!*"

"*Fermez-le, fermez-le, pour le bon dieu!*"

Shining in her eyes, a flashlight went dark.

"Stop!" Margy screamed. "Stop looking at me!"

276

She faced the wall and covered her eyes. Someone draped a blanket over her shoulders, and, swinging about wildly, she broke through the crowd on the run. Catching her toe on one leg-hole of her underpants, she stumbled and fell heavily to the ground. All of the dozen or fifteen people rushed to her side.

"No! Get your hands off me! Stay away from me! I don't want to be touched!"

Rising, she stumbled on the underpants again but just managed to push through the side door. Slamming it with a groan, she ran up the steps to her room.

Fred Misurella

24.

DREAMS

She stood in the center of a small hotel room taking off her clothes. Her mother and father sat in the corner staring at her feet. Just as she undid the bra-hooks at her back, Beverly Winters burst into tears, and Emory Winters started to laugh.

Margy kneeled before them begging forgiveness. Her father raised his hand to make the sign of absolution and changed into a Lutheran minister with a beret on his head. Her mother knelt beside him with a rosary in her hands and prayed aloud.

"Our blessed Margery, who art in Paris, come back to us with chastity intact. Thy will be done."

Beverly crossed herself, took off a long blue robe, threw it over Emory's head and, naked, wearing a gold chain around her waist, ran to the window, opened it and stepped into the air. Margy turned to her father for direction, only to find that he had disappeared. She ran to the window where she saw over and over as if from a stuck channel on a TV, not her mother but Marie-Thérèse hit the sidewalk below.

Not a sound came from the street--or from Margy or Marie-Thérèse either--as she witnessed the body break up on the pavement. Time after time the head rolled across the street, smashing through a dress boutique's window; again and again a torn-off limb landed in a garbage pail and almost tipped it over; the gold-chained torso, like a bladder full of blood, burst on the sidewalk and splattered, spraying layer after layer of red liquid and gold chain-links over the entire street.

The horrible sight appeared at least half a dozen times. Margy opened her mouth with each fall but could not utter a sound. She ran to the phone but could not lift the receiver. She suddenly noticed that her room had no doors and in fright went to the window again in order to climb out. But the sight of Marie-Thérèse's body breaking up on the

278

street forced her back, and she turned to look for her father again. He was not there, but her mother's robe seemed to move now. She approached it cautiously, poked it with her bare toe, and then snatched it from the floor. Beneath it she saw a black infant lying in a basket, its long legs and arms pushing and kicking against the robe.

"I wants you," said a sign pinned to the baby's diaper. "I be," said another in its beating hand.

Cooing but making no audible sound, Margy took the infant into her arms and brought it to her breast. It took her nipple into its mouth and bit it, as if it were a piece of candy. That pleased her, and it pleased her more when she let its hand play with her other nipple too.

"How's it feel, Miss Margery? Y'all like this here chocolate-flavor?"

She looked across the room. Josef stood before her flexing his muscles like a wrestler. He was large, grinning, and confident until she lunged at him and tried to put her fingers into his eyes. He dodged, dropping the blue robe over her head and, in the darkness, stuffing its end into her mouth as she tried once more to scream. Often she awoke at this point, puffing, staring at the ceiling with a bed cover clenched between her teeth. Sometimes she slept through it, however, and then she would dream that she was screaming in a plane, flying over the ocean toward home. The bomb bay opened and dropped her out just as she found her voice. She struggled awake from this part of the dream and found herself in bed, crying, aching from head to toe with chills and fever as she clutched the bedpost above her pillow.

She looked at the sun entering her room, shining brightly through the drawn curtains as the sounds of a garbage truck, delivery truck, or motorcycle came up from the alley below. She turned to the wall, covered her head with the pillow, and drew the sheet above her neck as, gradually, despite her attempts to blank it out, the memory of the evening of the 13th returned. When it did, when she arrived at the point where Josef ran off and the people stood gaping at her in the alley, tears poured from her eyes, and she found that she had to get up. Self-respect demanded it.

279

Terrible times, and, to make matters worse, she held everyone in contempt--French and American alike—willing to see no one except Marie-Thérèse. When the police arrived on the 17th to say that they had at last arrested Josef, she refused to speak to them, indicating that she would not go down to the prefecture to look at him or make a deposition for a trial. She identified him by a photograph and that was all.

From Marie-Thérèse she learned about other events of the night of the 13th and felt even more ashamed. Everet had been charged with attempted rape. He was the one who had come out of the rear hotel and chased Josef. Yet the police, looking for a black man, had stopped him while he ran along the quais near the Notre Dame. In the process Josef had escaped, last seen running somewhere near the church of Saint-Severin.

Everet carried no papers, and, when they called the hotelier down to the prefecture, he could only say that he had seen Everet run from the alley. Other witnesses concurred, and, since under French law suspicion was enough to make him guilty, they held Everet in jail until Margy told them who the real assailant had been. Three days later, they found Josef in a friend's apartment near Les Halles, not far from Marie-Thérèse's room on rue du Cygne.

Margy reacted strongly to the apprehension of Josef, but she held in her emotions until the police and Marie-Thérèse left. Then she lay in her bed all afternoon and cried. She asked the hotelier to send up newspapers from the last few days and saw with horror the coverage some had given the incident. Most had printed nothing or kept the story in the back pages, but one, *Le Cocorico,* specializing in sensational sex, published front page pictures of her and Everet (he hand-cuffed and headlined *"Le violeur noir"*) with a story that she had been raped and that at one time she had lived with Josef, whom they described as a student leader and noted importer of African goods. They made it seem like a simple underworld incident or quarrel and never corrected the story to identify Josef as the real *violeur.*

280

Marie-Thérèse visited Margy the following morning and dismissed the newspaper accounts immediately. She cleaned up the room, told Margy to be proud she had fought Josef off, and read to her in French from one of Marie-Thérèse's favorite novels. Everet visited around noon, but Margy could not face him and asked Marie-Thérèse to send him away. Being unable to see Everet depressed her even more, and, at the end of the week, thinking to change her life yet again, Margy decided to leave her room in disguise. She wore dark glasses, white makeup, and jeans, and her hair cut short. She clipped it herself with a pair of ordinary scissors, and the scruffy, uneven look, with sideburns and short, curly top, gave her the appearance, along with the makeup, of an adolescent Andy Warhol. *"Très, très androgyne,"* Marie-Thérèse said, with a grin, upon seeing her next afternoon.

She walked to an art store on rue Bonaparte and--though she did not need them--bought supplies, including stretchers, four or five meters of canvas, some brushes, oil paints and a palette, all costing about fifteen dollars. She decided against an easel for the present, choosing to use the one already in her room. She also bought several sketchpads and some charcoal, together with a lovely box of pastels that she wanted for outdoor Parisian scenes. Bundling everything in her arms, she took a taxi back to her hotel where she sorted out the equipment, put canvas on stretchers, and color-tested dabs of paint on the day's edition of *Le Cocorico*.

She admired the Impressionists passionately at the time; although she had never studied them systematically before, the first thing she tried was an impressionistic self-portrait. Careful, dark, and shady in the background, it showed great energy in the strokes, but not much detail, especially on the short hair and clownish, painted face.

She left the canvas unfinished because she grew impatient confined to her room. She took her box of pastels and the pad, left the hotel, and decided to sketch something by the Seine. The day was bright, lovely, and breezy, with the colors of the river and buildings showing a translucence perfect for pastels. But it was Paris after all, and, as had

281

happened many times before, nothing struck her as new or fresh. Finally, she left the quais and walked to the Luxembourg Gardens where she sketched a long row of chestnut trees at the west gate. It was an ordinary scene, but she liked the feeling of children playing among the trees, and to the little green concession stand on the left side of the path she added several balloons, painting them as blue, red, yellow, and purple lollipops riding the wind beneath the chestnut blossoms.

As she sat on an iron chair and drew, several young men stopped to admire her work. She shuddered when they came near, and, because she avoided answering them, the less stubborn drifted away. But then three young men drew up chairs together and surrounded her as if they wanted to see how long she could remain silent. They spoke to her in English and in French and tried one or two phrases in either German or Swedish. She made no sign that she understood them.

"*T'es américaine, n'est-ce pas?* Wow! 'ow are you? Okay?"

"*Non, non, non. Elle est blonde. Elle doit-être suédoise. Gooten tak.*"

"*Allemande, peut-être. Schlafst du mit mir?*"

Everybody laughed. She closed the pad, slid the cover over the box of chalks, and stared down the row of trees toward the exit. Folding her arms, she closed her eyes and tried not to shake.

Luckily, they stayed only another five minutes or so before going away. She sat, finished working on the scene and left too, taking a leisurely stroll along the river before she turned back to her hotel. That night she decided to stay in her room and work some more.

She felt as if she had not painted for months, and the accumulated energy of a whole year's work seemed to emerge in a matter of hours. Still life intrigued her particularly: books and luggage that somehow mutated into outsized tickets of travel, a bowl whose pieces of fruit took on the shape of petals on a flower, her closet with the doors open and clothes hanging from the bar metamorphosing into multicolored human ghosts ready to burst into life.

Around midnight she had already filled three canvases, finished one sketch pad, and was pages into the second. She felt as if she were on amphetamine, with little sense of passing time. She simply set objects before her, drew them, and hoped for accuracy--accuracy, at least, to her vision.

This work continued through the night and for two more days during which she hardly had more than one or two hours of sleep at a time. At sunrise on the 21st, she walked out to the Seine with her pastels again, trying for the light on the gray stone and purple windows of the Notre Dame. She returned to her room by eight with a dozen sketches and again took out her oils. She began her eighth and ninth canvases simultaneously, and, by the time she returned to the Luxembourg Gardens late in the morning, she had already fingered the last pages of her fifth sketch pad.

She stopped at the art store for more supplies but found it closed. To her surprise, when she looked at the clock through the window, she saw that it was after noon and she realized that she had not eaten well or slept completely in more than twenty-four hours. Still she did not feel tired. In a cafe on rue Bonaparte, she ordered a double express and croissants and sat in the window overlooking the square in front of Saint-Germain des Pres. The waiter, a young man with long sideburns, smiled pleasantly enough as she ordered, but, when he brought the coffee, he wore a strange expression on his face as if she had done something wrong.

Shrugging, Margy smeared the croissants with butter and jelly, dunked them into the coffee, and swallowed each in one or two large bites. She felt famished although she had not known it, and so she asked for more immediately. But when she ate them and called for a third order, the waiter disregarded her as if she were acting in bad taste. She waited five minutes as he took care of two other customers, then stood to command his attention and tipped the small table in front of her causing the small cup of coffee to turn over onto the floor. It was as if she were at the *Quatorze Juillet* party, crashing through the door with Josef again. Everyone in the cafe stopped talking to turn and look at her as cup, saucer, and utensils clattered at her feet. Coffee splattered her jeans, and, when she saw the stains, she burst into tears. Starting for the ladies room, she discovered she had no purse. She could not find it on the floor beneath the table, or with the sketch pad and charcoal on the seat beside her. Yet she was certain she had carried it from the hotel because she remembered vividly looking through it for her key as she left.

"*Je retourne,*" she called to the waiter, without explaining. She left the cafe and trotted across the square in front of Saint-Germain, intending to return to the Luxembourg Gardens where she must have dropped it in the grass near the tennis courts.

"*Mademoiselle! Mademoiselle!*" the waiter called. He burst through the door of the cafe and ran after her. "*Mademoiselle!*"

When she did not answer him, he blew a whistle, shouted for the police and called "*Au voleure! Au voleure!*" as he ran after her.

Mixing up her flight from the waiter with her flight from Josef, Margy dashed into the Metro station on the boulevard, and, when she reached the entrance to the trains, she could think only of getting away. She saw a woman checking for passenger tickets. Having none, of course, and with no money to buy one, she leaped the turnstile and ran down the stairs, past the woman's outstretched hand.

"*Mademoiselle! Mademoiselle! Votre billet, s'il vous plait. Votre billet!*"

"I need to get away!" Margy shouted.

A male agent standing at a bend in the tunnel to the trains stepped out from the wall and caught her arm. "*Arrêtez!*" he cried, but she freed herself and rushed up the stairs to the street level again. There, across the turnstile, stood two policemen talking to her waiter. She felt safe, just for a moment. One policeman wore a razor-thin mustache and clicked his heels as he saluted the waiter; the other

284

sported white gloves and smoked a cigarette in a calm, almost effeminate manner. But the waiter spotted her, shouting as he lunged across the barrier, and, before she could escape, the agent from below had caught up, the police had crossed the turnstile, and someone, she would never know who, took her arms and held her against the wall.

"*Arêtes! Arêtes-toi!*"

She did not struggle at first, but, when the three of them pinned her arms back, she kicked and screamed, shouting for her rights until they had knocked her off her feet.

"Get off! Get your hands off me! I'm an American!"

A blur of faces surrounded her. The woman who had checked for tickets tried to calm her with a soothing voice. Margy looked up the hall to the exit and blanked out everything but escape. The last thing she saw was the ceiling rising, a huge, empty canvas, its parabolic, soiled surface filled with the white gloves and blue caps of the policemen who held her to the floor as if to stop her from falling. Blue, white, red, the ceiling looked like paisley.

"*Mademoiselle, mademoiselle, calmes-toi! J'ai dit, je t'ai dit, calmes-toi!*"

"Fuck off! Fuck off!" she shouted.

***

"I don't want any! I don't want any!" she heard herself saying.

"What? You say something? What?"

"I don't want any. Get your hands off me!"

She heard the grating, mournful scream of a wheel turning against an axle and fell onto a pillow, complaining about the sun being bright in her eyes. Things were imperfectly visible, although sounds were bell-clear, and yet this person beside her and this man (who?--The name seemed to tease her as she heard his voice) kept asking her to repeat herself.

285

"The sun. The blinds. It's dark in here," she muttered. They looked at her strangely, or so she supposed. The gauze was much too opaque to tell.

"Turn on the lights, please. It's much too bright."

The person (a man; there was something about his voice, she could not quite...) placed his hand beneath her head and offered a glass of water as his breath grew thunderous in her ear.

"Go away. Take your mouth away. I don't want anything."

***

She moaned. A bright light broke into her eyes, and she felt a pair of hands thrashing at her wrists. She kicked, howled, caught a flash of that awful dirty ceiling again, but through the paisley design of red and blue fish swimming across it she also saw that the gloves holding her down were black instead of white. The person, a stranger, leaned across the canvas, seemed to bear a fist of needles, and the next thing she knew she was dreaming.

A vase, a little water. The black gloves set the vase beside her bed, and she began to sob. She gagged. The gloves brought the bowl to her. Vomiting into it, she brought up foul smelling liquid that hit the porcelain like heavy, pasty coins. The black gloves washed her face. She lay back and seemed to rise on air. She floated, hovering near the ceiling (whiter up close, yet flayed and marked like a game fish caught and cleaned) and her body swelled suddenly—she felt her hands and feet touching all four walls at once.

"Help! I'm exploding!—blowing up!"

Someone touched her arm and she seemed to contract, jetting around the room with a dry, embarrassing fart, like a balloon letting out air.

Black and pink gloves chased her, caught her, soothed her. Blankets smothered her. She blacked out, woke up, blacked out and awoke again, in a bed rather than on the station floor. A woman's face broke across the canvas, then the man with the black gloves, then her father and mother

286

behind. She could not believe this was happening; she knew it for a dream and laughed out loud as she tried to move her hand to pinch herself.

"A nightmare, isn't it? A vicious, awful nightmare. Somebody tell me that this isn't real."

Her parents looked mournful, as if she were dying. Her father, dressed in black, played with the brim of his hat, and her mother stared blankly into space as if she, like Margy, had been cornered.

"Pfff," said Margy, trying to snap her fingers to make them disappear.

"Margy..."

"Pfff," she said.

Her father stood at the bedside, placed his hand on her forehead, and mumbled something to the peeled skin of the fish on the ceiling. Margy turned her eyes to the wall and tried to wink everything away. Lights burned; she saw the black gloves bring a pillow. She screamed and tried to shrink away from them, but, as they moved closer to place the pillow under, not over, her head, she realized they were harmless. She opened her eyes to find them resting in the corner. They seemed to float in the white space of her gauzy vision—two dark fish ready to swim, two black birds ready to take flight.

"You all right?"

"Who's there? What?"

"I said, are you all right?"

"What's going on?" she said.

Rising, the gloves came to the bed, fluttered a moment, offering her a glass of water. Then they wiped her chin with a towel.

"You had a bad time."

"Are? Are? My parents...?"

"Oh, yeah. They'll be back in just a little--"

She blanked out. Then, dimly, beyond the gloves she saw a mask with a huge, grotesque white grin painted on it. It was like a clown, a sad clown, until it became pink and changed. It moved. It seemed to synchronize with the voice she kept hearing in the distance. It closed in, then drew

287

back, out of the gauze, until it became an ordinary unmasked face.

"Can you see me now?"

"M-m-m... "

She opened her eyes and for the first time picked out the wall, white, the light, yellow, the ceiling, and then the green chair in the corner. She realized she was in a room, a hospital room: bars on either side of her, gauze curtain between her and what must have been the door. She tried to move but could not lift her arms--or legs--from the mattress.

"Am I paralyzed? Oh, please, no!"

"No, no. You're all right. Take it easy."

The voice cooed. The gloves lifted the sheet--hands!-- and pointed to the belts on her arms and around her waist.

"We thought you were flying out the window at one point. You wanted very much to leave."

They went to the door, came back, and then the face behind them regarded her very carefully. The grin broadened again.

"You suppose we can loosen them a little?" it said.

"What?"

"The straps."

"Straps?"

She nodded.

"You're not going to break things anymore, are you?"

She shook her head.

"You sure?"

She nodded again, and the black hands loosened the belts a notch. They loosened her arms, her legs, her hips, her waist.

"How long?"

"How long, what?"

"Have I been here?"

"Three days. Your mother and father came in last night." The face looked at her closely. She recognized it.

"This is Paris, in case you need to know."

A finger went to the lips and then the whole set of images--black, white, a touch of pink--retreated to the chair. Then a huge man, a doctor, came from behind the screen

288

and looked into her eyes. A mauve face, and with it a bright, white, curly wig and well-trimmed, powdered goatee.

"Hmmm. Well, she cleared up rather suddenly, didn't she? Any dizziness? Any signs of passing out?" He turned to Everet and, after a silly grin, the mauve mask wobbled from side to side.

"I feel fine," she said.

"Good. Do you know who this man is?"

"No. Or rather, yes I do."

"Say his name, please."

She thought a moment, blocking out the name of Josef, which still forced itself on her tongue. Finally, she gave up and shook her head.

"So you don't know who he is."

"But I do," she said.

"Then say his name."

"Everet," she blurted out.

"Yes? And--?"

She hesitated, thought some more, and said, "I really don't remember his last name."

"Hamilton?"

She looked at him and muttered, "Right--I think."

"Perfect," said the doctor, without turning around. "Thank you. Thank you for your help."

She nodded; she did not know why.

"He is a very important, very loyal friend," said the doctor. "You remember that. Now let me take your pulse and listen to your heart and lungs. If you feel better after lunch, we'll let these straps stay off."

***

"Would you like to brush your teeth?"

"Please."

"That's good. Visitors will be coming soon."

Margy stopped, squeezing a measure of paste onto her brush. "Parent visitors?"

"Why, yes, how did you know?" The nurse smiled and tied a ribbon around Margy's neck. Actually, it had been intended for her hair but she had cut it too short to form a loop around it.

"I don't want to clean up. They're not going to like what happened to me here."

She put the brush and toothpaste aside, but the nurse brought in a basin of water anyway and, when Everet left the room, she began to wash. Afterward, the nurse straightened the sheets, and in half an hour or so Everet returned, trailing Emory and Beverly Winters behind him.

"Here she is, brand new," he said.

Gauze seemed to hang before Margy's eyes. She would always remember that. It smothered the room as her parents stood just at the split in the curtain and regarded her. Then her mother strode through the folds of gauze and kissed Margy's forehead. Margy burst into tears, automatically it seemed, and Everet retreated behind the curtain at once.

"Call me if you need me," she heard him whisper to her father.

"No, Everet, please."

"I just--"

"I don't want you to leave. There is nothing I wouldn't want you to hear."

Tears burned in her eyes, turning everything brighter. Years later she would recall how the colors in the room seemed to mix as Everet stepped into the clear light, looked at her and her parents, then shrugged and said he had to make a phone call. Her father told him to go ahead.

"No, Everet. Stay. Please. I'm afraid."

"I'll be back in a little while," he said.

He waved with a quick nod toward her parents, but, when Margy heard the loud click of the door, she saw her mother's eyes harden and her father drop his hat on the table while he moved to stand at the bottom of the bed.

"How are you?" he said, kindly, pressing her foot and smiling.

"I'm doing fine. Please don't touch me."

He put his arm around her mother's shoulders and, as if that movement should have brought them into sharper focus, asked if Margy knew who they were.

She laughed.

"Do you?" her father said.

"Yes, I recognize you, all right."

"You should. You gave us every reason to despair when you ran away."

Her mother began to whimper, yet stared with anger, not sorrow, in her eyes. To Margy, her parents looked out of place--or out of costume. Dressed elegantly for Europe, her mother wore pink-framed glasses that glinted and accentuated her angular features, creating rainbows from the overhead lights. She wore a gray turban wrapped tightly about her wrinkled forehead, and at the top of that a pale blue diamond pin shimmered in the ceiling light. In contrast, her father was dressed in dark gray, with white chalk stripes to disguise his rotund body, but, in an unusual choice for him, he sported a deep red silk tie under his jutting, rigid chin. Despite Margy's anger, his sad, tired expression tore at her heart. She knew she had disappointed him, and she had never been able to handle that.

"Well, it happened, didn't it?" she asked.

"What?" he said.

"The wonderful, talented daughter of pure parents has run away and smudged her family's reputation."

"Margy, we're here to help. This is not about reputation."

She looked out the window. When she turned back they were virtually the same although, in a slight switch of the tableau, her father's hand now rested on her mother's shoulder.

"Don't just stand there, Daddy. I ran away. I know you're disappointed. I am, too. Say it for a change."

Her father came to the bedside and put his hand on her arm. She felt it shake as he squeezed her.

"Margy, Mother and I are very sorry about this. Truly. We're not angry, but we hope you can learn from the experience and see better where you've gone wrong."

291

He patted her hand, looking directly into her eyes. As if he were a hypnotist, she angled her line of vision to the window in order to avoid his power. She wondered if she would always avoid a man who looked at her that way.

"We do love you. We always have," her mother said.

Margy remained silent. As she flexed her hands beneath the sheets, she wanted to say something but had no idea of what it should be.

"Don't you see how your actions have kept us away?" her mother said.

Margy laughed. "Actions?" she said. "Well, I'm appealing to you now, Mother. You too, Daddy. Yoo-hoo, come help me."

She continued to stare past her father, wondering if her mother were right, wondering if somehow she could have made a pact before she left, something that would have brought the three of them closer together. But the responsibility should not have been hers completely. She remembered the beatings her mother had given her, and she knew she could never forget them or let her mother forget them. She could not forget her father's recent abandonment of her either or the fact that neither of them ever praised her work.

"Margy?" her father called. "Are you really all right?"

She nodded, struggling to hold her head in place as he moved closer and stopped within inches of her face. She felt, not touched, but invaded with him so near. And she was fearful of lashing out now that the straps were off. If only her mother...

"Don't you hear your father? Don't you have the decency to answer him? You have a tongue; use it!"

Her mother stepped to the side of the bed, took Margy's shoulder, and--it was the only right word--hissed in her ear.

"Mother, please. Don't do that."

She held back, trying by will to pin her own body to the bed. It was as if those white gloves were in the room again, trying to press a pillow on her head. Her hands slipped from under the sheets without her wishing them to.

292

"Speak to us. You can't ignore that we're alive," her mother said. She shook Margy's shoulder, and it seemed to affect her vision. Suddenly, two hands shot out from the covers while balling into fists. But before they struck, her father pushed them back to the mattress and with a weird squint to his eyes covered her mouth with his hand. He shouted wildly; and as if in slower time, Margy saw two nurses and a doctor rush through the curtain around her bed. Along with her father they strapped her down as she kicked her feet. Margy's hair looked curly, clownish, compounding her hysterical look. Her stomach muscles heaved as if she were giving birth. Her arms and legs flailed and pushed as if she were struggling free of a heavy weight. In a violent, billowing sea, her head jolted left and right as gloves tightened the belts around her waist.

"I don't want you in this room--or this city," Margy shouted. "You make me sick."

"Margy, my girl--"

Her father leaned forward and jumped back as she swiped a hand at his face.

The doctor took her arm, inserted a needle into it, and, as Margy gasped in surprise, they all slowly faded away. She felt herself weaken, blubbering, wondering if she were going to reach the other shore. She mumbled words she herself could not understand, and soon the room turned into a gray translucent cloud. She floated through it slowly, seeing patches of light break through it here and there. Then Everet and the goateed doctor stood by her side. The doctor placed his thumb on her wrist.

"Now, who are you—and where?"

"I know, I know. I'm tired of knowing."

She could say no more. Her tongue stuck to the roof of her mouth and had the feel and taste of cotton. She could barely move her lips. The doctor wiped her forehead and put a stethoscope to her breast. She felt grateful. He lifted the stethoscope from her skin and left, motioning Everet to the chair beside the bed.

"Don't loosen those belts," he said. "Just keep her company."

293

The gauze faded now, and Everet clearly sat there, a round, soft, brown face instead of a painted mask.

"You're having a hard time," he whispered. "I'm sorry. I really am."

"Don't let them in," she pleaded. "Please don't."

"Who? Don't let who?"

She swallowed. How could he not know?

She mumbled. He leaned closer. It occurred to Margy that he had been around, in dreams or reality, for days, and now she tried to tell him that she was grateful, too. But she could only mumble again and never knew if he understood. He smiled, squeezing her shoulder in a very intimate way. Unable to verbalize, she splayed her fingers, pushing against the belt until he understood and took her hand.

"M-m-m-m. M-m-m-m. My... " she managed to blubber as he massaged her fingers with his thumb. She had intended to say, "My miserable life."

"Just rest and get your strength," he said.

He looked at the door again, and she squeezed his hand with all her might.

"Relax. Your mother and father--" He stopped and looked away. "I'll stay as long as you like."

***

Again, dream? She called for help or tried to, feeling her body expand and the walls close in until at a certain point her whole physical being seemed about to explode. Her voice would not come, and for a frightening instant Everet no longer held her hand. She felt the ceiling press against her stomach, she heard the goateed doctor bellow as if from far below. Someone pulled and pushed her arm. Then she felt a pinprick and jetted around the room head-first until she slammed into the corner and dropped, awake and, yes, crying in her bed.

"Hold it. Easy! I'm glad to be with you, Margy."

She tried to calm herself. She noticed the open window beside the bed. The wind blew cool, but now the sun warmed her skin. She felt good to be alive.

"I want to leave all this," she whispered.

"When you leave here, if you feel the same, I'll help you go."

She turned her cheek and her nose seemed to bump the ceiling. "Why do I always hurt so much?" she said.

The room altered: from the bed she saw Everet floating above her. She reached up and squeezed his hand. Not a glove. Beside her, bending and whispering in her ear: "Hey, Margy. I'm next to you. Right here. Calm down."

"Where? I can barely hear you. Where--?"

"Here, by the bed. I'm not sure how much you'll remember."

She glanced around the room. The light was clear. A breeze pushed through the window and blew the gauze away at once.

"I *do* want to leave this place," she said.

Everet smiled. She squeezed his hand and laughed as if she had made a joke. Grinning broadly as if he thought it was pretty funny too, he kissed her cheek. Margy felt something odd--her skin was splitting. When he kissed her again, she felt the muscles in her face open, crack and then turn out with joy.

25.

LEARNING

Margy tried to explain her parents to Everet, but never really could. And so at the time, his understanding of them boiled down to a couple of nasty incidents that she told him about.

One occurred while she was a sophomore in high school when Margy came home at three o'clock in the morning from a weekend dance. She had promised to return by midnight, but she and her date, Willie, drove into the farmlands beyond the school and on the way home she asked him to stop near the woods outside of town. With a searchlight in her hand, Margy led Willie to her favorite spot, the waterfall, and, as they sat on a rock overlooking the pool, she put down the flashlight, held hands with him, and talked about the future. He was a senior, an aspiring artist like Margy, and under a clear sky with just a slice of the moon they discussed college, marriage, and their careers. When they drove home, Willie parked a block away from Margy's house, and she spent half an hour necking with him. It was the first time she had ever let a boy touch her beneath her blouse, the first time she reached into a male lap and, while she did not exactly feel flesh, she felt its urgency in the lump beneath Willie's trousers. To her surprise, it caused just a moment or two of panic and then moved her enough to know that she would come back for more.

At home she looked into the glass of the storm door and saw that her hair was out of place. Bobby pins dangled from her sweater, and the wool plaid skirt was rumpled and twisted. She straightened herself as best she could, turned off the porch light, then took off her shoes and circled the living room coffee table before going into the kitchen. Her parents kept a nightlight burning there; as usual she turned it off before going to bed. But she heard a cough from the hallway, and, when she went to see who it was, she saw her mother with a pile of magazines in her arms.

"Do you know what time it is?" her mother asked, holding out the magazines as she stepped away from the staircase that led to the second floor.

Her mother waited up during most of Margy's nights out, and so the number of magazines was a gauge of the lateness of the hour. Margy stepped back and turned on the kitchen light. Her mother entered the room, tossing magazines onto the table.

"I've been doing more important things than watching the clock," Margy said.

"That's rare."

Margy turned off the light, leaving her mother in darkness. Then she started toward her room.

"Apologize for that, Miss."

Her mother took Margy's arm, backed her into the kitchen, and ordered her to turn the light back on.

"Emory," she called. "Emory! Come down here. Take a look at your daughter."

"Oh, Mother, are you going to start trouble again?"

Margy felt embarrassed. She knew her lipstick was messy, and she could almost feel the prints of Willie's fingers burning through her bra and showing on her blouse.

Her mother stood behind her picking a hairpin off Margy's shoulder.

When her father came down, Margy's mother held up the hairpin, pointed to the clock, and asked him to look closely at her.

"Just a little wrinkled," he said, stretching a little and tying the robe about his waist. With a yawn, he placed his hand on Margy's shoulder and asked her in a friendly voice if she had had a good night. Margy shrugged and nodded.

"Wonderful," he said, scratching his chin. "Now go upstairs."

He pushed her toward the hallway, and she, relieved and strangely regretful at the same time, began to leave the room. "Good night, Daddy," she said. "Thanks."

297

Then he took her hand and, turning her around, looked carefully into her eyes. "Tell me honestly, Margy. You haven't done anything that you would be ashamed of telling your parents, have you?"

He looked closely at her. His eyes darted to the wall behind her head, down to her feet, then carefully worked their way up to her eyes. She felt as though he were searching for clues. She also felt that her appearance must have provided them in abundance. The skin around her nipples still prickled with the memory of Willie's palms.

"Well," he said. "Have you?"

She looked down at her skirt and brushed away a wrinkle. Her father held his smile until it strained.

"Oh, come on, Margy. Tell me."

She looked away, then back to her feet.

"Well, what did you do with Willie tonight?"

"Daddy, that's personal."

"That's why we should know," her mother said.

"Beverly, let Margy answer. What did you do, Honey?"

"Nothing." She looked out toward the hallway. "Talked," she said.

"Until three o'clock in the morning?"

"That's understandable. There's nothing wrong with that. We--"

"Oh, Daddy, I know you understand. You always understand. But it never does any damn good."

"Watch your words, Miss. You just watch your words."

Her mother ran her fingers through Margy's hair and along her back. She picked off a second hairpin as if it were a louse and pointed to an inch or so of slip beneath the rear part of her hem. Then she, too, pushed Margy toward the door.

"Sweet, innocent little thing, isn't she? And talking all that time? She doesn't know enough. She doesn't have that much to say."

As she raised her hand to strike, Emory caught Beverly's wrist and pushed her into a chair.

"Go upstairs, Margy. Go."

But Margy made no move to leave. Usually, she avoided her mother at these times, but the talk with Willie had made her feel different, and she wanted to strike out at her mother instead. She stood with her fists raised, half-clenched, like a boxer.

Her father stood in front of her mother and waved his hand. "Go upstairs, I said. Do you want your mother to hurt herself?"

"Herself? That's a joke!"

"Margy, please... "

Margy slammed the door to the hallway and ran up to her room. She was exasperated. She was used to her mother's tantrums by now or should have been. Still, she suffered. Along with her mother's screams, she heard her father talk in a calm, soothing voice. There was a crash of dishes, then the thud of a piece of furniture hitting the floor, and finally her mother's shrieking voice rising and falling as she ran through the kitchen. Her father cooed and lowed until, with occasional warning shouts, he had made everything quiet. In pain, deeper pain than she ever thought she would bear, Margy knelt at her bedroom door and cried.

She could not pray; she had not prayed in several years, but that evening she fell to her knees and whispered to herself, wishing for better things. Her wishes led back to many childhood scenes such as the afternoon she broke the family's crystal platter and the night when, during an argument, her mother destroyed a roomful of furniture and threatened Margy with a knife. But her adolescence had become even more painful. As she grew from a bright, coordinated child with skillful hands (adored by her father) to a gangling, then increasingly graceful young woman, her mother became more jealous. In order to avoid humiliation, Margy kept her friends away from home, especially boyfriends, and she always dreaded the inevitable after-midnight confrontations when she returned after curfew.

Yet her father's discipline could be worse than her mother's because on the next day he would do whatever Beverly bid the night before. As Margy knelt near her bed that night, she could almost predict it. Her father would

299

knock on her bedroom door at six or seven o'clock next morning, enter with an expression of regret and, dressed for work while wringing his hat like a country peasant, lean over the bed to kiss Margy on the forehead and then mete out punishment as though it were nothing more than a listing of local fauna. She was sure that personally he favored her over her mother, but, because of some inner compulsion, concern for family hierarchy perhaps, he rarely showed that favor except through weak emotional expressions.

"You are my darling, you know. You are the only reason I stay in this house."

"I know, Daddy. It's hard for both of us."

He would take a deep breath, turn, stare at an empty square of light on the floor, and let the ax fall.

"I think that, for all concerned, Margy, it will do us good if you apologize."

"Apologize? For what?"

"Your mother is very sensitive."

"Daddy, so am I."

"But you are younger," he would say, as if that were an excuse.

He turned to the door, raised his hand to quiet her, and cast a wistful glance around the room. She kept two cut-out pictures on the mirror--one, a magazine photograph of Picasso; the other a photographic reproduction of a Georgia O'Keefe painting: "Black Cross, New Mexico." He strode across the room to look at them, but, after a moment of study, his eyes switched to Margy's in the mirror.

"I'm sorry. I'm only doing what I can, what I *have* to do," he said.

"Daddy... "

"Margy, I'm sorry. We've decided that you must stay in for the coming week."

"*We've* decided?"

"Yes, *we* have. And I must be firmer here--if you don't stay home, if you sneak out as you have several times recently, I'm going to be forced to take more drastic steps."

She laughed. "What more can you do?"

He looked down at his feet as if he were very tired. "Don't test me," he said as he left, and he added, just as he closed her door, "Cooperate, Margy. In a certain sense, you have no other choice."

Everet found it hard to believe these stories even though he had seen her parents' odd behavior in Paris. But there were more, many more things that took Margy a long time to tell: how during the two or three periods of months that Beverly Winters spent in a mental hospital, her father could be as relaxed and relieved as Margy about his wife's absence. Each of the separations provided a glimpse of how much better their lives might be. Margy painted and drew with more productivity and less restraint. She laughed often and felt no tension around the house. Most important, she spent less time with her friends and more with her father, whom she loved very much. Like a recent bride, as she described it for Everet, she looked forward to the end of the day when she could turn their evening meal into an adventure. Her father grew vegetables and herbs in back of the house, canning and drying large amounts of them through the fall and winter seasons. Margy loved them. She used them to create curry and other exotic dishes during their evenings alone. They went to films and concerts and took trips into Cedar Rapids and Iowa City to visit art museums.

On spring and summer weekends they camped out near the falls, birding, looking for catfish, and hiking over rocks beside the stream for miles until they had crossed the woods and come to the main highway leading north toward Wisconsin and Minnesota. Once, taking what started to be a day trip to Chicago to see some O'Keefe paintings at the Art Institute, they passed the night at a downtown hotel because they also visited the Sullivan Amphitheatre, the Carson Pirie Scott Building, and Frank Lloyd Wright's Robie House near the university.

It was the summer after her sophomore year in high school, the year she had read *Lolita*, sneaking the paperback version in and out of the house inside her jeans, and, when she and her father stood in the center of the hotel room,

301

watching the bellboy turn down the pale rose coverlet on a double bed and opening the blinds to show them a view of the city, she could not help thinking of Humbert Humbert and Lolita entering their first motel.

About that night, she could never give Everet all the details; but she told him most. They had not been able to get a room with separate beds, and through the night they slept uneasily. Margy clung to her side of the mattress, conscious that each time she moved and each time her father moved, their bodies made contact. It disturbed yet somehow excited her too. Once she opened her eyes to see him leaning over her, and, when she asked what the matter was, he simply shook his head and lay back again.

Toward morning her arm flew behind her, brushed against him, and for a fleeting moment felt something unmistakably alive and rigid. His hand came to her shoulder and steadied her. She started to excuse herself, but, when his fingers gripped her and began to move down her side, reaching the hem of her pajama top (they had just bought the pajamas, at Carson Pirie Scott, the previous afternoon), she found herself unable to speak. Her skin crawled. Her breath began to catch, and years later she would remember the sensation occurring again when she circumvented a description of the morning to Everet in Paris.

"Daddy... "

"Shhh... Don't speak."

She felt his lips against the back of her head, and then his hand slipped under the pajamas and rested on her stomach. When he turned her over to face him, Margy felt as if the whole room revolved with her. His complexion paled, but he was smiling. His hair was messy with strands frozen into stalks like birch trees crossed in a confusion of white, black, and gray as if someone had run through and knocked them to the ground. His mustache prickled when he moved his lips. He looked old and tired, but an excited expression brightened his eyes like the one she saw on the faces of boys she went out with. She recognized that expression with dread because, in her mind at the time, it seemed to imply something unnatural about her.

302

"How do you feel?" he whispered.

"Fine," she said.

He nuzzled her neck and touched his lips and mustache to her ear.

"What are you doing, Daddy?"

"Are you happy we stayed?"

She did not know what to say. She nodded, but at the same moment she pushed herself away, placing her hands on his chest and gently shoving. The flesh of his hand came away from the flesh of her rolling hip with a slight sucking sound, and she felt her face grow hot. Her eyes went from his to the sunlit window, to the chrome tap in the sink just beyond the bathroom door, to her hand against his chest, and then up to his eyes again.

She pleaded with him to stop. He flexed his hand, as if there were a cramp in his fingers. She felt an urge to fling the cover off, stand up and straddle him. She felt at fault (after all, she had touched him first), yet his reaction made it seem inappropriate to apologize. He reached out, draped his arm over her shoulder and drew her close. Their lips met, and, pushing hers open for a moment with his tongue, he said good morning.

"Do you know what we're doing, Margy?"

She shook her head, lying. Out in the hall someone passed talking loudly, and through the bathroom door the sound of a flushed toilet from another floor filled the room with an uncomfortable sense of soiled intimacy. Margy pulled away again, this time her father's hand sliding across her neck and cheek as she turned away and took her side of the mattress.

He sat up. As they remained silent for several minutes, she became aware of his breathing and the uncomfortable sense of wanting to be held at the same time she feared it. For a moment she remembered the rigidity on his body, and it filled—no, over-filled--her mind.

"Margy!" he whispered.

The mattress shifted. She wanted to touch him again, but she felt her arms shiver as he caressed her shoulder. Some ten or a dozen floors below a police siren wailed; like

303

the flushed toilet it brought out a sense of something terribly wrong. The sound seemed to start at the soles of her feet, push through her thorax, and issue from her own open, worried mouth as she hunched her shoulders and turned more completely away.

"I won't hurt you," her father said. "I don't want to hurt you."

She said nothing. But when his hand brushed her breast, she squealed, rolled off the bed and, on her feet, turned to face him. He looked gentle, innocent. She would remember that in her mature years. His expression was genuine, and later she would often wonder if the whole Chicago experience was not just a figment of an adolescent's over-developed imagination. Yet when he rose from the bed, circled the mattress and, hugging and caressing her, whispered, making her feel much more her girlish self again, his hand pressed her breast, and for another unmistakable moment she felt his erect penis against the palm of her hand. With boyfriends before Willie, she usually pulled away, but with her father's arms around her, she felt she could not.

"Daddy, please..."

"Don't feel bad," he said. "It will be all right."

"No!"

She hunched her shoulders, burying her face in his chest, hoping he would understand she loved him. She felt the strain of pulling away from him as he pressed against the small of her back and kept their bodies close.

"No, please!" she said.

"Margy!"

This was not a whisper. She looked up to see an expression close to anger upon his face. She would remember that as genuine too. Nevertheless, he let her go. She turned, ran into the bathroom and wondered if she should lock herself in. Ironically, she often did that when her mother came after her, and she had wished that he were there to protect her. At the exact moment that she turned the hotel doorknob, however, the phone rang twice, delivering her. Afraid that someone had called to complain about their immoral behavior, she listened carefully. The clerk was simply following instructions. Her father had asked to be awakened early, and, as Margy turned the tap on in the tub, she heard her father refuse breakfast, thank the clerk for the call, and then ask that their car be brought around to the entrance in half an hour.

"Let's get ready, Margy. We're leaving soon."

"After I shower, Daddy," she said.

They never spoke about it, either on the drive from Chicago that day or during the weeks that followed. In fact, except for her father, there was no one to whom Margy normally would confide such things, and for years she had a secret sense that she had caused the situation, disappointing him as well, and that there was an ominous note of warning in the experience that she should heed. She began to feel uncomfortable with him whenever they were alone, especially during the months when her mother was hospitalized. As she grew older, she became angry with him, but rarely allowed herself to express it—certainly nothing about the Chicago experience itself. She put his behavior down to grief over his life with her mother and berated herself for compromising their relationship with stupid behavior that morning. She had been young, but not that young: something firm between his legs indeed!

Everet literally turned pale when she told him some of it. He urged her not to see her parents anymore, and he wanted her to come home with him to Connecticut where she would, in his words, learn the benefits of healthy family life. She hesitated, wanting but afraid to tell him more.

For years after that incident, Margy lost her ability to draw and paint. The gift that had been so much a part of her (and her relationship with her father) seemed to dry up. As a matter of fact, she gained entrance into the university on the strength of drawings she had done as early as the eighth and ninth grades. But while she told Everet about that, she did not make him aware of other things, such as how the blocked condition came to an end in her freshman university year when Joseph Gardner entered her life: how he eventually led to her trip to Paris and how, through Marie-Thérèse, she fully regained her abilities.

Gardner was the professor of her first studio art class at the university. Forty-eight years old, short, and silver-haired, he wore a beard that sprouted from his face and chin in long, luxuriant curls that always reminded her of the famous cartoon self-portrait by Leonardo in his later years. And there was something in Gardner's pale blue eyes that reminded her of her father, although she could not say definitely what she saw.

He was kind to her, taking her under his wing almost from the very first day of class when they stood around a plaster-of-Paris torso and drew it from various angles. He had admired her firm hand with the charcoal, encouraged her use of shading around biceps and thighs, and particularly praised her attention to the intricacies of anatomical lines. After class he had asked to see more of her work, and, when she in embarrassment admitted that she had not done much of late, he had not been critical. When she returned to her room that afternoon, she began to work on things that she had only fantasized for the past two years. In a burst of energy, she brought out six or eight sketches that did not shame her.

"They're fine, quite fine," Gardner said when she showed them to him after the next class. He bought her a cup of coffee at the student snack bar, and, almost as if it were a part of a larger plan, she found herself running across his path from that day on: in the student room where she set up her easel to do extra work at night, along the walks beside the river that flowed through campus, or in the cafeteria line so that they often joined each other for lunch.

Always he proved thoughtful in his comments, interested in her life, and kind whenever she discussed a problem she had with painting. Hands behind his back, a curved pipe jutting from his mouth in an old world manner, Gardner's painfully expressive baby blues darted into hers, and then, when she had noticed, moved quickly into the distance where they seemed to swivel back and forth in search of something to set on. He seemed to be the quintessential trusted father she had wished for but never completely had. He invited her to his studio, where he

306

showed her the tools he worked with, offered her a cup of tea, and, regrettably, she felt, escorted her back to campus without so much as a word or look, let alone a touch, she could take as hint of something more.

Still his interest was clear, and, when Margy looked him up in the college catalogue, read his biography in the American *Who's Who*, or listened to student gossip whenever his name came up, she felt thrilled. True, he was married, but rumor had it he was unhappy. His wife was ill, a bitch, some said, and perhaps about to be hospitalized (shades of the jittery Winters family, she thought). He had a son in the university high school, a notorious discipline problem, and a daughter, his favorite, a year older than Margy, who was out of town attending Smith College in Massachusetts, making him lonesome at home. Professionally, Gardner had written several books on classical art, exhibited in Europe and the United States, and had work in the permanent collections of American museums from coast to coast. As a professor, Gardner's reputation among the students was enviable; he was sharp, they said, yet sympathetic, and above all, fair. He was not a pushover for grades, so it particularly satisfied Margy that he admired her work, and, when she received an "A" at the end of her first term with him, she saw the path of her future in art had cleared at last. Under his tutelage she gained respect, and both students and professors expected a lot from her after graduation.

Some said Gardner doted on her. He invited her to faculty parties that his wife could not attend. He introduced her to other artists traveling through the city. He helped show her work at special exhibitions in Cedar Rapids, Des Moines, and Minneapolis. Then one evening as they walked back from his studio, they embraced, went into his office at the top of the art building, and made love on an old torn couch while they listened to the footsteps and talk of other students and faculty out in the hall. They laughed silently, feeling apart from and above the others because of the secret of their love.

Gardner spoke to Margy about leaving his wife and living on a farm out in the country. He talked of changing

307

jobs, leaving America, and living permanently in Paris. The unspoken assumption was that whatever he chose, Margy would follow him. But toward the end of her junior year, just as he had decided to make the final break, his son spotted them walking together hand in hand along one of the back walkways of the campus. They did not hide, nor did Gardner hide his true relationship with Margy. He boldly placed his arm around her waist and introduced her to his son. Jed was the boy's name. He smiled, spoke pleasantly with them for several minutes and then left. But that night he wrote to her father, who wrote to the university's fine arts dean, and, a week later, as if he had been caught at something grossly immoral, Joseph Gardner decided that his duty called him home.

"But why?" she asked. "It's not as though your family was unaware. Your relationship with them is obviously failing."

"I'm sorry," he said. "I simply don't have the courage."

"But it's legal. I'm old enough," she told him. "Why should it take courage to try for happiness?"

He shook his head.

"You don't think we'd be truly happy, do you?"

"I think we could be ecstatic."

"Could be? Then why stop now?"

He said nothing. "I'm afraid," he murmured as he turned and walked away. "That's all there is to say. I'm afraid."

That was the last Margy saw of him. She stopped going to his class. She stopped drawing and painting in the student workshops. By April, with only a month till the end of junior year, she dropped out of the university and, without telling her family, went to live with friends on a communal farm outside Waterloo Falls. But her father found out and came to see her.

She argued bitterly with him, and, when he saw how much his fatherly leverage over her had weakened, he tried to make up for it with the gift of a summer tour in Europe. Margy refused at first, especially because it was part of a

Christian Youth Fellowship tour. But finally she accepted with the explicit idea of throwing the gift back in her father's face. She wanted to live alone; she wanted freedom to paint. Though Joseph Gardner would not be with her, she would begin her new life in art. In the old world of Paris, she thought, getting rid of her past would be the best way to start again.

26.

LEAVING AGAIN

In late September Margy's father called to say that he and her mother had returned from Italy and were leaving for the United States next evening. Somber, aloof, he wondered if he could see her alone. She was happy to agree, and they decided to meet at the Tuileries near Place de la Concorde not far from her parents' hotel. Since Margy had an appointment in the afternoon, they decided to meet around four o'clock, and, when she arrived wearing an informal shirt and sweater, she saw him dressed in his blue business suit and hat, combed and shaved as if ready to travel home at that moment. Waiting at the magazine kiosk near Cleopatra's Needle, he hardly smiled when Margy walked up.

"How is Mother?"

"She is not feeling well," he said, "and is anxious to get home."

"I'm sorry she's not happy," Margy said.

He shook his head but remained silent. She was relieved to talk to him again because he had not, in fact, phoned after their last meeting at the hospital. But as she stood on her toes to kiss his cheek, her father put out his hand to keep her away.

"Where can we have a cup of coffee?" he asked.

"It's awfully warm, Daddy. I'll take an ice cream from the vendor."

They walked to a stand in the gardens, ordered two large cones, and sat on a shaded bench away from the boulevard. As they watched traffic and occasional passersby, they ate their ice cream in silence.

"Dad, I just want to say—"

With his hand upraised again, her father stopped her.

"Margy, when there is nothing else, the only thing we have to fall back on is our quiet love. I admit I haven't been much of a father. But I have loved you very much, and I hate to lose you, especially this way."

"I'm sorry too, Daddy, but I'm not sure what 'this way' means."

He rose, tossed his unfinished cone into the basket and came back to the bench. He walked stiffly. After looking at her, his blue eyes turned toward the Champs Elysée and moved to Concorde.

"We're not enemies," she said. "I love you."

He smiled, but sadly. His eyes wavered a moment. As he glanced over her head toward Hotel des Invalides, he said, "What takes men like me and turns us into puppies? What takes a lovely young person like you, like your mother was once, and turns her into an unhappy woman?"

He took off his hat, wiped his forehead, then buried his face in his hands. A breeze blew through the chestnut trees surrounding them as Margy patted him on the shoulder. Finally, he looked up and took her hands.

"Daddy..."

"Your mother and I discussed this last night," he said.

He looked around and let her hands drop into her lap.

"Much as I hate to, I have to tell you what we've decided."

"Daddy, I'm afraid... What is this?"

"Now, listen. You are nearly twenty-one, and you are no longer our responsibility, at least not legally."

He looked at her guardedly, his voice trembling. Hiding her own feelings, Margy simply stared through the space in front of her. He took one of her hands again, then let it go in order to continue.

"Since you no longer choose to live with us, since you no longer want us to be your parents in effect, we have decided to reciprocate in kind. We will no longer be responsible for your bills or your illnesses. I will pay your hospital bill, but after that we will no longer be responsible for your problems. We will, in fact, no longer treat you as our child."

Her back stiffened, and Margy looked at the roadway in front of her. A civil guard passed. Then a young child followed, a whistle in her mouth, dragging a balloon behind

311

her. "Fine. That's the way it's been for the last year anyway," Margy said. "What else is new?"

"In fact, when we get home we will start formal, legal proceedings to end our relationship. Do you know what that means?"

Her father looked at her, uneasily, as if he was not really sure of his own words. Margy bridled at first, but the feeling subsided when she heard the little girl blow her whistle and the traffic along the Champs Elysée roared into her ears. For a moment she seemed not to believe her father, and, when he took her hand again, she let it lie in his limply.

"Daddy... "

"Confidentially," he interrupted, "you know your mother will forget this soon after we get home."

Remembering the unanswered cards and letters this past year, she pulled her hand away. Her father shifted uneasily beside her.

"You really have no backbone, do you? Not with her. You've never had one."

"Margy--"

"And you've never loved me either, despite what you tell me. You've wanted a pretty pet. Something to show off in company."

He shrugged. "I married badly. After that, there is nothing more to say."

"Oh, God. Well, I can say right now that you might as well begin those legal proceedings. I mean to be free of both of you. For good. I'm disowning you!"

"Don't be hasty, Margy."

"Don't touch me! I remember what it's like to be touched by someone as sick as you."

"God bless you, Margy."

She gasped, realizing what she had said, and almost expected him to strike her for it. Instead, he put on his hat and, with a stubborn yet defeated expression, left, beginning the walk toward Concorde. He turned up one of the side streets near the American Embassy, and Margy went after

312

him. But he walked fast, and, by the time she caught up, he was three-quarters of the way down the block.

"Why did you have me in the first place, Daddy, especially if you had a bad marriage? And why have you taken care of me all these years?"

He kept his head down doggedly, turned the corner at a brisk pace and, as she drew near again, stopped, whirling around and pointing a finger at her.

"I have nothing more to say to you. And I don't want to be bothered anymore either."

He looked miserable, yet still in charge. Then he seemed to break as he brought his hands up to his face and dropped them to his side. "I love you," he cried, choking.

"But inappropriately. And look how I turned out."

"You are what I came home to at night, Margy, what I loved about our life."

"Sure. So now you disown me."

He shook his head. "I love your mother too. I just don't know how to love very well. Not anyone."

His words affected her and moved her to shame when she remembered them years later. But on that day she hid the shame very well, saying only, "What a lovely thing to tell a daughter, Daddy. Do you tell that to Mother too?"

He turned, walked a little farther and without a sign went into their hotel. It had a plain, dark front with gold lettering. Through the glass door Margy saw that the lobby had an art deco mixture of mirrors, chrome, and crystal. Ready for a showdown, she followed her father indoors, but he stopped and waved her away at the elevator.

"Don't follow me," he warned. "I'll call the police. I won't tolerate it."

"Daddy, how could you? I'm still your daughter."

"I will not allow you to see your mother. It would be too disruptive. You are choosing to leave us, after all."

She charged the elevator doors, but they closed just as she reached them, leaving her with a vision of the car ascending into empty space. She went outside and sat in a cafe across the street for twenty minutes or more. Then she tried again to go up to their room but without success. No

313

one answered the phone, and the desk clerk refused to let her go up without her parents' permission. Her father had ordered it, he said.

Frustrated, she went out on the sidewalk again, looked up at the building, and saw them standing in the window a few floors above. With her mother beside him, her father looked grave, almost carefully unresponsive to the life on the street before them. But her mother looked even more curious because the afternoon light set a golden glow on the glass above her head. As the seconds passed, it seemed to envelope both in flames at the same time it gave them a formal, gilded veneer, as if to preserve them for passersby.

IV.

HOME AGAIN: 1974

27.

KENNEDY

Years later in Connecticut, during a week when she did nothing but sit in her room at the Caliban (or on its balcony), and write and sketch in her journal, Margy tried to restart her life. She had stabbed Everet, mortified herself with shame in front of her son, Kennedy, but after a week away she felt that she had to do something--confront her possible choices. Driving down the Thruway from Stratford gave her a sense of new life, and, when she saw the buildings of downtown Stoddard, she felt as if it were a family welcoming her home. She had not realized how lonesome she was.

At home she found Everet writing in his study, but, unlike the Stoddard skyline, the sight of him did not make her feel at home. Without a welcome or any sign of greeting, he informed her that Kennedy was still at his grandmother's house and pushed across his desk three telephone messages. She asked about Goldie. Everet looked up angrily, saying that he had not seen or heard from Goldie since she left. Then he returned to work.

He looked rested and, as usual, seemed to be in excellent physical condition. She wanted to ask about the wound on his neck, but she was afraid that would start an argument. It was covered with a piece of tape and a patch of gauze about an inch and a half square. Minor, apparently. She was grateful for that, but, disliking his gamesmanship, she sat on the couch across from him, and, when he still did not look up from his desk, she tried to startle him by saying that she was thinking of leaving.

"Leaving?" He raised his head, as if he were in deep thought.

"That's right," she answered. "Tonight."

"Oh, no problem at all." He leaned back, speaking as if she were going out for a stroll. "Go right ahead. We'll manage."

316

He returned to his writing pad without further comment.

"You're awful. You know that?"

"Look, I'm busy, you know? Come back when I have more time."

"Forget it."

"I have. So *you* forget it," he said.

Furious, she went up to their room (slamming the door, as usual, she thought), showered, and, after putting on fresh clothes, brought her pads and pencils up to the attic, where she opened the windows and tried to think. It was quiet in the neighborhood that evening, and she sighed happily, glad to be home, though not without regret. It was comfortable, and it was hard to remember why she had wanted to leave in the first place. She heard the usual spring night sounds of the Drive: a child crying, crickets mixing with the distant thump-a-thump of a stereo, an occasional door shutting on an outdoor conversation. Sounds of suburban life. But, oddly, except for the fish-eye blue of a television screen here and there, most of the windows on the street were dark. Goldie's room was still unlit, and the only visual sign of action on the street came from the headlights of a single automobile passing through. It rolled down to the cul de sac, paused, then turned around and went out again.

She looked at the phone messages (Everet had written no names on them, just instructions to call a number when she returned) and saw that one of them was from Foss. The other two were numbers that she did not recognize. She dialed them, hoping at least one would lead to Goldie, but she received no answer at either. She wondered if Foss might have some information on Goldie, and, although she was reluctant to call, it was with him that Margy's world finally resumed a part of its former shape.

"Hello, Foss?"

"Yes...?"

To her surprise, he sounded clear-headed. "This is Margy," she said.

"Well, well, well. Where have you been the past seven days?"

317

. "Just living--by myself. That's all."

"Hmmm... Sounds eventful. Word has it that the Mayor was calling out the National Guard."

"Foss... "

"Sorry. I shouldn't joke, At least I know it wasn't Goldie this time. He was here yesterday, also wondering what had happened to you."

"Is he okay? I haven't been able to reach him."

"He's all right. In fact, he's fine. He had a little run-in with Dan the Man and had to take off for a while."

"Again? Where did he go, Massachusetts?"

"I don't know where. But I think he's staying with some friends in New York. He's perfectly capable of caring for himself, Margy."

"What did you call me for, Foss? I don't want to get into another discussion about Goldie."

Foss blatted a crude raspberry sound into the phone, but, when he received no reaction from Margy, he sucked in air and stopped. In the silence Margy heard further heavy breathing and nothing else.

"Well, what did you call about?" she asked.

"I have to admit that I called to apologize."

She laughed. "You have to admit it?"

"I mean it."

"What did you do, Foss, get religion?"

"I mean it, Margy. It was an awful thing I did. An apology is the least I owe you."

She sighed. She did not believe him, but went along with what he said anyway, mainly because she felt too weak--too depressed--to argue. She also thought she should hold on to her friends right now. "Forget it, Foss," she said, lamely.

"I wish I could forget it, but I can't. And I have to tell you, you were right about that impotence thing."

"Oh, Foss, really..."

"Really," he said.

"Foss, I don't know what I was right about. It was an awful thing you did, and I got hysterical."

"Margy, I want to make up for it."

"Don't worry about it. I have other things on my mind."

"Margy, I wouldn't have called if I didn't mean it."

"I'm sure you do," she said. "But let's change the subject. I don't want to talk about old stuff. How are you feeling now?"

"One hundred percent better. I haven't touched a drop since Monday. I'm working again. Even got that canvas of 'Margy: La Primavera' out on the stretcher."

"That's great, Foss."

"Come on down and see it. By the way, I'd still like to have you pose."

"No, Foss. This is not the time for that."

"Yes, yes, yes--it is! I understand your feelings, especially after the other afternoon. But maybe just a couple of times?"

"Foss, do you know what is going on in my life right now?"

"I have some idea. Maybe posing will be good for you. No hanky-panky this time. I want to finish up this damn painting and get on to other projects. I'm through with chasing women and drinking liquor, Margy. At least for now. From now on, Foss will be a dynamo. Did I tell you that I finally got the word on the Guggenheim for Italy?"

"You did?"

"Yup. The approval came this week. I'll be leaving in the fall."

"That's really great, Foss." She smiled, despite herself.

"Florence. Oh, man, I can't wait to see those Botticellis again."

"Will you have a chance to help me with my show?"

"Oh, ho, ho! Look who's talking about other things in her life."

"You just said that you owe me something."

"Right--and I do. All right, bring your stuff to class. We'll go over it afterward. Maybe here."

"Not at your place, Foss. Not anymore."

"Suit yourself, Margy. It's your thing."

319

"It's going to be difficult... "

"Maybe you ought to forget about the show for now. You're under a lot of pressure."

"I think I can handle it."

"I'm sure you can." He paused. "But this is an important occasion, and you're having a lot of other issues."

"Foss, is that all you called for? To apologize?"

"Yeah. And to tell you that I'm straight again; and I still want you to pose."

She sighed. "Thanks. I'm glad you're feeling better, but I have to hang up now."

Laughing, he said, "Believe it or not, so do I. I'm busy too."

"So long, Foss."

"Hey, listen, I'll see you in class. Okay? We'll talk about this show some more."

"Thanks, Foss."

"Cheer up. We can work out something."

"Good-bye."

"Come on, Margy. I want you to do a real bang-up job."

"Good-bye," she repeated.

Somewhat disappointed, she hung up and dialed the two other numbers. Still no response. Margy sat at her desk doing nothing for a while, then went down to the kitchen for coffee, and from there called Kennedy in Bridgeport.

It would be an awkward call, she knew, one she wanted to avoid making, first because she knew she would speak to Ruth Hamilton, who would act surprised and delighted to hear from her, and second because when she spoke to Kennedy the awkwardness would likely get worse. In addition to being tired at this hour (nearly ten o'clock), he would be more than a little upset not knowing where his mother had been for the past week or so. She dialed anyhow, and she did get Ruth. But without a moment's pause, Kennedy came on.

"Are you all right, Mama? Are you home?"

"I am, Kennedy."

"When did you get there? And why--"

320

"Just a few minutes ago," she said. "Are you enjoying yourself at Grandma's?"

He sighed. "I guess. But I'm missing too many things because of you. Aunt Cora picks me up from school early to take me back to Grandma's. So I can't play softball. I told Daddy that I want to come home at night, but he said he has to work late. Can I come home tomorrow, Mama? Will you be there?"

"I'll be here tomorrow, honey."

"You sure?" She sensed the criticism in his voice, of course, and she made an effort to answer calmly.

"I'm sure. You come right back after the game, and I'll be waiting."

"Mama?"

"Yes, honey?"

"Daddy says... Daddy says that you weren't crazy when you stabbed him."

"Crazy? Oh, God, did you think that, Kennedy?"

"He says you did it because you were mad at him. Is that true?"

She thought a moment, suddenly feeling weak. "I guess so, honey. I'm ashamed, but I guess I was too angry."

"At what?"

"At what?"

"Angry at what?" he asked.

"Oh, Kennedy, Mama and Daddy have a lot of problems. I'm not sure I can explain. But it had nothing to do with you."

"I know that, Mama. I asked Daddy if it was because you didn't want him to be mayor. He said it was more than that--it was other things I wouldn't understand. Don't you think someone should tell me?"

"Being mayor is a big part of it, I think."

"Isn't it good for Daddy to be mayor? He'll be a good one."

"Of course, he will, honey. Only, as Daddy said, there are other things."

"What things, Mama?" He sounded impatient, and she hunted for something that she could explain.

321

"I just want to stop him from going away from me, honey. I need him."

"Oh, Mama, Daddy says he loves us—he loves *both* of us."

"Kennedy, what can I say? You're a little boy, and I can sense things better behind Daddy's words."

"Things? Daddy says he'll love us more if he's mayor. Don't you believe him?"

She thought a moment, trying to think of a way to say no. "You know how it seems when he says something seriously, and then you find out he's only been fooling? He doesn't do it all the time. But when he does, it hurts, doesn't it?"

"Yes," he murmured, grudgingly.

"Well, I feel like that when Daddy says he loves me. I don't know why. But I want him to make me feel that he's serious all the time. That he means it."

"But he does."

"Maybe--for you. But for me, I'm not so sure."

Margy felt depressed, yet might have continued. But Kennedy asked for quiet, and she decided to let her words lie for a couple of seconds. Finally, he said, "I never feel that way about Daddy loving me, Mama. I don't see why you should."

"Kennedy, there are things a woman wants from her husband that... Oh, I don't understand, and I don't see why you should."

"Mama!"

"Well..." She paused, trying to gather her thoughts again. "Maybe you would understand," she said. "Do you believe Daddy and I really need each other? Do you think he really needs me?"

She heard Kennedy fumble with the phone as he passed it from ear to ear. It was doubt, she thought, much like her own.

"Well, do you think we respect each other?" she asked, preferring that choice of words. "I know it's a hard question for a nine year old, but I think it's something you might try to understand."

322

"Sometimes I think you do," he said, "but a lot of the time you don't. You seem to fight each other then, and I don't like it."

"That's just it. We don't like it either, honey, which is why I had to go away. I love Daddy too much. I love him too much to fight with him anymore."

"That doesn't make sense to me, Mama."

Margy laughed. "I'm not sure it does to me, either," she said. "But it's the way I feel, and I think Daddy understands."

There was a long silence, Then, very quietly, he asked, "Does that mean you're going away again, Mama? I don't want you to."

A lump came to her throat. Margy sat on a kitchen chair and thought a moment. "Honey, I don't want to. But I have to talk it over with Daddy."

"Talk..."

"Well, he's angry at me, as I suppose he should be."

She heard him switch the phone to the other ear again. More hostile, he told her abruptly, "I want to go to bed, Mama. I'm tired."

"And now you're angry with me too," she said. "We'll have to talk about this another time. I told you I don't fully understand things myself."

"Well, think about them, Mama. I'm interested, you know."

"Good-night," she said, nearly sobbing. "I'm sorry to have to put you through this."

She hung up, feeling more depressed. Margy had expected Kennedy to feel angry, but she was not prepared for the sense of abandonment in his voice.

She went to his room and, straightening his bed, picked up a pair of jeans and put away a pair of his sneakers. There was a desk in the corner. Its legs trussed up a pile of sport books, magazines, and sheets and sheets of statistics on the past three seasons of baseball. She had put a bookshelf next to the desk, and Kennedy had filled it with volumes concerning sports, as well as adventure books and books on boats and navigation. He talked of attending the

323

United States Naval Academy, and, to encourage him, Everet regularly rented a sailboat to take him out for lessons on the Sound. Above the TV (also on the bookshelf), he had photographs of baseball players: Hank Aaron, Roberto Clemente, and two older ones of Willy Mays and Jackie Robinson. She thought with some regret of her own treasured photograph of Picasso and the reproduction of the painting by Georgia O'Keefe. She saw a reprint of a Remington painting hidden in the corner, but some lithographs of pioneers and hunting expeditions she had bought him were off the walls, probably gathering dust in his closet. His father's son, she thought, shrugging, as she stood at the desk and leafed through the pile of books and statistics. If he had been a little girl, if he had cultivated the least bit of interest in the world of art--? But she crossed that from her mind, and, after cursorily dusting the shelves and other bric-a-brac with her hands, she returned to the kitchen and called Kennedy again.

She heard a busy signal at first, but she dialed once more and Ruth Hamilton answered, again calling Kennedy right to the phone.

"Hello?"

"Honey, I'm sorry to wake you. And I know you're angry, but I just want to ask you a question."

"Mama?"

"One question. Do you... Do you respect me? I mean really respect me and like to have me around?"

"Mama, I do."

"You do. Are you sure?"

But she could not ask him if he loved her.

"Yes. You do such wonderful things for me..."

"Honey, go on. I really want to hear everything you say."

He paused, laughing. Still, she could not ask, but Margy sensed the hurt in him when he added, "Well, sometimes, Mama, you act as if I'm in the way. Like when you start worrying about your painting and forget about my stuff. I don't respect you then, you know."

"Oh, honey, no..."

324

"I try not to get in the way, or be a pain. I really try."

"I love you, Kennedy. You're more important to me than painting. I'm very happy to be your mom."

He laughed again, but bitterly. "Good, Mama."

"What, Kennedy? What's the problem?"

"Well, can't you show it more? I was in bed just now, and I was thinking, you wouldn't leave us now if you loved us. Or respected us. You wouldn't go away and not come back?"

Margy sighed. "I don't think so, Kennedy."

"Think so?"

"Oh, honey, I don't know. Really. Just remember, I'll always love you, no matter what happens. If I left I would always want to see you again. I would always want you to love me. But I might want something different as a way of life."

"Way of life? What..."

"Painting. I would want more of that."

She stopped, conscious of the contradiction in her words. She heard no sound on the other end, which she read as bewilderment, as well as disapproval. But after a long pause, Kennedy said he would always love her too. "No matter what you do, I'll love you. I have to love you. I can't help it," he said. "You're my mother."

At the sound of those words, Margy felt her stomach contract. As if someone had hit her, she sat down again.

"Oh, Kennedy, I'm so glad you told me that. Thank you."

"But I want you to stay, Mama. Daddy thinks I'm selfish, but I won't like it if you go away."

"Selfish? Oh, God. It wouldn't be selfish; it would be normal, natural. It would be wonderful. Thank you, for telling me, Kennedy. I'll have to talk this over with Daddy. Then I'll talk it over with you."

"I don't want you to leave, Mama."

"I'll remember that. But now you have to answer one more thing."

"Yes?"

"This isn't easy, but try to answer it honestly."

325

"Of course, Mama! I'm always honest."

She held her breath. "Would you rather have me unhappy at home, or happy living by myself. I ask myself that all the time."

He sighed. "Home, Mama. No question about it."

She was about to hang up when Kennedy took back his words. "I want you to be happy. I told Daddy that, but I still want you home. I don't understand why you can't be happy there."

Margy sighed. "Sometimes I don't either," she said. "It's difficult to understand, honey, and a difficult decision."

"It doesn't have to be difficult. It's all up to you."

He hung up politely, telling Margy he would see her next afternoon.

28.

EVERET

Margy felt drained and went into the living room where she opened a few windows. In about fifteen minutes, she tried Goldie again and, receiving no answer at the two numbers she had, dialed the Goldsteins. Dan Goldstein answered; Margy began to hang up, but he spoke sharply into the phone, apparently addressing Goldie, and she could not help listening.

"I know it's you, you little shit with attitude. I know you're just trying to bust me with these calls. Well, I'm glad you're gone. Don't come back unless you want to apologize. Go to the people next door. You disgust me sometimes, but they disgust me even more."

He hung up and Margy almost jumped away from the sound of the click in the phone. She sat for a while, uneasy, and then decided to take a walk. A damp, cool breeze blew against her face as, without saying anything to Everet, she stepped out the front door. Along with the fog from the Sound, the breeze carried a smell of plastic from downtown, and, walking beneath the streetlights' blotches of yellow mist, she reached the corner. Undecided where to go from there, she turned back toward the cul de sac. The two large houses at the end looked solemn: Dan's with one bedroom light high on the second floor, her own with Everet's study shining dimly on the lower right. The two windows looked like cat's eyes staring through the night. Feeling an eerie chill, she walked between the houses and past them into the small woods beyond until she reached the pool where Brenda Salerno made her attempt at suicide years before. She stopped and listened to the cicadas, shivering as an occasional nighthawk darted across the water. She circled the pool, passed Kennedy's school, then took a footpath out to the main road and followed it slowly back to Camels Back Drive. Her phone call with Kennedy almost demanded that she talk to Everet about staying, but, as she entered the house, she feared that he would embarrass her with further strategic delays.

"Everet?"

"Yes."

He was still at his desk when she entered the study. He bent over a yellow legal pad, reading something with a rapt expression. It made her feel that perhaps his busyness was not feigned.

"Can we talk?" she asked, trying to be pleasant. His face dropped when he looked up. Then he looked down at the pad and grunted.

"What does that mean?"

"Yes... I suppose."

"Good... I suppose."

"Look, would you mind waiting a few minutes while I finish this final paragraph?"

She nodded, still trying to be pleasant, taking the couch across from the desk and lighting a cigarette. She felt tense but determined to be civilized. He looked at home here, as always. He wore a blue button-down shirt open at the neck (earlier it had been closed with a tie so that she could barely see the bandage) and a pair of bifocals. He looked completely healthy, Margy noticed. Despite the injury, she could see him sprinting along the Sound, speaking before a crowd (although perhaps with a turtle neck shirt to hide the wound) and carrying out heavy physical and mental tasks without tiring. Sheer energy had always been his outstanding trait, she knew. She also knew she would never match it.

"Well, that's about it," he said, sighing as he underlined something, dotted what appeared to be an *I*, and scribbled a few more words. A cloud of smoke had begun to gather around his desk. He waved his hands unconsciously, and, like some dark Moses spotting the Golden Calf, dropped his legal pad and frowned. He rose and threw open the window without a word. At the desk, he grimaced, picked up the pad and began to read again, running his fingers through his newly trimmed Afro. Margy smothered her cigarette and left.

328

"Whenever you're ready," she called out from the living room.

Everet did not reply.

She went to the attic, jotted a few lines about him and Kennedy in her journal and arranged some canvases, watercolors, and drawings along the wall in order to work on them for the show. Everet's efficiency always spurred her on in her own work. It was a form of competition that she considered healthy. She worked for a while, made some more notes in her journal, then decided to call the two numbers. At the second, she found that Goldie indeed had stayed there but now had moved on to New York. She took down his new number and went downstairs to pour a glass of orange juice. Everet called when he heard her, and she returned to his study, finding him seated in his Barcalounger, leaning back with his shoes and glasses off.

"I'm sorry," he said, motioning toward the couch. "I had to finish something in my announcement speech."

"So you're going on with it. Good." She sat, smoothing her shirt over her jeans.

He nodded. "It's better for me to announce alone and have the state people back me a few days later. Looks less like a backroom set-up."

Margy smiled. He looked confident, glancing at her and exuding a sense of pride and accomplishment. The delays had not been strategic, she guessed, but, as she sipped the juice, she wondered if this friendliness was his way of preparing a first salvo.

"I'm glad you finally know your mind about it," she said.

"When have I not known my own mind about it?" he asked.

She shrugged, still trying to be pleasant.

"Remember, I don't want to argue," Everet said.

"Neutral topics," she answered, laughing. "Or should I say difficult ones which Margy responds to as neutrally as she can. What are you saying in your speech?"

He waved, proud. "'Make Stoddard a Home Again.' That's my slogan."

329

He smiled, fondly picking up the speech and reading some passages aloud. It was filled with high-flown, almost 19th century rhetoric, but, despite that, Margy felt his personality come through, especially since he had a rather deep, preacher's voice. The effect was powerful in a poetic, original way. He read several parts of it--about establishing a new community center, increasing jobs, making frequent use of public meetings and church organizations--and then he stopped in the middle, tossed the pad onto the desk and, smiling, leaned back in his chair. He rested his large brown hands behind his head,

"Congratulations," Margy said as she sipped her juice. After a moment she added, "You're making the speech alone, aren't you?"

"That's right."

"So--?"

"So, what? Come on, Margy. Speak up. What is it?"

Almost as an afterthought, she added, "You might have gone to Wiltshire with me. You could have made the speech another day."

He shook his head. "No, no, no. No. If I want it to make the Sunday papers, it has to be on a Saturday."

"M-m-m... "

"As I said in the letter, Margy, I'll go to Wiltshire when I feel that you and I are ready."

"That's exactly why I have to leave, Everet. When will we be ready, in your estimation?"

She put the orange juice down, opened her hands and placed them on her knees. Just a few light blows, she thought, looking at her nails and noticing that they needed painting. Yet definitely more than a simple sparring match. She thought of Kennedy's comment about selfishness and could not figure where Everet stood.

"What do you think?'" he asked.

"About what?"

"Us?"

"I think you're avoiding me, as always."

"Come on, Margy. I've been a damn committed husband, and you know it."

330

"Oh, really? Well, then, how do *you* feel about us now?"

"Terrific... Really terrific."

He laughed, placing a hand near the bandage on his neck. She remained calm for a moment, but she felt that, in his own way, he was getting to her. If this kept up, she would have to shout to reach him, and she did not like that. She kicked off her shoes and sat with both her feet under her on the couch. She tried to steel herself, as she had with Kennedy.

Pointing to his bandage, Margy said, "I'm glad that's not serious. I was really worried. I want to apologize."

He waved. "Some blood, but, really, not much of it."

"I'm very relieved."

He shook his head. "You're a child sometimes, Margy. That was one of the times when you were most childish."

She dropped her hands in her lap. "Everet, I don't want to be analyzed. Try to figure out your own failures."

"Failures?" He sat up, looking at her as if the word applied to him was an insult.

"Yes, that's the word. You're acting the part of a white man. That's a sellout as far as I'm concerned. It's also one definition of a failure."

His mouth nearly dropped open. "It always comes out, doesn't it?--even from you."

"What?"

"You know damn well what—this stinking racism."

"Oh, and what about your sexism, you bastard? The little woman, standing behind her man!"

He waved his hands above his head. "Hallelujah! Hallelujah! And de Lawd God brought feminists, hanging from the trees!"

"That's it--the way it always is! My problems are never as difficult as yours. You don't think my life is as important either."

"Hell."

"It's true. You don't even think I do significant work."

"For Christ's sake, has a woman ever been lynched or tortured because she was a woman? Has an artist?"

331

"Everet, you know better. What about rape? And wife beating? And censorship? My God, have you forgotten everything?"

He looked down at his hands. She slammed her fist on her knee.

"Furthermore, despite everything, you've had rewards. What do I get out of my work?—Nothing... a feeling of uselessness."

"And a provider and lover in me," he said plaintively.

"But because I'm a mother, not because I'm loved."

Everet threw up his hands again. "That's not true, and you know it. I love you very much." He leaned back, looking at her thoughtfully. "Margy, in a black man that useless feeling you're talking about is perceived as shiftlessness. We can't afford to be idle if we're going to be men."

She groaned. They stared at each other, the friendly veneer cracked and nearly vanished. Everet made a point of smiling, but then he seemed to think of something and turned away. "You may not care about this," he said, "but I'll tell you anyway. What you're doing, no matter how innocent, really hurts my chances for election. In this... "

"Everet--"

"But I don't care--really!" He put his hand up again to quiet her. "I really don't, Margy. Now, that might seem wrong-headed or stupid to you, but that's the way I feel. I want to be mayor, but I won't sell out for it."

"What about Gray? What--?"

"Please. Please, listen to me. When my family moved into our house in Bridgeport, my parents were stoned. People broke our windows and shouted ugly things. I never forgot that. Then, when you and I moved here, we had all that awful neighborhood nonsense to endure. Well, because of that I've tried to prove that I deserve to be where--and what--I am. I've succeeded more than I ever hoped, and I will continue."

"See?"

"But, Margy, two papers in this town would love to blow my private life to smithereens. The only reason they haven't is that I have Fred Gray on my side, and now, possibly, Buford."

"Everet--"

"Let me finish, will you?"

She slouched back in her seat.

"One headline like, 'Candidate's Wife Runs Off with Adolescent'... Or, better yet, 'Black Candidate's Wife in Weekend Tryst with Juvenile'.... Then I'm finished. They'd print it with a front page picture of you and me at that dinner and—"

Margy smiled. "Ultra-high contrast, no doubt. My little dress would come out very well next to your dark skin."

He shook his head. "It's not funny, Margy. I don't have to remind you that Buford, supporter that he might be, would not be hard to buy off, if I judge him correctly."

"He's a shit. You're a sellout, but he's a genuine, unmitigated piece of shit."

Everet looked in her eyes and shook his head again. "I have no choice. I have to work with him, so I can't complain."

"If you're not selling out, why do you have to work with him?"

Everet looked away, nodding. "Margy, I know that something went on between you two."

She said nothing.

"I don't mind," he said. "I really don't mind--mostly."

She remained silent. He folded his hands in his lap and continued. "Family is the staple of this country and this city, Margy. I believe in it. I know that you've had a bad experience yourself, but I believe it makes our country go."

She nodded, shifting uneasily. Margy felt unsure again, and she wanted to change directions. "I agree with you," she said. "But it bothers me. It makes me feel so left out, almost like an orphan."

He leaned forward, pointing at her. "Whether you agree or not almost doesn't matter. People will perceive our broken relationship as a threat to our community—and against the concept that black and white can live together.

333

Some would even see it as a weakness in my manhood; yes, and in my ability to administrate effectively. Gray says--"

"Gray says... I thought you didn't care about the election, damn it!"

"I *don't* care! I *don't!*" He rose, started to add something, then looked away. "You know damn well I care," he said.

She laughed, bitterly. He sighed, looking out the window. Rain had started to patter against the glass. Margy sipped the juice, grateful to have a point in her favor at last. Rather than take advantage of it, she decided to make an admission of her own. She unfolded her legs and sat with her feet flat on the floor.

"Everet, I came to a profound conclusion this past week. I thought about my past, my parents, Josef, and you--how we came together, I mean. And I came to see that my miserable life wasn't just the fault of my parents, as I, you--and my other friends--had always thought. It was mine, too, because I couldn't see the larger picture. I needed things too much, especially from men: first, my father, because my mother wouldn't, or couldn't, be there; then Joseph Gardner, because he gave me my first real recognition as a person; then I tried to depend on you and... And..."

Everet nodded. "And other men followed, because I didn't turn out as you expected either. I'm sorry."

"Yes." She looked disgusted, not quite sure if she should be angry with herself or him. "I admit there were other men," she said. "Just as my father probably slept around on my mother, especially when he was young--just as you must have slept around on me, too."

Everet sat up, bristling, his brown eyes wide and righteous. "Margy, I have never, ever, not once, been with another woman since I started seeing you."

"Never?" She looked at him. She was not completely surprised, but she did not want to give in on this particular point.

"Never," he repeated. "And I'm not saying I didn't have the opportunity--or the desire." He looked away. "I never gave in to it."

334

"Who did you do it for? Me?"

"What the hell is the difference? For you--and especially for Kennedy."

"Bullshit. You did it for yourself. To prevent the headlines. "

"There were no headlines to worry about ten years ago, my dear, because I had no possibilities."

He laughed, relaxing with a shift of his body as he played with a button on his shirt. "Simply speaking, Margy, I've been faithful, whatever the reason. That's more than most can say."

She waved her hand. "'Maybe it would have been better if you had played around."

"That stinks, and you know it."

"Tell me, if it turned out to be a disadvantage to you, what then?"

"What are you talking about?"

"If it turned out to be a disadvantage to be faithful, what would you have done?"

"But it didn't because I didn't believe in it."

"What if it were a political disadvantage—a lack of manliness?"

He shook his head, finally comprehending. "You can't do that, Margy. You can't turn it around on me."

"You know damn well—"

"Margy, I'm telling you that I have been faithful to you. It is *possible* that I genuinely love you and am unselfish. All the Wiltshire pseudo-honesty crap won't get you anywhere past that. "

He let out a long, slow sigh of discontent as if the conversation bored him. But at the same time his face weakened, folding his eyes, she noticed, in upon themselves, a position she would draw if she wanted to make him look close to tears. To her surprise, she was affected too, but she did not know what to say.

"It hurts to be slighted, doesn't it?" she said.

He shook his head, raising his hand to stop her, but the crumpled, folded look remained around his eyes. It moved Margy so much that she had to turn away.

"I'm sorry," he said. "The horns are showing, I guess." There was just a hint of malice in his voice.

He took out a handkerchief and wiped his brow. Then, speaking dully but with an anger that seemed to come from deep inside, Everet said, "You are a child, aren't you? Especially with men. But what I'm worried about now is your discretion. Something crazy, such as this past episode at the Grays, and with Goldie, could explode. It would be trouble for everyone, but particularly Kennedy."

"Come on, Everet."

"I mean it, Margy."

"Sleep with whoever I want, whenever I want, so long as it doesn't offend anyone's public standing? Is that it? You're asking me to keep everything secret?"

"I'm not talking about public standings! It's our son!"

His eyes burned. Margy stood up, crossed the room and put her hand on his bandage. It was white but a little soiled now, massive with the shirt open, and a shocking gray contrast to the skin just above the collar bone. She felt sorry, but like a boxer Everet parried her hand and then shoved her, not too gently, back toward the couch. He rose from the Barcalounger and faced her. "Is there anyone else?" he asked. "Someone who is really important?"

She shook her head. Everet raised his hand, then let it drop, going behind the desk and sitting in his chair again. She saw his hands tremble. He turned, reached for a picture on the wall behind his desk, and Margy, as if she were looking through layers of time, remembered his father doing the same thing, with the same picture, but on a different wall.

"Luke and Emma," Everet said. "My great, great grandparents."

Over his shoulder, Margy looked at them, an aged couple, posing on a porch of an old tarpaper shack with a large hole torn in its side. The photograph dated from about 1880. Emma sat on a rocker, a bandanna around her head, her hands folded on her lap, and, in an almost comic touch, smoked a corn cob pipe. Luke stood beside her, arm around her shoulders, his left hand holding what looked like a well-

336

thumbed Bible. He wore cotton homespuns, a dark silver-buttoned Union soldier jacket, and a flat-brimmed straw hat. Wrinkled yet healthy, they each had extraordinarily clear, bright eyes. The looks on their faces impressed Margy as knowledgeable about life but still idealistic for the future. She remembered how Everet's father's voice had changed when he talked of them:

"They were slaves, Margy, though they were both children of one white parent." It was 1964, October. Everet and she had just announced that they had decided to wed. She had not reacted when Everet's father took the photograph off the wall, but he smiled knowingly, perhaps seeing something in her eyes. "Be prepared," he said, "to have your children affected. They may not be slaves, but they'll still be niggers to a lot of people."

"Oh, no, Douglas, things have changed." Ruth Hamilton had walked across the room, placed her arm around Margy's shoulders, and stood up to her husband. "People aren't so pig-headed anymore," she said.

Everet's father laughed. "Like hell they aren't."

Douglas Hamilton turned toward them and, with what Margy thought of as wonderful slowness, recited the hangings, tortures, and executions that had occurred in America during the past ten years. She remembered him wearing a red and black checkered shirt with sleeves rolled up to his elbows. He looked vigorous and healthy although apparently even then he had begun to suffer the effects of hyper-tension. His wide, wallpapered office had been made in the basement of their Bridgeport home. It had a small desk in the middle of the floor, some file cabinets behind it in the corner, and a few photographs on the wall: Luke and Emma, one of himself with Fred Gray and Martin Luther King, and another older one, a magazine clipping really, of a chubby-faced black man in what looked like an admiral's hat--Marcus Garvey, Everet had told her later.

"Things may not seem so bad to you, Ruthy, but they ain't so good if you go out into the world." He hung up the picture and turned back to Margy and Ruth. "I haven't got anything against you, Margy. You seem like a fine, ambitious

337

girl, and I know that young people today don't mind integrated marriages as much as they used to. But my son must be *happily* married. I want him to do something with his life. I know how hard it is when you're with your own kind, but with someone of another color?—" He shook his head, sadly.

"Hey, Daddy, that isn't fair. I've seen things in life. I'm not doing this completely blind."

"Hah! My boy, you haven't been married yet. You don't know what it's like to be ambitious for yourself and your family. You are still naive."

Everet shook his head and stood closer to his father. "Idealistic, maybe, but definitely not naive. I love Margy, and I think we can make it go. This is not the 19th century after all."

Margy looked from the picture to him now--that is, behind his desk in 1974--and saw a newly troubled face in place of the youthful, idealistic one she remembered. It made her uneasy to watch him replace the picture on the wall. Perhaps the 19th century hadn't really finished.

"Six months, Everet. I spent six months really cheating on you. That's all."

He laughed. "*Really cheating?* I don't understand that at all."

She shook her head. "Don't be funny! It was while you were so busy working on the Democratic Convention. You absolutely disregarded me."

He folded his hands, cracked the knuckles, then, as if ashamed, extended his arms and gripped both sides of his desk. His forearms shook as he half rose from the chair. Then abruptly he shouted, his voice changing pitch suddenly as if he had lost his mind:

"I disregarded you! ... How far do you want to go, bitch! You're trying to--" He struggled to sit back, obviously with tremendous physical effort. Blue veins swelled out on his neck above the bandage. He had never hit her, but the look on his face right then made Margy lean back from the desk. He left his chair, and immediately she stood to defend herself. As he moved quickly toward her, she picked up an

338

ashtray on the table next to the couch and threw it at his feet. It worked or seemed to. After it shattered against the baseboard, Everet stopped and returned to the chair.

"Don't be aggressive with me, Everet."

"Aggressive... Margy, sit down. Just sit down--now!"

She took the juice glass, drained it, and threw it wildly. It missed his determinedly unflinching head but broke against one of the photographs behind his desk. Cringing, she began to sob, but he merely shouted at her:

"SIT DOWN, I SAID!"

He seemed to erupt from his desk, and, shrieking, she started for the door. With one hand upraised, he caught her, grabbed a fistful of her hair, and, just about to swing his open hand, stopped again. Margy could not speak. She looked at him, frightened yet somehow (later, she would dislike herself for this) curiously relieved. When she saw him drop his hand, she turned limp herself, sagging into the couch, and began to cry. Breathing deeply, he crossed the room and gathered himself beneath the pictures.

"Why didn't you hit me, Everet? I can take it."

Through gritted teeth, he said, "I'm not going to be an infant, you bitch! Don't push me."

"You're afraid of feeling, aren't you? You not only avoid--"

"Bullshit! That's Wiltshire double-talk, for petty ofay people trying to deal with three-hundred years of racist guilt."

"No! It's anger, maybe hatred--emotions you avoid because they open people up!"

She lit a cigarette, exhaling in desperate, exhausted breaths. Everet went to the windows again, threw open a sash, and pulled the curtains back. But the rod holding them came off in his hands, and after glaring at Margy as if to kill, he hurled it, along with the curtains, into the corner.

"Goddamn smoke stinks up the goddamn house. It's disgusting."

Margy laughed. "Oh, very peaceful, Everet. Very Martin Luther King."

339

He slammed his hand against the sill, stormed back to the desk, shoved the chair aside, and, throwing himself into it, almost tipped it over.

"Careful!" Margy shouted.

He leaned forward, just managing to regain his balance. She would remember the look on his face for years, and, no matter where she was--in the street, on the job, once even in bed with someone--, she always had to giggle. At first she thought he was having a heart attack. His head jerked back quickly, his eyes wide in panic before he tilted toward the desk.

"Ohhh-wohhh!Wo-ahhh!" he cried

He snorted, blew some spit and mucous from his mouth, but, after he regained control, giggled a little himself. Catching his breath, he leaned back once more and laughed harder. But this time as he threw his arms forward reaching for the desk, the wheels slid out from under him.

"Ohhh, oohhh, God!"

The back of the chair clattered against the wall and he sank along with it, head and shoulders first, the flesh of calves and ankles afterward, then finally the uplifted feet pedaling away in panic. Margy gasped, not knowing whether to laugh or cry out. He tried to rise immediately but hit the floor a second time, the up-ended chair sliding more deeply under the desk.

"I got to... I got to ... Help!"

He whimpered; giggled; then neither of them could stop laughing.

"Stop, Everet. Don't... Don't try again!"

He fell a third time despite, or because of, his struggle to regain his feet. His ass slid under the desk completely as the back of the chair shrieked against a fragment of crushed glass.

"You'll cut yourself," Margy shouted.

He fell a fourth time and, truly alarmed, she ran across the room to hold him down, embracing him, brushing aside shards of the shattered ashtray, and pulling the chair from under the desk.

He began to tickle her.

"Stop, Everet! I'm going to, oh, God, I'm going to pee!"

He went down a fifth time because Margy leaped to her feet just as he was about to roll both of them out of the chair. She hurried into the bathroom, dropped her jeans, and peed. Then she returned to the study, throwing herself onto the couch and howling into the pillow because she saw him trying and failing again. She heard a thud and looked, gasping for breath as he held his finger to his lips. On his knees now, Everet rose carefully, righting the chair but almost letting it fall a sixth time as the wheels skidded on a piece of glass. Finally he sprang to his feet, and she buried her head beneath the couch pillow, spasms of laughter shaking her stomach again.

"All right, all right. I know it's funny, Margy, but cool it."

He took the pillow from her head and held it in his hand, trying not to smile.

"Don't. Don't start again, please? I want to be serious." He raised his hand, palm outward, and pushed it toward her.

"I... I..."

She choked as she tried to swallow. He snorted, dropped the pillow onto the couch and walked back to his desk. When she looked at him, he was still grinning but more calmly. He went out to the kitchen, returned with a broom and a dust pan, and started sweeping up the glass. The practical hominess of it seemed to help. The tension between them cleared when Margy rose to hold the dust pan for him. Together they hung the curtains and straightened out the wall of pictures. They went together to clean other things in the living room.

"Hell," Everet said, dumping the contents of an ashtray into the dust pan. "What's the use of arguing? I've made mistakes, but you have too. This is the modern world." In front of the fireplace, Everet held the empty tray of a TV dinner. It looked a few days old.

"We'll have to talk about this further," Margy said. "It isn't settled." She went back to the study for the broom.

341

"Do you still want to do your show?" He stood behind her in the doorway to the study.

"Of course," she said.

"You're welcome to stay here, then."

She shook her head. "I said we'll have to talk about it. There are lots of things to take into account."

He nodded. "Important things."

His look sobered her immediately, and, when after a moment or two he said he loved her, she found herself moved enough to take everything back. Almost.

"I'm sorry," she said, finally. "I haven't treated you-- or Kennedy--well, but I love you both in my own way."

He nodded, clearly pleased. "I'm aware of that," he said, coming into the room. He stood next to her.

"I don't want to make you or him bitter."

"You won't make me bitter, Margy. When or if, you leave, you're the one who's going to be alone." He looked at her. "And you're the one who's going to have to explain this to Kennedy."

She winced, taking the broom into her hands. It had been lying across the desk. "I know. I've already promised to discuss it with him tomorrow."

He sat in the upright chair. They stared at it, but neither of them so much as grinned. "And you?" he asked, finally. "What will you do about money? That is, if you leave."

"I could use some." She carried the broom and dust pan into the kitchen. When she returned, he looked at her evenly.

"I'll help some," he said. "But this is not going to be happy for me, and, once you're on your feet, you're on your own. Don't even think of alimony. I'll fight it to the end."

That made her shrink inside, mainly because it showed he had been thinking such things through, and less than generously.

"Oh, no credit for the ten years I spent with you? Emotional support? The housework?" She looked at him as if she were judging something, and then she added, "For a closed mouth with the newspapers?"

342

"That will be..." His mouth dropped open. His eyes widened, and he looked almost as if he were falling in the chair again. "Try it," he said, placing his hands on the desk. "Just you try it."

"We can talk about it another time," Margy said. "I was only joking."

"Of course you were."

He turned to the wall. With a careful, trembling voice that shook Margy to the core, he added, "You know what the hell we're saying here, don't you?" She stared at him. "It's over. Isn't that it? If we really pay attention to what we're saying... " He snapped his fingers. "Ten years of our lives."

"Maybe not," Margy said. Yet as she thought about it, the certainty of it all moved her too. "Just in case," she added, "I want one promise."

He turned, guarding himself. "Yes?"

"If I stay, permanently or for a while, no matter what the reason, I want one condition."

He waved his hand. "Oh, Margy, let's not quibble now. I don't want any ultimatums."

"I mean it."

He sighed. "Okay. What is it?"

"No more political dinners, okay? No more parties with the Grays."

He let out a long whistle, dropping his palm onto the desk. With a grin, he spun around in the chair and, howling, rose. "You got it, baby. I promise—that's one agreement where both our interests are served."

She fingered the bandage on his neck again. He touched her cheek. Starting forward as if to kiss her, he stopped and turned to leave. At the door he stopped again and walked back to the desk to pick up his speech. Obviously fatigued, he seemed to need the final word.

"I suppose you'll be sleeping in the studio tonight," he said. "I've got to make some changes in this, so I'm going to keep it with me."

She nodded, not knowing how else to respond. "Good night." She slipped into the chair behind the desk.

"Good night," he said. "Sleep well."

Fred Misurella

She picked up the phone. He waved the yellow legal pad and left.

EPILOGUE:

29.

WATERLOO FALLS AGAIN

"Don't look back. Don't look back at anything in the past. Understand?" Marie-Thérèse said.

Margy nodded, realizing it would be impossible.

Goldie drove the little *Deux Chevaux* around the circle at the Arc de Triomphe, skittered between a taxi and a bus, slid over some cobblestones, and steered through Porte Maillot. Margy was on her way home again.

"When a parent dies, you always want to stop to gather all that up, to keep it close to your heart--like Proust, *n'est-ce pas?* But it is not there." Marie-Thérèse waved her hand, annoyed with her English. *"La vie,"* she continued, *"c'est toujours enface; devant toi. Tu comprends?"*

Margy nodded, looking out the left rear window to see what might be her last view of Paris. The Eiffel Tower hovered like a giant praying mantis above the lush woods of the Bois de Boulogne, and behind it, a fat ghost of twentieth century modernity that had not been there on her first arrival in 1964: the Montparnasse Tower boxed out a portion of the sky.

"Have you got your papers?" Goldie asked.

She nodded. "You can send back the canvases when you get a chance. I'll probably be in Iowa for about a week."

Goldie nodded, gravely. "Take it easy, heh? Don't put too much pressure on this visit."

"I'm fine." Margy smiled and leaned over to kiss him on the cheek. He was a man now, a young one still, with the tight blond curls balled around his head as ever, but with a firmer chin, a leaner look around the eyes, and a mouth that was thinner-lipped and more expressive. After all these years, he was not yet her lover. But maybe; increasingly she

345

felt maybe. Margy, still painting, but also free-lancing occasionally as a journalist, had come on assignment for a month to gather information for a series on the European art scene. Goldie lived in Paris, studying at the Ecole des Beaux Arts for more than a year. As had happened almost twenty years before, she had fallen in love with the city and decided to extend her stay.

They turned off the Périphérique now, and, headed northeast, Margy watched as the city skyline gradually moved farther and farther from the road. The new streamlined, technical, less aesthetically pleasing France, she thought. She was amazed at how many cars and trucks filled the road, how many square, white factories occupied the horizon, how many Swedish cranes stood on the roadside like poorly positioned Eiffel Towers erecting more square buildings. Those new buildings, miniature Towers of Montparnasse, gave the Paris *banlieues* the feel of a *papier-mâché* New York.

"I should write about this architecture," she said. "Marie-Thérèse, despite what you say, it's positively ugly. We went through this stuff years ago in America."

Marie-Thérèse tossed her dark hair, dispensing with her usual defense of post-1960s French life. She wore boots, tight jeans, and a sweatshirt with a picture of Mickey Mouse on it. In certain ways she looked more American than Margy.

"Give my regards to Gerard and *petit* Gerard," Margy said, meaning Marie-Thérèse's lover and son. "I'm sorry I can't say good-bye properly."

"*Petit* Gerard will miss you. But you will come again for sure, *n'est-ce pas?*"

Margy shrugged and said she could not tell. But she hoped that Marie-Thérèse would visit her in New York. "I have an apartment in a nice part of the city--West End Avenue. And there is always room for a friend."

Marie-Thérèse frowned. "I am a mother. When I can leave my two Gerards, maybe I will come see you in your country."

Margy smiled. They drove on, passing through some poorly cultivated farmland and, in another twenty minutes, followed a wide curve to the left and then straightened for a long descent at the bottom of which was a sign for the airport exit. A 747 roared in from their left, just missing the *Deux Chevaux*, it seemed, as Margy and Marie-Thérèse ducked, then landed beyond the rooftops of some buildings a few hundred yards away. Margy thought of Foss, checked her notebook for his new address (he still lived in Connecticut, but closer to Hartford), and searched for the slides of his most recent work, now on view in a couple of Left Bank galleries. He had experimented with photographic realism recently, creating silk screens that superimposed prints of Cezanne's *Mont Sainte-Victoire* paintings over realistic, detailed views of the same mountain and other portions of the Provence countryside. He called the works palimpsests. The Museum of Modern Art in New York had bought a series of them in blue and red, and the new Pompidou Center in Paris had bought another in orange and brown. His nude portrait of Margy had never been completed, but he had asked her to pose for him again when she visited him before flying to Paris. She had refused, of course, but she also knew that he and his work would be a central part of the stories she intended to write when she returned to the United States. Goldie and some other young Americans she had met would get some mention too.

With Marie-Thérèse directing, Goldie pulled the car into the short term parking area, and they carried Margy's baggage to the terminal. She checked in at Air France, reserved a seat in the non-smoking section, and then, with baggage accepted and place confirmed, she started for the boarding area. Since Goldie and Marie-Thérèse could not go with her, they said good-bye just before Margy entered the passenger inspection gate.

"I'll see you in a couple of months," Goldie said. "It's been nice. I'll call as soon as I get back to New York."

They kissed. She smiled, but then tears swelled from her eyes when she turned to Marie-Thérèse.

"Salut, ma vraie amie."

"Salut, Margy. Bon voyage."

347

"Oh, Marie-Thérèse, I wish I could put you in my bag and take you home with me. I've learned so much."

"We will meet again. Either here or in New York. And we can write each other, no?"

Margy nodded. "But I wish we could live nearer each other."

She took out a handkerchief to dry her eyes, and Goldie came close to take her arm. "Remember. Not too much pressure on yourself. Nothing is your fault. Don't let your parents, especially your father, get to you."

"I'm sure it's not going to be that way."

"*Tout droit*. Always to the front," Marie-Thérèse said.

"*Merci, mon amie.* And especially for keeping my memory and my pictures so long."

She embraced Marie-Thérèse and then turned to the gate, laughing, yet with tears rolling down her cheeks. She handed over her carry-on luggage, shoulder bag, an attaché full of notes, notebooks, and sketches, and, flashing her passport and boarding pass, stepped through the machine. No beep, but as she picked up her things, she almost wished she heard one.

"Good-bye."

"Good-bye."

Goldie waved. Margy acknowledged it, but, when she looked at Marie-Thérèse, she picked up her shoulder bag and attaché and walked to the escalator behind the gate. It took her up into a criss-cross of plastic cylinders where she stepped on a conveyor belt that vaulted over an open court and led eventually, after a long hallway lined with clothing and liquor advertisements, to the boarding area. Marie-Thérèse and Goldie waved until she disappeared over the open court, and then they went to the car.

The flight to New York proved uneventful through the full seven hours of daylight. Margy read, reviewed notes for her articles, and took occasional naps. At Kennedy she passed through customs easily (no liquor, gifts, or souvenirs) and then took a taxi into Manhattan. She reached home by three in the afternoon, entering the five-room apartment at 89th Street and West End that she shared with two other

348

women. Neither roommate was home. Both usually worked or took classes in the afternoon, and so she left an explanatory note on the refrigerator, phoned for reservations on a flight to Iowa and, after showering, called Everet in Stoddard.

"City Hall."

"The Mayor's office, please."

"Uh, I don't think he'll be in. Can I re-direct your call?"

Margy laughed. "He'll be in. Tell him Margy Winters is calling. He knows who I am."

"One moment, please."

It still felt funny to think of him as mayor, as if it were still a part of Foss's mocking humor. But in the middle of his third term, Everet's mayoralty was no longer a joke. In fact, articles in local papers hinted that he would run in the next Congressional election. He seemed to be the Democratic liberals' one last hope in Connecticut.

Still single, he lived with Kennedy on Camels Back Drive, but he had been seeing a black woman, a rising young lawyer who had defended cases in both New Haven and New York. Margy had met her in June at Kennedy's high school graduation. Her name was Blossom. With a tall, athletic body and a Shirley Bassey face, she looked as if she would make a good political wife and mother, if her own career did not interfere. Friendly to Margy, she had made a point of taking her aside so that they could talk alone for half an hour or more. It was a gesture that Emmy Gray would have made. Blossom was also caring to Kennedy and warm and sisterly in her affection for Everet. Nothing much had changed, as Margy saw it. A little jealous, she had whispered to Everet at one point in the evening, "In the public eye the sweet and sexy mama type still gets her man. Doesn't she?"

"Not funny, Margy. Not funny at all." He had hardly smiled.

"Anyway, she'll look terrific beside you on the podium."

Margy was surprised to see Blossom in a televised soft drink commercial just a few days afterward: A group of

349

young people were socializing in a college quad. A Frisbee floated through the air. A handsome, muscular black boy leaped, caught it, landed on his back; then, as he ran to a group of young women cheering him, he took a bottle of soft drink from one of them, chugged it, and handed it back, quickly kissing the girl on the cheek before going back to his game. The girl, blonde and lovely, raised her fist to urge him on; then she raised the bottle and, as the theme song blared, her head dipped back, her mouth opened, and she emptied the bottle of soft drink into it. Beside her, laughing and cheering everything--soft drink, drinker, Frisbee player, and perhaps the advertisement itself--sat Blossom, her bright eyes and infectious smile full of confidence and hope for the future as the camera centered on her face and the picture faded.

"Mayor Hamilton's office." It was a man, Everet's personal secretary, not Buford, but somebody very much like him.

"I'd like to speak to Everet, please. This is Margy."

"I'm sorry, but Mayor--"

"This is his wife, or former wife, calling. He's probably expecting me. If he isn't, tell him it's very important."

"I will see if His Honor is busy."

She waited a few minutes, still thinking of Foss's joke, and, since she was in her bedroom, she looked into the closet and tried to think of the clothes she would take to Iowa. It would be hot, yet events would most likely be formal. She had better bring skirts and blouses. Except for Everet's parents, she had never been to a funeral before.

"Hello, Margy?"

"Yes. I'm sorry to bother you at work."

"Did you just get in?"

"A few minutes ago."

"I'm sorry about your mother. Luckily I was home when your father called. I didn't know what to say. I didn't know if he knew that we were divorced. I just gave him the Paris number and let it go at that."

"He knows. My father has been writing Christmas letters for the past three years. Last year I started answering him."

"Good. That will ease the burden. What happened to your mother?"

"Oh, I don't know. Some awful accident at the nursing home. My father wasn't very clear. All I know is that I have to go out there, and I'm not looking forward to it."

"Look, I'd like to come out with you."

"Don't be silly. They never accepted you."

"It's not silly. And I'd like to bring Kennedy with me. I think he should know something about his grandparents, even if it's this way."

"Oh, Everet."

"Margy, he's almost eighteen. He's going to college in a little while. Besides, he's never met your parents. At least this way he'll know your father."

Margy sat on the bed and glanced out the window to the building next door. As in every issue having to do with Kennedy since their separation, she felt very uneasy. She saw him three or four times a month, and he still conveyed distant, dutiful expressions of affection only. It had been heartbreaking to see him become a tall, gangling--indeed, handsome--boy, with large hands and a moderate Afro. He managed to tower sullenly over her as if she were an impediment. She invited him into New York for exhibitions, to see plays, and to attend concerts. He rarely enjoyed them, more because of her than the things themselves, she thought. He was jealous of her relationship with other men (although he did not seem to mind Blossom), hostile toward the city, impatient with her interest in the arts, and generally uncommunicative to her roommates and friends. But his school grades were good, he was passionate about law and minority issues, and, according to Everet, he had developed a fine game of tennis. His dislike of her was clear, and that did not seem to forecast a comfortable or useful graveside visit to Iowa.

"Everet, it's going to be awkward enough for me out there as it is."

"Maybe we can help you along."

"It's been nearly twenty years since I've been back, and Kennedy--"

"Margy, Kennedy has been cut off from a lot of important things because of us."

"So have I. So has everyone."

"A case in point. I want him to know about the human links in his past—black and white. Mine have been important to me. If you're going out there, we should go with you. In certain ways, we are still a family unit."

She sighed. "I appreciate your saying that, especially for Kennedy. It has made my meetings with him at least tolerable."

"That's why we have to come out there, to affirm that."

"I don't know."

"Margy, we're coming with you. What's your schedule?"

"I'm leaving from La Guardia this evening. I should be in Cedar Rapids by ten o'clock tonight."

"Are you changing in Chicago?"

"Yes. For an 8:30 flight to Iowa."

"And how do you get to Waterloo Falls from the airport?"

"Cab--my father won't meet me because he can't drive at night anymore."

"Okay. I'll get my secretary on it right away. Then he'll let you know when we're coming out. We'll try for tonight's flight with you, but if that doesn't work out, we'll make it on our own. I just have to clean up some things around the office."

Reluctantly, Margy acquiesced and began packing. She called her father to let him know that she would arrive that evening, and, since he seemed eager to talk, she asked him for further details of her mother's death. He said a fire had accidentally started in one of the patients' rooms. It had spread quickly, at least through the portion of the building where Beverly stayed, and twelve people died of smoke inhalation. Margy's mother had been ambulatory, but she

352

was found wrapped in a blanket in her bed, her knees curled up to her chin, her hands behind her head. There was not a sign of struggle or movement.

"Ugh. It sounds horrible."

"Maybe. But at last your mother has some rest. It's her life that was the real tragedy."

Margy said nothing, feeling the old mix of pain and rage. In a certain sense, she knew, her father had to feel relieved by the death. But her own feelings were more complex, mainly because she had always hoped, even after all these years, that her mother's head would somehow clear and her life become fulfilled--more for Margy's own good than her mother's. She needed someone to look up to.

She hung up and, after packing, called a couple of editors to discuss her trip to Europe and ask for extensions in deadlines. Around five she heard from Everet's secretary, who said that Everet and Kennedy would meet her at La Guardia and take the same plane. Everet had already left the office and was getting himself and Kennedy ready for the trip. Margy called Iowa again, and her father seemed delighted by the prospect of finally meeting Kennedy. In an hour, dressed in gray and checking the note on the refrigerator to make sure her father's address and phone number were on it, she started for the airport.

The three of them sat together in the same row: Kennedy on the window, Everet on the aisle, Margy in the middle. They arrived in Chicago by 7:30, left there after an hour wait, and arrived in Cedar Rapids late that evening. It was a forty-five minute drive from there to Waterloo Falls. The cab passed through moon-lit farmlands and occasional woods where the trees, bare due to years of constant flooding from a nearby river, stood out like ghostly reminders of the dead. On the outskirts of Waterloo Falls, Margy asked the driver to take them past the nursing home and then felt strange when she saw it. One side of the building stood in perfect condition. The other was absolutely gutted. It had bright yellow fire lines around it. She thought of her mother trapped in there and moaned. Everet put his arms about her, and she turned her head away. After they drove off, she

353

remembered a small white chair lying on the curb, shining in the moonlight like some child's abandoned toy.

They went on, and, as the cab rolled down the street where she had lived, her anxiety increased. The house was dark when they arrived. The doorbell did not work, and they had to knock, loudly, several times. Finally, the light went on over their heads, and the door opened revealing her father-- tall, thin, frail, and greatly aged--in his pajamas. He let them in with a surprised flourish of his hands, as if he had not been expecting them, and went about the living room turning on the lights while they put down their bags. No one kissed, embraced, or exchanged greetings. Obviously there was nothing customary between them anymore.

Her father looked tired, his face haggard and his eyes curiously still and red-lined. His hair had turned completely white, and his unshaven face (for a moment, it looked bearded) gave Margy a momentary *déjà vu*: Joseph Gardner stood before her.

"Daddy, this is Kennedy... Hamilton. He's... " She stopped and looked at Everet. "He's your grandson."

Kennedy's chin hung low, but with a shuffle of his feet and a shy grin he leaned forward and shook hands. Her father embraced him, and, when he pulled away, he looked at Margy with misery-laden eyes. Everet shook hands too, and then the four of them, laughing at their own awkwardness, decided to find their places for the night. Her father led them past the dining room, through the living room, and up to the second floor. To Margy it was like seeing the old house on a film clip running in reverse. She recognized the chandelier over the dining room table, the sideboard that still held the family crystal, the wing-backed chair in the corner, the fireplace, a rocker; and then the very shadows on the stairs that formed familiar lace patterns from the moonlight shining through the trees and curtains on the second floor windows. But it all seemed slightly unsynchronized. First came her mother's room, on the right overlooking the backyard, then Margy's, on the left overlooking the front yard, and at the end, her father's study, which had a lamp over the desk showing a huge brown leather couch where he usually slept, two windows overlooking the fields beyond their property, and shelves of books he had been collecting since before Margy was born.

There were a few additional awkward moments as they sorted out beds and people. Finally, Margy chose her old room (the bed, barely long enough for her, would never suit Everet or Kennedy), while Everet and Kennedy took the twin beds in her mother's room. Her father stayed in his study. But it was clear that he would not sleep, and later, as she lay on her back uneasily, Margy heard his footsteps pacing back and forth in the hall. She rose around 2 a.m. and saw the study door still open. Her father held a book in his hand and stood near the desk with his head inclined over a pile of paper.

"My book on the town's history," he said. "I've never completed it. Maybe I'll be able to get back to it now."

She smiled. "Is there much about the falls?"

He nodded. "There should be, I've read enough about them—and the river."

He put down the book and took off his glasses. "You haven't changed much," he said as he smiled at her. "Still... Still lovely, although obviously older."

"I'm pushing forty, Daddy. From the wrong side."

He nodded, brushing back a lock of thick white hair that had fallen over his eyes. "It happens. You dress more neatly now, don't you?"

"I'm a working woman. At least when there is work. I can't afford to let people see all the paint spots on my clothes."

He laughed and crossed the room to sit on his couch. There was a pillow and an afghan on one arm, and on the wall above it a photograph of him and Beverly, taken long before Margy was born. Faded and brown, slightly over-exposed, it revealed no doubt about his handsome clear eyes, wavy hair, and dapper clothes. Beside him Beverly looked slightly disheveled but with fresher, smoother skin than Margy remembered. Her dark double-breasted suit looked too large for her slim frame while on her head she wore an outlandish white turban cap with a huge tassel

355

dangling over the left side of her face, partially hiding it. Strands of blonde hair fish-hooked out around her ears, and there was a slight smear to her lipstick. Still something haunting and unmistakably vulnerable stood out in her eyes.

Margy stepped into the room to glance around and saw that very little had changed. Her father's old Underwood sat on the table behind the desk (she had hunted and pecked at it as a child) and beside that a pile of books on county history, Waterloo Falls history, and Iowa history. She sat on the swivel chair and remembered the view behind the house: the large yard, the thin maple (long since dead of some disease, her father informed her), the toolshed back behind the garage, and after that, field upon field of wheat that used to undulate in the late summer sun.

"Remember when you tore out the pages of my book in here?" her father asked. "The one with antique prints of the river and the falls?"

Margy nodded, only dimly recalling. "Wasn't there a drawing I did to make up for it? Something you ripped up because you were angry?"

He shook his head. "I never ripped it up. I balled it up and threw it on the floor when I saw what you had done to my book. How old were you then?"

Margy shrugged. "Six, maybe seven. I don't remember."

"I remember. And you could draw beautifully, even then. See what I've done with the book?"

Her father handed Margy the volume he had been reading. It was a history of the town, published in 1937 as a W.P.A. project, but it had a new red leather binding.

"It's the same as the one you tore up. I found it at a used book sale a few years ago and had it rebound. I've always wanted to give it to you." He took the book, opened it to its final pages, and handed it back. "Look what I've added to it."

"Oh, Dad."

It was a photostat of her drawing. Reduced to the size of the book, it had been copied in high contrast so that the drawn lines stood out from the original folds and wrinkles.

Margy smiled. Here was an old wound, and she could feel that she still held a grudge, but she moved to the couch and kissed him anyway. He embraced her, then quickly withdrew his arms in order to take out a handkerchief. Margy put her arms on his shoulders as he turned away and wiped his eyes. He was over eighty, yet, she was proud to see, he had the appearance of a much younger man.

"You don't forget much, do you, Daddy?"

"Less than I'd like to," he replied.

Folding his handkerchief, he replaced it in his pocket and turned back to her with a fragile smile. "I try to stay busy, but for all my effort, things keep catching up to me. It's been a hard couple of years."

She laughed. "Like father, like daughter."

Margy looked down at the book. They sat in silence for a while as she turned the pages. Boards creaked throughout the house, and occasionally they heard a snore or a heavy breath from Kennedy or Everet. After reading several passages, she placed the book on his desk and asked what they would have to do next day.

"Nothing much. Most of the arrangements have been made." Her father looked down at his feet. "There will not be any..." He looked up. "There will not be any viewing."

"I gathered." Margy stared at her hands. The sight of the burned-out nursing home came back to her, along with the thought of her mother smothering in its smoke. She felt pity, but to her surprise the child in her, even after all these years, could not fully suppress--what?—her relief that this part of her life was over. She looked up at the photograph behind the couch and searched for a key to the people in it. She had become much different from her mother. She could not easily fit over her mother's facial outline as, say, Foss's photo-realistic Mont Sainte-Victoire could fit over Cezanne's, and, as usual, she was grateful for that difference. But along with the gratitude came a basic loneliness that she knew would never leave. In a sense her mother's death was a non-event in Margy's experience.

"We should get some sleep," she said. "The next few days are going to be difficult."

357

"Try to get some sleep, you mean," her father said. "I know I won't."

Next day they made final arrangements for the funeral and attended a public service for all who had died in the fire. Her father cried silently as first a priest, a minister, and then a rabbi gave their blessings. About one hundred townspeople attended, and something about the shared community sadness gripped Margy in a way that surprised her. She grew faint. When the minister pronounced her mother's name during his prayer, she had to grip Everet's arm and almost fell to her knees. Her knees trembled so much she could not stand, and, finally, Everet and Kennedy escorted her to the car while her father stayed through the rest of the ceremony. In the car both tried to comfort her.

"Goddamn it, goddamn this life," she kept saying. As she sobbed, Everet offered a handkerchief and held her close, but Kennedy, after hugging her, looked puzzled and distracted, as though he did not know who his mother was.

One undertaker served the town, and, because of the many denominations and types of services, the interments had to be set at different times. Her mother's was among the last, scheduled for the following afternoon. In the morning, while her father and Everet attended some of the other burials, Margy strolled through Waterloo Falls with Kennedy and tried to reconstruct her childhood for him. The town had changed a lot in twenty years. She had expected that but not quite so dramatically. A highway strip of shopping centers and stores went through the outskirts of town, assaulting her eye with unanticipated and unwanted splashes of new color. A housing development now stood just the other side of the strip, and together the new constructions split the town in two, effectively replacing the old Main Street as an axis with a highway and exchanging the town's slow, old-fashioned pace for the rush and push of contemporary pickups and semis. When she showed Kennedy the view from a hilltop near the falls, the town seemed to nestle in a fold of land as if it were in hiding. Now garden apartments rose beyond the highway. In the field behind her father's house she saw that not only the elm was missing, but also more than half of the fields of wheat she remembered. Factories and warehouses-- cement blocks and metal plates--had replaced them.

Yet she saw positive signs about the town as well. More black faces passed on the street, so that no one regarded with suspicion or surprise this blonde-haired lady, whom none of them remembered, walking along with the obviously mulatto young man. Also, women strode more certainly before her, showing more independence; and, although she felt nervous about bringing Kennedy to the falls, when she led him along the path a little more than a mile from the hill, she was pleased to see they had remained pretty much intact: the rock, to her childhood eyes, like a bird ready to take off, still occupied its perch near the spillover; oaks and maples around it looked about the same; and the pool, heavily rainbowed, still roared with the smash of falling water.

Afterward, she drove Kennedy to the county high school she had attended. The building, expanded by now, looked far smaller than she recollected, but the fields of corn and sorghum surrounding it looked as plentiful. At home, they found Everet and her father discussing afternoon plans. Margy sensed an intimacy among the four of them that had not yet fully bloomed but was deepening. Her father acted particularly happy with Kennedy, who responded, calling her father "Grandpa" and listening attentively to his stories about Margy's childhood. That touch of normality pleased her, pleasing her father too. Despite his age, the white hair and unsteady movements, he still had an air of certainty about the past, especially with a book or a paper in his hand and his reading glasses on. But it bothered Margy that her mother's life had been so negative that none of them-- husband, daughter, or grandson--could feel genuine remorse. When she read about the fire and service in the afternoon paper, she felt the communal sadness again, yet nothing but a bitter relief for the person whose name she read among the others: Beverly Winters.

They had a quiet, simple burial that afternoon. Mercifully, no minister attended, by her father's choice, since, as he said, Beverly had accepted no formal religious

359

ties in the end. At a cemetery just outside of town, the coffin slid into the ground as gravediggers, pallbearers, undertaker, the driver of the hearse, and Margy's remaining family watched. A railroad track passed just beyond the cemetery wall, and, as again by choice her father dropped a rose into the grave then pushed the first shovelful of rock and earth onto the coffin, an engine whistle blew. A short ten- or fifteen-car train rolled by, the porch on its yellow caboose holding three men in bibbed overalls and gray engineer's caps. In this scene from another time, the gravediggers began to shovel the rest of the dirt over the coffin, and Margy tried not to visualize the other funerals to come. She, Everet, and Kennedy each dropped a rose into the grave and then followed her father back to the car. Only Kennedy lagged behind, a look of puzzlement on his face as if he did not know how to react.

"I expected something different," he said, after they called him and he entered the car.

"We all do, son," said Everet.

"I mean from the ceremony."

"Anything else would have been hypocritical," her father said. "Sometimes it is better not to be remembered as we live."

Margy reached out and touched Kennedy's hand.

At home they sat in the dining room and ate a quick meal, prepared and served by Sophie, a maid whom her father had hired some months before. She came in each evening to cook dinner, serve, and wash the day's dishes. Mennonite, fiftyish, married, she had three grown sons and grandchildren whose number she could not keep straight. Sophie reacted silently when she saw Everet and Kennedy, but by the second night she served them without the slightest hesitation. Margy's father called her Sophie while she referred to him as "Sir," a very British, very Victorian relationship, especially with the dining room's somber furniture, swinging butler's door, and formal china and silverware that Margy remembered as showpieces only. Still, it pleased her to see this mark of relaxation and comfort in her father's life.

360

They remained in Waterloo Falls for three more days. Margy and her father had several long talks. By the time she, Everet, and Kennedy left, her father felt comfortable enough to place his hand on Margy's and ask to visit her in New York. She nodded, reminding him that he had always hated the city. He embraced her, then turned to Everet and Kennedy. With emotion grippIng his face, he said, "I've faltered awfully in the past, but I want you to know I'm committed to you, to all of you. If there is ever anything I can do, just let me know."

Everet thanked him. Margy did, too. But feeling very mixed emotions, she carefully and forcefully kept herself from too long an embrace. "We'll see you again," she said. "It won't be so long next time."

As they entered the Cedar Rapids Airport lounge, she remembered her last good-bye to her father here, and she realized that in addition to her mother's absence the model world she had stood before while she said a bitter farewell before going off to Europe was gone as well. It had been replaced by a wooden and glass partition and X-ray machine that would check her and her carry-on baggage before letting her on board. As they moved toward the machine, she watched her father embrace Kennedy then speak to Everet in a kind of panic.

"I can help with his college if you need it. We want him to have the best."

Everet smiled, not at all dismissive. "Thanks. He'll have the best, I assure you. Fortunately, we have that all taken care of."

They shook hands, then Everet moved toward the inspection gate and placed his attaché case on the conveyor belt. Feeling a sudden loss, Margy embraced her father before she followed with her overnight bag.

"Keep in touch, Daddy. I've enjoyed writing to you these past few months."

"So have I," he said.

She waved while Kennedy, hugging his grandfather, followed Margy through the gate. From there they walked through the boarding lounge and out of the building toward

361

the tarmac. Near the plane, they turned and saw her father among a crowd of people in the visitors' area. They stood at a large window, jockeying for positions close to the glass and waving to the departing passengers.

"Bye," Margy said as she watched Kennedy striding beside her. He paused a moment and waved to his grandfather. They continued for another 50 yards or so, mounted the plane's steps, and at the door Margy turned. She could not distinguish her father in the crowd at the window now. She thought she saw his white head once or twice, but with a glare on the glass and the distance she could not be sure which he was. She blew a kiss. Then she entered the plane, found her place with Kennedy and Everet, and settled between them in a row of seats.

"We've been through something, Margy," Everet said.

She nodded and, feeling she had to resist her emotions, she added, "So have lots of others."

"This should make us stronger."

Everet squeezed her hand and then reached across her body to pat Kennedy's knee.

"We've got a lot to think about, haven't we, son?"

"Yes, Dad. We do."

"I know that I do," Margy said. As the plane taxied down the runway, she took out her notebook and pen, but, when Kennedy waved out the window and the wheels thumped into the great metallic belly, she crossed her arms over her lap and gripped each of her companions tightly by the hand.

ABOUT THE AUTHOR

Fred Misurella has published *Only Sons*, a novel, *Lies to Live By: Stories*; *Short Time*, a novella about Vietnam; and *Understanding Milan Kundera: Public Events, Private Affairs*. His stories and non-fiction have appeared in Partisan Review, Summerset Review, Salmagundi, Kansas Quarterly, Voices in Italian Americana, L'Atelier du roman, The Christian Science Monitor, The Village Voice, and The New York Times Book Review. His essays on Primo Levi appear in *The Legacy of Primo Levi* and *Answering Auschwitz*. He is a Fulbright scholar and a graduate of the University of Iowa Writers Workshop.

Learn more: www.FredMisurella.com.

30532696R00221

Made in the USA
Charleston, SC
18 June 2014